Burns and Lambert

A popular manual of church history

New edition

Burns and Lambert

A popular manual of church history
New edition

ISBN/EAN: 9783741197949

Manufactured in Europe, USA, Canada, Australia, Japa

Cover: Foto ©Andreas Hilbeck / pixelio.de

Manufactured and distributed by brebook publishing software
(www.brebook.com)

Burns and Lambert

A popular manual of church history

A POPULAR MANUAL

OF

CHURCH HISTORY.

LONDON :

PRINTED BY ROBSON, LEVEY, AND FRANKLYN,
Great New Street and Fetter Lane.

A

POPULAR MANUAL

OF

CHURCH HISTORY.

A New Edition.

LONDON:

BURNS AND LAMBERT, 17 & 18 PORTMAN STREET,
AND 63 PATERNOSTER ROW.

1861.

Imprimatur.

N. CARDINAL WISEMAN.

West., *Oct.* 10, 1857.

CONTENTS.

———

CHAPTER XL

THE EIGHTEENTH CENTURY.

CHAPTER XII.

THE NINETEENTH CENTURY.

A SHORT

HISTORY OF THE CHURCH.

Introduction.

THE Church is that society which Jesus Christ set up tc
teach mankind the true religion, and to train and perfect in
holiness the future citizens of heaven. As these ends respect
the whole course of time, the Church must exist without in-
terruption to the end of the world; it must be always visible,
always pure in faith and in morals; it must always possess
saints, and supernatural charity can never cease within it.
"The generation of Christians," says St. Bernard, "can never
come to an end; neither can faith perish from the earth, nor
charity from within the Church."

Nevertheless, it was foretold by our Lord that the Church
should be persecuted by the powers of this world; that it
would be distracted and torn by heresies and schisms; that
scandals would arise within it; that "the wheat and the cockle
would both grow together until the harvest." And it is clear
that its existence amidst these assaults and perils requires the
succour of an almighty hand, no less than its first institution.
Hence our Lord foretold and promised that He would Himself be with it "all days;" that is, that He would succour it
with His continual invisible presence "even to the consummation of the world." Without this presence,—

1. It must have perished beneath the sword and fires of
persecution. For three hundred years the mightiest efforts

were made to root it out from the earth. But, instead of crushing it, persecution served only to deepen and extend it. The blood of the martyrs was the seed of the Church.

2. It would have perished beneath the assaults which a long succession of heretics have made upon the leading doctrines of the faith. But their efforts, though aided often by the secular power, have not only failed to change or adulterate the faith; they have been made the means of securing the clearer and fuller expression of the doctrines assailed. There have never been wanting holy doctors to refute and confound each error as it appeared; while by the voice of the bishops, with the Pope—the Vicar of Christ—at their head, all novelties have been condemned, and the truth declared in authoritative decrees, and in definitions which make equivocation and subterfuge impossible.

3. It must have perished by reason of the laxity and corruption which have, at times, crept in amongst its children, and even amongst its priests. But its standard of morality has never been lowered; it has never ceased to confront and oppose corruption with the holy laws of the Gospel; and, even in the darkest times, it has possessed saints, whose lives were a protest against prevailing disorders.

Thus the constant victory of the Church over the might of oppressors, over heresies and schisms and corruptions, is a standing and imposing miracle of God's power. "The floods came, and the winds blew, and they beat upon that house; and it fell not, for it was founded upon a rock." And what claims to our veneration has that Church which, in its enduring strength, no less than in its marvellous origin, bears the sensible impress of divinity! What can be more worthy of admiration than this spiritual kingdom, which, amidst the changes of all earthly institutions and societies and dynasties, is always one and the same? All things else crumble beneath the touch of time, if they are not shattered by outward violence; but this society has preserved through all time, and in spite of all assaults, its every essential note, prerogative, and privilege. It is the manifest fulfilment of the great words: "All power is given to Me in heaven and in earth. Going, therefore, teach ye all nations . . . . and, behold, I am with you all days, even to the consummation of the world." "There is nothing more majestic," says Bossuet, "there is nothing more divine, in the conduct of Jesus Christ, than His foretelling, on the one hand, that His Church should never know rest from attack, either by persecution from without, or by ever-emerging heresies and schisms, or through the relaxation of discipline induced by declining charity; and His promising, on the other hand, that notwithstanding all this, nothing should ever avail to destroy its life, or break the line of pastors who hand down from generation to generation the authority received from Him, the holy doctrine He taught, and the salutary Sacraments of grace. ' I have appointed you,' said He to His Apostles, ' that you should go, and should bring forth fruit, and that your fruit should remain.' This was His promise to twelve poor fishermen— ' their fruit should remain;' and surely this stamps all His words with the seal of truth."

What a glorious testimony to the truth of this prophecy, and how great a confirmation to our faith, that from Pius IX., who now holds the keys of this kingdom, the Church may be traced back to St. Peter, who received them from Jesus Christ Himself! Even on a mere human estimate, what authority can compare with that of the Catholic Church, which unites in itself the authority of all the generations which have preceded us, and all the traditions of our race to its very origin! Surely the simple fact of its existence bears witness to its supernatural character; and its exemption from the universal law of change and decay is itself sufficient to justify its claims on our faith, our obedience, and our love.

CHAPTER I.

FROM THE INSTITUTION OF THE CHURCH, A.M. 4004, TO THE CONVERSION OF CONSTANTINE, A.D. 312.

§ 1. Jesus Christ founds His Church.

WHEN the time appointed in the counsels of God was come, the Saviour, promised to Adam in the beginning, and announced by a long succession of prophets, the expectation and the desire of all nations, was born in Bethlehem of Judæa, A.M. 4004. At that time the Jews alone possessed the light of Divine revelation; and it was amidst this privileged people that Jesus Christ appeared—the only-begotten Son of God, equal in all things to the Father. A virgin, whose name was Mary, the purest and most exalted of creatures, received from heaven the sublime dignity of being the Mother of God, and brought forth the Redeemer of the world. Concealed for thirty years in the lowly house at Nazareth, and subject to Mary His Mother and Joseph His foster-father, Jesus began His mission by being Himself an example of all the virtues He came to teach and enjoin—of humility, poverty, and obedience; of perfect detachment from the riches and pleasures of the world. When He was thirty years of age, He went throughout the cities and villages of Judæa, preaching the Gospel of the kingdom of God, healing the sick, raising the dead, and dispensing blessings at every step. He selected for the pillars of His Church twelve poor fishermen; He devoted three years to instructing them; and then, His hour being come, the Lamb of the everlasting covenant gave Himself up into the hands of sinners, suffered a death of ignominy, and thus redeemed the human race with His own precious blood. He rose again from the dead on the third day, according to the prophets, and in fulfilment of His own promise to His Apostles. He appeared in the midst of them, triumphant over death; He instructed them in the things appertaining to the kingdom of God, that is to say, His Church; He established Peter as head of the college of Apostles, the chief shepherd of the flock, which He had purchased with His own blood. Then, promising to be with them "until the consummation of the world," He commanded them to await in Jerusalem the descent of the Holy Spirit, who would endow them with supernatural light and grace. He breathed on them and blessed them, and said: "Going, therefore, teach ye all nations; baptising them in the name of the Father, and of the Son, and of the Holy Ghost." Then He ascended into heaven in their sight, and entered into His glory.

They returned to Jerusalem, and continued in prayer in an upper room. With them was Mary, the Mother of the Divine Word made flesh, and about one hundred and twenty disciples. While they were thus awaiting the coming of the Holy Ghost, Peter proposed to appoint a twelfth apostle in the place of Judas the traitor. Two of the disciples present were found so equally endowed with the requisite virtues and gifts, that the Apostles implored the Lord to "show whether of the two He had chosen." The lot fell on Matthias, who was thus raised from the position of a simple disciple "to take the place of the ministry and apostleship, from which Judas had, by transgression, fallen."

On the tenth day, the day of Pentecost, while they were "all together in one place, there came a sound from heaven, as of a mighty wind coming; parted tongues as it were of fire sat upon every one of them; and they were all filled with the Holy Ghost." They immediately "began to speak with divers tongues," and to declare the wonderful works of God, "according as the Holy Ghost gave them to speak." Their souls were replenished with knowledge and with grace; they were no longer a mere assembly of individuals, but became the one mystical body of Christ, the Church of the living God.

§ 2. Preaching of the Apostles, and extension of the Church.

It was the will and command of God that the gospel should in the first instance be preached to the Jews, the heirs of the promises made to Abraham. Our Lord had signified this will of God in His treatment of the woman of Canaan: "I was not sent, but to the sheep that are lost of the house of Israel." Nor was this purpose of mercy changed by their rejection of Him; the first-fruits of the Church were gathered from amongst them. Jerusalem was full of strangers from every part of the known world, Jews by birth, who had come up to keep the Feast of Pentecost. To these the Apostles addressed themselves; and each listener heard them speak in the tongue most familiar to him. They asked in wonder who these men could be, these unlettered Galileans, who spoke so many languages with such fluency and power. St. Peter expounded to them the prophecy of which this miracle was the fulfilment. He preached to them the Godhead of that Jesus whom they had crucified; and declared that He was the Christ their fathers had waited for; and he exhorted them to seek remission of their sins through baptism in His name. Three thousand were converted and added to the Church. A short time afterwards, as Peter and John were going into the Temple, they healed a lame man. St. Peter again preached to the crowd assembled at the news of this miracle; and five thousand more were admitted into the Church.

The priests and Sadducees were "grieved that they thus taught the people, and laid hands upon them, and put them in prison." On the morrow the whole council of the nation sent for them, and asked: "By what power, or by what name, have you done this?" "Then Peter, filled with the Holy Ghost," answered boldly: In the name and by the authority of that same J. sus whom you have crucified. The members of the council were amazed at the firmness of these "illiterate and ignorant men;" but the man who had been healed was present, and they could not deny the reality of the miracle. They could only "threaten them that they speak no more in this name to any man." The Apostles replied with holy intrepidity: "If it be just in the sight of God to hear you rather than God, judge ye; for we cannot but speak the things which we have seen and heard." Having no pretext for detaining them, the council let them go. The Apostles returned to the faithful, and related what had taken place, and the whole assembly gave thanks to God, and besought Him to give them strength and fortitude to preach the gospel without fear.

God attested the preaching of His servants by many miracles, and especially by the wonderful efficacy of His grace in changing the hearts of those who were converted. "Great grace was in them all." On one occasion "they were all with one accord in Solomon's porch." The multitude "durst not join themselves unto them," but they could not refrain from honouring them when they beheld "the many signs and wonders wrought by the hands of the Apostles." Sick people were brought out and laid along the street, that the shadow of Peter might fall on them as he passed by; and "they were all healed." Then the high-priest, instigated by the impious Sadducees, "was filled with envy, and laid hands on the Apostles, and put them in the common prison." In the night an angel led them out, and charged them to "speak in the Temple to the people all the words of this life." In the morning the high-priest "sent to the prison to have them brought;" but though the prison was found securely locked, there were found "no men within." Then "one came and told them" that the men whom they had put in prison were "standing in the Temple and teaching the people." The officer of the Temple went in search of them; and when he had found them, he brought them "without violence, for they feared the people lest they should be stoned." When they were in presence of the council, the high-priest asked them: Did we not expressly forbid you to teach in this name? and yet you have filled Jerusalem with your doctrine, and intend to bring the blood of this man upon us. Peter, always the foremost of the Apostles and their spokesman, replied: "We ought to obey God rather than men." He then declared solemnly that God had raised up Him whom they had unjustly put to death, and had exalted Him to be Prince and Saviour. The council was on the point of condemning them to death, when Gamaliel, a doctor of the law, cautioned and advised them thus: "Refrain from these men, and let them alone: if this counsel or this work be of men, it will come to naught; if it be of God, you cannot overthrow it." This memorable advice was followed. The Apostles were scourged, and dismissed with a strict charge to abstain from "speaking in the name of Jesus." They went away, "rejoicing that they were accounted worthy to suffer reproach for the name of Jesus; and every day they ceased not in the Temple, and from house to house, to teach and preach Christ Jesus." It was in private houses that the Adorable Sacrifice was offered, and the Sacraments administered; for as yet the faithful had no places of meeting such as were afterwards raised in every part of the world.

The number of the disciples increased from day to day. When St. Luke wrote the "Acts of the Apostles," their num-

ber was already considerable. They were taken from every
rank, from every age. They were of one heart and one soul;
and so fervent was their charity, that not one was left destitute
among them; for as many as were owners of lands or houses
sold them, and laid down the price at the Apostles' feet,
"and distribution was made to every one according as he had
need." Soon the Apostles found themselves unable to attend
personally to this distribution; and they ordained seven
men, full of the Holy Ghost and of wisdom, as deacons, who,
amongst other sacred duties, should minister the alms of the
faithful in the different quarters of Jerusalem. The first of
these deacons was Stephen; and the splendour of his miracles, the zeal of his preaching, and his great success, drew
down upon him the special hatred of the unbelieving Jews.
He was brought before the high-priest on the charge of
blasphemy; but he confounded his accusers by words of divine wisdom and power, commemorating the mercies of God
towards His ungrateful people, and boldly proclaiming the
divinity of the Lord Jesus. He was dragged away from the
judgment-seat, and stoned without the city, praying the
while for his murderers (Acts vi. vii.). His prayer was to
have a speedy and a signal answer.

The martyrdom of St. Stephen was the signal for a general
and violent persecution of the infant Church. The faithful
were dispersed throughout Palestine, and diffused the light of
faith wherever they went. Thus, as ever, God overruled the
malice of His enemies to the accomplishment of His purposes.
Some went as far as Phœnicia, some to Cyprus, some to
Antioch. St. Philip the deacon converted many of the inhabitants of Samaria; while Ananias founded the church of
Damascus. But now a young man called Saul, who had
taken part in the martyrdom of St. Stephen, and who "yet
breathed out threatenings and slaughter against the disciples
of the Lord," went to the high-priest, and begged to be sent
to that city, with power to bring all Christians he might find
there, "bound to Jerusalem." While he was on his way, Saul
was suddenly dazzled by a light brighter than that of the
sun, and heard a voice saying to him, "Saul, Saul, why
persecutest thou Me?" He had fallen to the ground in terror
and awe, and answered humbly, "Who art Thou, Lord?" "I
am Jesus, whom thou persecutest." And Saul, "trembling
and astonished," asked, "Lord, what wilt Thou have me to

do?" "And the Lord said to him, Arise, and go into the city, and there it shall be told thee what thou must do." Saul arose, blinded by the splendour of that great light. He was led into Damascus, was instructed and baptised by that Ananias whom he had come to denounce and to put to death, "and immediately preached Jesus in the synagogues." A conversion so sudden astonished and irritated the Jews; but Saul "confounded" them, "affirming" with increasing strength "that this is the Christ." The Jews, enraged, conspired against his life; but the disciples delivered him out of their hands by letting him down from the city-walls by night in a basket.

Hitherto the Gospel had been preached only to Jews; but the kingdom of Christ was to include all nations. There was in Cæsarea a Roman centurion named Cornelius, a religious man, who feared God, and gave much alms to the poor. One day, while he was praying, an angel appeared to him, and told him that "his prayers and his alms had ascended for a memorial in the sight of God. And now," continued the heavenly messenger, "send to Joppe for a man called Peter; he will tell you all that you must do to be saved." Cornelius despatched three soldiers in search of this wonderful man. At the same time St. Peter had a vision which prepared him for this message, and removed his natural scruples. He went with the men whom Cornelius had sent. On his arrival, he preached to Cornelius and his family and friends the life, the doctrine, the miracles, and the redemption of Jesus Christ. While he was yet speaking, the Holy Ghost fell upon all who heard the word, and they began to speak with tongues, to the astonishment of the Jewish converts who had accompanied the Apostle. Then said Peter, "Can any man forbid water, that these should not be baptised, who have received the Holy Ghost as well as we?" Thus did he to whom had been given the keys of the kingdom of heaven, open its gates to the Gentiles, as he had already, on the day of Pentecost, opened them to the Jews.

The Church was now to undergo another persecution. Herod Agrippa, nephew and successor of the Herod Antipas who had clothed Jesus with a purple robe, "stretched forth his hands" against the disciples of the Lord, and killed James the Greater, the brother of St. John, with the sword. Seeing that it pleased the Jews, he proceeded to take Peter also, and threw him into prison; but in answer to the prayers of the Church for its chief pastor, he was delivered by an angel, and withdrew from Jerusalem. On the death of Herod, who, in the midst of his glory, was struck by God with a terrible disease, the keenness of the persecution diminished; and "the word of the Lord increased and multiplied."

God had selected Saul, whom we shall now call by his Roman name of Paul, for the especial office of the Apostle of the Gentiles. By the command of the Holy Ghost he and Barnabas were set apart for the work to which He had designed them. They went to Seleucia, to Salamis, and to Paphos, where St. Paul converted the proconsul Sergius Paulus. Thence they proceeded to Perga in Pamphylia, and to Antioch in Pisidia, preaching always in the synagogues, and making many converts. At Antioch, as elsewhere, the Jews contradicted and opposed the truth; then said the Apostles, " Because you reject the word of God, and judge yourselves unworthy of eternal life, behold we turn to the Gentiles." Upon this a furious persecution arose, and St. Paul and St. Barnabas were cast out of the city; but shaking off the dust of their feet, as the Lord had commanded them, they passed into Iconium and the cities of Lycaonia, whence, after enduring many tribulations, they returned to Antioch in Syria.

Some of the recently converted Jews, tenacious of the law of Moses, wished to subject the Gentile converts to its observances. Some of them came down to Antioch, and excited great alarm by teaching that the Gentiles who submitted to the faith could not be saved, unless they were circumcised and kept the law of Moses. St. Paul and St. Barnabas resisted them, and said that Jesus Christ had come to fulfil the law of Moses, and by fulfilling to supersede it; and that His grace would not profit those who continued to regard circumcision as necessary. It was resolved that the question should be remitted for decision to the Apostles. St. Paul and St. Barnabas went up to Jerusalem to consult them. St. Paul had undertaken this journey in obedience to a particular inspiration. He conferred with St. Peter, St. James, and St. John, the pillars of the Church; he compared with their doctrine that which he had taught to the Gentiles, and which he had received immediately from Jesus Christ. His teaching was approved, and his special mission to the Gentiles recognised. When the question was brought before the

Apostles, and had been argued on both sides, it was decreed: "It hath seemed good to the Holy Ghost and to us to lay no further burden upon you than these necessary things,— that you abstain from things sacrificed to idols, and from blood, and from things strangled, and from fornication."

Here we have an example of the Church for the first time meeting in council, and of the method she has ever since scrupulously followed. All questions pertaining to faith and discipline are determined by her sovereign authority. A grave dissension arises. The matter is referred to the college of the Apostles, with St. Peter at their head. They meet: the question is eagerly discussed; Peter rises, and delivers his opinion, to which James and the rest adhere; the decision is pronounced, reduced to writing, and goes forth—not as a simple human judgment, but as an oracle of God: "it hath seemed good to the Holy Ghost and to us." It is sent to particular churches, not to be examined, but to be received and obeyed implicitly. Thus speaks the Holy Ghost in the Church and through the Church; and accordingly we read that "Paul went through Syria and Cilicia confirming the churches; commanding them to keep the precepts of the Apostles and of the ancients."

Some years after this council, Ananus the high-priest took advantage of the death of the Roman governor to cite St. James the Less before a special council of the Sanhedrim. St. James was Bishop of Jerusalem, and was not only beloved by the faithful, but respected by the unbelieving Jews for the simplicity of his character and his eminent holiness. His life was one of great austerity. His clothing was coarse; he wore no sandals; his hair was never cut; and his only drink was water. He passed several hours daily in the temple, praying for the conversion of the people; and it is said that in consequence of his continual prayer, his knees were hardened like those of a camel. His charity and gentleness had obtained for him the surname of *the just*. When he appeared before the council, the high-priest said to him, "The people ignorantly take Jesus for the Messias. We wish you to dissipate this error; for every one is ready to believe what you say." He was then led to a terrace of the Temple to address the multitude. When he made his appearance, one of the council said to him, "Thou just man, whom every one believes, since the people err in following Jesus who was crucified, tell us what we are to think of Him." St. James replied with a loud voice, " Jesus, that Son of Man of whom you speak, is even now seated at the right-hand of the Sovereign Majesty as Son of God; and He will come on the clouds of heaven to judge the whole world." A testimony so solemn and explicit irritated the Pharisees, and they exclaimed, "What! the just man is himself led astray!" Then, in the blindness of their rage, they hurled the holy Apostle from his elevated position to the ground. St. James was not killed by his fall: he had still strength enough to raise himself upon his knees, and to say, "Lord, forgive them: they know not what they do." He was then assailed with a shower of stones; and a fuller in the crowd took a mallet, and with one blow perfected the martyrdom of the Apostle. So great was his reputation for sanctity, that the ruin of Jerusalem, which took place soon afterwards, was attributed to his death. He was buried on the spot on which he suffered, and a pillar was erected to commemorate him. St. James wrote one of the seven epistles called Catholic, because addressed to the Universal Church. In this epistle he affirms the necessity of good works in order to salvation, in opposition to some who taught that faith alone, without works, sufficed,—an error which made its appearance again in the sixteenth century.*

Besides the Apostle Jude, St. James the Less had another brother, whose name was Simeon. They were closely related to our Lord; and Simeon was raised to the see of Jerusalem by the unanimous voice of the Church. But the time was drawing near when the predictions of our Lord concerning the calamities and the dispersion of the Jews were to be accomplished. That generation was not "to pass away until these things came to pass." It is a tradition attested by the Talmud, that forty years before the destruction of Jerusalem, or about the time of our Lord's Passion, ominous and startling prodigies occurred in the Temple. An appalling voice is said to have issued from the holiest place on the day of Pentecost: "Arise, let us go hence!" The holy angels, guardians of the Temple, forsook it because it was rejected of God,—forsaken by the Presence which had been its glory and defence for so many ages. Four years before the war in which Jerusalem was destroyed, we are told by Josephus

---

* Hence the antipathy to the epistle of St. James expressed by Luther.

that another terrible warning was sent to the rebellious people. A man named Jesus, the son of Ananus, came from the country at the feast of tabernacles; and while the city was in profound peace, he cried, "Woe, woe to the city! woe to the Temple! A voice from the East, a voice from the West, a voice from the four winds of heaven: woe to the Temple! woe, woe to Jerusalem!" Day and night he went about the city repeating these ominous words. The magistrates commanded him to be scourged. He said not a word to excuse or to justify himself, but continued his fearful cry: "Woe to the Temple! woe, woe to Jerusalem!" He was led before the Roman governor, who commanded that he should be scourged still more severely. Pain extorted from him no cry, no tear, no supplication for mercy. At every blow he received, he repeated with wailing voice, "Woe, woe to Jerusalem!" They asked him whence he came, what he meant: his only answer was his monotonous "Woe!" During the last siege of Jerusalem, he reappeared in the city with his unceasing cry. At length, one day he exclaimed, "Woe, woe to myself!" and was killed immediately by a stone discharged from the besieging army.

The Jews had been for more than eighty years subject to the Romans; but they still chafed under the yoke of bondage. Pilate, who had condemned our Lord while acknowledging His innocence, was disgraced by Tiberius four years afterwards, and banished to Vienne, where he died A.D. 40. Several governors had followed him in succession, when the Jews broke into open revolt. The wiser part of the people left Jerusalem, to avoid the misery they foresaw, but could not prevent. The Christians retired to the little town of Pella, amidst the mountains of Syria; following thus the injunction of our Lord. The Roman army received a slight check, which emboldened the rebels; and it was deemed necessary to intrust to Vespasian the task of reducing them to submission. The Jews split into fierce and sanguinary factions, and Vespasian waited quietly while they destroyed one another. Being meanwhile raised to the purple, he left his son Titus to continue the siege. The young prince advanced to within a league of Jerusalem, and invested it closely. As it was near the feast of the Passover, a great multitude of the Jews were assembled in the city; and soon their provisions were entirely exhausted. Then were fulfilled the fearful predictions of the prophets, and horrors were perpetrated the bare recital of which makes us shudder. Titus gained possession of the Temple; a Roman soldier, impelled, says Josephus, by divine inspiration, set fire to it; and in spite of every effort to stay the progress of the flames, it was utterly consumed. A terrible massacre ensued; and all whom the sword and famine had spared were sold into slavery.

Thus were accomplished the predictions of our Lord. Titus himself was so impressed by the horrors of the siege, that he declared that he had been but the instrument of divine vengeance. Of the Jews eleven hundred thousand perished. The feeble remains of this wretched nation were scattered over the face of the earth, like the fragments of some awful wreck cast on every coast for warning and for instruction. Their crime can have neither counterpart nor parallel; their punishment is as unexampled as their crime. They had rejected and crucified the Lord of Glory; and in them were verified the words, "But woe unto them when I shall have departed from them!"

A new people, admitted to the covenant made of old with Abraham, and comprising all the nations of the earth, has succeeded to their position and its privileges, and shall endure "until the consummation of the world." Not alone within the limits of one land, but "from the rising of the sun even unto the going down, the name of God is great among the Gentiles, and in every place there is sacrifice; and there is offered to His name a clean oblation."

Still there is hope that, after the conversion of the Gentiles, the Saviour, whom Sion knew not, and the sons of Jacob rejected and despised, will have mercy upon them, and "take away the veil which is on their heart." Meanwhile they wander to and fro through the earth, bearing unwilling witness to the divinity of Jesus.

When the Apostles presented themselves to the heathen to announce the gospel, the Roman power extended over the whole world. God had thus gathered all nations under one empire to hasten the spread of the Church. It was a sublime and a perilous undertaking, and one which only men sent by God could have conceived, to preach to nations so corrupted the purity and holiness of evangelical morality. Nothing can be more sad than the details given us of the

deep degradation of society at that period. Vice was deified
in its most repulsive forms, and the worship was worthy of its
objects. Poverty was deemed a crime ; wealth and pleasure
were the chief good. The laws trampled on the most sacred
rights. More than half the population consisted of slaves,
who were treated as mere animals, employed in criminal or
degrading work, and liable, at the caprice of a master, to be
wantonly put to death. The chief delight of the Romans
was in the combats of gladiators, which took place at the
games which were celebrated on great occasions. It is said
that at these times 20,000 men were often butchered in the
course of a month. Remoter nations had not sunk so deep
in corruption, but they had been equally faithless to the old
patriarchal traditions. The empire was one vast Sodom. The
simple fact that the pure and persecuted faith of Christ made
such rapid progress amidst so corrupt a generation, is itself
an incontestable proof of its divine origin. It must be divine,
to have wrought a change so marvellous, without other aid
than the grace and protection of God, and the miracles which
accompanied the preaching of the Apostles.

Nothing can be more beautiful or more touching than
the picture which has been left us of the virtues of the first
Christian converts. The contrast of their lives with those of
the Pagans among whom they lived is a striking illustration
of the power of the grace of God. When once they had received holy baptism, there remained no trace of what they
had formerly been ; they began to live a new, an inward and
spiritual life ; and what had formerly seemed impossible to
them was now easy. They who had been slaves of lust became temperate and chaste ; the ambitious saw no longer any
solid glory but in the Cross ; earthly passions were subdued,
and Christian virtues flourished in their place ; they renounced the ease and the comforts of life ; they found a
special attraction in labours and fastings, in silence and retirement. Their principal occupation was prayer ; they obeyed
almost literally the injunction of the Apostle : " pray without
ceasing." Such a change is manifestly the work of that same
Power which drew forth the world from nothingness, and which
is then most glorious when it vanquishes and captivates the
human heart, without trenching on the freedom of the human
will. In the one case, God acts on inert matter, and meets
no resistance ; in the other, He wills that man should render

Him a free unconstrained obedience; and has therefore given him power to resist.

The Apostles, dispersed by persecution, preached every where the word of God; but before their separation, they agreed upon a brief symbol or formula of belief, which might serve to distinguish the faithful from Jews and heretics. This is the creed we say daily in our prayers, and which we call *the Apostles' Creed.* St. Peter founded churches in many places, and at length established his see in Antioch, the capital of Syria, in which the gospel had made great progress. It was in this city that the disciples were first called *Christians;* a title which they adopted, and by which they became known throughout the world. The Prince of the Apostles then went to Rome, to combat idolatry in the very centre of its power and influence. He had preached to the Jews of Pontus, Galatia, Cappadocia, Asia, and Bithynia, as we learn from the superscription of his first epistle. He sent some of his immediate disciples to found various churches in the West. Of these the most celebrated was St. Mark, who wrote his Gospel at Rome, setting down without regard to order of time what he had gathered from St. Peter. This Gospel is said to have been revised and approved by St. Peter himself.

Meanwhile St. Paul was preaching with great success. He passed through Phrygia, Galatia, Mysia, and Macedonia. At Philippi he founded a church, which remained unshaken in its attachment to the doctrine and the person of the Apostle. After gathering many souls into the Church on his way, he stopped at Thessalonica, the capital of the province, where he founded a church, which became a model of fervour and charity. Thence he passed into Achaia; and at Athens, standing in the centre of the Areopagus, delivered the celebrated address which was followed by the conversion of St. Dionysius and many others. From Greece the Apostle repaired to Ephesus, whence, notwithstanding the entreaties of the brethren, he returned to Jerusalem, where bonds awaited him. There his enemies raised an uproar against him, threw him into prison, and, unable to prove any thing against him, unjustly sought his life by assassination. St. Paul appealed to Cæsar; and was sent to have his cause adjudged at Rome. There he remained two whole years, under the guard of a soldier, in his own hired lodging. His friends having thus free access to him, the imprisoned Apostle was still able to preach the Gospel, and the faith of the Crucified God penetrated even into Cæsar's household. After obtaining his liberty, he continued to preach the gospel in various countries of the world; neither chains nor scourges, hunger or thirst, or the scorn of men, could abate the ardour of this valiant soldier of Jesus Christ; and ultimately he returned, as we shall see, to Rome, there to suffer martyrdom with the Prince of the Apostles.

So numerous were the conversions wrought by the preaching of the other Apostles, and so widely was the light of the gospel diffused, that at the end of the first century Christians were to be found in every part of the empire. A trustworthy tradition informs us that, during the lifetime of the Apostles, the faith was proclaimed throughout the whole world. Of the twelve who went forth from that *upper room*, we have seen two seal with their blood the truths they preached—St. James the Greater and St. James the Less. St. Thomas carried the gospel into Parthia and India, where the Portuguese are said to have discovered his remains, and transported them to Goa. St. Andrew preached amongst the Scythians, and from thence returned to Achaia, where he suffered martyrdom on a cross, uttering these beautiful and memorable words: "Happy cross, hallowed by contact with the body of Jesus Christ, receive me from the hands of men, and convey me to the arms of my Master—of Him who hath redeemed me." He is held in special veneration by the Russians, who now occupy the territory of the ancient Scythians. St. Bartholomew exercised his ministry in the Greater Armenia and part of India. Thither he conveyed the Gospel of St. Matthew, which was written long before the other Gospels. St. Matthew composed it for the use, and at the earnest request, of the faithful in Judæa; and it is said that he wrote it in Hebrew. This holy Apostle and Evangelist preached among the Ethiopians, and was noted for his extraordinary abstinence. St. Simon laboured in Mesopotamia and Persia; St. Jude in Arabia and Idumæa; St. Matthias in Ethiopia. Such are the notices preserved in the traditions of these several nations; and they show us with what reason St. Paul applied to the Apostles the words of the Psalmist: "Their sound hath gone forth into all the earth, and their words unto the ends of the world."

The Apostles and first disciples diffused a knowledge of the gospel by their writings as well as by their personal teaching. They have bequeathed us several books, which we call collectively the *New Testament*. Besides the four Gospels of St. Matthew, St. Mark, St. Luke, and St. John, we have the Acts of the Apostles by St. Luke, fourteen Epistles of St. Paul, one of St. James, two of St. Peter, three of St. John, one of St. Jude, and the book of the Apocalypse, written by St. John.

This blessed Apostle, whom our Lord loved in an especial manner, and to whom He confided His blessed Mother from the Cross, traversed Asia Minor and penetrated into Parthia. St. John was the first Bishop of Ephesus. He is said to have written his gospel at the earnest request of the bishops of Asia. Many false teachers having arisen who denied the Divinity of Jesus Christ, the Apostle dwells especially on the Incarnation of the Eternal Word. He wrote it A.D. 99, and his epistles were composed about the same time. So great was his zeal against heretics, that he could not endure to be in their presence except for the purpose of reclaiming them. One day, on entering a public bath at Ephesus, he found there a notorious heretic named Cerinthus: instantly he turned, and made his exit in all haste, exclaiming to those who were with him, " Let us fly, lest the bath fall upon us, while Cerinthus, enemy of the truth, is beneath its roof." Another incident is recorded which illustrates well the fervour of his charity. In the course of his apostolical journeys, after having preached to the faithful in one of the cities of Asia, he noticed a young man of pleasing appearance and promising abilities. Turning to the bishop, he said : " Take special care of that young man; I commend him to you in presence of the Church and of Jesus Christ." He then returned to Ephesus. The bishop instructed the young man, and prepared him for baptism. After having baptised him, and administered to him the Sacraments of Confirmation and of the Blessed Eucharist, he ceased to watch over him, and allowed him greater liberty. The young man became the companion of some dissolute persons of his own age, fell away into grievous sin, and at length became the captain of a band of robbers. Some years afterwards St. John returned to the city, and demanded of the bishop an account of the deposit he had left in his hands. The bishop was at first astonished, thinking that

St. John must mean a deposit of money. " I mean the young man I confided to your care," said the Apostle,—" I mean the soul of our brother." " He is dead," said the bishop, in confusion. " Dead!" exclaimed St. John; " by what death did he die?" " He is dead to God," added the bishop; " he has become a robber; he inhabits the mountains with a gang of miscreants as wicked as himself." At this intelligence the Apostle uttered a loud cry, and said, " Give me a horse and a guide." He left the city, and reached the spot frequented by the robbers. Their scouts seized him and led him to their captain, where he stood armed in the midst of his band. No sooner did he see St. John, than he was overcome with shame, and fled away. The holy Apostle, forgetting the infirmities of his advanced age, ran after him, and cried: " My son, why do you flee from me; from your father, an old man, and unarmed? My son, have compassion on me; fear nothing. I have still hope of your salvation. Gladly would I give my life for you, as Jesus Christ gave His life for us. Stop, it is Jesus who sends me to you!" At these words the young man stopped, threw down his arms, and burst into tears. The Apostle embraced him tenderly; prayed for him and with him; and did not leave him until he had fully reconciled him to God and the Church.

Our blessed Lady abode with the beloved disciple until her death, of the date of which there is no certain record. The Church celebrates her Assumption into heaven on the 15th of August. It is a tradition and a pious belief universal among the faithful, that her body was not suffered to remain in the grave, but, reunited to her immaculate soul, was gloriously exalted into heaven by her Divine Son.

§ 3. The Persecutions.

First Persecution.—The Church had suffered much at the hands of the Jews, as we have seen; and it had been violently opposed by the heathen; but these outbreaks were merely local and temporary. The Emperor Nero* was the first who

---

* Nero was the fifth in the series of Roman emperors. It is said that Tiberius, the son and successor of Augustus, having heard from Pilate the striking circumstances of our Lord's passion, wished to admit him into the number of the gods; but that the senate refused its consent. He was succeeded by Caligula, a cruel and dissolute prince, whose violent death gave the empire to Claudius. Claudius adopted as his successor Nero, the son of his wife Agrippina by a former husband.

formally opposed his sovereign authority to the advancing kingdom of God. He was irritated by the numerous conversions which were taking place even within his own household; and he was anxious to divert from himself the odium of having occasioned the great fire which had destroyed the larger portion of the city. The Christians were charged with this crime, and a fierce persecution began. Very many were put to death, not as being convicted on this charge, but as persons hateful to the human race, by reason of their religion. New and strange torments were invented. Some were sewn up in the skins of wild-beasts and torn by dogs; others were wrapped in garments saturated with pitch, hung up on lofty gallows, and then set on fire in the dusk of the evening.

It was during this persecution that St. Peter and St. Paul received the crown of martyrdom. It is said that the holy Apostles were imprisoned for nine months in a dungeon at the foot of the Capitol; that two of their guards were converted and baptised by St. Peter, together with forty-seven of their fellow-prisoners. The faithful of Rome contrived to convey to St. Peter the means of escape, that he might prolong a life so precious to the Church. The Apostle yielded at length; but as he reached the gate of the city, Jesus Christ appeared to him, bearing His cross. St. Peter asked in wonder: "Lord, whither goest Thou?"* Our Lord replied that He was going to Rome to be crucified a second time. St. Peter understood these words to mean that it was in the person of His earthly representative that the Lord was to be crucified; he returned to the prison, and was eventually condemned to the cross. At his own request, he was attached to the cross with his head downwards: he felt himself unworthy to die in the same manner and posture as his Divine Master. St. Paul, who was a Roman citizen, was beheaded. On his way to execution he converted three soldiers, who shortly afterwards suffered martyrdom. Such was the first persecution.

Second Persecution.—The wars in which succeeding emperors were engaged, and the pacific temper of Vespasian and Titus, afforded the Christians an interval of rest and peace. The second general persecution was begun by Domitian, the imitator of Nero's worst vices, and the inheritor of his hatred against the Christians. It had pleased God to prepare the

* A church stands on the spot hallowed by this meeting. It is called, from St. Peter's question, *Domine, quo vadis!*

faithful for this fiery trial. We may judge of the fury with which the persecution raged, from the treatment of persons of the highest rank, and even of members of the imperial family. The consul, Flavius Clemens, his own cousin, was put to death, and Domitilla his wife was banished, simply because they were Christians. Two of their slaves, Nereus and Achilleus, were beheaded, after having suffered excruciating tortures; and multitudes, besides, were killed or deprived of their possessions and banished. But the persecution under Domitian is chiefly remarkable from its connection with St. John. The holy Apostle was cited before the tyrant and brought to Rome; there he was plunged into a cauldron of boiling oil without sustaining the slightest injury. The glory and the reward of martyrdom were granted him; but our Lord willed to show that the hand of man could not touch His anointed without His permission. This miracle took place in front of the Latin gate; and a church has been built on its site. St. John was then banished to Patmos, an island in the Ægean Sea. There were granted him those wonderful visions which are recorded in the Apocalypse—visions in which, under the most sublime images, are foretold the downfall of idolatry and error, and the triumphs of the Church. On the death of the tyrant, St. John returned to Ephesus, where he died in peace, A.D. 101, the last survivor of the apostolic college. When so old and infirm that he could no longer either walk or preach, he would have himself carried to the church, to be present at the Divine Mysteries; and there, day after day, to the assembled brethren, he would repeat these few touching words, " My little children, love one another." Being asked why he always said the same thing, he replied, " It is the commandment of the Lord, and if this be fulfilled, it is sufficient."

St. Peter was succeeded in the see of Rome by Linus, Anacletus, and Clement. During the pontificate of St. Clement the church of Corinth was troubled by certain of the laity, who rebelled against the authority of their priests. Pope Clement wrote them a letter as touching as it is instructive. Next to Holy Scripture, it is the most beautiful relic of ecclesiastical antiquity. It produced the effect which the holy Pope desired; and he had the satisfaction of healing the incipient schism.

Nerva, the successor of Domitian, was a mild and just

prince. He recalled the bloody edicts of his predecessor, and the Christians again had rest.

Third Persecution.—The third persecution was begun by Trajan, the successor of Nerva. Among the first victims was the holy Pope St. Clement. Indeed, for a long succession of years, the Papal throne was a certain step to martyrdom. This persecution was less violent than the two former; but what it lacked in intensity was more than made up by its duration; and the number of martyrs was far greater. Trajan was, in other respects, a wise and clement emperor. He issued no new edicts, but simply put in force those which Nerva had suspended. His character and policy may be traced in his reply to Pliny the younger, then governor of Bithynia, who had written for instructions how to deal with the Christians. Pliny had no fault to find with them;* they were good citizens, and no other crime was laid to their charge, but that they were obstinate and refractory in the matter of religion. "Their only error is," he says, "this: on certain days they meet together before the rising of the sun, and sing hymns to Christ, whom they honour as their God. They further engage themselves by an oath to abstain from theft and from adultery; never to break their word," &c. He says that he had discovered nothing in their practices but what was simple and innocent; and he adds that "the contagion of this superstition" had reached every rank, every age, not in the cities only, but in remote country villages; so that the temples were deserted, and the victims fed for sacrifice found no purchasers. Trajan replied, that the Christians were not to be officiously sought out; but if they were brought before Pliny, they were to be put to death, unless they would deny their faith, invoke the gods, and burn incense before the image of the emperor. They were to be treated as adherents of an unlawful religion, who dared to insult the religion and defy the authority of the empire.†

Amongst the earliest martyrs was St. Simeon, Bishop of

---

* It is worthy of remark, that Pliny, nevertheless, put two deaconesses to the torture, to ascertain the real nature of these suspicious meetings (*per tormenta quærere*).

† Tacitus speaks of the Christian religion as *exitiabilis superstitio*, a deadly superstition; and of its professors as men held in abhorrence for their crimes (*per flagitia invisos*). The gentler Pliny regarded it as a dreary and overstrained superstition. For further notices of the Church by Pagan writers, see Newman, *Essay on Development*, pp. 204-242.

Jerusalem, who had reached his 120th year. He was denounced as a Christian, and as a descendant of David. He was crucified, after having endured various tortures with a fortitude which amazed the beholders. On his way through Antioch, Trajan summoned before him Ignatius, the bishop of that see. "Are you he," said the emperor, "who, like an evil demon, dare to disobey my commands and lead the people to destruction?" "Prince," replied Ignatius, "never has any one called Theophoros* an evil demon. Know that the servants of God are so far from being evil spirits, that evil spirits quail and fly before them." "And who is this Theophoros?" "I myself, and whosoever bears Jesus Christ in his heart." "Think you, then, that we have not gods in our hearts who war for us?" "Gods!" exclaimed Ignatius, "they are only devils! There is but one God, Creator of heaven and earth; and one Jesus Christ, the only Son of God, to whose kingdom I aspire." "Do you mean that Jesus whom Pilate hanged on a cross?" "Say rather that Jesus hanged on that cross sin and the author of sin, and that He gives from that cross power to all who bear Him within them to resist and destroy hell and its powers." "Do you, then, bear Christ within you?" asked the emperor. "Yes, undoubtedly; for it is written, 'I will dwell in them.'" Trajan cut short the inconvenient discussion by pronouncing judgment in these words: "We command that Ignatius, who boasts of bearing the crucified one within him, be put in irons and taken to Rome to be exposed to wild beasts." The saint clasped his hands and exclaimed: "I thank Thee, O Lord, that Thou hast granted me a perfect love of Thee, and that Thou dost honour me with chains like those of the great St. Paul, Thine Apostle." On his way to Rome the vessel touched at Smyrna, and St. Ignatius had the consolation of an interview with St. Polycarp, the disciple of St. John and bishop of that city. From Smyrna he wrote letters to the churches in Asia; and, fearing lest the Roman Christians might interpose to deprive him of his martyr's crown, he wrote to them to dissuade them from the attempt.

After a long voyage, the saint reached Rome just as the games were proceeding. He was led to the amphitheatre at once. He heard the roar of wild beasts, and the wilder shout of execration raised by the populace; but his countenance

* St. Ignatius was surnamed *Theophoros*, "the bearer of God."

was radiant with serenity and joy. Two hungry lions were let loose, and in a moment the martyr was with God. The few relics which remained of his bones were carefully collected, and sent to Antioch, with a letter in which these words occur: " We were witnesses of his glorious death . . . . that night we spent in tearful prayers to the Lord to strengthen our weakness. The holy martyr appeared to us as we were praying, encompassed with an ineffable glory. We make known to you the day of his death, that you may annually commemorate it."

Fourth Persecution.—The Christians were comparatively at peace during the reigns of Hadrian and Antoninus. The governors of provinces were sometimes compelled by the populace to put in force the still unrepealed edicts; but they did so reluctantly and seldom. The Church spread rapidly throughout the empire; and zealous missionaries preached the gospel with success in Armenia, Persia, and India, amongst the Sarmatians, Dacians, Scythians, and other barbarous nations.

The Emperor Marcus Aurelius, whom history has delighted to honour, was unhappily prejudiced against the Christians by false reports, and sullied by his cruelty towards them a character otherwise remarkable for justice and humanity. The persecution begun by this prince was exceedingly violent, and its victims were very numerous.

It burst forth in Smyrna. Many Christians of the neighbourhood were brought before the proconsul. " These holy martyrs," says the letter of the Church of Smyrna, " were so torn by scourges, that their veins and bones, and even their entrails, were visible. Yet they stood firm and unshaken, without uttering a groan or a cry. They stood calm while their blood was flowing in streams from a thousand wounds; they opened their lips only to bless the Lord. They seemed no longer in the body; they heard only the voice of Jesus speaking to their hearts; the joy of His presence rendered them insensible to their agony. They saw the things which no human eye hath seen; for they were no longer men, but angels. . . . A young man, named Germanicus, edified his fellow-sufferers by his fortitude. Before exposing him to the wild-beasts, the proconsul exhorted him to have pity on himself; but the martyr replied that he would rather die a thousand deaths than procure his life at the cost of his soul. Then,

walking boldly to meet the lion which was rushing towards
him, he spread his hands to welcome death, and laid down the
bleeding spoils of his body." This boldness irritated the crowd,
and they began to shout, " Bring forth the bishop Polycarp."
    The holy bishop was sought every where : yielding reluc-
tantly to the entreaties of his flock, he had concealed himself
in a neighbouring village. For some days he eluded their
search; until a young man, overcome by torture, revealed
the place of his retreat. When the archers came to seize him,
Polycarp might still have escaped ; but he refused to do so,
saying : " The will of the Lord be done !" He came down ;
and the archers were so struck by his venerable appearance,
that they said : " Why such eagerness to seize this good old
man ?" St. Polycarp gave them supper; and thus obtained
time to pray for the Church, and to prepare for his trial. He
was then mounted on an ass and led to the amphitheatre,
where the people had assembled on receiving tidings of his
capture. The proconsul, touched with pity, besought him to
respect his old age and to swear by the genius of the emperor.
The bishop was unmoved by his solicitations. " Curse Christ,
and I release you," said the proconsul. " Eighty-six years
have I served Him," replied the intrepid bishop, " and He
has done me nothing but good ; how, then, can I curse Him,
my Lord and my Saviour ?" When the proconsul pressed
him still further, he replied : " You are giving yourself needless trouble : *I am a Christian !* If you care to know the
doctrines we profess, I will gladly declare them to you." It
is clear that the proconsul would have gladly availed himself
of any pretext to spare the saint; but the wild cries of the
people compelled him to put the law in execution. As the
games were over, he was condemned to be burnt alive. Immediately Jew and pagan ran to fetch wood to form the pile ;
and the holy martyr mounted it with joyful calmness. When
they were about to secure him with chains, he said, " Leave
me thus ; He who has strengthened me to bear the flames
will strengthen me to stand firm at the stake." They complied with his request in so far that only his hands were tied
behind his back. As the fire was being lighted, he prayed
thus : " Almighty God, Father of Jesus Christ, Thy beloved
Son, through whom we have received grace to know Thee ;
I thank Thee that Thou hast brought me to this happy day,
on which I shall be admitted to the company of Thy mar-

tyrs, and drink of the chalice of Thy Son, to rise unto life everlasting. I praise Thee, I glorify Thee, through our great High Priest Jesus Christ, Thy Son, to whom with Thee and the Holy Ghost be glory, now and evermore. Amen." The flames ascended and formed as it were an arch over the head of the martyr, leaving his body untouched, like pure gold amidst the glow of the furnace; while an odour of surpassing sweetness filled the air. The irritated heathen pierced the martyr's body with a sword, and the flow of blood was so abundant that it quenched the flames. Those who stood by tell us that the heathen would not allow the body to be removed, *lest the Christians should forsake the Crucified to adore Polycarp;* and they add: "Do they not know that we can never forsake Jesus, who suffered for our salvation? We adore Him as the Son of God, and we justly venerate the martyrs as the faithful followers of their King and Master even to death." They then continue: "We saved some of his bones from the fire, regarding them as more precious than costliest jewels; and we laid them in a suitable spot, where we hope to assemble year by year, to animate ourselves by his example. Thus, from the earliest ages, the Church honoured the saints as the servants and friends of God, and preserved their relics with religious veneration as portions of the living members of Jesus Christ and temples of the Holy Ghost.

This persecution ceased in consequence of a miraculous interposition of Providence, obtained by the prayers of the Christian soldiers in the emperor's army. Aurelius was engaged in a campaign against the German tribes, and found himself entangled amidst the barren rocks of Bohemia, with countless troops of barbarians on every side. It was the height of summer; the heat was excessive, and the army was entirely destitute of water. In this emergency, the Christians knelt down and prayed to God amidst the mockeries of the enemy; but in answer to their prayers, the sky became suddenly charged with clouds, and an abundant rain fell around the Roman camp. At first the soldiers opened their mouths to catch the heaven-sent drops; then they filled their helmets, and, after quenching their burning thirst, gave their horses drink. At this moment the barbarians made their onset; but a violent storm of hail, accompanied with vivid flashes of lightning, furiously assailed them, while the gentle and

beneficent shower refreshed the Roman army. The barbarians threw down their arms, and fled in terror. The Romans regarded their deliverance as a miracle; and the legion
to whose prayers they ascribed it was known henceforward
as the Thundering Legion. The emperor wrote to the senate
that his army had been rescued from certain destruction by
the prayers of the Christians, and he forbade the governors
to punish or to search for Christians in future.

But this favourable disposition was of brief duration.
Three years later we find the persecution raging violently
in Gaul in the name and with the authority of the emperor.
Perhaps he had been persuaded that his deliverance was due
to the heathen gods; or it may have been but the caprice of
the local governors, who could at any moment put in force
the dormant laws. The stress of the storm fell upon Lyons.
Tradition affirms that the faith was carried to this city by
Trophimus, the first bishop of Arles, who was sent thither
by St. Peter. The faith spread rapidly and widely. The
heathen were filled with rage; they excluded Christians
from the baths, the market-places, and the public buildings.
Wherever they appeared, the populace insulted them, struck
them, attacked them with stones, and at length denounced
them to the magistrates. The details we are about to give
of this persecution are found in a letter of singular beauty,
written by the faithful in Lyons to their brethren in Asia
Minor. Those who were interrogated concerning their religion, confessed it boldly, and were kept in confinement until
the arrival of the president. A few days afterwards they were
summoned into his presence. The judge behaved so brutally,
that a young man named Epagathus could not restrain his
indignation. He was very young, but an austere and fervent
Christian. He demanded as a right to speak in defence of
the accused, and declared that he could disprove the charges
of impiety and atheism; but he was silenced by a thousand
angry voices. The judge asked whether Epagathus was a
Christian? The zealous young man answered in the affirmative, and was immediately numbered among the Christian
prisoners. His best eulogy is the sneer of the judge, who
called him *the Christians' advocate*. His example stimulated
the rest, and they suffered martyrdom with invincible fortitude.

Meanwhile search was every where made for Pothinus,
Bishop of Lyons, in whose old and decrepit body there dwelt

the vigour of an ever-youthful soul. He was soon found, and led before the judge amidst the execrations of the rabble. When the president asked him, "Who was the God of the Christians?" he replied, "You will know Him if you are worthy." For some time he was left to the mercy of the exasperated multitude; they buffeted him, they kicked him, they pelted him with stones : every one seemed to feel that it would be impious to abstain from insulting the enemy of the gods. He was finally rescued from the mob, and thrown into prison, where he died of the injuries he had received.

The next victims of the popular fury were Sanctus, a deacon of the church of Lyons; Maturus, a recent convert; Attalus; and a youthful slave, whose name was Blandina. The exceeding delicacy of Blandina's frame led the faithful to fear that she could never sustain the terrible ordeal; but, to the amazement of the multitude, the noble girl exhausted the patience and skill of her tormentors. From early dawn until night, every kind of torture was tried; and at length her executioners were constrained to acknowledge themselves baffled and defeated by a weak girl. At every renewal of her agony, she said simply, "I am a Christian; no evil is practised amongst us."

Sanctus the deacon also endured great torments. It was hoped that some expression unworthy of a Christian might be extorted from him; but his only words were, "I am a Christian." The judge was so irritated by his fortitude, that he commanded red-hot plates of copper to be applied to the most sensitive parts of his body. The martyr bore this exquisite torment without a shudder or a groan. When the baffled tormentors left him, his body was one universal wound; his appearance was scarcely human; all his members were dislocated or mutilated. The tormentors returned to the assault after a brief pause; but—wonderful to relate—their steel and their glowing copper did but heal the wounds they would have opened anew, and the body of the holy martyr became whole and sound as before.

Many expired under these torments; while others seemed endowed with a life over which man had no power. But what was most worthy of admiration was, the deep humility of these Christian heroes. Although they had suffered torments of which we can scarcely bear the recital, they would not allow that they deserved the name of martyrs. "When it happened that one of us applied this title to them, they were sensibly distressed, and rebuked us with kind severity. That glorious name, they said, belonged only to those who had finished their course, and whom Jesus Christ had taken to Himself at the moment of their confession of Him,—not to such vile creatures as they were." So strong was the impression produced by the fortitude and the exhortations of these confessors, that many who had denied our Lord from fear of man, on being brought back to the tribunal, avowed themselves Christians, and cheerfully endured all that the disappointed rage of their enemies could inflict on them.

After a few days, the holy martyrs were brought forth and exposed in the amphitheatre. As the beasts were not sufficiently savage to please the populace, they demanded that Maturus and Sanctus should be seated on iron chairs made red-hot. This was done; and, as they still breathed, their sufferings were ended by the sword. Blandina was suspended on a gibbet, with her arms extended in the form of a cross; but the wild beasts refused to touch her. Attalus was led round the amphitheatre with an inscription on his breast—*Attalus the Christian!* As he was a Roman citizen, the president would not gratify the mob by putting him to death; and he was sent back to prison, with others of the martyrs, until the pleasure of the emperor was known. Marcus Aurelius commanded that those only should be put to death who persisted in confessing Jesus Christ; and as all the prisoners continued firm in their confession, they were condemned to death. On the morrow, Alexander, a physician, and Attalus, were slain in the amphitheatre; and the remaining prisoners suffered during the public games. Blandina was enveloped in a net, and thrown to a bull, who tossed and gored her for some time; at length she was despatched with a knife. The bodies of the martyrs were thrown to the dogs; and the fragments were burnt and cast into the Rhone. The sacred relics were not, however, lost. They were recovered in consequence of a vision which disclosed the spot to which they had been borne by the stream, and placed under the altar of the church which is now called St. Nizier. The number of the martyrs was forty-eight; and the church of Lyons has preserved their names, together with a detailed account of their sufferings.

Very shortly afterwards, this same church had the glorious privilege of adding to the army of Christian heroes two young men, Epipodius and Alexander. They were both of distinguished birth, and were connected by a friendship based on their common faith. Having been denounced as Christians, they took refuge in the cottage of a poor widow in the adjacent country; but they were soon tracked and thrown into prison. Three days after their apprehension, they were brought before the judge, who asked them what religion they professed. They answered boldly that they were Christians. "What!" exclaimed the judge, "are the edicts of the emperor still disregarded? has not the warning you have received been sufficient?" They were then separated, lest they should derive strength from beholding each other's firmness. Alexander was led back to prison; and the judge, addressing Epipodius, who was young, and of feeble constitution, said, "Why will you rush on your destruction? We adore the immortal gods with joy, and feasting, and games; you adore a crucified man, whom you can please only by renouncing all the pleasures of life. Abandon this dreary austerity for those pleasures which are so much more suitable to your age." Epipodius calmly replied, "You know not that Jesus Christ rose again; and that, being God and Man, He has opened to His servants the kingdom of heaven. Know you not that man is composed of spirit as well as of flesh? Amongst us the spirit commands, and the flesh obeys. The pleasures to which you surrender yourselves in honour of your gods flatter and please the senses indeed, but they slay the spirit. We war against our bodies; but it is to secure the supremacy of our souls. And what is your end?—a dreary and hopeless death : while we enter upon everlasting life through the torments with which you slay us." The judge abstained from further discussion, and commanded that Epipodius should be racked, and that his flesh should be torn with iron hooks. The martyr was at length beheaded. The next day but one Alexander was brought forth. "Take warning from the fate of the rest," said the judge; "we have done our work so effectually, that you are, I believe, the only Christian we have left." Alexander replied, "I thank God that, in calling to my remembrance the holy martyrs, you animate me by their example. You are wrong in your calculations. The Christian name can never perish. I am a Christian; and a Christian I shall die." He was given into the hands of three executioners, who took it in turns to beat and torture him, until they were all wearied with the task. The governor then ordered him to be fastened to a cross, on which he speedily expired.

During this same persecution suffered St. Symphorian. He was a young man of high birth in the city of Autun. On occasion of the feast of Cybele, he had openly testified his contempt for the impious rite. He was seized and brought before the governor, who exclaimed on seeing him : " How have you contrived to elude my notice? I thought I had cleared Autun of Christians. And now, tell me why you refuse to adore Cybele?" " I am a Christian," was the reply; " I adore the one God whose throne is in heaven. As to the image of Cybele, I not only refuse to adore it, but if you will give me leave, I will break it in pieces." " It is your birth and your family, I suppose," said the judge, "that make you so bold. But are you aware of the emperor's command?" He then read the edict, and continued : " What have you to say to that?" " This idol," replied Symphorian, " is an invention of the devil to delude and devour souls. Our God punishes sin, while He rewards virtue. I can reach a happy eternity only by stedfastness in confessing His holy name." He was then beaten with rods and taken back to prison. After a few days the judge offered him a large sum of money and an honourable employment, if he would but adore the idol. " It is not the office of a judge," answered Symphorian, " to waste time in needless talk, or to lay snares for the innocent. I fear not death—we must all surrender our life to Him who gave it; and why should I not offer to Jesus as a free gift that which I must one day pay Him as a debt? Your offers are poison, proffered in pleasing form; but time, like an impetuous stream, bears away your cherished good; our God alone can bestow a perfect and an unchanging felicity. Remotest antiquity saw not the dawn of His glory, nor shall the latest future behold its setting." " You are exhausting my patience," said the judge; " sacrifice to Cybele, or you shall die this very day amidst horrible tortures." Symphorian replied : " I fear none but the all-powerful God who created me, and Him alone can I serve. My body is in your power—my soul is in my own." As he was led to the place of execution, his mother came to meet him ; not to unnerve him with her tears, but to animate and encourage him to suffer for Christ. " My son Symphorian, my beloved son," cried this worthy daughter of the Mother of sorrows, "remember now the living God. Summon all your courage, my child; fear not a death which leads securely to life. That you may not feel any regret at leaving this earth, lift your eyes to heaven; despise the torments which last but for a brief moment; persevere unto the end, and they will issue in changeless eternal blessedness." The faith which inspired these heroic words was surely not less than that which sustained the martyr in his agony.

After the death of Aurelius, the Church again enjoyed an interval of rest. His successors were too much engaged in their vile pleasures to care for the interests of paganism.

Fifth Persecution.—Severus was at first so favourable to the Christians and so indifferent to the rapid progress they were evidently making, that ten years passed without his noticing them. He then published edicts so sanguinary, and executed them so rigorously, that the faithful deemed the times of Antichrist had come. The persecution began in Egypt, and raged throughout Africa with unexampled violence. At Alexandria, Leonidas, the father of Origen, and seven of his pupils, were beheaded; but the martyrdom of the slave Potamiæna is the most striking and affecting episode in this tale of horrors. She might have purchased safety by the sacrifice of her honour; but she spurned the perfidious tempter. She was condemned to be thrown into a cauldron of boiling pitch. As they were preparing to strip her, she implored her executioners to allow her to retain her garments; they consented on condition that she should be lowered gradually into the cauldron. Her agony lasted three hours, and her rude guards confessed that the grace of Jesus did indeed sustain His disciples in a manner that was wholly supernatural. One of them, named Basilides, behaved kindly to the martyr, and shielded her from needless insult. She thanked him, and said she would pray for him when she reached her God. Shortly afterwards Basilides avowed himself a Christian. At first he was laughed at; but when it was found that he was serious in his avowal, he was denounced and put in prison. The Christians contrived to obtain access to him, and he was baptised on the eve of his glorious confession of Christ. One such conversion, at such a time, is a magnificent illustration and proof of the power of divine grace.

The persecution raged violently at Carthage; and amongst its victims were St. Perpetua and St. Felicitas. Perpetua was twenty-two years of age—a mother, with an infant at her breast; and she had to struggle, not only with the dread of tortures and death, but with the purest and holiest human feelings. Her mother was a Christian; but her aged father was a pagan. Again and again he implored her with tears to pity his gray hairs, and not to expose him to such shame amongst men. " My father's gray hairs," she wrote, " pained me, when I thought that of all my family he alone would not glory in my sufferings." Felicitas was prematurely delivered of a daughter on her return from examination. The gaoler said to her, " If you suffer so much now, what will you do when you are thrown to wild-beasts?" To which she replied : " What I suffer *now*, I suffer in my own person ; *then,* Another will suffer with me and for me, because I shall suffer for Him." On the appointed day, after having been torn by wild-beasts, their sufferings were ended by gladiators who despatched them with their knives.

Irenæus, a disciple of St. Polycarp, had succeeded Pothinus in the see of Lyons ; and in consequence of his zealous labours, the number of the faithful had increased greatly. In this persecution the soldiers were let loose upon the Christians, and ordered to slay all who would not deny Christ. St. Irenæus received the crown of martyrdom, and with him many thousands of his faithful flock. The firmness of these Christians amidst the most exquisite tortures showed, as the letter of the church of Lyons beautifully says, " how they were bedewed and refreshed with those living waters that flow from the Sacred Heart of Jesus : that nothing can inspire fear where the love of the Father dwells, nothing can be painful where the glory of Christ reigns."

 . *Sixth Persecution.*—From the death of Septimius Severus (A.D. 211) to the accession of Maximin (A.D. 235), the Christians enjoyed rest. Alexander Severus was even favourable to them. He was a young man of amiable dispositions, and a professed philosopher. In his private chapel, amongst pagan gods and heroes, in company with Apollonius of Tyana and with Orpheus, stood a bust of Christ. He was especially pleased with the words, " As you would that men should do to you, do you also to them in like manner;" and he caused them to be written up in his palace. He was put to death by Maximin, who then usurped the purple. It is said that the immediate motive of this emperor's persecution of the

Christians was the refusal of a Christian soldier to wear a wreath of laurel on his accession. The Christians were now so numerous that their extermination would, it was feared, depopulate the empire; and hence the fury of Maximin was directed against those who *taught* and *governed* in the churches. It was hoped that the people, when deprived of their pastors, would be easily reclaimed. Thus the stress of this persecution fell on the bishops and priests. Pope St. Pontian was one of the first sufferers. His successor, Antherius, occupied the see of St. Peter for six weeks only, and is generally believed to have suffered martyrdom. We read of churches being destroyed by fire; from which it appears that the Christians had been encouraged by twenty-four years of peace to erect public buildings for worship. This persecution was keen but brief, as Maximin was murdered by his own soldiers.

Seventh Persecution.—No sooner had Decius become emperor than he published a bloody edict against the Christians, and sent it for execution to the governors of all the provinces. It was his design to suppress Christianity altogether. Imprisonment, scourgings, fire and wild beasts, melted pitch, burning pincers, and other tortures, were used to shake or to punish the constancy of the faithful; but while many quailed and consented to sacrifice to idols, many more were made strong by grace to endure to the end. At the head of these were the Pope St. Fabian, St. Alexander Bishop of Jerusalem, and St. Babylas Bishop of Antioch. We read of one who was torn with pincers and burnt with red-hot plates of iron until his body was one continuous wound. He was then smeared with honey, and, with his hands tied behind his back, exposed to the rays of a burning sun, and to the tormenting stings of flies, bees, and other insects. The spirit which animated the martyrs of that day may be seen in a letter written from their prison to St. Cyprian by some confessor of Rome. "What lot more blessed can be ours, by the grace of God, than to confess Jesus Christ amidst pains and torments—to confess the Son of God with lacerated bodies, but with souls free and triumphant even in the agonies of death—to become sharers of the Passion of Christ by suffering in His name? If we have not yet poured out our blood, we are ready to do so. Pray, then, that the Lord may more and more confirm and strengthen each one of us, and that the

Captain of our salvation may lead forth to the battle us, his trained and veteran soldiers, armed with weapons divine and unconquerable." Many of the leading bishops and priests withdrew from persecution, acting on our Lord's injunction, and fearing that their presence might exasperate the heathen still more against their flocks. The persecution increased in severity, until an insurrection in Macedonia and the war with the Goths occupied Decius with cares of greater political importance. He was killed in the latter war (A.D. 251), and a brief respite was granted to the Church.

A pestilence, which ravaged the empire was the occasion of renewed persecution under the Emperor Gallus, when Popes Cornelius and Lucius, and many more, were sacrificed to appease the supposed wrath of the pagan deities.

Eighth Persecution.—For several years his successor Valerian (A.D. 253-260) left the Christians in peace, until, at the instigation of his favourite Macrinus, their sworn enemy, he published an edict against them, to render the gods propitious to his expedition against the Persians. The exercise of the Christian religion was forbidden under pain of death, and sentence of banishment pronounced against the bishops and pastors of the Church; so, it was vainly imagined, this *strange superstition* would die out of itself. This seems clear from the first examination of St. Cyprian. But no power of earth can sever the spiritual tie between a bishop and his flock; and the emperor found himself baffled by these obscure and despised men. Wherever they were banished, the bishops not only continued to rule their flocks, but they gathered new churches around them. Thus Dionysius, Bishop of Alexandria, who was banished to Libya, says: "We were at first insulted and stoned; but soon some of the pagans forsook their idols and turned to God. God sent us thither expressly to sow the seed of the Divine word." Thousands of confessors sealed their faith with their blood; but, furious at the resistance he encountered, the emperor issued another and a still severer edict in the year 258, by which it was ordered that "bishops, presbyters, and deacons should be at once put to death by the sword; senators and knights were to forfeit their property and their rank, and, if they still continued obstinate, were to be put to death; women of rank were to be banished. Those Christians who were in the service of the palace were to be put in chains, and set to work on the imperial estates."

Pope St. Stephen and his successor St. Sixtus II., together with four deacons, amongst whom was St. Laurence, were sufferers under these edicts. As Pope Sixtus was being led to martyrdom, Laurence followed him, and said with tears: "Whither are you going, my father, without your deacon?" The saint replied: "My son, a nobler conflict is reserved for you. You will follow me within three days." The holy deacon hastened to distribute amongst the poor all the money in his hands. Then the prefect of the city, knowing that the Church had great wealth, sent for Laurence, and said to him: "I do not wish to punish you; I am content to ask for what you can well give. I know you have vessels of gold and silver for your sacrifices; give me these treasures; the prince needs them to pay his troops." St. Laurence made answer: "I admit that the Church is rich, and that the emperor himself has not treasures so precious. You shall see them if you will give me a little time to set them in order." Three days were granted him; and the saint employed them in collecting all the poor whom the Church maintained; then he told the prefect that every thing was in order. The prefect accompanied him; and when he saw this crowd of blind, and lame, and crippled poor, he turned with fury to St. Laurence. "Why are you so angry?" said the saint; "gold is but a vile metal, and the occasion of countless evils: the *true gold* is the divine light which enlightens these poor. This is the wealth I promised to show you." "Is it thus you presume to mock me?" exclaimed the prefect. "I know that you Christians pride yourselves on despising death. But I will make you die by slow degrees." The agony of the saint was begun with severe scourging; then he was stretched on a gridiron and slowly roasted alive. So great was the strength granted him, that his pain seemed but a refreshment. After a while he said calmly to the judge: "I am roasted enough on this side; turn me over on the other." Then, with a holy irony, he added: "My flesh is now sufficiently roasted; you can eat of it." He then prayed for the conversion of Rome, and gave his soul into the hands of God.

It was during this persecution that the great St. Cyprian, Bishop of Carthage, received the crown of martyrdom. He was born in Africa, of a distinguished family, and taught rhetoric in Carthage with great success. It was in his riper age, and after long examination, that he became a Christian.

" When the water of regeneration had washed away the de-
filements of my past life," he writes, " and my cleansed heart
had received the Divine light, all my difficulties disappeared;
and what I had deemed impossible, became easy to me." He
was soon raised to the priesthood, and, on the death of the
bishop, was elected his successor. The humble priest fled to
evade a responsibility so great; but he was discovered and
brought back, and compelled to submit. In the heat of the
Decian persecution he had concealed himself; but during his
concealment he had ruled and watched over his church, and
on his return he continued his indefatigable ministry. He
was at first banished, together with many other bishops and
priests; but, having been permitted to return, he was again
seized, when the persecution became more virulent, and condemned to death. On hearing his sentence pronounced, he
joyfully exclaimed, " God be thanked !" When led to execution he prostrated himself on the ground and prayed fervently for a short time. Then, as a token of his forgiveness,
he gave the executioner twenty-five pieces of gold; and,
after with his own hands bandaging his eyes, he knelt down,
his arms crossed on his breast, and so awaited the fatal blow;
while the faithful spread handkerchiefs and cloths around to
catch the martyr's blood.

We have an interesting account of the martyrdom of St.
Montanus and his eight companions, begun by themselves,
when they were in prison, and completed by an eye-witness.
Some also refer to this persecution the martyrdom of St. Denis
or Dionysius, who was the first Bishop of Paris. This holy
bishop was called the Apostle of Gaul, from the zeal and success of his labours. An unbroken tradition points to the hill
called Montmartre (*Mont des Martyrs*), near Paris, as the
spot on which he was beheaded, together with Rusticus a
priest, and Eleutherus a deacon. At Cæsarea in Cappadocia
a child, whose name was Cyril, displayed an unusual and edifying fortitude. He had the name of Jesus continually on
his lips; and in pronouncing it felt a sweetness and a strength
which made him insensible alike to praises and to threats.
His pagan father, after treating him cruelly, turned him out
of doors, because he would not worship idols. The governor
of the city then sent for him, and said : " My child, I am willing
to overlook your fault in consideration of your tender age.
You can easily regain your father's favour and all the comforts

of your home; renounce your silly superstition!" The child
made answer: "God will take me, and I shall be better off
with Him than with my father. I care not for being thrust
out of my father's house; I shall have one much larger and
more beautiful. If I am poor now, I shall be rich in heaven;
and if I die, I am not afraid, because there is a better life
after this." He spoke these words with a clearness and a
courage which showed that it was God who spoke in him.
The governor then tried to frighten him: he tied his hands
together, and told the officers to make ready a pile to burn
the child. Cyril moved not a muscle, but walked steadily
onwards to the flames. He was brought back to the governor, who said to him: "Well now; you have seen what fire
is, and what the sword is: will you be a good child now, and
let your father take you home?" Cyril replied: "I wish
you had not brought me back. I am not frightened at the
fire, or at the sword. I want to go to a better home. I want
God to receive me, and welcome me home: kill me at once,
that I may go to Him." The bystanders shed tears at this
moving scene, while he spoke words of reproof and of consolation to them. He was then led off to execution; but the
acts of his martyrdom do not inform us of the death he suffered. "Out of the mouth of babes Thou hast perfected
praise, O Lord, because of Thine enemies" (Ps. viii. 3)

Ninth Persecution.—In the year 260 the Emperor Gal-
lienus published an edict, by which he secured to the Church
the free exercise of its worship, and the undisturbed possession of its buildings, lands, and burial-places. Macrinus,
however, had usurped imperial authority in Egypt and the
East; and it was not until his overthrow (A.D. 262) that this
edict of toleration put a stop to the persecutions which were
going on under the edict of Valerian. Eusebius, in his history, records an instance which gives an insight into the position of Christians at that time. Marius, a Christian soldier
of Cæsarea in Palestine, was about to be made centurion.
Just as the staff of office was being given to him, another
soldier, who was next in order of promotion, stepped forward
and said that Marius was incapable of holding rank, because
he was a Christian. Three hours were granted to Marius to
decide whether he would sacrifice to the gods. The Bishop
Theotecnus, leading him into the church, pointed to the soldier's

sword, and at the same time presented him with the book of the Gospels, bidding him choose between them — his rank and his faith. Without a moment's hesitation Marius grasped the Gospels in his right hand. "Now," said the bishop, "cleave fast to God. Go in peace." He was beheaded at once.

The Emperor Claudius II. renewed the persecution, causing two hundred and sixty of the faithful to be put to death in the amphitheatre by the arrows of his soldiers. Many other martyrs suffered about the same time.

The Emperor Aurelian (A.D. 270) was not at first hostile to the Church; but at length he thought he should gain the favour of the senate and of the people by persecuting the enemies of their gods. "It was fortunately," says Lactantius, "towards the close of his reign; so that the edicts had not reached the remoter provinces before his death." Still the known inclination of the emperor was the occasion of many martyrdoms.

Tenth Persecution. — The Church had peace for twenty years; during which time the numbers of the faithful rapidly increased. But with security came a decay of piety; and God permitted a new persecution to arise, at once to chastise the infidelities and to rekindle the fervour of His people. This was the last and crowning assault made by the imperial power on the Church of God. Dioclesian was emperor of the East, and Maximian of the West. In the year 303 the former published at Nicomedia an edict, in which he commanded the churches to be pulled down, and the holy Scriptures to be burnt. Maximian had already preceded him with characteristic ferocity in the West, where the persecution had long raged. Torments previously unknown were employed to intimidate the Christians. They were suspended by the feet over a slow fire; they were stripped naked, and with a fork stuck through one leg left to expire by lingering torture; sharp reeds were thrust beneath their nails; their flesh was scraped from the bone with broken pots, and molten lead poured into their open wounds. In Phrygia a city was invested and set on fire by the pagans, and men, women, and children perished in the flames, calling on the name of the Lord Jesus. Eusebius, who was an eye-witness of some of these scenes, tells us that their barbarity was without precedent. All the earth, says Lactantius, was drenched in blood

from the East to the West. The persecution invaded even
the emperor's palace. Several of his most distinguished officers
were Christians, and it was resolved that they should be compelled to sacrifice to idols. One of them named Peter endured
with unshrinking firmness torments which we cannot read of
without a shudder. He was first thrown from a considerable
height; his bruised and shattered body was then beaten with
heavy sticks, so that the bones in some parts were laid bare.
His wounds were then washed with salt and vinegar. After
which he was slowly roasted; and, in order to protract his
agony, withdrawn at intervals, and then again put to the fire.
The glorious martyr endured his torments as calmly as though
he were insensible to pain. The persecution raged with greatest
fury in the East; but the West also furnished many martyrs.
It was at this time that the holy virgin, St. Agnes, and the
heroic soldier, St. Sebastian, sealed their faith with their blood.
In Gaul St. Quentin was barbarously tortured, and then beheaded. He was racked, and beaten with heavy chains; boiling oil and pitch and grease were poured upon him; lighted
torches were applied to his body. He received his crown in
the town to which he has bequeathed his name—St. Quentin
in Picardy. The slaughter of the Theban legion is referred
to this persecution. Bede records the death of St. Alban, the
first English martyr. Alban was a citizen of Verulam, and
a pagan, when compassion led him to shelter a Christian
priest fleeing from his enemies. He admired the piety of his
guest, listened to his teaching, and was at length baptised.
The priest was, after some time, tracked to his hiding-place;
and Alban, to save his teacher, surrendered himself to the
soldiers, clothed in the priest's garments. He gave his name
when examined, boldly avowed himself a Christian, and refused to sacrifice to the gods. He was scourged, and beheaded
on a little eminence outside the town. When the persecution
ceased, a church was built over the spot of his martyrdom;
and in 793 Offa, king of Mercia, founded on the same spot
the noble abbey of St. Alban's. This fierce persecution was
the last. It had been proved that the Church could not be
crushed by brute force. It was now to triumph visibly, to
overthrow paganism, and to become the religion of the empire, which had struggled against it in vain.

Lactantius has left a treatise on the deaths of the persecutors. Nero was proscribed by the senate, and stabbed

himself to avoid the disgraceful fate which awaited him (A.D. 68). Domitian was assassinated by his own wife, aided by some officers of his palace (A.D. 96). Septimius Severus died of grief at the ingratitude of his son, who had twice attempted to kill him. Maximin was put to death by his own soldiers (A.D. 237). Decius perished miserably in an expedition against the Goths (A.D. 251). Valerian was taken prisoner by Sapor, king of Persia. When Sapor mounted his horse, the emperor was compelled to stoop, that the king might step on his neck and so reach his saddle. At last he was flayed alive; and his skin, dyed red, was hung up in the temple, in derision of the Romans. Aurelian was killed by his secretary. Maximian was put to death by order of Constantine, for having conspired against that prince. Dioclesian had shared the empire with Galerius, whose cruelties went far beyond those of any former persecutor. He was smitten with a loathsome and incurable disease; his flesh rotted from off his bones. He lingered for a year in excruciating torments, and died in agony. Dioclesian starved himself to death (A.D. 307).

Barbarians poured in upon the empire, as if to avenge the insulted Church. The Goths overran Thrace and Macedonia and Greece; the Germans advanced as far as Ravenna; others traversed Gaul, and poured into Spain; the Sarmatians devastated Pannonia; the Parthians ravaged Syria; while the Empire was every where internally distracted by the struggles of its numerous competitors. There were earthquakes, inundations, droughts, and famines; men wasted with hunger fell dead in the streets, and there were none to bury them; while a virulent ophthalmia threatened a plague of blindness.

The Bishop of Alexandria writes of the plague of A.D. 262, that there was not a house free from death and mourning. "It was," he adds, "an occasion for the Christians to display the most heroic charity. The sick were visited, instructed, assisted, and fed; and many fell victims to their self-devotion; while the heathen fled, leaving their dearest friends uncared for. The Church honours those who perished in this noble work as martyrs of charity."

§ 4. Christian writers and apologists.

The triumph of the Church was as signal in the field of literature as in the amphitheatre. Learned men defended it eloquently and solidly. The earliest apology or defence of Christianity which has reached us is that of St. Justin; he prefixed his name to his work, and addressed it to the Emperor Antoninus and his two sons. Justin was a pagan by birth. It was not until his thirtieth year that he became a Christian, after long investigation. One day he was wandering, lost in thought, when he was accosted by an aged Christian, who showed him that the heathen sages were wrong in their first principles, and knew not God; that they only were really wise whom God had inspired. This discourse stirred up in Justin the desire to study the holy Scriptures; his heart was touched by Divine grace, and the sight of the constancy of the martyrs completed his conversion. He became a Christian. About A.D. 148 he wrote his apology, which is valuable, not only as a defence of religion, but as a record of many points of faith and practice. He wrote other books on religion, and at length sealed his testimony with his blood.

While the fifth persecution was raging (under Septimius Severus), Tertullian, a priest of Carthage, a man of keen intellect and burning zeal, of vast learning and singular eloquence, published his apology. He sets forth the doctrines of the gospel boldly and clearly, in contrast with the incoherent traditions of heathenism. "Were we disposed to resist you," he exclaims, "think you we should lack men or courage? We are but of yesterday, and already we fill your cities, your castles, your hamlets, your fields, your palaces, the senate: we leave you nothing but your temples! But it is our duty to suffer death rather than inflict it. Besides, we need take no deeper vengeance than to withdraw beyond the limits of the Empire; we should leave you appalled by the solitude that would surround you." He draws a beautiful picture of Christian life and manners in the third century.

Some years later, under Alexander Severus, Origen attained great celebrity as a writer. He was a martyr's son, and had been educated with care; his father was more struck by the manifest grace of God in him even than by his brilliant abilities. During the persecution in which his father suffered, he was with difficulty prevented from giving himself up as a Christian. He wrote to his father just before his martyrdom: "Fear not for us your children; God will take us up." The family was reduced to poverty by the confiscation of their goods, and Origen began to teach grammar. He became at length the head of the great catechetical school at Alexandria. He then sold his profane books, and applied himself to the study of the sacred volume alone. His lectures were well attended; many were converted to the faith, of whom not a few afterwards suffered martyrdom. He was himself thrown into prison, where he was subjected to great tortures in the hopes of overcoming his constancy, and by his fall leading many to abandon the faith.

Amongst his many writings is a volume against Celsus, a pagan philosopher, who had given vent to calumnies against the Christians. It is regarded as the completest defence which antiquity has transmitted to us. In many of his works, however, he has put forth extravagant and dangerous opinions which have left a shade on his memory. The limits of this little work will allow no more than a record of the name of Athenagoras, who addressed an apology to the Emperor Commodus, St. Clement of Alexandria, and Arnobius.

In these learned and temperate apologies reason and faith combined to crush paganism; it showed itself unable to reply, save by renewed violence and persecution.

§ 5. Conversion of Constantine.

Amidst the fiercest and most general persecution the Church had ever known, God, who sets bounds to the fury of the wildest storm, had decreed the triumph of His Church over the powers of the world. Dioclesian and Maximian were compelled to relinquish the purple to Constantius Chlorus and Galerius, who had long held the second rank as Cæsars. Constantius Chlorus was the first instrument in God's hands to pave the way to the peace and triumph of the Church. To him was intrusted the defence of Gaul, Spain, and Great Britain; but the seat of his government was in Britain, which he ruled with mildness and impartiality. His character may be gathered from the following incident. There were many Christians in the palace when the edict of Dioclesian appeared. In his inferior office of Cæsar, it became his duty to communicate to them the emperor's command. He accordingly summoned them into his presence, and informed them that they must either sacrifice to the gods, or give up their situations. Most of them protested that they loved their faith more than place, and wealth, and life itself; but some, corrupted by the atmosphere of a court, consented to sacrifice. Then Constantius avowed his own intentions; he extolled the noble firmness of the one party, and with withering reproaches rebuked the dastardly compliance of the other. " How," he exclaimed, " can I expect that you will be true to the emperor—you who are traitors to your God ?" He drove them from his palace in disgrace, and honoured with his fullest confidence those who had loved their faith more than the world. Under such a prince the Church in Gaul repaired the losses it had sustained under Maximian; and the soil, fertilised by the blood of martyrs, yielded an abundant harvest to the many labourers who went forth when the storm had passed over. Constantius died at York, A.D. 306, and was succeeded by his son Constantine.

The young emperor was about thirty-one years of age, of handsome form, with good abilities, and a wisdom in advance of his time. He was a pagan, for we find him in 308 offering sacrifice in the temple of Apollo, probably at Autun in France. The crisis of his fate, however, was drawing on. Maxentius, the son of Maximian, desiring to subdue the whole West to his obedience, declared war against Constantine, and sought to secure victory to his arms by practising the most cruel and abominable superstitions. Constantine, whose forces were far inferior to those of his adversary, feeling the necessity of aid from on high, bethought him of the Christians' God, and prayed that He would reveal Himself to him, and give him victory in the battle. His prayer was heard. At noonday, while he was marching at the head of his army, a cross of fire was seen in the calm and cloudless sky, and on it these words: *In hoc signo vinces*—" Through this sign thou shalt conquer." It was visible to all the army. During the ensuing night our Lord appeared in vision to Constantine, and commanded him to make a standard like the cross he had seen, and to bear it at the head of his troops. Accordingly he caused one to be made of costly materials, covered with gold. On its top was a regal crown blazing with jewels, and bearing the first two letters of the word *Christ*. A veil of cloth-of-gold hung from the transverse arm of the cross. The standard was called the *Labarum* ; and fifty of the bravest soldiers were chosen to guard it and bear it by turns. Sending also for Christian bishops, he inquired of them the meaning of the vision he had beheld, and received from them an exposition of the doctrines of the faith. Then, confident of the Divine protection, he marched to Rome, where he attacked and utterly defeated the tyrant Maxentius, who was drowned in the Tiber while attempting to escape. Rome opened her gates to the youthful conqueror, and he entered in triumph.

Although Constantine did not at once become a Christian, or even declare himself a catechumen of the Church, he in every way protected a religion of the truth of which he was intellectually convinced. He published an edict of toleration; and although he does not appear, in the first instance, even to have contemplated the abolition of paganism, nevertheless he placed various restrictions on its exercise, forbidding the abominable sacrifices performed in private dwellings, and afterwards demolishing certain of the temples where immoral rites were practised. He proceeded to remedy the wrongs inflicted by his predecessors. He recalled the Christians who had been banished, restored the churches, enriched them with magnificent ornaments and vessels, honoured the ministers of religion, and conferred upon them special privileges. He gave the Pope, who had been hitherto the special object of hatred and of persecution, the palace of Lateran, and turned an adjacent palace into a church. This is the beginning of the patrimony of St. Peter; it is now the church of St. John Lateran.

The affrighted Christians could scarcely believe for joy. Their religion protected by the emperor, their worship held in honour, their churches glowing with unwonted splendour, their confessors liberated, their exiles recalled—they could but exclaim, "This is the Lord's doing; and it is marvellous in our eyes!" The Church had become honourable in the eyes of the heathen. The standard of the cross was placed in the right hand of the emperor's statue; and thus, that which had been an object of scorn and detestation, became the proudest decoration of the Cæsars.

REFLECTIONS.

It pleased God to show that the Church is the work of His hand, by establishing it in spite of obstacles which were apparently insuperable. The new religion humbled human reason by the depth of its mysteries, and thwarted human passions by the strictness of its laws. If we consider the state of those to whom it was preached, the position of its preach-ers, the claims made by men of low condition on a generation so enlightened, so polished, so proud and disdainful, and so corrupted, we feel that, had "this work been of men," it must have "come to naught." It was of God; and its tri-umph shows that "the weakness of God is stronger than man." On the wreck of the older civilisation arose a new society, youthful, and energetic, and virtuous; despising all that the former had venerated, and venerating all that it had despised. The foundations of this new society were laid in martyrdom, during three hundred years of almost continuous persecution. The Lord had foretold all this: His disciples were to be persecuted; brought before governors and before kings for His sake; scourged and slain for "the testimony of Jesus." And no sooner did the Church appear on earth than the Gentiles began to rage, "and the kings of the earth stood up against the Lord, and against His Christ." Sense, and passion, and interest were on their side; theirs was the religion of pleasure and license. How could the religion of Christ, with its restraints and prohibitions, find favour in hearts so polluted? The Christians refused to share the impure feasts of paganism, and became the objects of public detestation. Again, the very interests of the empire were deemed to be at stake; the Roman polity was assailed in its foundations when its gods were set at naught. Rome gloried in being a city holy in its origin, indebted to religion for all its successes in war; it boasted of having led captive the na-tions under the invincible protection of Mars, the god of war. To disown its gods was to deny the fundamental principle of the state. Hence the Christians were looked upon as the enemies, not only of the gods, but of the republic itself; it was more important, therefore, to exterminate them than to quell Parthians or Dacians. Accordingly we find that the Church was persecuted even by those whom history calls the good emperors. Hence any calamity, public or private, a reverse of arms, a famine, a pestilence—any thing served as a motive. Now and then there was a pause and a lull; but on both sides the conflict was felt to be mortal. The fiercer the persecution, the swifter the advance of the hated *superstition*; the blood of the martyrs yielded fruit an hundredfold. To the fury of the oppressor they opposed an invincible patience. Never did they use force, where force would have seemed both justifiable and lawful, to free themselves from the hateful tyranny that oppressed them. They were as unresisting under Dioclesian, when they filled the empire, as they had been under Nero, when they were but a scattered few. Their vocation was to suffer and to die. God would show that His Church owed nothing to human agency. The triumph was to be won by the cross. Aged men, delicate maidens, men in the strength of manhood, all alike braved torments, endured death with calm intrepidity. The baffled persecutors were compelled at length to stay their hand lest the empire should be depopulated.

Herein is the finger of God visible.[2] We cannot read the acts of the martyrs without feeling that at the root of their endurance lay a *supernatural* power; a courage and fortitude inspired by God, and therefore indomitable. Surely that men could thus, during 300 years, suffer for their religion, is a proof that that religion is of God, and that man did not build what man was powerless to overthrow. The Catholic Church plainly subsisted then, as, in fact, it has subsisted ever since, without earthly support, and in spite of earthly opposition. It has weathered every storm, and abides with its hierarchy unbroken, its rights and spiritual powers unimpaired, as it received them from the hand of Jesus Christ. A body which has survived the overthrow of all its enemies, and is still strong with the strength of immortal youth, unchanged and unchangeable, can have none but God for its author.

CHAPTER II.

FROM THE CONVERSION OF CONSTANTINE, A.D. 312, TO THE FALL OF THE WESTERN EMPIRE, A.D. 476.

§ 1. Constantine and his successors down to Julian the Apostate.

THE first public act of the first Christian emperor was one of grace and pardon. The prison-doors were thrown open, and those who had opposed the conqueror were restored to their liberty. The spirit of the Church began to pervade the laws: the punishment of the cross was forbidden; the forms for

emancipating slaves were simplified; the condition of prisoners
was alleviated; provision was made for the maintenance of the
destitute children of the poor.   Constantine even attempted,
though without success, to abolish the gladiatorial. combats.   He contributed largely to the erection and adorn-
ment of churches, and to the support of the ministers of religion.   Very soon after his victory over Maxentius, he sent
more than 10,000l. to the Bishop of Carthage for the clergy
of Africa; and, in the letter which accompanied this munifi-
cent donation, he said, that if the bishop found this sum too
little, he might apply to the steward of the imperial domain,
who had received orders to provide him at once with every
thing he wanted.   He welcomed bishops to his table, received
them in his palace, and was always accompanied by some
priests, whom he called his soul's guards.   In the year 321 he
made the observance of Sunday obligatory; all the courts of
law were closed, and all ordinary occupations forbidden.   His
pious care extended to the spots hallowed by the visible presence of our Lord, and he proposed to build a magnificent
church in Jerusalem.   His mother, St. Helena, a native of
Britain, had a peculiar devotion to the holy places; and, although she had reached her eightieth year, she made a pilgrimage to the Holy Land.   On reaching Jerusalem she felt
an eager longing to discover the cross on which our Redeemer
had suffered for our sins.   The search was not easy; the heathen had covered Mount Calvary with a vast quantity of
earth, and built upon it a temple to Venus, in order to prevent Christian pilgrims from visiting the sacred spot.   But
no obstacles could discourage the pious princess.   She held
consultations with aged persons who remembered the site in
its former condition; and she was assured that our Lord's
sepulchre would be recognised by the discovery of the instruments of His passion.   It was the custom in those days to
bury near the body of a criminal the instruments of his death.
The pagan temple was demolished, and excavations were
made in every direction.   Soon the cave of the holy sepulchre was discovered.   Near it were three crosses, and the inscription recorded by the Evangelists; with the nails which
had pierced the sacred hands and feet of our Lord.   All that
remained was to identify the cross of Jesus Christ.   A lively
faith is fertile in expedients.   By the advice of Macarius,
Bishop of Jerusalem, the three crosses were borne to the

house of a person who had been long lying sick of an incurable disease. Each was applied to the body of the sufferer,
and earnest prayers were offered that our Lord would deign
to show which of the three had been moistened with His precious blood. The whole city was greatly excited; two of
the crosses were applied without effect; but no sooner had the
third touched the sick person, than she arose perfectly healed.
Sozomen the historian says that it was applied also to a dead
body, and that the dead returned to life: and St. Paulinus
confirms this statement. The empress was transported with
gratitude and joy.* She detached a portion of the cross to
be presented to her son, and enclosed the remainder in a
shrine of silver to be preserved in the church of the Holy
Sepulchre. This church arose with a splendour befitting its
site. Within its foundations were comprised both the sepulchre and the hill of Calvary. St. Helena built two other
churches—one on the spot from which our Lord ascended into
heaven, the other at Bethlehem, on the site of the Nativity.
Nor was her charity restricted to the material temples of the
Lord. Wherever she went she bestowed abundant alms on
the poor, the orphan, and the widow. She manifested a special affection towards the virgins dedicated to God; and on
one occasion she assembled all those in Jerusalem, and served
them herself as they sat at table. She did not long survive
her pious pilgrimage, but died soon after her return, in the
arms of the emperor her son.

Our Saviour had foretold that His Church would be
always persecuted, and always victorious. No sooner did
external persecution cease, than deadly heresies arose within
it. The devil, unable to crush the Church, aimed at adulter-
ating its faith and breaking up its unity. There had, indeed,
been heresies from the beginning. To pass over the earlier
sects who strove to combine portions of the faith with their
private opinions, Montanus had taught doctrines opposed to
the mildness and tenderness of the gospel. The eloquent and
intrepid Tertullian was perverted by this heresy. Manes, the
leader of the Manichæans, had broached the impious doctrine
that there were two Gods—one supremely good, and one
thoroughly evil. Other heresies had arisen from the incapa-
city of human reason, unaided by grace, to receive the mys-

* The Church has hallowed the memory of this discovery by instituting
the festival of the Invention of the Holy Cross, May 3.

E

tery of the Incarnation. They had, however, rather retarded
the spread of the Church than perverted its~members. It
was otherwise with Arianism.

Arius was a priest of Alexandria; modest in demeanour,
austere in life, but full of ambition, and a lover of novelties.
It is said that he had aspired to the see of Alexandria; and,
that, when his hopes were crushed by the election of Alexander, his envy and anger led him to deny the teaching of his
superior, and to set forth a new and more acceptable doctrine.
He ventured to assail the Godhead of Jesus, and to teach that
the Son of God was not in all points equal to the Father.
Dexterously as this teaching was insinuated, it excited great
alarm; and he was accused by the people of blasphemy.
St. Alexander, a mild and loving prelate, strove to reclaim
Arius by affectionate remonstrances, and the most indulgent
patience; but when he saw that his gentleness was regarded
as an indication of weakness, he used the powers intrusted
to him, and, in a synod of his suffragan bishops, excommunicated Arius as a heretic. This decisive blow surprised but
did not crush Arius. He withdrew into Palestine, and collected partisans of his heresy even among the bishops. St.
Alexander now wrote to all the bishops, and especially to the
Pope St. Sylvester, to justify his own conduct, and to warn
them against the innovator. Arius betook himself to Nicomedia, the city in which the emperor usually resided, and the
bishop of which, Eusebius,* was already a favourer of his
heresy. Strong in the support of Eusebius, he began to
speak out more clearly, and to diffuse his teaching amongst
the lower classes, by writings and songs adapted to their capacity. The common people swallowed the poison greedily,
and became disputatious and irreverent. The emperor was
grieved and displeased at this dissension; and the more so
because Eusebius persuaded him that the dispute was merely
one of words, and originated entirely in the antipathy which
Alexander had conceived against Arius. The emperor wrote
a letter exhorting both disputants to silence, which he sent
to Alexander by Hosius, Bishop of Cordova, in whom he had
entire confidence. The letter, a singular document, was read
in synod; but neither the faith nor its opposing heresy could
be silenced by the mere will of the emperor. Hosius re-

---

* This Eusebius must not be confounded with the historian, of whom we
shall have to speak presently.

turned, leaving the conflict where it was before. Arius would not relinquish his supposed right to think what he pleased, and to say what he thought; and Alexander felt that it was his highest duty to guard and transmit the deposit of sound doctrine. The report which Hosius gave of the affair opened the eyes of the emperor to the extent of the evil which threatened the Church.

The evils which threatened the Church, rendered it expedient to summon an *œcumenical* (that is, a *general*) council; which was accordingly done, with the sanction and by the authority of the Pope. Constantine assisted the Church in the assembling of this council, by offering the city of Nicæa in Bithynia for its deliberations, by sending letters of invitation and safe-conduct to the bishops, and by providing for the expenses of their journey, as well as for their lodging and maintenance, while the council lasted. Three hundred and eighteen bishops assembled from all parts of Christendom, accompanied by a multitude of priests and deacons. Hosius, Bishop of Cordova, presided, as the representative of Pope Sylvester, whose great age prevented his undertaking so long a journey. St. Alexander, Bishop of Alexandria, was attended by a young deacon whose name was Athanasius, and who took a prominent part in the debate. It was a striking assembly. Most of the bishops were men advanced in years, eminent for sanctity, and many were covered with the glorious scars they had received in their sufferings for the faith. Amongst others was Paphnutius, a bishop of Upper Egypt, whose right eye had been plucked out during the persecution. The emperor showed him peculiar attention, and on one occasion kissed the mark of his honourable wound. Previous to the opening of the council Arius was invited to a private conference, at which he boldly maintained his detestable errors in presence of the assembled bishops, who no sooner heard the words of blasphemy issue from his lips than they stopped their ears in token of their indignation and horror. Nevertheless, both on this occasion and before the council, the unhappy man was allowed ample opportunity to explain and justify his doctrine. The impious novelties were refuted with consummate ability from the Holy Scriptures and the traditions of the Fathers. On this solid foundation was based the Church's decision. The council declared that Jesus Christ is really and truly the Son of God, equal to the Father in all respects; His power, His image, subsisting in Him from everlasting, true and very God. And, as the Arians were ingenious and fertile in evasions, the council employed the word *consubstantial* to express the indivisible unity of the nature of the Father and the Son This word admitted no escape. It became therefore the touchstone of orthodoxy, and the object of the bitter aversion and opposition of the Arians. They withdrew condemned, but unsubmissive; and the fathers of the council proceeded to draw up the profession of faith which is known as the Nicene Creed, and which is said in the holy Mass. All the bishops, except five Arians, subscribed this creed, and joined in the anathema pronounced against Arius and his heresy. The emperor employed his temporal authority in support of these decisions, and condemned Arius to be banished. Such was the result of this council, the memory of which is held in so much veneration by the Church.

The Arians were silenced, but not humbled. They wrote to the emperor, affirming their readiness to subscribe the Nicene decrees and confession; and they prevailed so far that they were recalled from exile. They then endeavoured to fill the mind of the emperor with suspicions of the Catholic bishops, and especially of Athanasius, who had succeeded Alexander in the see of Alexandria, and whose learning and ability made him their most dreaded enemy. They assured the emperor that Arius had been condemned simply because he had not explained his meaning clearly; and they said that, as he was really orthodox in faith, it would be a thing pleasing to God to order Athanasius to take him back into the church of Alexandria. It was an artful device. They well knew that the bishop would not be imposed upon by the dissimulation of Arius; and they hoped that his refusal to reinstate him in his office would be regarded as an act of disobedience to the emperor. The treacherous counsel was followed: Athanasius was commanded to receive Arius, on pain of deposition. Nor did the Arians stop at this point. They accused him of crimes so heinous in character, that the emperor deemed it necessary to inquire whether charges so grave were founded in truth. A synod of bishops was assembled by his order at Tyre; and Athanasius was commanded to appear and exculpate himself. The Arians, who, under the protection of Constantine, had again taken possession of their sees, contrived that the judges should be more or less favourable to their party, and Athanasius was treated with every indignity. They affected to regard him as a criminal on trial; they refused to allow him to sit amongst them; they compelled him to stand forth as a culprit while the examination was carried on. The holy prelate listened calmly to all the accusations brought against him, and refuted them all convincingly. The Arians were reduced to silence; and in their mortification would have torn him in pieces, if the emperor's commissioner had not rescued him from their hands. As Athanasius felt that his life was not secure, he resolved to seek the emperor at Constantinople, the recently built capital of the empire. In his absence the Arians pronounced against him sentence of deposition from his see; and they incorporated into their sentence the calumnies which had been so completely refuted. They then went to Constantinople, and accused Athanasius of having threatened to stop the export of corn from Alexandria, in case of his condemnation. It was in vain that the holy bishop denied this charge. So great was the credit his accusers had obtained with the emperor, that he banished Athanasius to Trèves, a city of Gaul, distant from his see about 800 leagues.

Emboldened by this signal success, the Arians proceeded to reinstate Arius in his dignities at Alexandria. The heresiarch attempted to enter the church; but the Catholic population refused him admission; and the tumult was so great, that the emperor was obliged to order Arius to return to Constantinople. By way of compensation for his rejection at Alexandria, the Arians resolved that their chief should enjoy the honour of a public and most brilliant reception in the church of Constantinople. The bishop of the imperial city was an aged and venerable prelate, orthodox in faith. He refused again and again to admit Arius to communion; and the enraged heretics obtained an order from the emperor to compel him. The day was fixed; they were radiant with hope; the hour of triumph was at hand. The holy bishop had no resource on earth; he turned the more imploringly to heaven. He went into his church and prostrated himself before the high altar, and prayed with tears: " Lord, if Arius is to be received to communion in this church, I beseech Thee to withdraw me first from this world; but if Thou carest for Thy people and this church, as I doubt not Thou dost, suffer it not to become a reproach."

On the morrow the partisans of Arius met with exulting eagerness, and went to seek their master, that they might escort him in procession to the church. Their march was one of triumph; and they indulged as they went in insulting jests against the bishop. Just as they drew near the church Arius turned deadly pale, as though from sudden illness, and retired apart. As he was absent longer than they expected, they went to seek him. He lay dead on the ground, in his own blood, and his bowels had gushed out. Deep was the horror of the multitude; and the place where this terrible death occurred was long pointed out as a monument of the Divine vengeance. The rumour spread far and wide; and the next day, in presence of a vast multitude, the bishop gave solemn thanks to God; not for the awful death of the heretic, but because He had averted from His sanctuary so foul a pollution. The emperor was led to reflect on his conduct. He saw in this death the judgment of God; he was about to recall Athanasius, when death prevented his signing the order. He gave it verbally, almost with his latest breath. He died at Nicomedia, in 337, after having received holy baptism.

Constantine left three sons to divide the empire: Constantine, Constantius, and Constans. Constantine, within whose jurisdiction Gaul now passed, restored Athanasius to his see with expressions of profound respect. He wrote to the Alexandrians a letter, in which he says that, in reinstating the holy prelate, he did but execute his father's wish. "When, then," he adds, "Athanasius arrives, you will know with what honour we regard him; and you will not wonder at it; for we have been witnesses of the affliction his absence has caused you, and of his distinguished virtues." The holy patriarch of Alexandria passed through Syria, and at length reached his beloved and rejoicing flock. The clergy and the faithful poured out in crowds to see him and to welcome him, and the churches resounded with songs of thanksgiving. His enemies were stung to the quick. They said his return was contrary to the canons; only a council of the Church could restore him. They invented fresh calumnies, heaping together every falsehood which the ingenuity of malice could invent. They contrived to gain the ear of Constantius, Emperor of the East; and they represented Athanasius to him as a restless, turbulent man, who had done nothing since his return but excite the people to sedition; and they said he had appropriated to his own use the corn destined for the support of the widows and poor. It was easy to disprove the charges; but it was not easy to dissipate the suspicions of Constantius. That unhappy prince had adopted the heresy and the cause of the Arians; he would hear nothing in defence of Athanasius, while he implicitly believed all that was reported to his prejudice. The Arians soon succeeded in inducing the emperor to command the election of another patriarch instead of Athanasius. The priest of their choice, named Pistus, had been excommunicated by the Nicene Council, together with the bishop who pretended to consecrate him. When tidings of this schismatical consecration reached the Pope, he refused his communion to the intruded patriarch. Thereupon he was disclaimed by the whole Catholic Church, and never took possession of the dignity he would have usurped. The Church has ever regarded schism with deep horror. It has always rejected with intense aversion those who seek to take possession of a see while its true pastor is still living, and in communion with the Church. It declares that such usurpers have neither power nor jurisdiction, and are not shepherds of Christ's flock, but robbers, who have climbed up some other way, wolves who have crept in, to lay waste and to devour.

The Arians now withdrew Pistus, and begged the Pope to summon a council to examine into the charges alleged against Athanasius. To this the Pope consented. The Arians, however, had resolved on having another patriarch. They selected Gregory, a native of Cappadocia; and, armed with the imperial authority, compelled his reception by the church of Alexandria. Then was displayed the real spirit of heresy and schism in its hour of seeming triumph. The forcible intrusion of Gregory had stirred the whole city. The faithful filled the churches and were earnest in prayer. The emperor's commissioner gathered a crowd of Jews and abandoned persons, and commenced an attack on the Catholics. Some were trodden under foot, some despatched with clubs, some slain with the sword. The priests who refused communion to heretics were scourged. The same, and even a worse fate, awaited the consecrated virgins. And, worst of all, these horrible impieties were perpetrated in Holy Week.

On Good Friday Gregory marched into one of the churches, and scourged and imprisoned thirty-four persons who would have resisted his entrance. The Catholics were compelled either to absent themselves from the churches, or to communicate with the profane rabble of heretics.

Meanwhile Athanasius himself had been enabled to effect his escape; and repaired in person to Rome. The Holy See was then occupied by Julius, who received his visitor with distinguished kindness. He summoned a council as the Arians had requested, but at which, when summoned, none of them attended. Athanasius was declared innocent of the crimes alleged against him, and confirmed in the possession of his see; but eight years elapsed before the death of the intruder facilitated his return. The letter written by the Pope to the Alexandrian church after the council is still extant. This is but one of many instances in which we see that the last appeal in all grave causes was made to the Pope, as the successor of St. Peter, and supreme visible head of the Church. The Church has ever recognised in the Pope, not simply a pre-eminence of place and honour, but a primacy of jurisdiction and authority. This primacy or supremacy is the centre of the Church's unity, and a fundamental article of the faith.

About this time, A.D. 350, took place the cruel persecution under Sapor II., king of Persia, which was excited by the jealousy of the magi. The cruelties perpetrated on the Catholics were without precedent; and the number of martyrs exceeds calculation. Sapor was at war with the Romans; and, while he was besieging Nisibis in Mesopotamia, St. James, bishop of that city, besought the Lord to confound the enemy of the Christian faith. His prayer was heard. A plague of gnats was let loose on the Persian host. They stung the elephants, the horses, and other animals to madness. The infuriated creatures broke their bridles, cast off their riders, trampled down the foot-soldiers, and threw the army into hopeless disorder. Sapor was obliged to raise the siege and retreat. In revenge, he ordered an indiscriminate torture and massacre of the Christians throughout Persia.

Constantine II. died in 340; his brother Constans survived him ten years; and Constantius, who had been compelled by Constans to permit Athanasius to return to his see, at length found himself sole master of the Roman Empire. One of his earliest acts was to issue an edict commanding all the bishops

of Christendom to subscribe the condemnation of St. Athanasius, on pain of banishment. The faith of Nicæa was, as it
were, impersonated, and assailed in its ablest defender. The
emperor assembled the bishops first at Arles, and then at
Milan; and condescended to' perform, in his own person, the
office of accuser. The bishops replied that they could not
condemn Athanasius, without violating the sacred canons.
"My will is a sufficient canon," exclaimed the enraged emperor; "obey, or go into exile." The bishops represented to
him that the empire did not belong to him, but to God, who
had delegated its rule to him for a time; that he ought to
fear the judgment of God, and not confound the spiritual and
temporal powers. This reply served only to irritate Constantius still further; he drew his sword, and commanded the
foremost speaker to be led forth to execution. He soon recalled his order, however, and contented himself with a sentence of banishment. Those who refused to subscribe were
driven from their sees, and replaced by Arian bishops. Constantius, however, could not remain satisfied so long as the
Pope refused to condemn Athanasius and communicate with
the Arians; but finding that neither promises could win nor
threats intimidate, he sent the Pontiff into banishment to
Berœa. This outrage on the Vicar of Christ was the signal
for a furious persecution against the Catholics. An armed
force was sent to Alexandria, and the scenes of cruelty and
of sacrilege were renewed. Athanasius concealed himself
among the monks in the desert of Thebaid, while one George,
a Cappadocian, a man devoid of education and a heathen in
manners, was intruded into the patriarchal chair. The persecution was more or less general throughout the empire,
while in the eastern capital, Constantinople, the Arian faction
reigned triumphant.

At length the discontent of the Roman people at the banishment of their Pontiff and the intrusion of an anti-pope
forced Constantius to recall Liberius. The calumny, invented
by the Arians and supported by subsequent forgeries, of his
having subscribed one of their equivocal formularies and condemned Athanasius, to obtain his liberation, is now an exploded error. Soon after, the emperor, finding himself unable
to settle by violence the affairs of the Church, but still bent
on victory, summoned a council at Rimini in Italy, and another at Seleucia in the East. Of course neither of these

councils represented the Catholic Church, seeing that the Pope had no voice either in its convocation or its deliberations. The latter, which was numerously attended by the Arians, soon dispersed without coming to any practical conclusion. The former upheld the Catholic faith as long as its deliberations were free from control; it refused to admit any other creed than that of Nicæa, from which it declared there was nothing to retrench, and to which there was nothing to add; and it anathematised Arius and his faction. The bishops, to the number of 328, signed this decree; and the dissentient Arians were condemned and deposed. But the emperor refused to allow the council to be dissolved until the bishops had signed a form of belief in which the decisive word *consubstantial* did not occur. The greater part of the bishops, wearied and worn out, intimidated by the threats of the emperor, and willing to do any thing to secure the peace of the Church, —believing, too, that the sense of the word *consubstantial* might be as forcibly expressed in other words,—in an evil hour subscribed a formula of which they saw not the pernicious consequences. The Arians raised a shout of triumph; the bishops at once saw their error, and were loud in expressions of indignation and regret. They protested against the interpretation which the Arians affixed to their compliance, and declared their unwavering adherence to the Nicene faith.

Although the bishops at Rimini had allowed themselves to be surprised into this act of unfaithfulness, the Church herself was in no wise committed to their error. Pope Liberius, at the head of all the Catholic bishops, including those who had been so recently led astray, disavowed the acts of the council, and declared its decrees void of effect. Hence we find St. Athanasius writing to the Emperor Jovian, within two years of the Rimini council, in these words: "The Nicene faith, which we confess, is the faith of all time; all the churches embrace it: those of Spain, of Britain, of Gaul, of Italy, of Dalmatia, of Dacia, of Mysia, of Macedonia; those of Greece, of Africa, of Sardinia, Crete and Cyprus; of Pamphylia, Lycia, Isauria, of Egypt and Libya, of Pontus and Cappadocia—all profess the same faith, with the exception of a small and insignificant minority." The number of heretics was, in reality, very small; their zeal and loquacity, and the support of the emperor, made them appear numerous and influential. The faith was deeply rooted in the mind and heart of the Church; and neither the council of Rimini nor the persecutions of Constantius could change or corrupt it.

It pleased God to raise up in the Church of Gaul an intrepid defender of the Catholic faith, in the person of St. Hilary, Bishop of Poitiers. This holy bishop was to the West what Athanasius was to the East. He opposed the Arian heresy with learning, eloquence, and untiring zeal. He remonstrated with Constantius on the injustice of the persecution he was inflicting on the churches; and he resisted the intrigues of Saturninus, the courtly Arian bishop of Arles. Constantius replied by banishing the bishop to Phrygia; but this banishment was overruled by God to the accomplishment of His will. The emperor soon after convoked the council of Seleucia, mentioned above, with intent to procure the repeal of the canons of Nicæa. As the heretics were divided against themselves, St. Hilary was invited to the council, and so ably maintained the faith of Nicæa, that the heretical faction became powerless for evil. He then went to Constantinople, and demanded a public audience of the emperor, offering to discuss the errors of the heretics in his presence. "Ever since the holy council of Nicæa," he writes, "those whom you honour with your confidence have done nothing but draw up fresh creeds. Their faith is not the faith of the Gospel, but a belief resting on their own conjectures. Last year they changed their profession of faith four times; for with them the creed varies according to individual opinion; and doctrine depends on the whim of the moment. Every year, nay, every month, they bring forth a new symbol; destroying all they had done before, and anathematising the opinions they have just abandoned. They talk much of Holy Scripture and of the faith of the apostolic age; but it is only to deceive the unwary, and to discredit the teaching of the Church."

These observations apply to other heresies and schisms which have sprung up since the time of St. Hilary. The Arians dreaded his zeal and controversial ability too much to accept his challenge; and, in order to rid themselves of so inconvenient an adversary, they besought the emperor to send him back to his own diocese. The holy bishop traversed Illyria and Italy on his way, and every where rekindled the faith and ardour of the Catholics. On his arrival in Gaul his first step was to excommunicate Saturninus, and depose him as tainted with heresy and other crimes. The effects of his presence were soon visible every where: the faith was set forth in all its purity, discipline was administered with its ancient vigour, scandals were removed, and peace succeeded to tumult and violence. At length the death of Constantius, in 361, deprived the Arians of their greatest support and most powerful argument.

Amongst the disciples of St. Hilary, the most illustrious was St. Martin of Tours. He had been a soldier in early life, but had maintained the purity of his morals. He was, remarkable for tenderness towards the poor and suffering, and distributed all his money amongst them. One day, during a severe frost, he met a beggar at the gate of Amiens, who was almost naked and benumbed by the cold. The charity of Martin was excited, but he had with him nothing except his arms and his military cloak. He immediately drew his sword, cut off with it the half of his cloak, and gave it to the shivering beggar. At night, Martin, who had not yet been baptised, saw in vision our Divine Lord clothed with the half of his cloak, and heard Him say to the angels who surrounded Him: "Martin, while but a catechumen, has clothed Me with this cloak." This vision decided Martin to seek holy baptism; and on being baptised he felt impelled to quit the profession of arms. He was attracted to St. Hilary by his reputation for holiness; and he built within two leagues of Poitiers a monastery, to which he retired with a small number of disciples. From time to time he left his retreat to preach in the neighbouring villages, where idolatry was not yet extinct; and God confirmed his preaching by numerous miracles. His fame now spread throughout Gaul, and the church of Tours demanded him as their bishop. His elevation made no change in his simple mode of life. He preached throughout the whole of Touraine; and his sermons and miracles effected the conversion of great multitudes. His memory is held in deserved honour in the Church, and especially in France.

§ 2. The monastic life.

Among the multitudes of heathen who followed the example of Constantine and professed themselves Christians, it was scarcely to be hoped that some would not do so from motives merely human. Many of the noble and wealthy, in submitting externally to the Church, had not learnt to abandon their vices or subdue their passions; while even many who had long been Christians lost the fervour of their love in the luxury of repose. In this state of things it pleased God to provide for His faithful servants a refuge in which they might perpetuate in the Church the model of primitive holiness. Multitudes withdrew from the world to live apart in the desert. From the beginning of the Church's history there had been many who, under the name of ascetics, had renounced the business and the pleasures of the world, and devoted themselves to meditation and prayer; but now communities were formed of those who wished to lead a higher life. St. Antony was the originator of this new institute. He was an Egyptian of noble birth, and had been brought up by his pious parents in the love and practice of religion. He was, however, left an orphan at an early age; and hearing one day in the church the words of our Lord, "If thou wilt be perfect, go, sell what thou hast, and give to the poor, and thou shalt have treasure in heaven,"—he applied them to himself, returned to his house, sold all his possessions, and distributed the proceeds amongst the poor. He then retired into a solitary place, and applied himself to the exclusive contemplation of heavenly things. He used severe penitential discipline to control and chastise the flesh, and toiled with his own hands for his subsistence, and to procure somewhat for the relief of the poor. Whenever he heard mention made of any eminent servant of God, he sought him out to gain some lesson or some hint for his guidance in the spiritual life. He soon became an example of every virtue; and the enemy of souls employed every temptation to overcome him—but in vain. The youthful solitary overcame the tempter by prayer and fasting, and mortification of the flesh; his bed was but a mat, and it was often relinquished for the bare ground; he ate but once a day, and then only bread and salt; his drink was water; his clothing consisted of a hair-shirt, a cloak of sheepskins, and a hood. As the Spirit of God destined him to people the solitary places, he was led farther and farther from the haunts of men. He penetrated into the deepest recesses of the Thebaid. There God imparted to him the gift of miracles; and a crowd of disciples were attracted to him to live under his direction. It was necessary to build several monasteries to receive the fervent novices. Antony instructed them, sometimes in private, often in public; and he laid down the rules which they were to follow. "Never," said he, "lose sight for one moment of the thought of eternity. Think each morning that you may not live until evening; and at evening think that you may not see the morrow. Perform each action as if it were the last of your life; watch unweariedly against temptations; resist manfully the assaults of the devil; our enemy is impotent when we know how to disarm him; he dreads fasting, prayer, humility, and good works; the sign of the Cross is alone sufficient to break his spell and scatter his illusions. Yes, the sign of that Cross, which broke his usurped power, is enough to make him tremble and fly." Formed on such instructions as these, the disciples of St. Antony were a wonder to St. Athanasius himself. "Their monasteries," says that great saint, "are like so many temples in which life is spent in singing psalms, in reading, praying, fasting, watching; in which all human hopes rest on the world unseen, and all are united in perfect charity; in which they toil less for their own subsistence than for the poor. It is a vast region severed from the common world, whose blessed inhabitants have no other care than their growth in holiness."

St. Hilarion, his disciple, did for Palestine and Syria what St. Antony had done for Egypt. His parents were idolaters; but this child of election was drawn to become a Christian in his twelfth year. He was then at Alexandria, whither he had been sent to study. In order to attain perfection he sought out St. Antony, and remained for some time with him, forming himself on his method of prayer, and penitential discipline, and toil. From this school of holiness he returned to his own land with a few monks, in order to establish the same rule there. He found his father and mother dead; and he abandoned all his patrimony to the poor. He then retired with his companions into the desert, which, beginning near Gaza, extends to the sea. It was full of robbers, who lay in wait for travellers, and pillaged those whom stress of weather drove to seek shelter near the coast. Hilarion had not been long on their territory before the brigands entered his cell. He accosted them with so self-possessed an air, that they were taken by surprise. "You fear us not, then?" said one of them. "Why should I fear you? I possess nothing in the world." "But we can take away your life." "When a man cares for nothing in this world, it costs him but little to leave it." And, in truth, Hilarion had nothing but a coat of skins and a bag, the gifts of St. Antony. His cell was of the smallest dimensions. Six ounces of black bread and a few herbs were his daily food. He employed himself in tilling the ground and making baskets of reeds. While at work he pondered the Holy Scriptures, which he knew by heart. His miracles and his graces attracted to him a multitude of disciples, and the institute was soon spread throughout Palestine. Wherever he went he was followed by a crowd of sick people, and of persons possessed, imploring aid at his hands; so that he exclaimed: "Alas! I have returned to the world; I have received my reward in this life." Although his life had been so penitent and so crowded with good works, the fear of God's judgment lay sore on him in his dying moments, and he strove to reanimate his confidence by saying: "Go forth, my soul, go forth. Thou hast had the bliss of serving Jesus Christ these seventy years, and thou fearest to die!"

The object of these solitaries was to attain Christian perfection through the practice of the evangelical counsels, of continence, and of poverty. They used four principal means to reach their end: solitude, manual labour, fasting, and prayer. They went far from any human dwelling, into deserts so remote that it was several days' journey to reach them. These deserts were not vast forests or uncultivated land which might have been reclaimed and rendered productive; they were places, not only void of inhabitants, but utterly uninhabitable—burning plains of sand, rugged mountain-tops, frightful precipices. They always set up their abode near running water. There they built huts of wood or of reeds; and there, removed from every thing on which human passion can fix, they strove to attain that purity of heart to which is granted the vision of God; to destroy all vices within themselves, and to practise all virtue freely and fully. They vanquished avarice by their voluntary poverty, and by their community of goods; they subdued indolence by continuous toil; and they selected a kind of work the least likely to occasion distractions and to interrupt their converse with God—the making mats or baskets of reeds. They thus attained two great ends—the avoiding indolence, and the living without being a burden to any one. As their expenses were very small, they gave abundant alms; their whole sur-

plus was expended on the poor. They fasted throughout the
year, except the Sundays, and during the Paschal season.
Bread and water composed their food. Twelve ounces of
bread a-day were found by experience to sustain life, and to
support their strength for work. They slept but little. And
this austere regimen was found to lengthen their days, and to
keep them free from sickness; St. Antony lived more than a
hundred years. Their hours of prayer were regulated with
the same practical wisdom. Twice in the day they assembled
for common worship; the rest of their prayer was private and
mental. Obedience was the remedy against pride; and they
were docile as children to their superiors. The deserts were
peopled with persons practising an heroic penitence; and so
numerous did they become, that the more advanced solitaries
were driven to seek a solitude yet more profound. The
Church of Christ has thus ever been as rich in examples as in
precepts of holiness; and her teaching has proved its sanctity
by training multitudes of saints. This same austere life is
retained to our own day by the Carmelites of both sexes, and
the Trappists.

§ 3. From Julian the Apostate to Theodosius the Great.

The Emperor Constantius was succeeded, in 361, by his
cousin Julian, known to after-ages as the Apostate. Educated by the Arians, and then by heathen philosophers, he
had lived an obscure life, studying at Constantinople or
Athens on the same bench with St. Basil and St. Gregory of
Nazianzum. The latter is reported to have exclaimed to his
brother saint, "What a monster the Roman Empire is cher-
ishing in its bosom!" and the after-life of Julian did not
belie the prediction. Being sent into Gaul to repel the Allemanni, Julian distinguished himself by military successes,
and by a wise administration. When recalled by his uncle,
he caused himself to be proclaimed emperor at Lutetia, the
modern Paris, and marched against Constantius. On his
way from Gaul to Constantinople he abjured Christianity at
Sirmium, in Illyria, and opened again the heathen temples;
thus, as he impiously said, to efface by his sacrifices the stain
he had contracted in his baptism. When he reached Constantinople, Constantius had been dead for several days, and
he took peaceful possession of the empire.

Could the Church have been overthrown, it would have

been under Julian—so ably devised were his plans of attack.
He began by according to all the free exercise of their religion, and by recalling all who had been banished in the late
persecutions.   He acted thus, not so much to gain the affection of his people, as to reflect discredit on the government of
Constantius.   St. Athanasius availed himself of this edict to
return to his diocese.   His entry into Alexandria was a complete triumph.   The people poured forth a day's journey to
meet him; so great was the concourse that the trees by the
wayside and the roofs of houses were crowded with persons
eager to catch but a glimpse of his beloved countenance.   But
this joy was not of long duration.   The emperor had resolved
to restore the worship of idols every where.   To attain his end
more surely he again banished St. Athanasius.   In the main,
Julian employed seduction rather than violence; he fomented
the divisions between Catholics and heretics; hoping to
weaken both parties, and to crush both the more easily.   The
religious liberty which he professed to allow the Catholics,
was, in fact, a wretched slavery.   He did not, indeed, condemn them to death, but he adopted the surest means of
crushing them.   He lavished his favours profusely upon the
heathen; the portion of the Christians was contempt and
derision, vexations and insults.   He laboured assiduously to
debase the clergy, and every thing connected with the religion
he hated.   He suppressed all privileges accorded to ecclesiastics, and confiscated the pensions of the consecrated virgins
and others.   He said, with a sneer, that he acted thus to
bring them back to the perfection of their state, to evangelical poverty.   He plundered the churches, and applied the
sacred ornaments to the service of idols.   He compelled the
Christians to rebuild the temples which had been cast down.
The clergy suffered exceedingly; they were imprisoned, and
put to the torture, to compel them to deliver up the sacred
vessels and ornaments.   The tombs and shrines of the saints
were thrown down, their relics scattered to the winds.   Julian
was lavish of promises to the weak and wavering in faith.
Firmness and fidelity to God were regarded as treason; while
those who bartered away their faith were loaded with honours
and with wealth.   Apostasy was a passport to imperial favour, and a qualification for all public employments; it imparted genius where there was none, and brought latent
merits to light; it effaced all past crimes, and bestowed im-

punity for the future. Julian passed a law to exclude Christians from all judicial charges, under pretext that the Gospel forbade them to use the sword; he stripped them of almost every right of free citizens, and refused them permission to plead at his tribunals. "Your religion," he said, "prohibits all law-suits and contentions." The cities which displayed any zeal for idols were assured of his protection and favour; those which remained true to God were degraded and ruined. He would not admit their deputies to an audience, nor listen to their requests. He prohibited Christians from teaching arts or sciences; because, he said, they ought to remain in contented ignorance, and believe without reasoning. It was a system more fitted to attain its end than the cruelties of Nero and Dioclesian. But God, who orders all things for the accomplishment of His adorable will, allowed this impious prince but a short career, and baffled this diabolical scheme by the death of its contriver.

In the course of his efforts to destroy the Christian religion, Julian furnished an additional proof of the truth of its living oracles. He was acquainted with the prophecies which announced that the ruin of Jerusalem was to be final and irreparable; he knew that Jesus Christ had said one stone should not be left upon another. In order to falsify the prophecy, he undertook to rebuild the Temple, and invited the Jews to aid him in this attempt. He furnished the requisite funds, and intrusted the work to one of his most confidential officers named Alypius. The Jews gave eager assistance, and a countless multitude of workmen were soon employed on the site of the Temple. The space was cleared, excavations were commenced, and all was ardour and animation; aged men, children, and women took part in this great work. Meanwhile Cyril, Bishop of Jerusalem, smiled at their impotent efforts; he quietly remarked that the time had come when the prophecy would receive its fullest accomplishment, that not one stone should remain upon another of the once glorious Temple. The works proceeded until the old foundations had been removed and broken up; and then there came an appalling earthquake which filled up the excavations, scattered the accumulated materials, overthrew the adjacent houses, and killed or mutilated the workmen. Still Julian's obstinacy induced him to renew the impious attempt; and then flaming balls issued from the ground, melted the very tools of the workmen, and buried them beneath the ruins. Again and again this terrible outburst of fire dispersed the labourers; the spectators were astounded: many Jews and pagans were led to recognise the Divinity of our Lord, and to seek admission into His Church. The emperor, alone blind amidst such marvellous portents, was defeated but unmoved.* Soon after he set forth on an expedition against the Persians, in which he perished miserably. His death was regarded as a judgment of God, and a token of His special providence over His Church.

On the death of Julian the soldiers decreed the empire to Jovian, the captain of the imperial guard; a man of courage, prudence, and capacity. As the Roman army was criti-. cally placed in Persia, an emperor of this character was peculiarly needed. It is more to the purpose of this history to record that he had given many proofs of the sincerity of his faith and of his zeal for the interests of religion. When Julian was entering on his campaign against the Persians, he said to Jovian: "Either sacrifice to the gods, or give me your sword." Jovian at once laid his sword at the emperor's feet; and Julian, unable to dispense with his services, was compelled to return it to him again. Before assuming the insignia of empire, Jovian assembled the troops, and proclaimed that, as a Christian, he would not lead idolaters to battle, men who were not shielded by the Divine protection. With one voice the soldiers shouted in reply: "Fear not; they whom you command are Christians. The reign of superstition has been too short to efface from our hearts the faith we learnt from the great Constantine and his sons." The position of the army was so desperate, that Jovian deemed it wise to accept the terms offered by the Persian king, and save his troops at the expense of some fortresses and provinces.

The emperor now set himself to heal the wounds of the languishing Church. He recalled St. Athanasius, and reinstated him at Alexandria; and the letter which he wrote to the holy confessor attests the esteem and veneration with which he regarded him. Athanasius once more forsook his

---

* This miraculous intervention is recorded not only by ecclesiastical writers, but by heathens—such as Ammianus Marcellinus. St. Gregory of Nazianzum and St. Chrysostom mentioned it in their homilies in presence of many who must have been eye-witnesses; and no voice was raised to contradict them.

wild retreat, and made his appearance in Alexandria. The Arians renewed their intrigues, but in vain; the cause of Athanasius was that of the Catholic Church. The emperor besought the saint to write for him a simple, concise statement of the Catholic doctrine. Athanasius complied with this request, and expounded the Nicene faith so clearly, as to convince the emperor that the pacification of the Church could only be effected by carrying out the decrees of the council.

And now the Church began to breathe freely once more; no such repose had been known since the accession of Constantine. Their privileges were restored to the clergy, the widows, the consecrated virgins; and the subordinate governors were commanded to protect the faithful, and to provide all that was necessary for the splendour of divine worship and the instruction of the people. But this peaceful time was too bright to last long. Jovian, who was but thirty-two years of age, was found dead in his bed. The fumes of charcoal which was burning in his chamber had suffocated him; and his death renewed the strifes and the sorrows of the Church.

The empire was now conferred on Valentinian, who unfortunately chose his worthless brother Valens as his colleague. The former reserved the West for himself, with Milan for his capital; and, as he was sincerely attached to the true faith, the Western Church had peace and prospered. But Valens began a vigorous persecution of the Catholics throughout the East; he decreed the expulsion once more of St. Athanasius, and of the other bishops who had been deposed or banished by Constantius, and who had again taken possession of their sees. After four months Valens recalled his order for the banishment of Athanasius. But this favourable change is attributable either to the intervention of Valentinian, who held the saint in great veneration, or to his fear of the people of Alexandria. Thus Athanasius once more occupied his episcopal throne; and after having been five times banished and five times recalled, he passed the remaining six years of his life in peace. One instance may be selected to illustrate the treatment of Catholics in the East under this unhappy prince. The faithful of Constantinople, feeling assured that the emperor could never sanction the atrocities perpetrated in his name, sent to him a deputation of eighty pious priests to represent their grievances and implore redress. Valens heard them quietly, and manifested no displeasure; but he gave secret orders to Modestus, the pretorian prefect, to put them to death. The prefect, dreading a tumult if this sanguinary order was executed in the city, pronounced against them sentence of perpetual exile. They were put on board a vessel, and as soon as they were out of sight of land, the captain set fire to the ship, according to his orders, and made off with his crew. Not one of the doomed ecclesiastics escaped. When tidings of these trials reached the monasteries, the monks issued from their retreats, and went from place to place, to sustain the faith and the fortitude of their brethren. At Antioch one of them, a man venerable for his age and sanctity, was brought before the emperor, who from a balcony had seen him pass on his way to join the Catholics, who, driven from their churches, met to worship in the open fields. " Whither are you going?" asked the irritated Valens. " Why cannot you remain in your cell, instead of running about to stimulate people to rebellion?" The old man replied calmly: " Prince, I remained in my cell so long as the sheep of the heavenly Shepherd were in peace; but now that I see them scared and scattered, and about to be devoured, would it become me to abide still in my retreat? The young virgin who lives at home secluded, ought she to remain tranquilly in her chamber when she sees her father's house on fire? Ought she not to cry for help, and seek to extinguish the devouring flames? This, then, is what I am now doing. You have kindled a conflagration in the Church of my God; from my remote cell I saw its frightful glare: I am but trying to extinguish it."

Valens encountered a powerful adversary in St. Basil, Bishop of Cæsarea in Cappadocia, a learned, holy, resolute prelate. The emperor sent Modestus, the pretorian prefect, to him, to gain him to the Arian cause, by promises or by intimidation. The prefect arrayed himself in his rich official robes, grouped his lictors around him, and thus received the intrepid bishop. The saint entered the presence-chamber with a serene and unembarrassed countenance, and was cordially welcomed by Modestus, who proceeded to express his hope that he would yield to the emperor's request and admit the Arians to communion. When civility had failed, Modestus began to threaten: "Can you really be mad enough to resist that imperial will before which the whole world bows? Do you not dread the indignation of the emperor? Has he not power to deprive you of your goods, to banish you, to take away your life?" "Such threats move me not," said Basil, calmly. "He who has nothing to lose, need not dread confiscation of goods. You cannot exile me, for the whole earth is my home. As for death, I do not fear it; it would be the greatest kindness you could do me; for it would be my passage to the true and real life. Long years have I been dead to the life that now is; torments cannot harm me; my body is so weak and so frail that one blow would end my life and my sufferings together." It was the first time that the ears of the courtly prefect had heard so much truth so boldly delivered. "Never," he said, "has any one dared to address Modestus with such freedom." "Perhaps," suggested Basil, "Modestus never before measured his strength with a Christian bishop?" The prefect could not refrain from admiring the manly firmness of St. Basil. He told the emperor that the bishop was as insensible to threatenings as to promises; and that the only resource was violence. This Valens could not venture to employ; the people of Cæsarea were too formidable a body to provoke.

It was not only by the clergy that this heroic courage was displayed during the Arian persecution; men and women from amongst the laity were equally firm. For instance: Valens had banished the Bishop of Edessa in Mesopotamia, and appointed an Arian bishop in his stead. He charged Modestus to compel the priests and deacons to communicate with the new bishop, on peril of being exiled to the extremity of the empire. Modestus employed caresses, but in vain. They replied with one accord, "We have one pastor with lawful jurisdiction; we can recognise none other:" and they were exiled accordingly. The people refused to receive communion at the hands of the schismatical bishop. They assembled in the fields at the customary hours of worship, and prayed in common. The emperor commanded the soldiers to charge the refractory assemblage; but Modestus, who had conceived a liking for persons so firm and courageous, sent them a private warning not to meet on the following day, because the emperor had resolved to punish all who were found assembled in the fields. This warning brought the Catholics in greater numbers and with more eager zeal to the appointed place. The prefect was perplexed. He marched towards the congregation, and commanded the soldiers to make as much noise as possible, hoping that the Catholics would be intimidated and disperse. As he was issuing from the city, he saw a poor woman running along with her child, and with her cloak trailing behind her in disorder. Modestus ordered her to be arrested, and asked her whither she was running in such haste. " I am going to the field in which the Catholics meet." "I suppose you do not know that the emperor has given orders to kill all who meet to-day ?" "I know it; and that is why I am so eager to get there, lest I should miss the blessing of martyrdom." " But why take your child with you ?" " That he may have his portion in the same glorious privilege." Modestus returned to the palace and assured the emperor that success was impossible, while failure would be dishonourable. Such were the feelings of the faithful towards Arianism. They knew the words of our Divine Lord, " He that entereth in by the door is the shepherd of the sheep; and the sheep follow him because they know his voice; but a stranger they follow not, but fly from him." And so they remained inseparably attached to the bishop whom the Church had sent, and were ready to die rather than communicate with an usurper.

On one occasion the emperor, being at Cæsarea on the Feast of the Epiphany, resolved to go to the cathedral church to join in the worship. He went in state, attended by all his guards, hoping that all this power and splendour would overawe the holy bishop. But when he saw the overflowing congregation heedless of his presence; St. Basil standing at the altar insensible to every thing but the mystery he was celebrating; the priests and deacons ministering devoutly in their places,—Valens felt that there was a power on earth greater than his own, and was profoundly moved. At the offertory he summoned courage and would have presented his offering, but not one of the deacons would come near him; they knew that St. Basil would not receive it. The emperor trembled, and would have fallen to the ground had he not been supported by one of the priests, who noticed his emotion. St. Basil, hoping to gain the emperor, received his offering; and Valens was softened so far as to change his tone towards the bishop, and to discuss with him the matters in dispute.

St. Basil spoke with entire freedom, and imposed silence on a courtier who threatened him in the emperor's presence. Valens gave the bishop land to found a hospital at Cæsarea; but the Arians wrought so upon him that he resolved to banish St. Basil. At this crisis his son was seized with a violent fever, and the physicians declared his case to be hopeless. The emperor was smitten with remorse, and sent for St. Basil. The bishop came; he assured Valens that his child would not die, if he would pledge himself that he should be brought up in the Catholic faith. The pledge was given; St. Basil prayed, and the child recovered. Valens broke his pledge; an Arian bishop baptised the child; and in a few days it sickened again and died. The emperor's heart was hardened. He resolved again to banish the saint; but when he attempted to sign the order, his hand shook so that he could not write. Soon after he perished in battle, and his body was never found. It was said that, being wounded with an arrow, he had been borne into a cottage, which the enemy set on fire.

St. Basil was united in closest friendship with St. Gregory of Nazianzum, who was equally zealous for the purity of the faith. Their friendship, formed while they were studying at Athens, became stronger and more tender as they grew in years. "We had both the same end," says St. Gregory; "we were in quest of the same treasure; we resolved to make our affection everlasting by preparing for a blissful eternity; we watched over each other; and mutually exhorted each other to piety. We held no intercourse with those of our fellow-students who led dissipated lives; we visited those only who could edify us by their modesty, their reserve, and their wisdom; for we knew that no contagion is so virulent and so diffusive as bad example. At Athens we knew two roads only—one led to the church, the other to the school; as to those which led to the theatres and to worldly feasts, we knew nothing about them." What an example to Christian youth! St. Gregory of Nazianzum passed the greater part of his life in retreat, until the urgency of his friend drew him forth, and procured his elevation to the episcopate. On the death of Valens he was called to Constantinople to govern that important church, and to stay the torrent of Arian blasphemy. His piety, his poverty, his humility, did but excite first the contempt, and then the rage of the heretics. He was stoned by the rabble, and accused before the authori-

ties of raising a sedition. To all the insults and outrages
of his enemies he opposed only an unconquerable patience.
His life was austere and mortified; and the greater part of his
time was passed in intercession for his flock, and in meditation on the Holy Scriptures. By degrees he won the affections
of the people and their unbounded veneration. His profound
knowledge of the Scriptures, his exact and cogent reasonings,
his fertile and glowing imagination, his wondrous fluency of
speech, and the purity and beauty of his style, attracted the
admiration of the whole city. He defended the truth tri-
umphantly, and edified the Church by his virtues; but contentions arising respecting his election to the see of Constantinople, he availed himself of the opportunity to put into
execution the desire he had long entertained of withdraw-
ing to his beloved retreat. A great number of the homilies
preached by this holy bishop are still extant. They are not
unworthy of the glorious mysteries of which they treat, and
justify the title given to St. Gregory of *the Theologian.*

The death of Valens put a stop to the ravages of Arianism in the East; but ere that heresy disappeared, it produced
another, which impugned the Divinity of the Holy Ghost.
The author of this new impiety was Macedonius, a semi-
Arian, who had usurped the see of Constantinople. It had
for years lurked behind Arianism, and had escaped notice
until the Divinity of our Blessed Lord had been solidly vindicated. But at the very beginning of the reign of Valens,
St. Athanasius, whose eagle glance nothing escaped, detected
it, and wrote a treatise in its refutation. In this work the
holy doctor proves that the Church has ever held and taught
that there is in the Unity of the Divine Essence a Trinity of
Persons. He shows, by induction from the Scriptures, that
the Holy Ghost is God; and he protests that this doctrine
formed part of the deposit of the faith handed down from the
Apostles. When the Arians began to decline in importance,
the Macedonians attracted more notice. Their lives were
regular, their demeanour grave, their conduct free from reproach. And as the common people are easily deceived by
outward appearances, the Macedonians formed a sect which
numbered many adherents in Constantinople, and spread
throughout Thrace, Bithynia, and the shores of the Hellespont. The Emperor Theodosius, who had succeeded Valens,
applied himself to the extirpation of this heresy. Soon after

his baptism he issued an edict, in which he fixes on communion with the Roman Church as the sure criterion of truth and touchstone of error. "It is our will," he says, "that all our subjects should follow the religion taught by the Prince of the Apostles to the Romans, and observed by the reigning Pope Damasus; that so, in conformity with the gospels and the apostolic teaching, we may all believe one only indivisible Godhead of the Father, the Son, and the Holy Ghost. We decree that those alone who thus believe be called Catholic, and that those whose rash and insane impiety we condemn be reputed and called heretics, and that their places of meeting be not called churches."

Theodosius, however, well knew that something more than an expression of the imperial will was needed to pacify the Church. He resolved to convoke a council, as Constantine had done. Constantinople was selected as the place of meeting, and provision was made for defraying the expenses of the bishops summoned. They came from all parts of the East, to the number of 150, besides 36 who belonged to the Macedonian heresy; and Meletius, Bishop of Antioch, was chosen to preside over the deliberations of the council. When the bishops were presented to the emperor, he besought them to restore peace to the Church; and promised to give legal effect to their decrees; so that what was in itself binding in conscience, should be enforced by the civil power.

The council was opened with due solemnity. Attempts were made to win back the Macedonians, and Theodosius exhorted them to return to the faith and communion of the Church; but they refused and withdrew from the council. Their heresy was then formally condemned; the decrees of the Nicene Council were confirmed; and a few words were added to its creed, to declare more explicitly the teaching of the Church concerning the Incarnation of the Son of God and the Divinity of the Holy Ghost. On the former point the Nicene Creed had said: "and was incarnate, was made man, suffered," &c. The creed of Constantinople added: "and was incarnate by the Holy Ghost of the Virgin Mary, and was made man; He was crucified also for us," &c. In regard to the Third Person in the Adorable Trinity, the Creed of Nicæa had said simply: "We believe in the Holy Ghost." The Creed of Constantinople unfolded the truth implicitly contained in this article, thus: "We believe in the Holy

Ghost, the Lord and the Lifegiver, who proceedeth from the Father, who, together with the Father and the Son, is adored and glorified; who spake by the Prophets." The emperor received these decrees as the oracles of God, and gave them legal effect. It is to be noted that this council was composed exclusively of Eastern bishops, and had been neither convoked by the Pope nor presided over by his legates. The subsequent confirmation of its decrees (with the exception of the third canon) by the Roman Pontiff, and their acceptance throughout the West, alone entitle it to be regarded as an œcumenical or general council.

The temper of Theodosius was rash and impetuous, though he was readily appeased. In the year 387 a sedition broke out in Antioch, on occasion of a new and odious tax. The populace, in its blind rage, threw down the statues of the emperor and empress, and dragged them through the streets. When Theodosius heard this he was exceedingly irritated, and in his rage would have buried the inhabitants of Antioch beneath the ruins of their city. When his anger had cooled down, he appointed two commissioners to investigate the outrage on the spot, and gave them power of life and death. Meanwhile the populace had become aware of the gravity of their crime, and were so alarmed that they scarce dared appear in the streets. Flavian, their bishop, was deeply grieved for them. He spent his days and nights in prayer that God would touch the emperor's heart, and mollify his resentment. At length the saintly old man went to the emperor and implored him to forgive his flock; they had sinned not through malice, but in the heat of passion. The emperor recounted the benefits he had conferred on the city of Antioch, adding to each succeeding instance the words: "And is it thus I have deserved this outrage?" Flavian replied: "Prince, we merit severest punishment; reduce Antioch to ashes; our punishment would be less than our crime. But consider the example of our God; let that be your model. His creatures have despised and offended Him; He pardons them, and opens to them the kingdom of heaven. If you pardon us, we shall owe our lives to you, and your clemency will give a brighter lustre to your glory. Unbelievers will feel how great is the God of Christians. Nor need you fear that our impunity will set a bad example. Our very fears are a warning to others, and the worst of punishments to us. Nor deem it beneath you to yield to an old man; I speak to you as God's minister and representative. In His name I warn you, and in His words: 'If you will not forgive, neither will your Father that is in heaven forgive you your sins.'" Theodosius was touched, and said with tears: "Can I refuse pardon to men, my fellow-creatures, when our Divine Lord implored pardon for those who put Him to death? Go, father; hasten back to your flock; bid them be of good cheer."

Some time afterwards Theodosius forgot this lesson. The inhabitants of Thessalonica had revolted against their governor and had put him to death. The emperor, in the first transports of his rage, ordered a general massacre of the city, and 7000 persons were slain. Theodosius was then at Milan, and St. Ambrose, bishop of that city, wrote to him to point out the enormity of his sin, and to tell him that, until he had repented, he could not be allowed to partake of the sacred mysteries. Theodosius put the matter to the test by going to the church; but St. Ambrose met him at the door, and said: "Pause, O prince; you do not yet feel the heinousness of your guilt: how can you enter into the sanctuary of God? The innocent blood is on your hands: how could you receive the body of our Divine Lord? Withdraw, and add not sacrilege to homicide." The emperor alleged the case of David. "You have imitated him in his sin," said St. Ambrose; " imitate him now in his repentance." Theodosius retired in confusion, and kept himself secluded in his palace for eight months. As Christmas drew near his grief became more poignant. "Alas," he said, " the temple of the Lord is open to the lowest of my subjects, and I am forbidden to enter it !" He went to the holy bishop and requested absolution. St. Ambrose required a public penance, and the suspension, for a month, of the execution of all sentences of death. Then the excommunication was taken off, and the emperor entered the church. There, prostrate on the earth, the master of the Roman empire smote his breast, and repeated aloud the words of David:* " My soul hath cleaved to the ground; quicken Thou me according to Thy word." The people, moved by this touching spectacle, united their tears and prayers with those of the august penitent, and Theodosius was admitted to communion.

Meanwhile Arianism, silenced in the East, raised its voice

* Psalm cxviii. 25.

in the West, under the auspices of Justina, mother of the Emperor Valentinian II. This princess was anxious to make over some of the churches to the Arian faction; but she met in St. Ambrose a vigilant and formidable antagonist. Justina finding that nothing could corrupt or intimidate this great prelate, had recourse to violence. But her punishment was not long delayed: her son was driven from his empire by the usurper Maximus, and five years afterwards was strangled by Arbogastes, one of his generals, who set up another aspirant to the crown. Theodosius defeated these tyrants as they arose, and became sole master of the empire. This great prince may be said to have given the final blow to idolatry; the universal contempt into which it had fallen enabled him to prohibit it altogether. Accordingly its revenues were sequestered, the sacrifices ceased, the pagan ceremonies were neglected, the priests and priestesses were dismissed, and the temples were abandoned.

At this time the Church was troubled by the schism of the Donatists; a schism which desolated the Church of Africa for more than 200 years. It dates back to the reign of Constantine. The spark which kindled so furious a conflagration was the simple question, whether Cæcilian, Bishop of Carthage, had been validly consecrated. A few bishops, with Donatus at their head, alleged that the consecration was not valid, and they withdrew from his communion. The question was referred to the Pope, who pronounced in favour of Cæcilian. This judgment was supported by Constantine; but Donatus and his adherents refused submission: they erected altar against altar, and established a schismatical bishop at Carthage. They then sent letters in all directions to induce the faithful to break communion with Cæcilian. This unhappy rupture occasioned endless disorders and miseries throughout Africa. The Donatists disregarded the Church's excommunication; they had wilfully separated from the Church, and boasted of having formed a separate and distinct body. To excommunicate them, was but to do that which they gloried in having already done. Their party grew by degrees, and exercised cruelties towards the Catholics, which would exceed belief, if the Church's history were not full of proof that the spirit of heresy and schism is essentially uncharitable and ferocious. They seized the churches by force, drove away the bishops, broke the altars and the vessels of the sanctuary. They rebaptised by force all who had received the Church's baptism; as though the Church had no existence beyond their pale, and were confined to the little corner of Africa they occupied. Those who refused their baptism were treated with revolting cruelty. The Catholic bishops endured these outrages with wonderful patience, hoping that the fury of their opponents would wear itself out. St. Augustine, Bishop of Hippo, who afterwards became so celebrated in the Church, wrote numerous books to refute their errors, and convince them of their schism. His success in converting a large number only rendered the remainder more furious and cruel. They lay in wait for him as he went visiting the churches of his diocese; and he escaped their snares by a succession of merciful interpositions of Divine Providence. At length the Catholic bishops found themselves obliged to claim the protection of the civil power, and the emperor published an edict of great severity against the Donatists.

The orthodox bishops were far more eager to convert than to punish their erring brethren; and they besought the emperor to adopt milder measures towards them. They recommended a conference; and, on receiving the emperor's concurrence, all the African bishops, Catholic and Donatist, were assembled at Carthage; and representatives were chosen by each party to confer together on the questions in debate. Seven bishops were selected on each side; four notaries were appointed to record the debates; and four bishops to superintend and correct the notaries. When all was thus arranged, the Catholic bishops put in writing the following pledge: "If our adversaries gain the advantage over us in this discussion, we hereby consent to resign to them our sees, and to submit to their guidance; if, on the other hand, the Donatists are convinced and induced to submit to the Church, we promise to make them our coadjutors in the episcopate. And if the simple faithful be scandalised at seeing two bishops in one see at the same time, we will gladly relinquish our sees to them. For us it is enough to be Christians; we are bishops for the sake of our people; and if it be for our people's advantage that we should cease to be bishops, we consent with all our hearts." St. Augustine was the originater of this magnanimous proposal. The conference lasted three days, and was conducted with great order. St. Augustine proved irrefragably that there never could be any lawful reason for forsaking the Catholic Church; that it is mortal sin to break its unity; that in its bosom alone is there promise and hope of salvation; that outside the Church there is neither true sanctity nor true justice; that the true Church, the bride of Jesus Christ, is, according to the prophesies and promises, that which covers the whole earth, and cannot be circumscribed within a corner of Africa; that here on earth the evil and the good will be found in its external communnion; that, while we are bound not to communicate with sinners in their sins, we have no right to decline their external communion; the separation is made at the great day. The blessing of God accompanied the arguments of the holy doctor; the greater part of the schismatical bishops and their deluded flocks eventually returned to the unity of the Church.* Theodosius did not live to witness the extinction of this schism; he died at Milan in 395, exhorting his children to be faithful to the duties of religion, and forgiving all who had borne arms against him in the East.

§ 4. From the death of Theodosius to the fall of the Eastern Empire, 395-476. *

Theodosius left two sons: Arcadius, who was eighteen years of age, and Honorius, who was only ten. The empire was divided between these two princes: Arcadius took the East, and the West fell to the share of Honorius. Those who administered government in their names followed the example of Theodosius, and protected the interests of religion. But the sleepless enemy of the Church had prepared for it new trials and new conflicts. Christ has promised constant victory, but not without perpetual warfare.

The Donatist schism was scarcely healed when the Pelagian heresy renewed the sorrows of the Church. Pelagius was a native of Britain, an acute, subtle, indefatigable man. He came to Rome, and began cautiously to teach a new doctrine which flattered the pride of man by denying original sin and the necessity of grace. He feared at first to alarm the orthodox by an open disclosure of the consequences of his heresy, and he wrapped it up in obscure and ambiguous words. He attached to himself an able disciple, named Celestius, who contributed greatly to the diffusion of his impious tenet. Ce-

---

* On the Donatists see an instructive article in Cardinal Wiseman's Essays, vol. ii. p. 201.

lestius crossed over to Africa, and, being bolder and more
enterprising than his master, he there taught, without any
reserve or concealment, that the sin of the first man does not
in any way affect his descendants; and that man is perfectly
able to fulfil the law of God without the aid of grace. St.
Augustine refuted these positions with admirable learning and
skill: he proved, from the words of Holy Scripture, and from
the very Sacrament of Baptism, that we are born in sin; and
that the effects of Adam's sin are felt by all his descendants;
he showed from the prayer our Lord has taught us, that we
all have need of grace to dispose our wills, and to aid them
in their labour and conflict. Celestius was condemned at
Carthage; and, as he persisted in his heresy, he was excommunicated.

In the mean time Pelagius had gone to Palestine, and had
succeeded by his artful reasonings in perverting many bishops
of that country. Encouraged by their support he sent to St.
Augustine a defence of his teaching, and vaunted the success
he had had in the East, and the esteem in which he was held.
This scandal stimulated the zeal of the African bishops, and
two councils were held, one at Carthage, the other at Milevis,
and both in 416. In these it was defined, in accordance with
the Catholic faith, that the sin of Adam has been transmitted
to his descendants; and that, without Divine grace, we can
neither will nor perform any good work, or obtain salvation.
The assembled bishops then wrote to Pope Innocent to request his confirmation of their decrees. In his reply to their
synodal letters the Pope applauded their zeal in maintaining
the purity of the faith; he laid down clearly the ancient doctrine of original sin, and the necessity of grace for every
action of the Christian life; he then solemnly condemned Pelagius, Celestius, and their followers, and declared them excommunicate unless they renounced their errors. St. Augustine's words on receiving this judgment are memorable:
" Rome has spoken: the judgment of the bishops of Africa has
been sent to the Apostolical see; the letters of the Pope have
arrived, and confirm that judgment. Rome has spoken: the
question is at rest; discussion has ceased; God grant that the
error may cease likewise."

St. Augustine's desire was not granted him; the heresy
continued to exist, notwithstanding its condemnation. Pelagius sought, not to submit to the judgment pronounced

against him, but only to efface the stain which it cast upon him in the eyes of men. Pope Innocent was now dead. Pelagius addressed a respectful letter to his successor Zozimus, together with a declaration of his faith. Celestius even went to Rome, and presented to the Pope a similar declaration drawn up with great care, with a promise that he would condemn all that the Holy See condemned. The new Pope asked a few questions, which Celestius answered with apparent simplicity and straightforwardness. The Pope seemed satisfied, and pronounced Celestius innocent; not, be it observed, approving his heresy, but because he judged him orthodox in intention, and ready to withdraw any obnoxious proposition. Zozimus wrote a letter to the bishops of Africa, in which he says that he is convinced of the sincerity of Pelagius, and reproaches them with undue severity; still without one word to favour the impious heresy. The African prelates perceiving that the Pope had been imposed upon by the craft of these wily heresiarchs, at once summoned a council. Two hundred and fourteen bishops responded to the call; the whole case was laid before them; the latent and subtile venom of the heresy was laid bare; and dogmatic canons were drawn up and sent to Rome, with the words: " We decree that the sentence pronounced by Pope Innocent against Pelagius and Celestius is in full force, until such time as they shall state in plain terms that the grace of Jesus Christ is necessary in order that we may know and follow the laws of justice in our every action, in such sort that, without the aid of grace, we cannot have, or think, or speak, or do any thing that is truly pious and good. It is not enough that Celestius has, in vague terms, professed his submission to the Holy See; to remove scandal, it is needful that he should, without ambiguity, anathematise the propositions in his writings which have been censured, lest the simple be led to imagine, not that the heretic has relinquished his heresy, but that the Holy See has approved it."

This representation had its due effect. The Pope saw that he had allowed his fatherly tenderness to carry' him too far; he read the writings of the heretics, and issued a sentence which confirmed that of the African bishops. And then it was seen how little sincerity there is in the protestations made by heretics to avert their condemnation. The Pelagians appealed to a general council; but St. Augustine proved decisively that this appeal was nugatory. The assembled Church could but reaffirm what had been decided by the African bishops, and approved by the Pope; the heresy had been sufficiently condemned; all that remained was to repress it. The emperor assisted this decision by the aid of the civil power, and added the penalty of banishment to that of excommunication.

The Pelagian heresy was withered by the censure of St. Peter's successor, and gradually died away; but from its ashes arose another sect, which softened the repulsive features of its parent heresy, and followed a middle course between the doctrine of Pelagius and the Catholic faith. This mitigated Pelagianism was taught first by some priests of Marseilles, and its followers acquired the name of Semi-Pelagians. They admitted original sin, and the necessity of grace in order to do good; but they affirmed that the beginning of faith and the first desire of virtue were to be ascribed to the mere powers of nature and of man's free will; that grace is the consequence and the reward of these first movements of the will towards good—of which God is not the author; and thus that man himself begins the work of his salvation, and obtains the first grace of God by his own unaided efforts. St. Augustine pursued the wily heresy into this its last lurking-place. He wrote two treatises, in which he shows clearly that not the increase only, but the very beginning of faith, is the gift of God; that the first grace of all cannot be ascribed to our own merits in any sense whatever. He alleges many passages of Holy Scripture which teach that it is God who disposes the human will to good; that grace is needful for the first step in the way of life, as much as for all subsequent steps; that God calls men, not because they believe, but that they may believe. He draws attention to the fact that the Church has ever shown by her prayers that she expects grace merely of the Divine mercy, and not in reward of our merits; and that grace would cease to be grace, were it not simply gratuitous. Why are children baptised, he asks, but to call them into possession of that grace which they could never have merited? Where is the faith, where are the works, which precede the sumptuous grace of baptism?

Despite this lucid exposition of the truth, the Semi-Pelagians continued to maintain their errors, and to impute to St. Augustine, after his death, opinions he had never held.

Whereupon Pope St. Celestine wrote to the bishops of Gaul, calling upon them to repress these obstinate impugners of the faith, and at the same time passing a high eulogium on the writings of the great Bishop of Hippo. In his letter he quoted against the Semi-Pelagians the definitions of the African bishops, as approved and confirmed by his predecessors, by which Pelagianism itself had been condemned. These disputes, however, were not settled until the celebrated decree of the second council of Orange (A.D. 529), at which St. Cæsarius, Bishop of Arles, presided. It runs thus: "If any one shall affirm that either the increase or the beginning of faith, and the first movement of the heart by which we believe in Him who justifies the sinner, is not an effect of the gift of grace, but that this disposition of the heart is the effect of our own natural powers, he contradicts the teaching of the Apostles; for St. Paul says, 'We are confident that He, who hath begun a good work in you, will perfect it unto the day of Christ Jesus;' and again, 'By grace you are saved through faith; and that not of yourselves, for it is the gift of God.'" This decree was approved by Pope Boniface II. in the year 531.

St. Jerome, one of the most illustrious doctors of the Church, aided St. Augustine in his contest with the heresy of Pelagius. He was born in Dalmatia about 331, of Christian parents. As they were wealthy, they sent him to Rome to cultivate his remarkable genius. He there made rapid progress in literature and eloquence; but as the esteem of men was the motive of his efforts, he was suffered to fall away into sin. After a time he came to himself; and in 374 he withdrew into a desert on the confines of Syria and Arabia. Smitten with fear of the judgments of God, Jerome devoted himself to the most rigorous austerities; and still further to divest his thoughts from all external things, he occupied himself in most laborious studies, applying himself to the acquirement of the Hebrew tongue, under the guidance of a learned monk, who had been a Jew. Being pursued even into these solitudes by the controversies of the day, he retired into Palestine; whence, however, after a time he repaired to Antioch, and was ordained priest. Shortly afterwards he went to Constantinople, and passed some time with St. Gregory of Nazianzum, with the aid of whose instructions he devoted himself specially to the study of Holy Scripture. He then went to Rome; and Pope Damasus kept him at his side to

answer those who consulted him on the sense of Scripture, or
on points of moral theology. At the Pope's suggestion he
corrected the Latin version of the New Testament; he also
translated the greatest part of the Old Testament into the
same language. This translation is that known as the Vulgate. On the death of the Pontiff he returned to Palestine,
and fixed his abode at Bethlehem, where he wrote his com-
mentaries. When Pelagius came into Palestine, the pious
monk, alarmed at the perils which threatened the faith,
deemed it a duty to write in its defence. Pelagius attempted
a reply; but failing in this, excited his followers to pillage
and burn the monastery in which St. Jerome resided. Many
of the inmates were killed by the heretics, and the saint himself escaped with difficulty to a fortified tower. He died in
420 at the age of ninety-one.

Contemporary with him was the great St. John Chrysostom, Archbishop of Constantinople, who laboured so assiduously to reform the clergy and people of that luxurious and
degraded city. He rebuked with unwavering zeal the avarice of the rich, the luxury of the women, and the pride of
the great. The court was not safe from the shafts of his
eloquent indignation. His episcopal fidelity raised him
many enemies. The empress Eudoxia was especially irritated against him because of a sermon which was supposed
to have been pointed at her. St. Chrysostom was banished;
but the very day after his departure there was a violent earthquake, which so alarmed the empress, that she requested the
immediate recall of the saint. St. Chrysostom returned in
triumph; but soon there arose a fresh storm. A silver statue
of the empress was erected near the principal church of Constantinople; and the inauguration was accompanied with su-
perstitious practices and with public shows and dances, the
noise of which interrupted the divine service. Against this
abuse the bishop raised his warning voice; and the empress,
deeming herself insulted, resolved upon his ruin. He was a
second time deposed, and banished to Cucusus, a petty town
of Armenia. He reached his lonely and sterile place of exile
after seventy days' journey. He there applied himself vigorously to the exercise of his ministry; and so great was his
success, that his enemies procured an order for his removal
to a small town on the eastern shore of the Euxine Sea, on
the very borders of the empire. He was removed under the

care of two brutal soldiers, who had received a hint of reward
if the saint died on the way. After three months of journey-
ings, sometimes through heavy rains, sometimes under a
scorching sun, which caused him the greatest sufferings, St.
Chrysostom was seized with a violent fever at Comana in
Pontus. That night he saw in vision St. Basiliscus, a martyr bishop of Comana, who said to him, "Fear not, brother;
to-morrow we shall be together." On the morrow he died.
In him the Church lost one of her most holy bishops, most
learned doctors, and most eloquent preachers. His eloquence
procured him the name by which he is commonly known—
St. John *Chrysostom*, or, St. John *of the golden mouth*. At
the earliest request of the clergy and faithful of Constantinople, his remains were translated from their obscure resting-
place at Comana to the imperial city. The emperor Theodosius II. advanced as far as Chalcedon to receive them, and
implored the pardon of God for his guilty parents, who had
driven the saint into exile.

　　When the spirit of error had recoiled baffled from his
attacks on the mystery of the ever-blessed Trinity, original
sin, and grace, he made renewed and more subtle efforts to
shake the Catholic faith in the great mystery of the Incarnation. It had ever been believed in the Church that Jesus
Christ is the Divine Word made flesh, and that there are
consequently in Him *two natures* and *one person*. Nestorius, Bishop of Constantinople, began in an evil hour to teach
that there are in our Divine Lord *two separate persons*. As
he feared to assail openly the Catholic dogma, he began by
teaching that the Blessed Virgin should not be called *Mother
of God*, but only *Mother of Christ*; thus drawing a distinction between the Person of the Eternal Word and that of
Christ. This novel doctrine was so opposed to universal belief, that it occasioned great scandal both amongst the clergy
and the laity. The first time that the faithful heard this
teaching, they fled from the church, to testify their abhorrence
of the blasphemer who had uttered it. This instinctive movement of faith is a thing much to be noted. The multitude
may not always reason soundly, but they believe implicitly
and feel keenly; their souls shrink sensitively from heresy,
they know not why. They detect it by a divine instinct, by
the unction from the Holy One. Nestorius was a great man.
He was Patriarch of Constantinople, then beginning to be

regarded as the second see in Christendom; he was high in favour at court; he was their own bishop; but no sooner did he utter words of heresy than his simple flock fled shuddering from him. It has pleased God to permit these successive heresies; and at the very moment of the Church's need He has raised up and prepared for the conflict some saintly doctor to defend the truth impugned. The instrument chosen of God to overthrow Nestorius was St. Cyril of Alexandria. When this holy bishop heard of the impious novelty broached at Constantinople, he published a treatise in which he states clearly and simply the mystery of the Incarnation. "I am astonished," he says, "that any one can doubt whether the Blessed Virgin should be called the Mother of God; for if our Lord Jesus Christ is God, the holy Virgin Mother must be Mother of God. This is the faith the Apostles have handed down to us, this the teaching of our forefathers in the faith; not that the nature of the Divine Word had its origin in Mary, but that in her was formed, and animated with a reasonable soul, the sacred Body to which the Divine Word is hypostatically united: and hence we say that the Word was born according to the flesh. Thus, in the natural order, though a mother has no part in the creation of the soul, she is regarded and called the mother of the whole man, and not of his body alone." This treatise of St. Cyril was soon spread throughout the East, and reassured the faithful, whom the new-fangled heresy had scandalised. St. Cyril wrote privately to Nestorius to bring him back to the faith. He exhorted him to appease the indignation of the Church by giving to the ever-blessed Virgin the title of Mother of God. Unhappily this letter had no effect;—the conversion of the leader of a heresy or schism is one of the rarest miracles of grace. The holy bishop then applied to Pope St. Celestine; ne drew a melancholy picture of the state of the Church in Constantinople, and implored him to apply a remedy to the evil. Nestorius had also sent to the Pope his writings, authenticated by his signature. The Sovereign Pontiff thereupon held a council at Rome to examine the writings of Nestorius; his teaching was found to be plainly opposed to that of the Fathers, and was condemned without a dissentient voice. St. Celestine notified this decision to the Eastern bishops; and in the letter he wrote to St. Cyril he applauds his zeal and diligence; declares that he accepts his statement of the Catholic doctrine of the Incarnation as perfectly accurate; and adds, that if Nestorius did not, within a time assigned, retract and anathematise his heresy, he should be cut off from the Church as a dead branch.

Nestorius was intractable; like all other innovators, opposition irritated his pride and hardened his obstinate heart. In spite of the strong protectors he had at court, Theodosius the younger felt that the tumults at Constantinople could not be allayed until the question was finally settled, and he resolved to convoke a general council at Ephesus: This resolution gave universal satisfaction; and nearly two hundred bishops, from all parts of Christendom, assembled at Ephesus. St. Cyril presided as legate of the Holy See; Nestorius came, accompanied by the Count Candidian, one of his principal supporters. He refused, however, to attend the sittings of the council, although he was three times summoned. He pleaded as his reason for non-attendance that the Patriarch of Antioch and his suffragans had not arrived. Meanwhile the council was opened. On a raised throne in the middle of the church was placed a copy of the four gospels, to represent the presence and illumination of Jesus Christ, who has promised to be with those who are gathered in His name. This solemn circumstance has been imitated in all succeeding councils. The bishops were ranged, according to their rank, on either side of the church. As Nestorius refused to appear in person, the council could ascertain his doctrine from his writings alone. These were read, and when the reading was finished, there was one unanimous cry: "Anathema to these impious errors; anathema to all who hold or teach this doctrine! It is contrary to the Holy Scriptures and to the writings of the Fathers." They then read the letter of Pope Celestine to Nestorius, and several passages of St. Cyprian, St. Athanasius, St. Ambrose, St. Basil, and others, which were contrasted with the propositions of the heresiarch. Meanwhile the greatest excitement prevailed in the city. The doors of the church were besieged by an impatient crowd. The decision was pronounced—the ever-blessed Virgin was declared to be the *Mother of God*.* The glorious tidings were taken up and repeated from mouth to mouth. Blessings were in-

* The word θεοτόκος, or *Mother of God*, was thus the touchstone of Nestorianism, and the compendious symbol of the Catholic faith; just as the word ὁμοούσιος, or *consubstantial*, had been in the Arian controversy.

voked upon the fathers of the council, and the city was illuminated to express the delight of the inhabitants at this confirmation of the glories of the Mother of God. The bishops wrote to acquaint the emperor with their decision; but Candidian, who had been sent to protect the council, intercepted their letters, and conveyed a false report to the emperor. Every means was employed to conceal the truth from Theodosius, until the bishops bethought them of intrusting their despatches to a mendicant, who kept them concealed in the hollow of a cane which he held in his hand as he begged alms on the road. The emperor thereupon banished Nestorius to Oasis in Egypt, where he died miserably in a short time. The council of Ephesus was held A.D. 431.

Out of the heresy of Nestorius was evolved another, equally fatal to the Catholic doctrine of the Incarnation. Eutyches, in refuting Nestorius, was led into an opposite extreme, and equally wandered from the truth. He taught that after the Incarnation there was in our Lord Jesus Christ only *one nature*. So weak is the reason of man, that it seems unable to escape from one error but by rushing into another; only the Church of the living God, infallible because led by the Spirit of God, condemns all errors, and is affected by none. Nestorius had divided the one person of our Divine Lord; Eutyches confounded the two natures. He was the superior of a monastery near Constantinople, and had manifested a most laudable zeal in maintaining the oneness of our Lord's Person against Nestorius. The new heresiarch at first developed his views to a few friends in conversation; he then proceeded to teach them in his monastery. His friends used their utmost efforts to reclaim him from his errors; but in vain: Eutyches displayed the inflexible obstinacy common to all heretics. He was then denounced to St. Flavian, Patriarch of Constantinople. After the holy prelate had exhausted every means of persuasion, he called together the bishops who happened to be in Constantinople, and cited the innovator to appear before them. Eutyches persisting in preferring his private fancies to the infallible wisdom of the Church, his teaching was condemned, and he was deprived of the charge of his monastery. He found at court a supporter in one of the principal officers of the emperor. This favourite, whose name was Chrysaphius, was a handsome barbarian, avaricious, cruel, and unbelieving; yet he had obtained an extraordinary influence over the young prince, and was the virtual ruler of the empire. He persuaded Theodosius to allow the teaching of Eutyches to be reconsidered in an assembly of bishops, and to name as president Dioscorus, Bishop of Alexandria, who was a friend of Eutyches and hostile to Flavian.* Chrysaphius overruled the assembly with threats of violence, and succeeded in inducing them to absolve Eutyches, and to condemn Flavian. Many refused to sign this iniquitous decision, and were sent into exile; amongst them was St. Flavian, who was so ill-treated on the journey that he died within a few days. The emperor did not long survive him. The glory of his reign was tarnished by the blind confidence he reposed in his profligate favourite, whose true character he discovered only when it was too late to repair the evil he had done. He was succeeded by Marcian, a religious prince, whose first care was to maintain the purity of the faith.

St. Leo, who then occupied the chair of St. Peter, was painfully affected by the wounds inflicted on the Church by Eutyches, and applied himself to their remedy. With the co-operation of Marcian he convoked a general council at Chalcedon, one of the suburbs of Constantinople. Three hundred and sixty bishops† assembled there in the church of St. Euphemia, and the first session of the council was held on the 8th of October 451. St. Leo sent three legates to preside in his name, and the book of the holy gospels was enthroned in the middle of the church. The proceedings were opened by an examination of the conduct of Dioscorus. He was convicted of having, in his treatment of St. Flavian, violated the canons; and sentence of deposition was pronounced upon him. They then read the admirable letter which St. Leo had written to St. Flavian on the first mention of the new heresy, expounding with luminous precision the Catholic faith touching the Incarnation — the oneness of our Divine Lord's person, and the distinction of His two natures. The bishops exclaimed with one voice: " This is the belief of us all; this is the faith of the Apostles, this is the faith of our forefathers: Peter has spoken by the mouth of Leo; this is the orthodox doctrine: anathema to him who impugns it !"

---

* This tumultuous assembly was held at Ephesus in August 449. Its iniquitous and violent proceedings have procured for it the name of *Latrocinium*, the *council of robbers*.

† Some writers state the number of bishops at 520, and the number of papal legates at four.

The council then drew up a confession of faith, in which, after recapitulating the creeds of Nicæa and Constantinople, they express themselves thus: " We declare that we confess one and the same Lord Jesus Christ, who is perfect and complete in His Godhead, and perfect and complete in His manhood, truly God and truly man,—consubstantial with the Father as to His Godhead, consubstantial with us as to His manhood, in all things like unto us, sin alone excepted; begotten of the Father as to His Godhead, and in these last days, for us men and for our salvation, born of the Virgin Mary, Mother of God, as to His manhood: we confess one and the same Jesus Christ, the only-begotten Son of God, in two natures, unconfounded, indivisible, immutable, inseparable; the difference of the natures being in no wise taken away by the union; on the contrary, the property of each is preserved, and concurs in one person and one hypostasis; so that He is not parted or divided into two persons, but He, one and the same, is Son and only-begotten, God the Word, our Lord Jesus Christ."

The emperor was present at the sixth session of the council, and protested that he came, not to influence their decision, but to lend to their deliberations the sanction of his temporal authority. He requested them to read their confession of faith; and when he had heard it, he inquired whether they were unanimous in this statement. The bishops exclaimed as one man, " We have all but one doctrine; this is the faith of the Church's doctors; this is the faith of the holy Apostles; this is the faith which has saved the world." Thereupon the emperor ordered the decrees of the council to be incorporated into a law of the empire; and in its preamble he says truly that he who would wish to re-open the question after the Church had decided it, could wish only to find a lie. And thus the heresy of Eutyches was cast forth, and the true doctrine of the Incarnation more clearly defined by the very heresies which aimed at its overthrow.

Meanwhile the political state of the empire was becoming worse and worse. From about A.D. 400 we may date those inroads of barbarians which ultimately broke down the Western Empire, and cleared the ground for the modern European monarchies. During the reign of Honorius, the terrible Alaric, king of the Visigoths, swept over Italy, and covered it with ruins. Scarcely had he retired, when a suc-

ceeding wave of invasion reached still further. It was then
that Honorius fixed the seat of empire at Ravenna, his last
stronghold. In the night of the 24th August 410, Alaric
took Rome by storm; it was sacked and pillaged; but the
barbarians respected the church, into which the affrighted
population had fled for refuge. Valentinian III. succeeded
his uncle Honorius in 425. While the Vandals, Visigoths,
and other tribes were ravaging Spain and Gaul, Attila marched
southward at the head of 700,000 Huns; and after spreading
devastation throughout the north of Italy, he advanced upon
Rome, which was just rising out of the ruins left by Alaric.
The emperor in alarm convoked his senate and consulted the
Pope, and it was resolved to send an embassy to Attila to
avert the fearful scourge. St. Leo took on himself this perilous mission; he dreaded Attila no more than he had dreaded
Eutyches. He acquitted himself with a calm intrepidity before which the wild savage conqueror quailed. Attila was of
low stature, with a broad chest, a head of enormous size,
flashing eyes, little hair or beard, a flat nose, a dark complexion, and a manner at once proud and menacing. Before
him came the simple ambassador of Christ, armed only with
Divine power, and speaking respectfully indeed, but with a
vigour and truthfulness to which Attila was little accustomed. The king remarked to his officers: " I cannot imagine why that old priest's words have touched me so much."
He was induced to listen to the propositions made him by
the emperor, and withdrew his troops from Italy. Three
years later St. Leo exerted his influence, with like success, on
Genseric, king of the Vandals. When this cruel conqueror
had already reached Rome, St. Leo went forth to meet him,
and wrung from him a doubtful promise that he would employ neither steel nor fire; that both the inhabitants and the
buildings of the doomed city should be spared. The booty
collected and conveyed away by the barbarians was immense,
and thousands were carried off into captivity.

It was but a putting off of the evil day. St. Leo could
only retard the inevitable catastrophe. Valentinian had been
murdered by Maximus, a senator, whose usurpation lasted but
a few months, A.D. 455. The last of the Western emperors
was Romulus Augustulus. In 476, Odoacer, king of the
Heruli, speaking in the name of the barbarians generally,
whether in the pay of Rome or opposed to her, demanded two-

thirds of the soil of Italy. On the refusal of the regent, he took Ravenna, exiled the youthful emperor into Campania, sent the insignia of empire to Constantinople, and assumed the title of King of Italy. The remaining provinces became the prey of the boldest and most rapid of the invading hordes; all were eager to share the spoils of the great nation which had pent them up so long in the solitary forests of the chilly north.

Thus came to an end, 1228 years after its foundations were laid by Romulus, the mightiest empire the world has seen: a memorable lesson of the instability of earth's strongest fabrics. Not only does one generation flourish on the decay of that which preceded it, empires and kingdoms wax and wane; one only institution knows no decay—the Church founded upon the Rock—Jesus Christ, the same yesterday, to-day, and for ever.

REFLECTIONS.

To be ever in conflict and ever victorious is the destiny of Christ's Church on earth. Like her Divine Head, she is made perfect through suffering; and when outwardly weak, is then most really strong. Thus we see that she no sooner has rest from persecution than her own children become her worst enemies, and grieve and rend her by heresies and schisms. On every page of Church-history we read the record of these conflicts; but we read also of the triumphs and extension of the Church, and the consolidation of her dogmatic teaching. Had not the strong arm of God been uplifted in her defence, she must have perished in the Arian controversy. In the period we are now closing, there were, notwithstanding the general peace, a multitude of martyrs, the victims of pagans in provinces nominally subject to the empire, or of independent countries, such as Persia and Africa. The Vandals were especially conspicuous for their cruelties. They had been brought up in Arianism, and they hated Catholics with a deadly hatred. But the blood of the martyrs obtained the recognition of the Divinity of Jesus Christ. "They overcame by the blood of the Lamb, and by the word of the testimony; and they loved not their lives unto death."[*]

During this period also a new spectacle was presented to

* Apoc. xii. 11.

the world.   Multitudes of men, most of whom were largely
endowed with the best gifts of this world, abandoned all, and
withdrew into the deserts of Egypt and Palestine to practise
the evangelical counsels in their sublimest degree.   Of their
own free will, unconstrained but by the desire of penance,
they embraced poverty, toil, and silence; despising the world,
with its illusory charms and treacherous gifts, for the sake of
"the things not seen, which are eternal." Their number is
almost incredible.   The deserts and the desolate places were
almost too narrow by reason of the inhabitants.*   And what
a protest did they thus make against the luxury which was
sapping the virility, and eating out the very heart of the
effete and exhausted empire!   But their protest and their
example were in vain.   The Romans refused to sacrifice their
vices at the foot of the Cross; and God swept them away, to
make room for another generation.

CHAPTER III.

FROM THE FALL OF THE WESTERN EMPIRE TO MAHOMET,
A.D. 476-622.

§ 1. Progress of religion in the West—England and France.

IT is now time to turn back and inquire into the state of
England and France, the two parts of the empire which were
destined to so glorious a future.   It is certain that the Gospel
was preached in Britain during the second century; but amidst
conflicting accounts it is impossible to decide to whom it owed
the light of faith.   It is contended by some that St. Paul
himself visited our land; but no certain reliance can be placed
on these unsupported legends.   The earliest authentic notice
we have occurs in Bede, who tells us that in the pontificate
of Eleutherius—that is, between 177 and 181—a British king
or chieftain named Lucius sent messengers to the Pope with
a request that he might be admitted into the Church.
    In the beginning of the third century, Tertullian numbers
amongst the conquests of the Gospel " Britain, unconquerable by the Roman arms, but reduced to the obedience of

* Isaias xlix. 19.

Christ." Other fathers also mention the Church in Britain. We then come to the persecution under Dioclesian and Maximian, at the beginning of the fourth century. There was a fearful persecution of Christians throughout Britain; and it was then that St. Alban received the martyr's crown. We next find British bishops in the councils of Arles in 314, of Sardica in 347, and of Rimini in 359. The heresy of Pelagius made great progress in the British Church. Gildas tells us that the British were always itching for novelties and changes; and that every heresy found patronage in Britain. Pope Celestine sent Germanus, Bishop of Auxerre, and Lupus, to crush the heresy, as the English bishops had raised a cry of distress. And this is all we know of the primitive British churches during the first five centuries.

Then came the invasion of the idolatrous Saxons, the ravages of the Danes and others; and the faith was almost extinguished. Its torch was kept dimly burning in the mountainous parts of Wales. While St. Gregory was still a deacon, he felt drawn to attempt the reconversion of England. One day, while he was passing through the market-place at Rome, his attention was arrested by some slaves of fair complexion who were exposed for sale. He asked who they were; and on hearing that they were idolaters from the distant isle of Britain, he said with a sigh, "Alas! that men of such radiant countenances should be in the power of the spirits of darkness." He then inquired the name of their nation, and being told that they were Angles—"Angels rather," he exclaimed, "if only they were Christians." He would himself have attempted the conversion of their country, but was prevented by his superiors. Still he never abandoned his design; and on his accession to the chair of St. Peter, his first care was to provide for the English. He sent over forty missionaries of the order of St. Benedict,* with St. Augustine at their head. This heroic band reached the coast of Kent, not far from Sandwich, in the year 596. The king, Ethelbert, had married Bertha, daughter of Charibert, king of Paris; she was a Christian, and had with her a chaplain named Luidhard. The king consented to receive the missionaries in the open air, where, he believed, incantations and spells could not injure him. St. Augustine and his monks moved in procession to the place of meeting, preceded by a

* See the account hereafter given of St. Benedict and his order.

crucifix of silver, and chanting litanies for the conversion of
England. The king courteously requested them to sit down;
and St. Augustine told him that he came to announce to him
very joyful tidings. God, who had sent him, was willing to
bestow on Ethelbert a kingdom far more glorious and lasting
than that of Kent. The king replied to him with kindness
and discretion: that the words he had spoken were fair and
promising, but that they were new and strange to him; that
he could not abandon the religion of his fathers without further knowledge and reflection. Meanwhile they might preach
where they pleased, and he would protect them as long as
they chose to remain. Not only so, he would provide for
their maintenance, since they had had the kindness to come
from afar to do him and his people good. The missionaries
began to preach in good earnest. Their simplicity and purity,
their disinterestedness, and their numerous miracles, touched
the hearts of many of the heathen, and they were baptised.
At last the good king yielded to the power of grace; and
his conversion was followed by that of a vast number of his
subjects. Ethelbert became most zealous for the spread of
the Gospel, and St. Augustine was obliged to curb his impetuosity, by reminding him that the service of Christ must
be free and unconstrained. The king contented himself with
giving his confidence to those who became Christians, and
intrusting to them the most important offices of his kingdom.

In order to give the rising Church its proper form and discipline, St. Augustine went over to Gaul, and was consecrated
by the Bishop of Arles, who was the legate of the Holy See in
Gaul. He returned to England with the title of Archbishop
of Canterbury, and renewed his labours with increased zeal
and success. On Christmas-day he baptised 2000 persons at
Canterbury. So widespread was his fame and so unbounded
his influence, that the Pope wrote him a letter, in which we
find the following beautiful words. After congratulating him
on his success and on his great gifts, St. Gregory writes:
"This joy, beloved brother, is not unmixed with fear; for I
know that God has wrought great things by your hand. Let
us often remember that when the Apostles cried with exultation
to their Divine Master, 'Lord, the devils themselves are subject to us in Thy name,' He answered them, 'But yet rejoice not that spirits are subject unto you; but rejoice in this,
that your names are written in heaven.' While, therefore,

God is working through you outwardly, do you, beloved brother, judge yourself severely within, and know well who and what you are. And if ever you have offended God, let the memory of your sins repress any secret complacency you may feel. Reflect that the gift of miracles is not given you for your own merit, but for the sake of those for whose salvation you labour. You know well what the Truth Himself has said: 'Many will say to Me in that day, Lord, Lord, have not we prophesied in Thy name, and cast out devils in Thy name, and done many miracles in Thy name? and yet I shall profess unto them, I never knew you.'"

The Pope continued to send fresh missionaries to labour in a field so fruitful. He had collected a number of promising young English, and had them taught and trained in Rome; these now became of the greatest service in the conversion of their countrymen.

The zeal of this holy Pope embraced the whole Church, and he watched over its interests with unslumbering eye. Notwithstanding the feebleness of his constitution, he allowed himself no rest. Every where he corrected abuses, and redressed grievances, and upheld discipline in its purity. Every where he was the protector of the weak and the restrainer of the oppressor, the helper of the poor and the needy. Although overwhelmed with public business, he never omitted the regular instruction of his flock. He has left us a large collection of writings, in which he expounds the doctrines and the morals of the Gospel with solid learning and in an attractive style. His unceasing toil wore him out, and he entered into his rest in the year 604. He is one of the greatest Popes who have ruled the Church, and one of her most voluminous writers. His name is enrolled amongst those whom the Church has canonised as saints, and reckons among her four principal doctors; while the influence he exerted in his day, his wisdom, and his virtues, have obtained for him, even in secular history, the title of Great.*

As the time drew near when the Western Empire was to be broken up into fragments, it pleased God to provide for the conversion of Gaul, the modern France, by calling to a knowledge of His grace Clovis, king of the Franks, and founder of the French monarchy. The Franks had already

* For some account of the conversion of Ireland and Scotland see Appendix.

gained a footing in Gaul, and Clovis had married a Christian princess of great piety, named Clotilda. She spoke to him often of the Christian religion, and brought him to a sense of the vanity of paganism; but the king would move no further. He allowed their infant son to be baptised; and as the child died a few days afterwards, Clovis became enraged, and charged his queen with having drawn on him the vengeance of his gods. Clotilda endured in silent resignation, and continued fervent in prayer. She had a second son, who also was baptised. The child fell ill; and the king renewed his reproaches, declaring that the boy was sure to die as his brother had died, because he was baptised. Clotilda had recourse to prayer, and God was pleased to restore her son to health. Clovis was no mere barbarian; rather he was the very perfection and ideal of human nature, unrefined by civilisation and unmoulded by grace. So noble was his character, that he won the hearts of all his subjects; prayers were every where offered by the Christians for his conversion; and it pleased God to bend this iron will by a miracle similar to that which had brought about the conversion of Constantine.

The Allemanni, a warlike tribe of Germany, had crossed the Rhine, and were advancing to conquer Gaul. Clovis marched to meet them; and the opposing armies met in the plain of Tolbiac, in the duchy of Julien. Before his setting out, Clotilda had assured him of victory if he would invoke the God of the Christians; but Clovis disdained this resource. The battle commenced; the troops of Clovis were broken, and fled in confusion. The Allemanni advanced with triumphant shouts, believing the victory gained. In this moment of anguish, Clovis bethought him of Clotilda's words; and lifting up his hands to heaven he cried, "O God, whom Clotilda worships, aid me now; if Thou wilt grant me the victory, I will worship no other God but Thee." Scarcely had he ceased speaking when the tide of battle turned mysteriously; the Allemanni, seized with a panic, took to flight, and all who escaped the sword surrendered at discretion.

The warlike Franks felt that this victory came from above, from the God of Clotilda, the Lord of Hosts. Clovis retraced his steps, and hastened to perform the vow by which he had bound himself. During the march he found at Torl a certain priest of great repute for piety and learning; and he induced the holy man to accompany him and instruct him in

H

the mysteries of the faith. Clotilda was filled with joy, and
went as far as Rheims to meet her husband—hers now in a
deeper, truer sense. St. Remigius, Bishop of Rheims, who
has well deserved to be called the Apostle of France, completed the instruction of Clovis. The king was convinced;
he assembled his army, and exhorted the soldiers to follow
his example, to renounce their dark and gloomy demons for
the God who had given them victory in the day of doubtful
battle. He was interrupted by a unanimous shout: "We
renounce all mortal gods; we are ready to adore the true
God, the God whom Remigius preaches." Clovis immediately asked the saint to appoint a day for his baptism, and
Remigius fixed upon Christmas-eve. It was his wish to
impress the minds of the Franks by the splendour of the Catholic ritual: the church and the baptistery were hung with
costly tapestry; spices were mingled with the wax of the in-
numerable tapers, so that the church was filled with a most
fragrant perfume. The catechumens came on in long procession, headed by the book of the gospels and the crucifix,
and singing litanies as they went. St. Remigius had the
consolation of baptising the king and two of his sisters, together with upwards of 3000 soldiers whom the example of
the king had induced to become Christians. When Clovis
reached the baptistery he formally begged for baptism. Then
the holy bishop said to him: "Haughty Sicamber, bow thy
head; burn all that thou hast hitherto adored, and adore
what thou hast burnt." He then required of him a confession
of faith, baptised him, and anointed him with the holy chrism.
     The tidings of the conversion of Clovis diffused joy through-
out all Christendom. Arianism was rampant in high places, and
Clovis was the one only Catholic sovereign. To his conversion
at that critical moment we owe the illustrious church of France.
     About this time a holy maiden, named Geneviève, was
famed throughout Gaul for the purity of her life and the
splendour of her miraculous gifts. She was born at Nanterre,
near Paris. St. Germanus, Bishop of Auxerre, noticed something so remarkable in her, as he passed through Nanterre,
that he exhorted her to consecrate herself to God, and himself received her vows. On the morrow he asked her if she
remembered her promise; and when she replied that, by the
grace of God, she would perform it, he gave her a medal, on
which was stamped a cross, and forbade her to wear any

ornament of gold or jewels. Her life became one of singular
austerity and prayer. When Attila was marching upon
Paris, Geneviève exhorted the inhabitants to avert the anger
of God by repentance, by fasting, and by prayer; and assured
them that the oppressor should not enter Paris. Her prediction was verified; and Geneviève was regarded with veneration
as a saint of God. She obtained money to erect a church in
honour of St. Denis and his companions; and during a severe
famine she undertook a long voyage to procure provisions for
the city. She died in the year 511, in her 90th year. Her
body was laid by the side of that of Clovis, in the church of St.
Peter and St. Paul, the same which is now called St. Geneviève. The aid she had given to her beloved city was not
withdrawn after her death: to this day she is invoked as
the patroness of Paris, and her relics are numbered among
the most precious treasures of the city.

The monastic life received a new impetus from the virtues
and miracles of St. Benedict (A.D. 480-543). This great man
was born of noble parents at Norcia, in the duchy of Spoleto.
He was sent to Rome to study; but the vices of the youth
amongst whom he lived induced him to withdraw to a hermitage forty miles from Rome. There he passed three years
unknown and undiscovered but by a holy monk, who supplied him with food. After three years he became celebrated
throughout the country. The sick were brought to him to be
healed, and all united in asking his intercession with God.
The religious of an adjacent monastery chose him as their
abbot; but Benedict refused, and told them that they would
never agree to the rules he should enforce. Overcome by
their solicitations and promises, he at length consented; but
soon, wearied of his unsleeping vigilance, some among them
determined to rid themselves of him by mixing poison in his
wine-cup. When the cup, according to custom, was held towards him to bless, St. Benedict made over it the sign of the
cross; when instantly the vessel broke in pieces without the
slightest noise. The man of God at once perceived the cause
of what had happened; and turning to the monks, he said
to them with unruffled calmness: "Brethren, why have you
treated me thus? Did I not say you would weary and re-
pent of your choice? Seek, then, a superior to your mind.
Farewell!" And he returned to his solitary cell. Soon a
large number of penitents gathered around him, and many

of them besought him to undertake the direction of their
souls in the ways of God. He then built twelve monasteries, and placed in each twelve monks under a superior,
retaining with himself those who needed further instruction and discipline. The young were attracted to him in great
numbers; and many of the most distinguished families of
Rome confided the education of their sons to him. Amongst
these were Maurus and Placidus, sons of two of the leading
senators, who became great saints.

The principal establishment of St. Benedict was at Monte
Cassino, in the kingdom of Naples. When the holy abbot
went there for the first time, there still remained on the mountain an ancient temple of Apollo, who was worshipped by
some of the ignorant peasants. When Benedict arrived, he
broke to pieces both idol and altar, and succeeded in converting these neglected people. God then bestowed on him the
gifts of prophecy and of miracles. Totila, king of the Goths,
was so struck by the accounts he received of this extraordinary abbot, that he expressed a wish to see him. He came to
Monte Cassino; and, in order to ascertain whether the saint
could discover things that were concealed, he sent him word
that he was about to pay him a visit, but despatched in his
stead one of his officers clothed in royal apparel, and accompanied by a numerous retinue. Benedict, who had never
seen Totila, said quietly to the officer, "My son, lay aside
the robes you wear; they do not belong to you." The officer
returned, and told what had happened. Then the prince
went himself, cast himself at the saint's feet, and did not
move until Benedict bade him rise. The saint gave him
much useful advice, and predicted to him the leading events
of his life. Totila commended himself to the saint's prayers,
and was observed to be more humane in his conduct than he
had previously been. A short time afterwards he took Naples, and treated the prisoners with a kindness unusual in a
barbarian conqueror. St. Benedict sent several of his disciples to found monasteries of their order in France. He
foretold the hour of his death some time before his last illness;
he even caused his grave to be prepared. This done, he fell
ill of a fever; and when the hour of his death drew near, he
caused himself to be carried into the church, received communion, and calmly expired in his 63d year (A.D. 530).

The rule which St. Benedict made for his order was regarded by St. Gregory as a masterpiece of divine wisdom. It indicates a man perfectly skilled in all that pertains to salvation, and inspired by God to lead others on to the most sublime perfection. It was found by practice to be so wise, so full of discretion, that it became the universal rule. The celebrated Cosmo de' Medici, and other skilful legislators, frequently studied the rule of St. Benedict as a treasury of maxims for those called to govern others. This great order conferred blessings beyond price on the Church and on civil society. Besides the glorious examples of sanctity it afforded, it furnished the chroniclers and historians of the middle ages, the patrons and students of literature and the arts. The labours and the learning of the sons of St. Benedict have passed into a proverb throughout Europe.

§ 2. The Eastern Church, from A.D. 480-630.

While the Roman empire in the West was breaking up beneath the blows of barbarian invasion, it continued to exist in the East, with Constantinople as its capital. Leo I., successor of Marcian who displayed such zeal for the Catholic faith at the council of Chalcedon, issued several laws favourable to the interests of the Church: he confirmed the privileges enjoyed by hospitals, monasteries, and ecclesiastics; and he forbade all judicial business and public spectacles on Sundays and festivals. Zeno, his successor, did little but embroil religious questions. Justin I. not only promoted the temporal welfare of his subjects, but protected the Catholic faith from the ever-renewed assaults of the Eutychians. This sect had ventured to raise its head in Egypt, and had committed many acts of violence. Its partisans were too numerous, and too well supported by those in authority, to be successfully put down. Their great aim was to discredit the authority of the council of Chalcedon, which had condemned them. Justinian, the son of Justin, was raised to the throne in 527; and during his reign the heretics pursued their ends with great adroitness. A controversy arose, which long agitated the Church, and which is known in history as that of the *Three Chapters*, from the three subjects or heads which formed the matter of the dispute. In the times of Nestorius, there had appeared certain treatises favourable to that heresiarch: the dissertations of Theodoret, bishop of Cyrus, against St. Cyril; the

letter of Ibas, bishop of Edessa; and the writings of Theodore, bishop of Mopsuesta. All these works were indeed heretical; but the authors (at least the first two) seemed to
have tacitly retracted them by making an orthodox profession of faith at Chalcedon. The fathers of the council, not
being assembled to examine the Three Chapters, passed them
over in silence, and demanded only that their authors should
anathematise Nestorius. Theodoret and Ibas complied; Theodore had gone to his account; the council therefore recognised
the prelates as Catholics, and pronounced no judgment on
their writings. The Eutychians now made this silence a
ground of accusation against the council; and by their repeated entreaties, induced the Emperor Justinian to condemn
the Three Chapters. Although the Catholics knew that the
writings contained errors, they feared that their condemnation would injure the authority of the council of Chalcedon,
and give a seeming triumph to the Eutychians. The dispute
was carried on with great warmth. Justinian called the Pope
to Constantinople, who, in the hope of restoring peace to the
Church, declared the writings heterodox, and condemned them;
reserving, however, the authority of the council, and prohibiting further discussion of the question. This judgment satisfied
neither party, and violent commotions arose. Whereupon Vigilius withdrew his declaration, and agreed to convoke a council at Constantinople for the termination of the controversy.
None of the western bishops, however, obeyed the summons;
and Justinian then urged the Pope to condemn the Three
Chapters in conjunction with the eastern bishops alone. This
Vigilius refused; and the emperor took upon himself to issue an
edict of condemnation in direct contravention of the Papal prohibition, and of the compact he had entered into with Vigilius.
Against this edict the Pontiff openly protested, and excommunicated the bishops who had signed it. Justinian would have
had recourse to violence, but was intimidated by the resistance
offered by the people, who assembled in defence of the holy
father; and Vigilius escaped from the city. Then was beheld a signal proof of the respect inspired by the dignity and
authority of the vicar of Christ, even when exiled and oppressed. The bishops returned to their allegiance, and begged
pardon for the past. The Pope again took up his abode at
Constantinople, and consented that a council should be summoned, to consist of an equal number of Greek and Latin

prelates. Still the western bishops did not arrive; for they distrusted Justinian's disposition towards them; and the council met without them on the 4th of May 553. The Pope, fearing a schism between east and west, refused to attend an assembly so composed. Trusting, however, to render the continuance of the council unnecessary, and to heal the widening breach, he addressed to the emperor a constitution in which he condemned the writings of Theodore, but passed no judgment on him personally. At the same time he forbade further discussion on the writings of Theodoret and Ibas, as of men absolved by the council of Chalcedon. This constitution was never delivered in by the emperor to the council, which had already begun its sessions. The bishops declared solemnly their cordial acceptance of the four general councils; thus classing Chalcedon with the others, and upholding its authority. They then examined and condemned the Three Chapters, and at the same time anathematised Theodore of Mopsuesta by name. The Pope still refused to recognise their acts, for the causes already assigned. Finding, however, that the schism he dreaded did not follow, and that the minds of men were growing calmer; seeing also the ill use which the Nestorians were making of the writings in question, he proceeded within six months, after due examination, to confirm the decrees of the council, which thus, by virtue of the papal confirmation, came to be regarded as the fifth general council of the Church.

Throughout this controversy, it is to be observed, no doctrine of the faith was at issue. In this both parties were agreed; Pope and bishops, east and west alike. The question was wholly whether, in the then state of the Church, it was prudent to condemn writings which the council of Chalcedon had not condemned, and to anathematise a man whom that council had not anathematised. The question thus being one of prudence, not of faith, the Pope changed his measures as circumstances altered, deeming one mode of action advisable at one time, another at another.* Here also we may note the sovereign power claimed and exercised by the Church of examining suspected writings, condemning those which are erroneous, and requiring the faithful to submit to her judgment. This authority, indeed, is essentially necessary

* The learned reader may consult with profit Palma's *Prælectiones Historiæ Ecclesiasticæ*, vol. i. pp. 372-394.

to her as the guardian of the truth; she is charged with the mission of teaching all nations; and one of the duties of this office is that of denouncing and prohibiting all writings contrary to faith or morals.

Heraclius succeeded to the empire of the East in 610. During his reign the Persians vigorously assailed the empire, and extended their ravages as far as Antioch. A Roman army, which they fell in with on their march, was cut in pieces; and the Persians, under Chosroes, penetrated into Palestine. The banks of the Jordan were strewn with ruins; the inhabitants fled in all directions; the monks were put to death, after having been subjected to abominable outrages. The invading army then marched upon Jerusalem, and the garrison fled in consternation at their approach. The city was given up to pillage, and a great number of priests and religious of both sexes were massacred. The remaining inhabitants were put in irons, to be carried away beyond the Tigris. The Jews were spared, because of the antipathy they displayed towards the Christians; and it is said that on this occasion they bought more than 80,000 captives, and put them to death. The bishop was led into captivity; the Holy Sepulchre, and the other churches of Jerusalem, were pillaged and set on fire; the sacred vessels, and all the wealth accumulated by the devotion of the faithful, were carried off; and the true Cross was borne away in malicious triumph. The Persians took it away in the shrine which enclosed it, and which was secured by the bishop's seal. Some of the instruments of the Passion were rescued by an officer of the emperor, and carried to Constantinople, where they were exposed for four days to the veneration of the Christians. The holy Cross was kept at Tauris in Armenia; and the ruins are still shown of the castle which contained a deposit so precious in the eyes of the Christian, but an object of contempt to the heathen, in comparison with the jewels and gold which fell into their hands.

On the retreat of the barbarians, a feeble remnant of the people returned to Jerusalem. Modestus administered the see in the absence of the captive bishop, and laboured to restore the ruins of the holy places. He was aided in this pious work by large contributions from John, patriarch of Alexandria, surnamed the Almoner. Many of the fugitive inhabitants of Palestine had found refuge in Alexandria, and had been received by the holy bishop with paternal care.

They were lodged in the hospitals, where their wounds were dressed, their sorrows soothed, and their wants supplied, by the good patriarch. His inexhaustible charity sufficed for every thing. He sent money, provisions, and clothes to Jerusalem; and mitigated in every way the sufferings of the hapless population of the Holy City.

The Emperor Heraclius deemed it advisable to sue for peace; and the insolent Chosroes demanded as a preliminary, that he should abjure Christianity and worship the sun. This indignity determined Heraclius to contend even to death for his empire and his religion. In an address to his soldiers, he drew a touching picture of the miseries inflicted on the empire by the Persians,—the fields laid waste, the cities plundered, the altars desecrated, the churches razed to the ground. "You see," he added, "the kind of foe with whom you have to do. They make war on God Himself; they have burned His altars and defiled His sanctuaries. But be of good courage; God will fight for us: faith is stronger than all earthly fears, or death itself." The blessing of God attended the Christian arms; and, encouraged by the presence of their emperor, his troops were victorious in four successive campaigns. He carried the war into the enemy's country, and compelled the proud Chosroes, who had vowed destruction to the Roman empire, to fight in defence of his own. In one decisive battle Heraclius was wounded, and narrowly escaped with his life; but the Persians lost more than half their army, and a great number of officers, while only fifty Romans were missing. The Persian monarch, compelled to fly from town to town, still obstinately refused to listen to terms of peace. Seized at length with what seemed a mortal illness, he named as his successor a younger and favourite son. The elder son rebelled against his father, threw him into prison, and left him to die of hunger. The new king of Persia sent overtures of peace to Heraclius; he restored all the captive Christians with their bishop; and, above all, the holy Cross, which had lain disregarded for nearly fourteen years. The Persians had not even broken the seal, which was authenticated by the bishop; and the precious relic was received with joyful gratitude. The emperor's return to Constantinople had all the appearance of a triumph. He rode in a chariot drawn by four elephants, and preceded by the true Cross, the noblest trophy of his victory. Early in the spring, Heraclius went to

Jerusalem to return thanks for his successes, and to restore
the holy Cross to its place in the Church of the Resurrection.
In humble imitation of our Divine Lord, the emperor bore the
cross on his shoulders all along the way of sorrows to the top
of Mount Calvary. It was a solemn feast for the church of
Jerusalem; and its memory is still preserved in the festival of
the Exaltation of the Holy Cross, September 14th.

CHAPTER IV.

FROM MAHOMET TO CHARLEMAGNE, A.D. 622-814.

§ 1. History of Mahomet and his doctrine.

GOD had renewed the face of the West by means of the barbarian invasions. A new life was infused into the exhausted
empire; and although history records many disorders and
crimes, such as may be expected from wild barbarians imperfectly subject to the Gospel, it abounds likewise in traits of
magnanimity and generosity. Far otherwise was it with the
decrepit East, sunk in the lowest sensuality, and incapable of
renovation; the centre and home of all heresies, the arena for
all kinds of wretched disputations. God had prepared for it
one of those startling scourges whereby He instructs and warns
the nations. After having let loose upon the West the hordes
of Northern Asia, Huns, and Tartars, and Goths, He called
from the south the predestined agents of His vengeance upon
the East—the Arabians, under the guidance of Mahomet,
their pretended prophet. And before entering upon this striking history, let us pause to note and to adore the wisdom
and the goodness of the counsel of God in kindling the light
of faith in new countries, ere it sinks into extinction in the
old; so that the Church remains ever visible, ever Catholic,
gaining in one direction far more than it loses in another.
Eastern Christendom was about to be laid waste; many ancient and venerable churches were to cease to have any but an
historical existence; but the barbarian invasions of the West
were so overruled as to lead to the conversion of the northern
nations, and by the foundation of new Christian kingdoms to
make magnificent compensation to the Church for the losses
she had sustained.

Mahomet was born at Mecca in Arabia, about the year 570. His parents died while he was still young; and he was educated for commerce by his uncle. He eventually married a rich widow, whose affairs he had managed. When he was forty years of age, he declared himself inspired by God to reveal His will to men; and he drew up a new religion, compounded of Judaism and Christianity, with an admixture of some notions peculiar to pagan Arabia. Thus he taught that there was One only God; but he denied the adorable mystery of the Trinity. He rejected the Incarnation and its consequences; he admitted circumcision, and enforced abstinence from wine, from blood, and from swine's flesh; while he allowed the true believer as many wives as he pleased to have; and, to encourage him by his own example, took as many as ten at once.

His admonitions to his fellow-townspeople to abandon their idolatry were at first received with contempt. At length the heads of the tribe became alarmed, and passed a sentence of banishment on all who should embrace his doctrines. Mahomet's life was threatened, and he fled with some of his followers to Medina. This is the *Hegira*, or flight from Mecca, which is the foundation of the Arabian chronology, and the point from which the Mahometans date their • religion. It took place A.D. 622. Hitherto Mahomet had relied on argument and persuasion to make proselytes; he now declared that he was commissioned to propagate his religion by the sword; promising his followers unlimited wealth and pleasure in this world, and a paradise of unpalling sensual delights in the world to come. A doctrine so captivating attracted to his standard numbers of robbers and dissolute persons, and runaway slaves; and he soon formed a compact body, of which he constituted himself at once the general, the legislator, and the prophet. He deigned at first to pillage the caravans which traversed Arabia, and thus accumulated much wealth. When he deemed his army strong enough, he marched against his unbelieving countrymen, and, after various successes, not unaccompanied with defeat, at length surprised and captured Mecca. He smote down with his own hand the 360 idols of popular worship; and thus purified from idolatry the spot on which tradition asserts that Abraham had offered sacrifice.

This capture made him master of Arabia. Its various

tribes submitted without a blow. Islamism, as his religion was called, spread rapidly. True to his principles, Mahomet loosed his adherents from all obligations of treaties made with pagans or with Christians, and thus gave them the whole world as their spoil. The prospect was too goodly to be resisted; and Mahomet soon found himself in a position to send an army against Syria. The troops had scarcely left Medina, when he was seized with a mortal illness, the result, it was supposed, of poison administered some time before by a Jewish woman. But ere he expired, he uttered his last commands: "Carry on the holy war in the name of God; and if any refuse to believe, slay them on the spot." He was buried at Medina, where a magnificent mosque contains his tomb.

As Mahomet could neither read nor write, he dictated his pretended revelations to a secretary. These were collected and put in order by his successor, and were entitled the *Koran*, or "the book." He was subject all his life to epileptic fits; and he caused them to be regarded as ecstasies occasioned by the visits of the archangel Gabriel, who came to disclose to him the everlasting truth. It is not our purpose to write the history of his religion. It is enough to say, that his energetic successors were true to the traditions of their chief, made numerous conquests, and founded an extensive empire; and whereas the Apostles conquered the world by imposing a restraint on human passions, and allowing themselves to be put to death, Mahomet succeeded by giving full scope to every passion, and slaying those who refused their submission. On the one side is the triumph of nature, on the other the victory of grace.

§ 2. The Eastern Church, from A.D. 630-814.

The joy felt by the Church at the recovery of the true Cross was soon troubled by a violent storm. The subtle Greeks devised another heresy, or rather revived that of Eutyches, with some slight modifications. They taught that in our Divine Lord there was but one will and one operation; hence their name of *Monothelites*, or asserters of one will. On the other hand, as the Catholic Church recognises in her Lord two distinct though inseparable natures, she recognises also two distinct wills,—the divine will and the human will, which can never conflict one with the other, yet can never be confounded. The error of the Monothelites was eagerly and obstinately maintained by Sergius, patriarch of Constantinople, and derived great weight from his support and influence. He insinuated himself craftily into the good graces of the Emperor Heraclius, who supported him by the celebrated edict called the *Ecthesis,* or exposition. St. Sophronius, patriarch of Jerusalem, perceived the magnitude of the evil, and published a treatise, in which, after establishing solidly the distinction of the two natures in our Lord's person, he lays down the constant doctrine of the Church in regard to the two wills and their operations. As Sergius dreaded the vigilance and clear-sightedness of the Pope Honorius, he wrote him a letter, with the view of extracting from him some reply which would seem to favour his heresy. The letter was one of artful dissimulation. Suppressing the part he had really acted, he pretended to consult the Pope in all simplicity and humility on a matter of difficulty which might be the occasion of scandal; employing terms calculated to mislead the Pontiff as to the true question at issue. The reply of Honorius was in accordance with the interpretation he put upon the letter of the wily heretic; who, however, never ventured to quote it in support of his pernicious opinions. But after the death, both of Honorius and of Sergius, an attempt was made to use it to the prejudice of the Pontiff's memory, as though he had connived at or favoured the Monothelite heresy. If Honorius failed in any way, it was in too readily crediting the good faith of the artful Sergius, and not making strict inquiry before committing himself to a reply. As for his orthodoxy on the point in question, it was abundantly vindicated by Pope John IV., and by St. Maximus, the holy abbot of Constantinople, who bears special testimony to his zeal against Monothelitism. Severinus, who succeeded Pope Honorius, condemned both the heresy and the imperial edict which favoured it; and this judgment was confirmed by Pope St. Martin, whose zeal and energy cost him both his liberty and his life. The Emperor Constans, successor to Heraclius, had issued a second edict in favour of the Monothelites, and he seized on the person of the Pope. The holy father was put in chains, led off to Constantinople, and treated with contempt and barbarity. He was then sent into exile, and died within two years of the hardships he suffered in his captivity; yet he never breathed a murmur, or remitted his pastoral exertions. St. Maximus imitated the zeal of the Pope, and was persecuted in like manner; he was beaten most cruelly with thongs, his tongue was cut out at its root, and he consummated a tedious martyrdom in exile.

The Emperor Constantine Pogonatus resolved to attempt the pacification of the Church by means of a general council; and to this end, wrote to Pope Agatho to request his concurrence. The Pope consented, and named three legates to preside in his name. The new heresy had made no impression on the practical mind of the Western Church, and all the bishops, without one exception, were opposed to it. The emperor received the papal legates with every mark of distinction, and the council was held in a room of the palace. The book of the Gospels was enthroned according to custom; and the emperor attended the sessions of the council. It was opened by the papal legates, who laid before the assembled bishops the point at issue. " For more than forty years," they said, " Sergius and others have taught that there is in our Lord Jesus Christ only one will and one operation. The Holy See has rejected this error, and exhorted its advocates to renounce it, but in vain. Let us therefore examine the question anew." The canons of preceding councils, and the writings of the Fathers, were examined with care. It was found that the new teaching was opposed both to Scripture and to tradition, and the Monothelites were convicted of having mutilated and falsified their quotations from the Fathers. The letter written by St. Sophronius against the heresy was examined, and declared to be in perfect conformity with the true faith, with the teaching both of Apostles and Fathers. After this careful examination, the council proceeded to draw up its confession of faith. Having recited their adhesion to the canons of preceding councils, the bishops say : " We decide that there are in Jesus Christ two wills, and two operations, naturally distinct; and we prohibit the contrary teaching. We detest and reject the impious doctrines of the heretics, who admit but one will and one operation, because we find their teaching opposed to that of the Apostles, to the decrees of councils, and to the teaching of all the Fathers." The council then pronounced an anathema against the authors of the heresy; and its acts* were subscribed by the Papal

* No allusion has here been made to the supposed condemnation of Pope

legates, and by 160 bishops. The blow was fatal to the
heresy; it was thrust forth from the Church, and all agitation
subsided. This council of Constantinople was held in 680,
and is regarded as the sixth œcumenical, or general, council.
The successors of Constantine Pogonatus were brutal
and stupid princes, whose chief occupation was bloodshed.
In seventy years eight emperors died a violent death. Then
Leo III., surnamed the Isaurian, from the place of his birth,
a warlike prince, was raised to the throne. Other emperors had patronised heresy; but Leo displayed to the astonished world the spectacle of an emperor becoming the founder
and head of a sect. He had been born and nurtured in the
camp, and his ignorance was profound; yet he indulged the
childish fancy of becoming a reformer of religion. He had
conceived a prejudice against the use and veneration of images,
and pronounced the Church's custom idolatrous. He resolved
to destroy them altogether; and he commenced his undertaking by issuing an edict commanding the images of our
Lord, of the Blessed Virgin, and of the saints, to be removed
from the churches. This attempt, so opposed to the principles and practice of the universal Church, excited the indignation of the Christian world; and the inhabitants of Constantinople openly expressed their discontent. Germanus, their
patriarch, boldly opposed the imperial innovation. He tried
at first to enlighten the obstinate Leo in private conferences;
he pointed out to him that the *cultus* paid to the sacred
images was paid to those whom they represented, just as people
honour the portrait or the statue of the emperor; that this
relative *cultus* had ever been rendered to the images of our
Lord and of His blessed Mother from the earliest ages; and
that it was an act of impious audacity to assail a tradition so
venerable and so universal. But the emperor had not light
enough to perceive his own darkness, and stubbornly persisted
in his error. The patriarch referred the question to Pope St.
Gregory II., who thanked him for his zeal in combating the
rising heresy. The Pope then wrote to the emperor, exhorting him to revoke his edict, and reminding him that he was
not competent to decide on such a question, or to innovate in

Honorius by this council; recent research having satisfactorily established
the fact, that some of its acts were falsified by those who had an interest in
so doing. *Annales de Philosophie Chrétienne,* vol. viii. série iv. pp. 54-60,
415-438.

any way upon the faith or discipline of the Church. The emperor replied as men are wont to reply who can wield force more readily than argument. He burnt all the sacred images in one of the public places of the city, and whitewashed the walls which were covered with paintings. He ordered the large crucifix, which had been put up by Constantine at the entrance of the palace, to be hewn down. Some women who were on the spot implored the officer to desist from his impious task, but their prayers were disregarded; he mounted a ladder and began to strike with a hatchet the Divine countenance of our Lord. The women, beside themselves with grief and indignation, drew away the foot of the ladder, and the officer fell down and was killed on the spot. The women were condemned to death, with ten other persons suspected of having encouraged them. The patriarch was driven from his see, and died in exile, in his ninetieth year. These events took place in 737.

Constantine Copronymus, the son and successor of Leo, followed in his father's steps, and went beyond his example in reckless impiety. Educated without religion, his violent character led him to persecute with savage fury those who honoured the sacred images. Death or mutilation was their portion. Their eyes were torn out; their noses were cut off; they were lacerated with scourges, and then cast into the Bosphorus. The emperor's rage expended itself with special violence upon the monks. It would be difficult to recite the various torments to which these holy men were subjected; their beards were steeped in pitch, and then set on fire; the sacred images were broken on their heads. Constantine took a wild delight in these atrocities. Not content with the report of the cruelties exercised by his order, he was eager to share in the sanguinary pastime. He caused a platform to be erected at one of the gates of the city; and there, surrounded with all the pomp and retinue of empire, he feasted his eyes with the agonies of the tortured Catholics. There lived near Nicomedia a holy abbot, named Stephen, whose virtues were held in great esteem by the people. The emperor was anxious to win the holy man to his party, and sent for him to Constantinople. At first he tried to argue with him; for the emperor, like most heretics, piqued himself on his dialectical skill. He began thus: "O stupid man, why can I not trample on a crucifix without offending Jesus Christ?"

Stephen held up a coin which bore the emperor's effigy : " I may, then, stamp upon this image without insulting you." He then threw the coin on the ground, and set his foot upon it; and as the courtiers rushed forward to chastise his in- solence, he said with a sigh, " Well, then, it is a crime to profane the image of an earthly king; and it is no crime at all to throw into the fire the image of the King of kings!" The emperor, embarrassed for a reply, ordered Stephen to be put to death. Nineteen officers were accused of sympathising with the holy martyr in his torments, and expressing their admiration of his fortitude and patience; they were ordered to be similarly tortured, and the two principal of them to be beheaded. The persecution extended into the provinces; servile governors courted the favour of the emperor, by the wanton barbarity with which they hunted down the stedfast Catholics. They made war, not only upon the images of the saints, but upon their relics; they tore them from the sepul- chres and sanctuaries; they threw them into the rivers and into common sewers; they burnt them together with bones of animals, so that their ashes might be hopelessly profaned : no outrage was deemed too gross to be inflicted on those sa- cred remains in which the Holy Spirit had dwelt, and through which such wonders had been wrought.

After the death of Constantine Copronymus, and his son Leo IV., the sovereign power devolved on Irene, as regent during the minority of her son. Then the distracted Church enjoyed an interval of rest and a gleam of hope. The em- press detested the impiety of the *Iconoclasts*, or breakers of the sacred images, and was firmly attached to the Catholic faith. In her anxiety to heal the wounds inflicted on religion during the late reigns, she consulted the Patriarch of Con- stantinople, Tarasius, who advised her to write to Pope Adrian, and request him to convoke a general council. The Pope ap- proved her pious wish, convoked the council, and sent two legates to preside over its deliberations. It was at first in- tended to hold the council in the imperial city ; but, as a col- lision with the Iconoclasts was dreaded, it was transferred to Nicæa, which was celebrated throughout Christendom as the city in which the first general council was held. Three hun- dred and seventy-seven bishops were assembled from all parts of the empire ; two imperial commissioners maintained order in the city, and the bishops were enabled to deliberate in peace

I

and safety. Eight sessions were held. In the first was read the letter of the Pope, in which he stated and defended the tradition of the Church in regard to the veneration due to sacred images, and explained the nature of that veneration, or *cultus;* letters were read from many eastern bishops, who were unable to attend the council because they were under the sway of the Mahometans. Their doctrine coincided with that enounced by the holy father. They then drew forth the testimony of Scripture and of the Fathers; the objections of the Iconoclasts were met; their heresy was refuted; and judgment was delivered in these words: "We decree that sacred images shall not only be set up in our churches, and graven upon the vessels of the sanctuary and on all ecclesiastical ornaments, but in private houses and by the wayside; for the sight of the images of our Lord Jesus Christ, His holy Mother, the Apostles and Saints, disposes our hearts to remember, and to honour those whom they represent. We are bound to render to them honour and reverence, but not the worship due to God alone. We may burn tapers and incense before them, as is usual before the Cross and the holy Gospels, because the honour paid to the image is referred to its original. And this is the doctrine of the Fathers and of the Catholic Church." The Iconoclasts were smitten with anathema; and the decrees of the council were signed by all the bishops present, with the legates of the Pope at their head. Thus the sanguinary heresy was silenced for a time, to revive again with all its odious characteristics amongst the so-called reformers of the sixteenth century.

The empress Irene, after a reign which ill accorded with this its commencement, was deposed by the usurper Nicephorus, and died in poverty and neglect (A.D. 802). Nicephorus died in 811, in an expedition against the Bulgarians, after having persecuted the Catholics with unrelenting cruelty.

§ 3. The Western Church, from A.D. 680-814.

The light of faith, like the sun, is never extinguished in one place but to shed its beams on another. In proportion as it faded away in the East before the conquering Mahometans, it waxed broader and brighter in the north, through the apostolic labours of numerous missionaries. Foremost of these was St. Boniface, archbishop of Mentz, and the apostle of Germany; we may mention with complacency that he was an Englishman.* From his childhood he displayed indications of the high destiny reserved for him. Some missionaries, who were one day entertained by his father, spoke to him of God and of heavenly things; the impression never faded away; he felt a strong desire to forsake all, and to devote himself to God, as they were doing. He entered a monastery, and was there formed and trained for the toils ot missionary life. By day and by night his soul groaned over those who were unblessed with the light of faith, and he pined for the day when he might be permitted to devote his life to their instruction and salvation. At length he went to Rome, and offered himself to Pope Gregory II., who recognised his vocation as from God, and sent him with ample powers to preach to the Germans. It was a slow and difficult task to bend to the gentle yoke of Christ these haughty and warlike barbarians; but in due time came an abundant harvest to cheer the weary husbandman. He began with Bavaria and Thuringia, where he baptised great numbers of pagans. The idol-temples were every where thrown down, and churches were raised on their sites. Great were the sufferings of the holy missionary; for the scenes of his toil were often swept by predatory bands of Saxons, and his flock was reduced to abject poverty and want. He next visited Friesland, where he remained three years, and gained many souls to Jesus Christ. Thence he went into Hesse and Saxony, where he reaped a plentiful harvest of souls. At this period of his labours the Pope sent for him, and conferred on him episcopal consecration. The saintly bishop returned into Hesse, where he built many churches and monasteries. Thence he passed again into Thuringia, where he reformed several abuses which had been introduced by certain among the bishops and priests whose disorderly lives were a scandal to their flocks. Finally, the Pope appointed him his legate in Germany, with power to do whatever he might deem necessary for the well-being of the rising church.

The fame of St. Boniface was spread throughout Europe, and his prodigious labours attracted many servants of God to

---

* This great man was born at Crediton, in Devonshire, in the year 680. His name was Winfrid. On his consecration the Pope gave him the name of Boniface, by which he is known in history. Most of his fellow-labourers were natives of England.

associate themselves with him. The holy archbishop, feeling the infirmities of age, chose a successor, resigned to him the see of Mentz, and devoted his remaining days to farther inroads on the waste of paganism. He could not rest while he knew that there were souls to whom Jesus was unknown; and he panted to pour out his life's blood for the faith. He had long felt a presentiment that this would be his lot, and he knew that it could not now be far distant. Having set all the affairs of his church in order, he departed with some zealous companions to preach the gospel to a nation of idolaters at the extremity of Friesland. He converted many pagans and baptised them. He then fixed a day for their confirmation; and as they were too numerous to be contained within any building, he bade them assemble in a neighbouring field. He ordered tents to be pitched, and came with his retinue on the appointed day. While he was engaged in prayer waiting for the arrival of the Christians, a troop of pagans appeared, armed with swords and spears. They rushed on the tents, and were met with determined resistance on the part of the attendants. When St. Boniface heard the tumult, he summoned his clergy, and taking in his hands the Book of the Gospels, and certain relics which he always carried with him, he issued from his tent, and said to his followers: "My children, cease your resistance; Scripture forbids us to resist evil; the long-expected day is come at length; let us put our hope in God; He will save our souls." He then exhorted them to suffer with fortitude a momentary pang, which would admit them to the everlasting kingdom. His example was even more efficacious than his exhortations. Scarcely had he ceased speaking, when the barbarians fell upon him, and slew him with all his attendants, to the number of fifty-two. The body of the holy martyr was transported to the abbey of Fulda, which he had founded; and God honoured his servant by working many miracles at his tomb. It may help us to form some notion of the extent of the labours of St. Boniface to know, that in Bavaria alone he baptised more than 100,000 pagans.

Without entering into details which pertain rather to secular history, we may remark here that in 750 Childeric III., the last descendant of Clovis, was deposed and succeeded by Pepin, the founder of the Carlovingian race of French kings. Pope Stephen appealed to him for protection against the fe-

rocius Lombards.   Pepin hastened to his defence, and generously restored to the Pope the territories which the Lombards
had seized, and which had previously put themselves under
the Pontiff's protection.   This is generally regarded as the
time when the temporal power of the Popes became consoli-
dated.   Pepin was succeeded (A.D. 768) by his son Charles,
to whom has been universally awarded the distinguished
name of Charlemagne; a prince who seems to have been
especially raised up for the interests of the kingdom of God,
and the defence of the Apostolic See.   Very early in his reign
he published, at the request of the bishops, a code of laws
for the maintenance of ecclesiastical discipline.   He likewise
protected the Holy See from the Lombards, and crushed their
dominion in Italy.   He drove back the Saxons, who had long
ravaged the French territory ; and his conquest was followed
by their conversion.   They resisted the faith for a long time ;
but yielded at length to the efforts of the missionaries sent
to them by Charlemagne.   Witikind, one of their principal
chieftains, was the most dreaded of their leaders, and the
most hostile to Christianity.   In a conference at Attigny,
where the king was holding his court, the rebel-chief was
subdued by the majesty and goodness of Charlemagne, and
submitted to his authority.   He also examined the new religion; he began to love it ; and, by the grace of God, was
led to embrace it, and to request to be baptised.   Charlemagne was his sponsor at the font; and Witikind, who was
a brave and upright soldier, became one of the most loyal
of subjects, and a most zealous propagator of the faith he had
hated with so deadly a hatred.   The pious monarch ordered
a day of thanksgiving for the conversion of the Saxons and
their chief.

   When Charlemagne ascended the throne, he found France
sunk in gross ignorance.   The fury of successive invasions had
swept away all taste for letters, and destroyed the opportuni-
ties and means of study.   The king knew the value of science
and art, and laboured assiduously to provide a remedy for
the ignorance that prevailed.   He opened schools ; procured
the ablest instructors; drew to his court the most learned
and celebrated scholars of Europe, and attached them to himself by his munificence.   Of these, the most distinguished
was an Englishman named Alcuin, whom he loaded with
wealth and honours.   Alcuin was looked upon as the most

learned and able man of his day; he had long successfully taught both profane and sacred science in England,
when he yielded to the urgent solicitations of Charlemagne.
Acting on his suggestions, the king established schools in
every town and in every monastery of the realm. He took
especial care to secure the services of intelligent men as copy-
ists : for in those days books were multiplied by hand with
incredible toil. He collected manuscripts of the sacred volume, and had them revised, corrected, and multiplied. He
procured the revision of the Liturgy, that every thing in
it might befit the majesty of Him to whom the Church's
worship is offered. He sent to Rome for persons competent
to teach the plain chant in its purity; and he caused all the
ritual-books of his kingdom to be corrected after their model.
And as example is more effective than bare precept, and
emulation one of the strongest of stimulants, he formed an
academy in his own palace for the instruction of the young
princes and the children of his nobles. Nor did the sovereign
deem it unworthy of his rank to take his seat among the disciples of Alcuin. The effect of this policy was incalculable.
There arose a universal desire for education throughout
France. Soon a body of learned students arose, who formed
amongst themselves a sort of literary society, and communicated to each other the results of their labours and inquiries.
This was the origin of the University of Paris.

Charlemagne's sway extended over almost all the pro
vinces which had composed the Western Empire; Germany,
Gaul, and the greater part of Spain and Italy, were subject
to him. The reality of empire was his; he wanted but the
name. And now an act was to be performed which should
inaugurate a new era in the history of the Church and of the
world. On Christmas-day, in the last year of the eighth century, Charlemagne, ignorant of what awaited him, was prostrate before the high altar of St. Peter's at Rome, when Pope
Leo III. approached him and placed upon his head the imperial crown. The act was at once understood and ratified by
the clergy and the assembled people; and the sacred building rang with the oft-repeated acclamation, "Long life and
victory to Charles, the most pious Augustus, crowned by God
the great and pacific emperor of the Romans!" At the same
time the Pope bestowed the sacred anointing upon him, as
well as upon Louis his son, and was the first to acknowledge

and to honour the exalted dignity he had himself conferred. Thus was re-established, in the person of Charlemagne, after three centuries of decay and desolation, that empire of which the Cæsars who ruled at Constantinople, had by their treachery or weakness shown themselves unworthy; or, rather, in him was created and consecrated a power which had never yet existed,—that Holy Roman Empire which, so long as it was true to its origin and vocation, should be the defence of the Apostolic See, and of the rights and liberties of Western Christendom. Such was the light in which Charlemagne regarded the dignity with which he had been invested by the Holy Father; calling himself, "Charles, by the grace of God king and ruler of the realm of the Franks, devout defender and humble auxiliary of the Holy Church of God." The emperor stayed the winter at Rome, where he enriched the churches with costly presents; and returned after Easter to Aix-la-Chapelle.

It was a happy epoch for the Church. The administration of Charlemagne forms a bright interval between the long years of tyranny and rapine that preceded him, and those of anarchy and barbarism that followed his orderly and prosperous reign. In 814 this illustrious emperor was removed from his sorrowing subjects. He was seized with a violent fever, and feeling himself in danger, he received the last sacraments with fervent devotion, and commended his soul to God, in the seventy-second year of his age. Posterity cherishes his memory as one of the mightiest of kings, one of the most zealous defenders of the Church—a hero in the eyes of the world, and almost a saint in the esteem of the Church.

REFLECTIONS.

Heresies and schisms were the second trial and test to which the Church was to be subjected. An apostle has told us that there must be heresies for the probation and perfection of the faithful; and never were the ravages of heresy so fearful as when the assaults of heathenism ceased. It was as though the great enemy summoned all his strength to rend and destroy by division that mystical body which persecution was powerless to crush. Scarcely had the Church drawn breath on the accession of Constantine, when the deadly

heresy of Arius renewed her anguish, and menaced her dissolution. Constantius, in the name of Christ, persecuted Christians,
with a virulence as intense as that of the pagans themselves.
Valens followed, and improved on his wretched example.
Other emperors protected other heresies with equal zeal and
cruelty. Christians were taught, by sad and long experience,
that the Church's trust was not in the arm of flesh, nor in
the smile of princes; and that she must defend with her life,
not only Christianity as a whole, but each separate article of
her creed. There is not one vital doctrine which she has not
seen assailed by those to whom she had communicated the
breath of spiritual life: the Godhead of our Lord Jesus
Christ, His Incarnation, His grace, His sacraments,—all
have been the watchwords of melancholy strife. But the
providence of God was over His suffering Church. He made
her as invincible in the conflict with heresy as in the endurance of pagan violence. Each dogma, as it has been attacked,
has been solemnly defined, and guarded, and confirmed: the
pure gold has issued yet more intensely purified from the
fiery furnace. She has seen, according to her Lord's promise, heresy follow upon heresy; she has seen them rise, and
swell, and threaten, and perish at her breath, in spite of emperors and kings, and the wild wayward will of man. Constantius was as impotent as Nero to crush the Church's life;
Valens could no more shake her faith than Dioclesian. Although the progress and diffusion of heresy have much of
solemn mystery in them, yet never has error prevailed; the
dominant teaching has been that of the Catholic Church;
with her alone has been the authority which men have recognised to be of God; and if here and there a rotten member
has dropped off, she has lost nothing of her universality.

So when heresy has robbed her of her children in one
direction, her missionaries have restored her tenfold in another.
She is like a mighty tree, from which the storm may rend a
feeble or dead branch; the pruning but quickens her vitality
and enriches her fruit. She alone has been apostolic. She
can ascend step by step from the existing Pope to St. Peter,
the prince of the Apostles; whereas each sect mounts up no
farther than its human originator, who separated from the
One Body. Even the heathen were struck with this; the
Church was the parent stem, the great church, the Catholic
church. Never has it borne any other name; never has he-

resy or schism been able to appropriate this glorious title. Every sect has borne on its brow the sentence of its condemnation; it was a novelty, a revolt. Never have they been able to shake off the name of their authors. Arians, Nestorians, Pelagians, have made the attempt; but the world spoke naturally and simply, and called them by their true names. And if you ask in any town of England now, Where is the Catholic church? you will not be pointed to the places of meeting of any of the sects, but to the church whose pastor receives his mission from St. Peter's see. This has been a constant and unfailing note. St. Augustine employed it against the Donatists 1400 years ago; it has lost none of its cogency now. The ineffaceable stamp of novelty, of separation, of a human origin, brands every schismatical body. So, too, the branches severed from the tree have withered fruitlessly away. They spread no branches; they strike no root. The work of man comes to naught, however great the earthly power which upholds it; the work of God abides firm and immutable. The Church has been as victorious over heresy as over idolatry in the generations that are past. And so it shall be to the end of time. Sooner or later they shall droop and wither, and their place shall know them no more. Her past victories are the pledges of victories yet to come. For the promises which form her precious dowry are for ever and for ever. "Thou shalt seek them, and shalt not find the men that resist thee; they shall be as nothing; and as a thing that is consumed, the men that war against thee."*

CHAPTER V.

FROM THE DEATH OF CHARLEMAGNE TO THE FIRST CRUSADE, A.D. 814-1095.

§ 1. Conversion of the Northern nations, A.D. 829-1002.

THE successor of Charlemagne imitated his zeal for the interests of the Church and the conversion of the heathen. It was under Louis le Débonnaire that the light of the Gospel reached the farthest north of Europe. The Saxons were the

* Isaias xli. 12.

first-fruits of this harvest, and became its most zealous and successful labourers. St. Anschar, a monk of Corbie, preached with great success in Denmark. He bought large numbers of young slaves, whom he trained in the knowledge and fear of God, and then employed to labour under his direction. The king of Sweden next requested Louis to send him some missionaries to preach the Gospel in his dominions. The emperor sent Anschar as the fittest leader of so great an enterprise, and associated with him another monk of Corbie. The missionaries were stopped by pirates and robbed of the presents with which Louis had charged them for the king of Sweden; so that they reached the scene of their labours with nothing but the message and boon of salvation. They were well received by the king, and made many conversions. Among the first was the governor of the city, a man beloved and confided in by the king. The new convert built a church, and lived a life of consistent and fervent piety. As the Christians increased in number, an episcopal see was established at Hamburg, and St. Anschar was appointed to it. He laboured with great diligence and success in this new field; his life was of the simplest and most austere kind; his food consisted of bread and water alone; and he often withdrew to the solitude of a little hermitage he had constructed in the neighbourhood, to be alone with God. His miracles were numerous; and when some one mentioned them in his presence, he said, "Had I any power with God, I would not ask of Him any miracle but this, that He would make me a holy man." When his last illness approached, he expressed great regret that he had not been permitted to lay down his life for the Gospel. "Alas," he exclaimed, "my sins have deprived me of the grace of martyrdom!" The infant Church suffered much from the ravages of the barbarians; but the good seed remained, and continued to yield abundant fruit.

The Eastern empire was often harassed by the incursions of the Sclaves, a barbarous people, who inhabited a part of the modern Poland. In the course of their depredations they acquired some knowledge of the Christian religion, and felt a desire to embrace it. They therefore sent a request to the empress Theodora,* then regent in the name of her son, that she would send a missionary to instruct them. They

---

* Theodora was the wife of the Emperor Theophilus, a violent iconoclast. He died in 842.

promised to requite this favour by abstaining from their
wonted ravages. The selected missionary was named Constantine. On his arrival, he set about acquiring the language
of the people, and translated for them the Gospels and many
other portions of Scripture. His labours were rewarded by
the conversion of the entire tribe. This opened the way to
the Russian territory, and the light of the faith soon spread
throughout it. The emperor Basil concluded with its savage
inhabitants a treaty of peace, conciliated them by numerous
presents, and sent them a bishop consecrated by Ignatius,
patriarch of Constantinople. A striking miracle, wrought by
the new bishop, facilitated his labours. The chieftain had
collected his people to deliberate whether they should abandon their hereditary religion, and, naturally enough, wished
to know what it was proposed to give them in exchange for
it. The bishop was sent for; he showed them the four Gospels, and narrated to them some of the miracles of the Old
and New Testaments. The wild assembly heard them all
with great interest; but the account of the three Hebrew
children in the fiery furnace made the deepest impression on
them. "If you can show us a miracle like that, we will believe that you are telling us the truth." "I dare not tempt
God," replied the bishop; "but if you wish a proof of his
great power, ask what you will, and He will do it." The
Russians demanded that he should throw the sacred volume
into a fire kindled by themselves; if it were not consumed,
they would become Christians. The bishop raised his hands
towards heaven and prayed: "O Jesus, Son of God, glorify
Thy holy name in presence of this people." The book was
thrown into the glowing furnace, and was left there for some
time; the fire was then extinguished, and the book was found
unconsumed and uninjured. The people submitted at once;
and, after being instructed, were admitted to baptism. Thus
from time to time God has repeated, and still repeats in our
own days, those miraculous interpositions which attended the
Church's origin. His arm is not shortened, and when He sends
missionaries to a new race, or would revive the languid faith
of an old one, He shows forth His wonders as in times past.

The Bulgarians* had been defeated by the emperor Theo-

* The Bulgarians were of Tartar origin, and inhabited the country
between the Don and the Danube, north-east of the Black Sea. It has
preserved its name, and is occupied by their descendants.

philus in a pitched battle; and among the captives was found
the sister of the vanquished king. The princess was brought
to Constantinople with the other prisoners of war, and detained there for thirty-eight years. During this interval, she
was instructed in the Christian faith, and baptised. On the
death of the emperor, the Bulgarian king took advantage of
Theodora's regency, and declared war against her. Theodora
replied, that if he set foot on the territory of the empire, she
would march to repel him, and hoped to conquer him; but
that even were he successful, there would be but little glory
in overcoming a woman. The king, surprised at her firmness, requested only that his sister might be restored to him.
On her return, she spoke to him of the Christian religion;
and the providence of God concurred with the solicitations
of the pious princess. A pestilence broke out in Bulgaria;
the distressed king had recourse to the God of his sister,
and the scourge was immediately stayed. The king was now
quite convinced; but he was deterred from avowing himself a
Christian by his fear lest his subjects should revolt. It pleased
God to terrify him into submission. He was decorating a
gallery in his palace, and had commanded the painter to choose
a subject of terror. The artist, who was a Christian, represented on the wall the last judgment, and the torments of the
lost, with every circumstance of awe and terror. The ex-
planation he gave of the painting made the king shudder;
he renounced idolatry, and sent to Theodora to beg her to
send him a priest to baptise him. The empress joyfully acceded to his request; and the bishop whom she sent baptised
the king privately in the night. But in spite of every precaution, the tidings were soon spread abroad; the Bulgarians
broke out into revolt, and attacked the palace; but the king,
confiding in the protection of God, sallied forth at the head
of his household, and scattered the rebel-troop. Having
quelled the rebellion, he pardoned its instigators; and this
clemency led to their conversion. The king then sent to the
Pope, as the head of the Christian Church, requesting an
ecclesiastical staff and regulations for the religious affairs of
Bulgaria. Pope Nicholas I. received the ambassadors with
paternal tenderness, acceded to all that the king requested,
and sent two bishops immediately to set the rising church in
order (A.D. 866).

While the kingdom of Jesus Christ was thus extending

into remote lands, a fresh invasion was impending over Europe, and threatening to cover it with ruin. The tenth century, so memorable for its calamities, beheld the Normans, the Hungarians, and other hordes, traverse Germany, France, England, Italy, and Spain, and bring desolation wherever they came. Flourishing cities were laid in ruins; monasteries were pillaged and burnt; studies were abandoned, sciences and arts almost forgotten. Ignorance produced its fatal consequences, in a corruption of morals and a relaxation of discipline. Scandals abounded; the most sacred laws were set at naught; the evil had infected those who governed the Church; and Rome itself was not free from its taint. The Church groaned beneath a trial heavier far than her heaviest persecutions; but God was pleased to turn her mourning into gladness by the conversion of those whose ravages had been the occasion of these evils; and nothing more clearly manifests the protection of her Divine Head than the fact, that in an age when she seemed so enfeebled and so corrupted, she was enabled to make fresh and important conquests, and bow to her sway the hordes who had laid her waste.

The Normans had ravaged France for seventy years, when it pleased God to arrest this torrent of miseries and sins. There were no outward indications of the impending change; Rollo, the bravest of the Norman chieftains, seemed more furious than ever. Charles the Simple, king of France, deemed it advisable to make a treaty with him, and offered him the province of Normandy, which constituted a large portion of ancient Neustria, together with the hand of his daughter, if he would cease his depredations and become a Christian. Rollo accepted the terms, and the treaty was concluded. The Archbishop of Rouen instructed the prince in the mysteries of the faith, and baptised him in the beginning of the year 912. Though political motives had determined this conversion, the grace of God made it a thorough and sincere one. The new duke was no sooner baptised than he asked the archbishop which were the most venerated churches in his province. The prelate mentioned Nôtre Dame of Rouen, of Bayeux and Evreux, the church of Mont St. Michael, that of St. Peter at Rouen, and Jumièges. "And what saint is most revered in these parts?" asked the duke. "St. Denis, the apostle of France." Accordingly, before dividing his territory amongst his leading captains, he set apart a portion for God, for the Blessed Virgin, and for the saints named by the archbishop. He endowed their churches with lands; he caused all his officers and vassals to be instructed in the faith; and soon the character of the whole people was changed. No arm less strong than that of our Divine Lord could have curbed the ferocity of these Normans; no power but that of grace could have effected such a transformation. Rollo became as remarkable for gentleness and prudence as he had been for ferocity and rashness. He showed that he was not only a formidable warrior, but a wise legislator; and that he was as able to control his impetuous people with wholesome laws, as to coerce his foes by the strength of his arms. He restrained the predatory propensities of his subjects by severe penalties; and so great was the terror inspired by his name, that no one would venture even to pick up any thing he found on the highway. It is related that on one occasion the duke hung up one of his bracelets on an oak-tree, under which he was reposing after the fatigues of the chase. He went away, and forgot it altogether; and it remained hanging on the tree three years. No one had presumed to touch it, so strong was the feeling that nothing could escape his vigilance.

The Hungarians, a ferocious horde from Scythia, had ravaged Germany with horrible cruelties. Churches were burnt, priests slain at the altar, and great numbers of Christians dragged into slavery, without distinction of age, or sex, or condition. But the Gospel put forth its might, and subdued these wild barbarians, and rendered them docile and humane. One of their kings felt a mysterious liking for the Christians. There were none in the neighbourhood; and he invited them by a public proclamation to settle in his dominions, with assurances of his favour and protection. He inquired into their religion, yielded to its power, and was baptised with all his family. He had one son, to whom the Bishop of Prague gave the name of Stephen. The young prince was educated with care, and manifested in his early years a true piety. He became subsequently the apostle of his people, and on his accession employed all his power to effect their conversion. He met at first with great opposition; a rebellion broke out in defence of idolatry; but the king marched forth with the banner of St. Martin, to whom Pannonia, the land of his birth, had a great devotion. The rebels were defeated; and with their possessions the king founded a monastery in honour of St. Martin, to whose intercession he ascribed his victory. When peace was restored, he devoted himself with redoubled zeal to the diffusion of religion; he bestowed abundant alms, and prayed with unusual fervour; he was often found in the church prostrate on the pavement, interceding for his people with groans and tears. He sent in all directions for missionaries, and at length had the consolation of destroying idolatry throughout his states. Hungary was then divided into six bishoprics, of which Strigonium on the Danube was the metropolitan see, and a monk named Sebastian the archbishop. In confirming this arrangement, the Pope testified his gladness and esteem for the king, and his appreciation of his zealous labours, by sending him a crown and a cross of gold, and with these the title of *apostolic* king, which was ever after borne by the kings of Hungary. Stephen and his queen were then crowned with great solemnity. He had an especial devotion to the Mother of God, and placed under her protection his person and his kingdom,—an example afterwards followed by Louis XIII. of France. The fervour and devotion of Stephen and his queen increased with years. On his deathbed, he charged the nobles and bishops of his realm to maintain the Christian religion in its purity. He died in 1038, and his last request was granted: Hungary never abandoned the faith.

§ 2. Troubles in the Church of Constantinople, A.D. 858-1053.

While God was consoling His Church by the progress of religion in the North, He permitted it to be harassed by the scandalous intrusion of Photius into the see of Constantinople. Photius was a man of distinguished birth, learning, and ability; he had been honoured with many important public offices in the court; but his ambition and his intriguing disposition tarnished all his good qualities. He was the favourite of Cæsar Bardas, the uncle of the youthful emperor, Michael III., and prime minister. Bardas had been excommunicated after many useless remonstrances by Ignatius, patriarch of Constantinople, for his scandalous life; and had sworn to ruin the faithful prelate. He abused his influence over his nephew to procure an order for the banishment of Ignatius. He then endeavoured to induce Ignatius to resign his see; and when all his efforts were in vain, he named Photius, a layman, to the patriarchate. A promotion so irregular scandalised the Church. The suffragan bishops at first refused to recognise the usurper; but eventually some were gained over to the cause of Photius, and the others were banished. Photius was eager to have his appointment confirmed by Pope Nicolas; he wrote an able and crafty letter to announce his election: it was opposed to his wish, he said, and in spite of his utmost resistance; he had yielded with tears to overbearing force. He added, that Ignatius had retired of his own accord to a monastery, in order to pass the last days of a holy life in tranquil preparation for death. His letter was accompanied by one from the emperor, confirming these statements. Ignatius, meanwhile, was shut up in a loathsome and unhealthy prison, and treated with studied indignity. He was accused of conspiring against the state; no proof was forthcoming; but he was loaded with chains, and sent off to Mitylene in the island of Lesbos. These events had been carefully concealed from the Pope; but the affair had a suspicious look; and Nicolas declined to decide on the election of Photius without examination. He sent to Constantinople two legates charged to investigate the facts of the case. On their arrival at the imperial city, the legates were put under surveillance, and cut off from every source of information, except the creatures of the court. They were threatened with the extremity of punishment, if they refused to recognise Photius as patriarch; and although they resisted for a long time, they at length yielded to the will of the emperor, subdued by solicitations, promises, and menaces. A synod was held, at which Ignatius was deposed, the papal legates concurring, with every circumstance of ignominy.

The usurper, however, could not rest satisfied until he had obtained from Ignatius an act of resignation. To this end he had him shut up in the tomb of Constantine Copronymus, under the charge of three ruffians, who treated him with the most revolting barbarity. After brutally striking him on the face with their fists, they stripped him naked, and during the severest weather made him lie on the cold pavement, with his arms extended and his face to the ground. They then kept him for a whole week in a standing posture without food and without sleep. As this did not subdue the old man's fortitude, they set him astride on the arched roof of the monument, and, tying heavy stones to his feet, made him pass a

whole night in that position, while they diverted themselves
with his sufferings. In the morning they threw him down
with such violence, that the pavement was bespattered with
his blood. Then, as he lay exhausted and all but lifeless, one
of the wretches, forcing a pen into his hand, made with it
a cross on a blank sheet of paper, which they immediately
carried to their employer. Photius wrote above it an act of
resignation, couched in the most abject terms, which he sent
to the emperor. Ignatius was now, by Michael's orders, set
at liberty, and at last found means to inform the Pope of his
position, and of all that had taken place at Constantinople.

Photius was not yet content, and he obtained an order from
the emperor that Ignatius should be compelled to read his own
condemnation in public; and that he should then have his eyes
pulled out, and his right hand cut off. The holy confessor,
however, was apprised of his enemy's designs, and contrived
to escape, in the disguise of a slave, even through the midst
of the guards who were sent to apprehend him. After wandering about from place to place in constant peril of his life,
he was at length recalled to Constantinople in consequence of
a violent earthquake, which struck, not only the citizens, but
the emperor and even Bardas himself with consternation.
By this time the Pope had been informed of all that had
passed, and he despatched letters to the emperor, to Photius,
and to the bishops, in which he condemned and disavowed the
acts of his legates, and declared that he recognised Ignatius
as the lawful patriarch, and regarded the election of Photius
as null and void. Photius got possession of these letters and
suppressed them; he then substituted forged letters, in which
he made the Pope say that he regretted having suspected and
opposed him, and promised him his constant friendship. The
imposture was too gross. But Photius went still farther in
his daring impiety. He drew up with great skill the acts and
decrees of a council, which he declared to have been held to
examine the conduct of Pope Nicolas. The document was in
perfect order; nothing was wanting to it. There were the
charges brought against the Pontiff; the testimony of witnesses on their oath; there was the able speech of Photius
in behalf of the accused. He would not condemn an absent
Pope; but he yielded at length to the judgment of the
fathers of this imaginary council, and concurred with them
in a sentence of deposition and excommunication. He even

found twenty-one bishops base enough to sign these fictitious acts and decrees; and he forged about a thousand additional signatures. The seals of the supposed subscribers were imitated; and he degraded the emperor by representing him as confirming this judgment by his signature. Photius had the impudence to send this document to Louis le Débonnaire, king of France, with a request that he would aid in the expulsion of the Pope from his see. He addressed to all the bishops of the East a circular letter full of complaints against the Latin Church; he asserted that the doctrine of the Procession of the Holy Ghost from the Father and the Son was a heresy, although this doctrine had been long taught by the Greek fathers, as well as by the Latin, and approved by several councils. At the same time he reproached the Roman Church with corruption in some points of discipline which he had up to that time regarded as free from blame. This was the fatal germ of the deplorable schism which has sundered the churches of the East from the centre of Catholic unity.

Photius did not find the same favour with the Emperor Basil as with Michael, his predecessor. The new emperor declined to patronise the intruder, and summoning a synod of all the bishops who happened to be in Constantinople, he gave effect to their decision, that Photius should be expelled from his usurped see and shut up in a monastery. It was on this occasion that the acts of the supposed council were discovered; the paper was brought before the senate; and the imposture was exploded amidst the ridicule and horror of the people. Immediately afterwards Ignatius, the rightful patriarch, returned to his church, and induced the emperor to convoke a council to repair the late scandals. The emperor applied to the Pope, and requested him to send two legates. The council was held at Constantinople in 869. Pope Adrian, who had succeeded Nicolas, named three legates, and intrusted to them two letters—one for the emperor, the other for the patriarch. Their entry into Constantinople was made with great pomp; and every respect was paid to the pre-eminent dignity of the Holy See. They occupied the first place in the council; next to them came Ignatius, and then the representatives of the other patriarchs in order of dignity. The legates read a document as the basis on which all might unite, and it was accepted unanimously. This document stated the supremacy of the see of Rome, denounced anathemas against all heresies, and condemned Photius by name, together with all his adherents. Pardon was granted to those bishops who had been surprised or intimidated into joining the faction of Photius. The schismatical usurper was cited to appear; but it was found necessary to use force to bring him before the council. He assumed, with consummate effrontery, the attitude of an innocent and unjustly oppressed man. He refused to answer most of the questions put to him; and when at length he spoke, he used the words which our Divine Lord had pronounced before His judge. He was sent away amidst the indignation of the council. The last session was a very numerous one. The emperor and his two sons were present. The decrees of the Popes Nicolas and Adrian in favour of Ignatius were confirmed; and as the usurper persisted in his obduracy, he was excommunicated, together with his faction. The emperor then spoke, and required all who disapproved of any decree of the council to state their complaints and reasons before it separated, as he was resolved to allow no discussion or disobedience afterwards. Lastly, two letters were written: one addressed to the Pope, requesting him to confirm the decrees of the council, and thus stamp them with the Church's divine authority; the other, addressed to the whole body of the faithful, requiring their acceptance of them and submission to them. This was the eighth general council.

Photius was banished; but the daring heresiarch did not cease to disturb the peace of the Church. His partisans were numerous; and by his writings he laboured, not without success, to keep alive the spirit of revolt, and to attract commiseration to himself. With Basil, however, he made no way, until he flattered the imperial vanity by forging a genealogical tree, in which the low-born son of a Spartan farmer was made to figure as a descendant of the royal house of Tiridates, king of Armenia. In the year 878 St. Ignatius died; and Photius immediately took forcible possession of the patriarchal chair. Partly by violence, partly by promises, he silenced or conciliated many of his opponents; he then sent deputies to Rome, who were bearers of a letter, signed by several metropolitans, in which he lamented with feigned humility that compulsion alone had obliged him to resume the patriarchal authority. The emperor, on his part, begged the Pope to sanction the re-instatement of Photius, if only for the sake of

preventing a deplorable schism. Moved by this consideration, and also by the perilous position of Italy, then menaced
by the Saracens, Pope John VIII. consented to remove all
censures from Photius on this condition, among others, that
he should declare his adhesion to all the acts of the eighth
general council, and his submission to all the judgments of
the Holy See, and should protest before a synod his sorrow
for his usurpation and other crimes. A synod was accordingly held, at which three papal legates were present, but at
which Photius himself presided; and, instead of acknowledging his past offences, the mendacious heresiarch read a pretended translation of the Pope's letter and his instructions to
the legates, in which all mention of the papal condition, with
reference to his own retractation, was omitted, and in its
place was substituted an eulogy of himself, and an express
condemnation of the acts of the council and the previous judgments of the Holy See. The legates were base enough to
connive at this falsification; and the Pope, deceived by their
report and by a letter they bore from the emperor, approved,
conditionally, the re-instatement of Photius; but as that heresiarch confessed, or rather boasted, in a letter sent at the
same time, that he had not made the disavowal required of
him, the Pope withheld his sanction from all acts of the council which were not in accordance with his instructions to the
legates. He then despatched the deacon Marinus to Constantinople, who, after ascertaining the real acts of the council on
this and other matters, condemned it by virtue of his legatine
authority, and confirmed all the censures previously pronounced against Photius. For this bold deed the emperor
threw him into prison; but without effect. Pope John confirmed his acts; and this same Marinus, when shortly after he
succeeded John VIII. on the papal throne, again repudiated
the Photian council, and condemned the arch-schismatic himself; which condemnation was repeated by Popes Adrian III.,
Stephen VI., and Formosus. On the death of Basil, Photius
was compelled to abdicate the patriarchal chair; but the fatal
seeds of schism never were eradicated.

Almost two centuries later, in 1053, there arose a dissension more grievous still; its author was another patriarch of
Constantinople, Michael Cerularius. The wound inflicted on
the Church by Photius had never been healed; a feeling of
jealousy remained in the hearts of the successive patriarchs

of Constantinople; they were, in fact, discontented with their position. Why should Rome retain its prerogative of being the first see, the see of St. Peter, the centre of unity, the source of all jurisdiction, the foundation-rock of the Church? Rome was now in decay; Constantinople was the seat of empire.' Michael Cerularius thought that the ecclesiastical dignity should attend, as its shadow, on the splendour of the throne; and being more impetuous and reckless than Photius, he ventured upon an absolute rupture with Rome, and a separation from the central see. To give some colour to this scandalous schism, he raked up all the grounds of quarrel which had ever existed between Rome and Constantinople, and all the falsehoods of Photius. He prohibited communion with the Pope; closed the churches against the Latins; and carried his fanaticism so far as to rebaptise all who had received baptism in the West. Pope St. Leo IX. exerted himself to stay this scandalous outbreak, and to allay the irritation of the Easterns. He condescended to a refutation in detail of all the charges brought forward by the patriarch; he showed him that a difference of customs need not induce a breach of unity. He even sent three legates to Constantinople to confer with the patriarch on the reunion of the East and West. The legates were cordially welcomed by the emperor; but the patriarch would neither hear them nor see them. Thereupon they executed their commission by pronouncing sentence of excommunication against Michael Cerularius, and by laying a copy of the sentence on the high altar of the principal church; they then shook the dust from their feet, and departed, saying, "May God judge between us!" They were admitted to take leave of the emperor, who censured the patriarch, but had no power to constrain him to obedience. Michael published an act of excommunication against the Pope and the whole Latin Church. From this epoch dates the great schism of the Greeks, which, despite some partial attempts to bring about a re-union, continues to the present day.

§.3. Re-establishment of discipline in the Western Church in the Tenth Century.

Never were the buoyancy and self-renovating power of the Church more conspicuous than during the lawlessness and corruptions of the tenth century. Let us turn to our

own country. The Danish invasion had swept away the monasteries and schools of Ireland and England; the institutions which had formed a Bede and an Alcuin, and had furnished multitudes of learned men and devoted missionaries.
The efforts of Alfred the Great contributed much to the spiritual, no less than to the intellectual regeneration of his
people. He himself translated the Ecclesiastical History of
Bede, and the Treatises of St. Gregory the Great on the Pastoral Care; but barbarism returned after this brief diffusion
of light, until God raised up Odo, archbishop of Canterbury,
to reform the disorders of the Church and relieve the darkness that prevailed. He drew up and enforced wise laws for
the clergy, the nobles, and the people. He was supported
in his reforms by the king, and met with the usual fate of
·reformers—the hatred of the patrons of evil. The good work
he had so vigorously begun was continued by his successor,
St. Dunstan. The calumnies with which the character of
this great and holy man has been aspersed have yielded
slowly to a more profound and candid study of history. He
was of noble family; endowed with great natural ability;
learned, and gifted with various and unusual accomplish-
ments. He traversed the whole of England, bringing back
the clergy and people to a stricter life; redressing grievances and correcting abuses. The vigour and unction of
his preaching wrought extraordinary effects; and he was
unwearied in every part of his pastoral work. Through his
efforts, and at the cost of much hatred and obloquy, he
raised the clergy of England from their state of ignorance
and degradation. His courage and firmness were remarkable. One of the most powerful lords of the realm was
living in sin with a very near relative, and refused to listen
to St. Dunstan's remonstrances. The saint forbade him to
enter the church; the earl complained to the king, who sent
an order to St. Dunstan to remove the prohibition. St. Dunstan was amazed at the facility with which the king had
allowed himself to be imposed upon; and finding no trace
of repentance in the earl, he replied, "When you are truly
penitent, I will gladly obey the king; as long as you are hardened in your sin, God forbid that any mortal man should
induce me to violate the law of God, and render void the
censure of the Church." This unexpected vigour so affected
the nobleman, that he renounced his unlawful pleasures, and

voluntarily repaired the scandal he had given, by a public and mortifying penance. He then threw himself at the archbishop's feet, and received the Church's pardon. Nor was St. Dunstan's firmness less remarkable in his treatment of the king, who had fallen into a great crime. He rested not until he had brought the monarch to repentance, and to testify, by an appropriate penance, his sorrow for the past. St. Dunstan was ably supported in his efforts at reformation by some of the bishops, especially by Ethelwold of Worcester.

At the same time many illustrious and pious bishops were labouring, under the auspices of Otho the Great, to stem the torrent of corruption in Germany. St. Bruno, brother of the emperor, was one of the most energetic and successful reformers. He had received an education suited to his rank, and was as remarkable for piety as for learning. The slightest indecorum during divine worship wounded him deeply. One day he rebuked Prince Henry for speaking to the Duke of Lorraine during Mass, and threatened them with the displeasure of God. All who loved religion were beloved by him; and any work was sure of his efficacious protection which had the glory of God and the salvation of souls for its object. On Bruno's return from Utrecht, where he had studied, the court became a school of royal and Christian virtues. St. Matilda, the emperor's mother, had retired into a monastery, where she practised in a supereminent degree all the virtues of a true religious. Among the first of St. Bruno's labours was that of setting in order certain of the monasteries, which he brought back to a sound discipline, and ordered with singular wisdom and prudence. His zeal had wider scope when he was raised to the see of Cologne; and he devoted himself to the restoration and purification of religion throughout Germany. He restored peace and concord, and regulated the divine offices with scrupulous care. So great was his wisdom and his renown, that when Otho set out for Italy, he left Bruno to administer the government of his kingdom. The saint discharged his trust with fidelity. Every where he restrained the evil, protected the weak, succoured the poor, and encouraged the good. He built or restored a great number of monasteries and other useful institutions. He was assiduous in preaching the Word of God, in appointing learned, pious, and laborious bishops through-

out the provinces, and in assisting them to root out all abuses.
His rule of action was, that the most powerful means of
reforming a corrupted people were the instructions and the
examples of their pastors.

The most efficient instrument in the re-establishment of
discipline and piety in France was the foundation of the celebrated monastery of Cluny, from which issued a long series
of apostolical, learned, and holy men for the work of the
Gospel. The origin of this congregation is due to the blessed
Bernon, a member of a noble family of Burgundy. He had
embraced the monastic life in the abbey of St. Martin d'Autun,
and was taken thence to rule the monastery of La Baume in
Burgundy, where he restored the utmost regularity. Some
officers of William, duke of Aquitaine, who had received in
passing the hospitality of this edifying house, spoke so highly
of it to the duke on their return, that he formed the design of
establishing in his states a monastery on the same plan, and
intrusting its government to Bernon. He requested Bernon
to come to see him at Cluny, an estate he possessed in the
Mâconnais. Bernon went thither, accompanied by his most
intimate friend, Hugh, a monk of St. Germain d'Autun. The
duke requested them, after much preliminary conference, to
select a spot for this new abbey. The two saints replied,
that no place could be more suitable than that where they
then were. The duke objected: it was his best hunting-
ground; he kept his kennel of hounds there. "Well, my
lord," said Bernon, with a smile, "it is only to drive away
the dogs, and let in the monks." The duke made the sacrifice, and requested that the monastery might be dedicated
to St. Peter and St. Paul. He drew up on the spot the necessary deeds, which were still in existence before the revolution. We may give an extract as a specimen of these do-
cuments, and an illustration of the tone of mind of the tenth
century. "Being desirous to make a holy use of the blessings God has bestowed on me, I have deemed it my duty to
seek the friendship of Christ's poor, and to make my work
permanent by founding a religious community. Where-
fore, for the love of God and of our Saviour Jesus Christ, I
give my estate of Cluny as the site of a monastery to be
built in honour of the blessed Apostles St. Peter and St. Paul,
to be for ever a retreat for those who, forsaking this world's
wealth, shall seek in the religious life the treasures of holi-

ness." The intentions of the pious founder were fulfilled. This community was remarkable for its undeviating regularity of discipline, for the extraordinary merit of its abbots, and for the blessings it diffused around it. From this central house the true spirit of the religious life was spread throughout France. There were but twelve monks at Cluny at first; but so great was their renown, that many other monasteries requested to be placed under its rule. This celebrated house has given to the Church several of its greatest Popes, and to France many holy bishops, who restored the early glories of religion by exemplifying its primitive piety and zeal.

St. Odo, the second abbot, gave the last touch to the rules of the congregation. He was a noble of Maine, and was educated at Paris, where, in spite of the troubles of the times, learning and piety were kept alive by a succession of professors. Urged by a desire to consecrate himself to God, he resolved to go to Rome, hoping to find there some fervent community in which he might attain to more perfect holiness. He passed through Burgundy, and was struck by the piety of La Baume. Here was what he sought; he renounced his journey to Italy, and petitioned to be admitted into the monastery. His great qualities and gifts soon procured his elevation to the post of instructor of the young, who thronged to the monastery for education. He was eventually selected as abbot of Cluny; but his resistance was so great and protracted, that only the threats of his bishop compelled his acceptance of the proffered dignity. He yielded; and under his administration the abbey surpassed its ancient fame for exactitude and holiness, learning and charity. Great numbers of persons, more or less distinguished in the world, embraced the religious life under his direction. Laymen of the highest rank came to make their retreats in the house; and even bishops resigned their sees to enter into the monastic state. The dukes of France eagerly sought to place their monasteries under the rule of Cluny, that the holy abbot might carry out the reforms that were required. Odo was not allowed to confine himself within the precincts of his own house; he became one of the leading reformers and restorers of discipline, not only throughout France, but even in Italy, whither he was summoned by the holy father himself. The results of his unwearied labours were prodigious; the face of Christendom was changed. His successors were not unworthy of him; they edified the whole Church by their holiness, and completed the great work of reformation. The monasteries returned to their primitive fervour; and their example stimulated the religious of Belgium and Lorraine to exertions which were crowned with like success.

Pope Leo IX. (1050) exerted himself strenuously to restore ecclesiastical discipline throughout the Church. He applied himself especially to root out two monster evils which were afflicting the Church—simony and incontinence. He undertook several journeys into France and Germany; assembled councils, and issued decrees for the extirpation of these scandalous crimes. The guilty were deposed; and if they resisted, were smitten with the spiritual sword of excommunication. The successors of this excellent Pope followed in his footsteps, and repressed the vices of the clergy with equal vigour. Their labours were marvellously aided by a holy man whom God raised up at that unhappy period to oppose the prevailing disorders. St. Peter Damian was born at Ravenna on the Adriatic Sea. Bereft of both his parents at an early age, he was brought up by an elder brother; and God, who destined him for a great work in His Church, enabled him to find means to acquire learning as well as holiness. His studies were accompanied with severe mortifications; he prayed, and fasted, and watched continually. At length he renounced the world altogether, and embraced the religious life in a monastery of Umbria, where the monks occupied separate cells, and devoted themselves exclusively to prayer and to study. Four days of the week they ate only bread; to which a few vegetables were added on Tuesday and Thursday. Peter became a living exemplification of the rule; and was remarked for his fervour in all penitential exercises, and in the practice of all virtues. The Popes, foreseeing how much good he would be able to effect, raised him by degrees to the highest dignities; he became cardinal and bishop of Ostia. There he laboured with unwearied zeal and a holy freedom to combat relaxation, and to carry out all the rules of the Church's discipline. He was employed in various legations, and was every where the inflexible opponent of abuses. The reform of ecclesiastical communities, decreed in a council held at Rome by Alexander II., was one of the fruits of his zeal. Ever since the fourth century there had been communities of clergy who lived together under the bishop's eye, possessing all things in common, and submitting to a common rule. Dwelling as they did in the great cities, they led a life, as far as their laborious functions permitted, of retirement from the world and severe austerity. This institution obtained and merited the eulogy of St. Ambrose : "They form a holy and angelical band of warriors, day and night singing the praises of God, without neglecting the people confided to their care. Their minds are ever occupied either in study or in toil. Can any thing be more worthy of admiration than this life, in which sufferings and austerities are repaid with peace of mind and heart, sustained by mutual example, alleviated by constant habit, soothed by holy and unceasing occupations? This life is neither troubled with temporal cares, nor distracted by the anxieties of the world, nor embittered by the visits of the idle, nor relaxed and cooled by intercourse with worldly people." St. Augustine held the institute in equal esteem, as may be seen in his two treatises on the excellence of a community life,—treatises which have served as the basis of the rules observed by canons. By degrees this discipline was relaxed; and it was almost abolished by the incursions of the barbarous tribes in the tenth century. It was restored to its primitive perfection in the time of St. Peter Damian, and those who followed it were called canons regular.

Some years later, in 1084, a new order of solitaries sprang up, destined to edify the Church by the splendour of its sanctity, and the fervour of its penitential exercises. St. Bruno, its founder, was born at Cologne. He grew in grace as he advanced in learning, and he was regarded as one of the profoundest theologians of his time. He was rector of studies and chancellor of Rheims ; but, fearing the dangers of the world, he resolved to retire into solitude, and devote his life to the practice of penance. He communicated his intention to a few friends, and inspired them with like sentiments. They then applied to St. Hugh, Bishop of Grenoble, who placed them in a wild desert called *La Chartreuse*. Then were renewed once more before the eyes of men the wonders of the Thebais. The new solitaries, said an enthusiastic contemporary, were angels rather than men. "Each occupies a separate cell, and has one loaf with a few vegetables which are to last him a week ; but they assemble on Sundays, and pass the day together. They wear a very simple dress, and beneath it a hair-shirt. Every thing about them bears the

stamp of real and extreme poverty; even their church contains neither gold nor silver, except one chalice. They observe silence so rigidly, that their communications are by
signs. They live by the labour of their heads, especially by
copying manuscripts." The report of their holiness roused
the slumbering world, and induced many to follow their example. Persons of every age and condition thronged to the
desert to bear the cross of Christ, and many similar communities were established in different countries. Ere St. Bruno
had passed six years in this solitude, he was summoned to
Rome by Pope Urban II., to aid him with his advice on ecclesiastical matters; but the saint could not bear the tumult
of a great city, or the constant pressure of affairs. In vain
the Pope pressed on him the archbishopric of Reggio; the
pious solitary knew no rest until he had received permission
to leave Rome. He then retired into Calabria, where he
founded a new community; and there ended his days in
prayer and in penance. When he found his end drawing
near, he assembled the brethren, and addressed them thus :
" I believe in the Sacraments of the Church; and, in particular, that the bread and wine consecrated upon the altar are
the very real Body of our Lord Jesus Christ, His true flesh
and His true blood, which we receive for the remission of our
sins, and in hope of everlasting life." The dying saint uttered these words wittingly, as we shall see. His spirit still
lives on in his spiritual children; his order, by a fidelity of
melancholy infrequency, has never degenerated from its first
fervour, and during the eight centuries of its existence has
never needed the hand of reform.

§ 4. Heresy of Berengarius. Disputes about Investitures.

In the eleventh century Berengarius, archdeacon of Angers,
acquired a miserable notoriety by assailing the mystery of
the Holy Eucharist, and asserting that the Body and Blood
of our divine Lord are not present therein really, but only
in figure. At once there arose one universal protest against
a doctrine so contrary to the uniform faith of the Church.
Catholic doctors refuted the rising heresy with great learning ; and letters came from all parts of the Church denouncing
the error and bearing witness to the truth. The celebrated
Lanfranc, archbishop of Canterbury, addressed a letter to the

innovator to recall him to a better mind. "I conjure you," wrote Adelman, bishop of Brescia, "not to trouble the peace of the Catholic Church, for which so many myriads of martyrs and doctors have contended unto death. We believe that the true Body and Blood of Jesus Christ are in the Blessed Eucharist. This faith has been held by the Church from the beginning, and this faith she holds now all over the world. All who are called Christians rejoice in the assurance that in this Sacrament they receive the Body and Blood of our Lord and Saviour. Ask of those who know our holy books; ask of the Greeks, the Armenians; ask of Christians any where,—all confess that this is, and ever has been, their belief." He then establishes the true faith by the testimony of Holy Scripture; and, as Berengarius had said that he could not comprehend *how* the bread could become the Body of our Lord, Adelman added : "The just man, who lives by faith, is not careful to cross-examine the word of God, nor to seek to understand what is, from its very nature, above the reach of his understanding; he loves to *believe* the sacred mysteries, hoping to receive one day the reward of his faith. It is as easy to our divine Lord to change bread into His Body as to change water into wine, or to call light into being by His word." In order to silence the innovator, a council was held at Paris, and the letters he had written on this holy doctrine were read. The assembled fathers could scarcely restrain their horror at a novelty so blasphemous, and condemned Berengarius unanimously. Pope Nicolas II. then assembled a council at Rome. Berengarius appeared, but dared not maintain or defend his error. He promised to sign the confession of faith drawn up by the council. It ran in these words : "I anathematise all heresies, and in particular the heresy of which I am accused. I protest with my mouth, and believe in my heart, that I hold concerning the Blessed Eucharist the faith which the Pope and the council have prescribed to me on the authority of the Gospels; to wit, that after their consecration, the bread and wine offered on the altar are the true Body and the true Blood of Jesus Christ." Berengarius confirmed his profession by an oath, and threw his books into the fire. Shortly afterwards it was found that he had relapsed into his errors, and was teaching that the substance of the bread is not changed into the substance of the Body of Christ, but that

the bread remains in union therewith. Cited again to Rome
(A.D. 1078), he himself drew up and signed with his own hand
a still more explicit confession of the true faith; and in the
following year he subscribed, in the presence of 150 prelates,
a formula so worded as to admit of no possible subterfuge, in
which he declared that the bread and wine placed on the altar
are, in virtue of the words of Jesus Christ, changed substan-
tially into His true and proper Body and Blood; so that the
Body received in communion is the very same which was
born of the Virgin Mary, suffered on the cross, and is now
seated on the right hand of the Father. But scarcely had
he returned to France, when, besides publishing a false report of what had occurred at Rome, he reasserted all his
former errors. Once more summoned before a council held
at Bordeaux, he a fifth time, and at last, it is believed, with
sincerity, submitted to the teaching of the Church; and re-
tiring to a small island in the Loire, spent the remaining
eight years of his life in practices of penance. The heresy,
thus abandoned by its inventor, was repressed for the time, to
reappear when Protestantism revived so many exploded and
condemned opinions.

Simony and incontinence, it has been said, had become
widely prevalent, and nowhere had they struck deeper roots
than in Germany and Lombardy. The source of the evil
was in the tyranny of the secular power, which made an ill
use of the extensive patronage it enjoyed; conferring benefices on worldly and time-serving prelates, and even selling
episcopal sees and abbeys to the highest bidders. It was
customary also for the emperor to put bishops and abbots in
possession of their temporal domains by delivering to them
the crosier and the ring; and this was called the *right of investiture.* As the ring and the crosier were the symbols and
badges of a spiritual power, this practice became a great and
mischievous abuse; leading men to imagine that the temporal ruler conferred the spiritual authority; an idea which
ambitious and irreligious emperors took care to foster and
strengthen. Henry IV., emperor-elect, then occupied the
throne of Germany. To almost every other vice he added
that of profound dissimulation. His desire was to bring the
Church into the position of a feudatory vassal of the empire;
but as his cruelty, profligacy, and ill-government excited the
hatred of his subjects, who rose in revolt against him, it be-

came his policy to affect in words a dutiful submission to the Pope, while in reality he continued to adhere to his sacrilegious and tyrannical practices. Gregory VII., one of the best and most able of a long line of Pontiffs, was, on his part, determined to assert and maintain the discipline of the Church, and to put a stop to an abuse which seemed to constitute the emperor the source of jurisdiction in spiritual matters. Towards Henry he never ceased to act as a tender father and friend, while there existed only the smallest hope of reclaiming him; but when his obstinacy and hardened ungodliness became too apparent, and he even proceeded to publish, with the concurrence of his creatures in the episcopate, an act of deposition against the Supreme Pontiff, this holy Pope, with sorrowful regret, pronounced sentence of excommunication against him. Excommunication in those days deprived of all civil rights; and an excommunicated sovereign could not reign over Catholic subjects. A year and a day was, however, always granted before it became incumbent on the people to withdraw their allegiance. When the truce was nearly expired, Henry, seeing himself abandoned by his outraged subjects, pretended to seek a reconciliation with the Pope, crossed the Alps in the depth of winter, and repaired to Gregory at the castle of Canossa in Lombardy; the Pontiff being on his way to Germany, to mediate, as he had been requested, between the emperor and his people. Here he presented himself humbly in the penitential garb usual in those days, confessing his guilt, and feigning the most profound humility. Gregory's heart was touched; and notwithstanding Henry's many former proofs of insincerity, he, on the fourth day, admitted him to reconciliation, and absolved him from the censures of the Church. Henry soon threw off the mask. His subjects, impatient at the Pope's forbearance, and without waiting for his decision, elected Rodolph of Suabia in the place of Henry; and now civil war, with all its horrors, devastated Germany. Rodolph being slain in battle, Henry passed rapidly into Italy; created an anti-pope, Guibert, archbishop of Ravenna; and marched upon Rome to receive from his hands the imperial crown. The Romans loved their Pontiff, and shut their gates against the emperor. After repeated sieges, he must have ultimately failed, had he not by bribes and cajolery induced the inhabitants to admit him within the walls (A.D. 1084), the Pontiff taking refuge in the castle of St. Angelo. An avenger was at hand. The Normans of Italy, Gregory's feudal subjects, came to his assistance, led by Robert Guiscard. They took Rome by storm, and delivered the Pope; but Gregory, his paternal heart filled with grief at the chastisement which had over taken his treacherous subjects, retired to Salerno, where he expired the following year. Before his death he uttered these words: "I have loved justice, and hated iniquity; therefore I die in exile." He was answered by words more memorable still: "Vicar of Christ, in exile thou canst not die; thou hast received the nations for thine inheritance and the uttermost parts of the earth for thy possessions."

The lawful successor of Gregory was Didier, abbot of Monte Cassino, who took the name of Victor III., and was solemnly enthroned in 1085, on the expulsion of the anti-pope Guibert. The subsequent life of Henry IV. was regarded as a judgment for his impiety. Though he was for a long time victorious over his enemies, his worst foes were found within his own family. His eldest son, Conrad, maintained with him a struggle of eight years' duration. On the death of Conrad, Henry V., his second son, took up arms in his turn, deposed his father, and allowed him to die at Liège in misery, and almost in want. Such was the melancholy end of a prince whose genius and valour were displayed in more than sixty battles; but who by his sensuality, his contempt for religion, his sacrilegious traffic in spiritual things, and his perfidious cruelty, has earned for himself an infamous celebrity in the Church of God.

The affair of the investitures was subsequently settled by a change in the symbols by which the feudal dominion attached to the great benefices was conveyed.

REFLECTIONS.

The tyranny exercised by the great feudal powers induced so many disorders, and such relaxation of discipline, that those who should have been patterns and examples to their flocks became their scandal. Hence the enemies of the Church have ever found in the tenth century an unfailing supply of reproaches and calumnies against her. But these scandals ought rather to strengthen than to shake our faith. Never was it more obvious that the Church was guided, not by man, but by the strong overruling hand of God. Had the Church been a human institution, the tenth century would have been its destruction and its tomb; and this remark applies also to other melancholy periods in her history. The weaknesses and the sins of the pastors of the Church do not compromise her Divine origin and mission; while, in times of the worst corruption, and amidst the greatest troubles and disorders, there have ever been, not only those chosen souls—few in number, but eminent in sanctity—to whom has been accorded the distinguished title of saints, but multitudes whose lives were models of all Christian virtues, and a reproach to the world around them. Those who were abandoned and scandalous in conduct were so, not on account of their faith, but in spite of it. The moral teaching of the Church remained unlowered, and her creed untouched. Her voice of remonstrance and rebuke was ever audible amidst the tumult of violence and iniquity; in every council admirable disciplinary laws were decreed, and their observance commanded and enforced. Even when apparently most powerless, the Church was enabled by her inherent Divine energy to heal the wounds inflicted on her by the barbarian hordes, and to subject a new race of persecutors to the yoke of Christ. She vanquished the vanquishers of the empire. True it is that many years were needed to tame their haughty natures, and to disperse the darkness of their ignorance; but the work was at length accomplished, and the Christendom of to-day is the monument of her triumph. Sciences and arts still found a shelter amongst the clergy and in the monasteries. The palaces of bishops and religious houses became public schools, in which knowledge was preserved from extinction. While the nobles were ravaging the empire, humble monks were transcribing in the quiet of their cells those precious remains of antiquity which they had rescued from the hands of the barbarians. It is in her bosom that the goodly treasures of antiquity were preserved, and in her various institutions that the waning light of knowledge, both sacred and profane, was fed and rekindled. To her the world, unwilling to acknowledge its debt of gratitude, owes, not only the custody of the faith, and the Divine morality of the Gospel, but the revival of secular literature, science, and the fine arts. The unbiased judgment of one great man, himself opposed to the teaching of the Church, is enough to silence a whole herd of inferior cavillers. "It was the Christian Church," says Bacon, "which, amidst the inundations of the Scythians on the one side, and the Saracens from the East, did preserve in the sacred lap and bosom thereof the precious relics even of heathen learning, which otherwise had been extinguished, as if no such thing had ever been."[*]

CHAPTER VI.

FROM THE FIRST CRUSADE TO THE DEATH OF ST. LOUIS, A.D. 1095-1270.

§ 1. The first Crusade, 1095-1099.

WHATEVER judgment may be formed of the political wisdom of the Crusades, they certainly offer a grand and impressive spectacle,—the rising of Europe as one man to wrest from the infidel the desecrated sepulchre of our Divine Lord. The Arabs had pushed their conquests to the very gates of Constantinople; Egypt and a portion of Africa were subject to their rule; they had formed extensive settlements in Spain; and but for Charles Martel would long ere this have been masters of Europe. And now a tribe issued from Turkistan, and insensibly supplanted the Arab race. This new nation of conquerors took Jerusalem in 1086, and exercised upon the Christian inhabitants, and upon the numerous pilgrims from every part of the world, the most revolting cruelty. The eastern emperor had long sounded the note of alarm, and invoked in vain the aid of the West. France was governed by the dissolute Philip I., the third successor of Hugh Capet; Germany was cruelly oppressed by Henry IV.; in England William Rufus was busied in strengthening his power and oppressing the Church; Spain was slowly rising from her ruins, and had to struggle for her existence with the Moors and Arabs; Italy was rent by intestine factions; the Latins could not combine to drive back the insulting infidel. But religion did what politics could not do: a poor monk hushed the dissensions of Europe, and combined its divided forces

[*] Advancement of Learning.

against the common enemy.   Peter the Hermit, a priest of
Amiens, had gone in pilgrimage to Jerusalem, and returned
saddened by the profanation of the holy places by the infidel.
He conferred with the patriarch of Jerusalem; and these two
ecclesiastics were bold enough to conceive a plan for delivering
the Holy Land from the slavery under which it had groaned
for ten years.   It was agreed that the patriarch should write
to the Pope, and that Peter should convey the letter, and
support its petition.   He did so; and represented to Pope
Urban II. the desolation of Sion in terms so touching, that
the Pope resolved to appeal to the princes of Christendom
for aid.   He had already convoked a council at Clermont for
the settlement of certain points of ecclesiastical discipline; and
there he addressed the assembled prelates with such pathetic
eloquence that they burst into tears, and exclaimed : "God
wills it; it is the will of God !"   The cry was caught up, and
reverberated throughout Europe, and long struck terror into
the infidel who heard it shouted amidst the fury of battle.
They who bound themselves to take part in this expedition,
assumed, as the badge of their engagement, a red cross sewed
on to the right shoulder : hence their name of *Crusaders*.
The bishops exerted themselves in their dioceses with a success which seemed miraculous.   Peter the Hermit traversed
province after province to enkindle and direct the popular
enthusiasm; his zeal, his disinterestedness, his austere life,
gave to his person the appearance, and to his words the authority, of a prophet.   Soon France, Germany, and Italy
were in movement from one end to the other; nobles and
people were affected with one common enthusiasm.   En-
mities and feuds and wars were all forgotten; peace and justice seemed to have descended again upon the earth.   The
noblest heroes of Christendom led the several bands; a host
powerful enough to have subjugated the world, had it been
possible to secure union of counsel, and to preserve the discipline of the troops.   The famous Godfrey of Bouillon, one
of the most distinguished leaders of the Christian forces,
combined the prudence of age with the energy of youth, and
was as fervent in piety as he was intrepid in battle.   Although
his rank was inferior to that of many of the Crusaders, his
army was the largest and best appointed, as his reputation
attracted to his standard multitudes of youthful nobles, eager
to learn in his service the science of war.

The Crusaders, thus divided into several detachments, appointed Constantinople as their rendezvous; but unhappily multitudes perished on the march from disregard of discipline and consequent excesses and disorders. Godfrey alone brought his army to Constantinople in good order. The Greek emperor, Alexius, alarmed at the number of the Latin forces, began to distrust the defenders of Christendom more than he feared the infidels; and from that moment the conduct of the Greeks towards their allies was marked by meanness, duplicity, and perfidy. Crossing the Hellespont, the combined forces laid siege to Nicæa in Bithynia, in order to open their way into the Holy Land. Though its garrison was strong, this city could not withstand the impetuous assault of the Crusaders. It surrendered at discretion. A few days afterwards, the Christian host was surrounded during its march by a countless multitude of infidels. The Crusaders fought with the energy of enthusiasm, and defeated the enemy with great slaughter. But victory did not avert all the dangers of their enterprise. The country had been carefully laid waste by the enemy, so that neither provisions nor water could be obtained. A great number of soldiers and almost all the horses perished from famine and thirst. At length the army reached Syria, and invested Antioch, at that time one of the largest and strongest cities of the East. The enemy had provided it with abundance of provision and with every kind of implement of defence, in anticipation of this siege. The siege lasted seven months; and the Crusaders were beginning to despair of reducing the place, when a Greek renegade admitted them within the walls. The enemy, however, still held possession of the citadel; and a large army of the infidels, advancing to the relief of the town, besieged the Christians in their turn, and so hemmed them in, that, unable to obtain provisions, they were compelled to eat the flesh of their beasts of burden. In this dire necessity, when all hope was fled, He in whose cause they were enduring such straits vouchsafed a miraculous token of His favour. It was revealed to a certain priest, that under the pavement of a church within that very city lay concealed the lance that opened the Saviour's side. The holy relic was discovered and exposed to the veneration of the faithful; and now, assured of the Divine protection, the Christians sallied out upon the beleaguering hosts and defeated them with great slaughter. The conquest of Antioch struck terror into the whole of Palestine, and the Crusaders reached Jerusalem without further molestation. The city might have sustained a long siege, the infidels had made great preparations for defence; but the valour of the assailants was irresistible. Within five weeks they took Jerusalem by storm, and entered it on a Friday, at 3 p.m.; a circumstance remarked with pious awe, as it was the hour when our Lord had expired on the cross. In the flush of victory there was an indiscriminate massacre; but the associations connected with the holy city soon calmed their rage. They cast off their blood-stained garments, and went, barefooted and smiting their breasts, to visit the spots hallowed by the sufferings of the Redeemer. The feeble and oppressed remnant of Christians left in Jerusalem accompanied them with shouts of joy and thanksgiving. Eight days afterwards, the chieftains of the Christian army assembled to elect a king able to retain this important conquest. Their choice fell on Godfrey, the most valiant and pious of the captains. He was led in procession to the church of the Holy Sepulchre, and there proclaimed with due solemnity. When a crown of gold was presented to him, the pious hero put it aside with the words, "God forbid that I should wear a crown of gold in a city where the King of kings was crowned with thorns!" This important capture was made A.D. 1099.

From the Crusades sprang the great military orders. The most ancient of these was that of the Knights of St. John, who survived until the last century under the name of Knights of Malta. The first house of this celebrated order was a hospital built at Jerusalem, to receive pilgrims and to shelter the sick. It was founded by some merchants of Naples, while Jerusalem was still in possession of the infidels. Gerard, a native of Provence, a man of extraordinary prudence and virtue, was superior of this hospital when the Crusaders became masters of the city. The new king, Godfrey, took it under his special protection. Many of the young nobles and others who had accompanied the expedition were so edified by the charity displayed towards the pilgrims and the sick, that they consecrated themselves to this good work; but as they could not lay aside their military ardour, they often took arms against the infidel. Their fervour of piety gave additional strength to their arm in battle; but terrible as they were in presence of the enemy, in the hospital they were the humble servants of the pilgrims, the most tender nurses of the sick. They were austere only to themselves, and lavish in their charity to others; while their own food was the coarsest bread, they procured the finest and best for those under their care. In order to place this institution on a permanent foundation, they resolved to bind themselves by vows; and their resolve was sanctioned by the patriarch, before whom they took the three usual vows, to which they added a fourth,—to fight against the infidel when called upon. Pope Pascal II. confirmed the institute, and granted it great privileges. They thus formed a body which was at once monastic and military; and the new order became so popular, that it multiplied its numbers and its possessions in a short space of time. The bravest of the Christian youth were eager to obtain admission into a community so renowned; and as long as the kingdom of Jerusalem stood, they were its firmest supporters. After its fall—it lasted only ninety-six years— they removed to the island of Rhodes; where, in 1522, they maintained against Soliman, the Turkish sultan, a siege for ever memorable in history. They then removed to the island of Malta, which the Emperor Charles V. ceded to them; and where likewise, under the celebrated grand master La Valette, they made a glorious stand against the vast armament of the infidels. They retained possession of the island until its capture by the French under Napoleon in 1798; in 1800 it was taken by the English, who still retain it.

The order of Templars was instituted in 1118. Baldwin II., king of Jerusalem, granted them a house near the Temple of Solomon; and this is the origin of their name. Their object was the defence of Jerusalem against the infidels. When Palestine was abandoned, they degenerated from their first fervour and strictness of discipline, and became the objects of popular animadversion. The gross charges propagated against them were seized upon as a pretext by the King of France for their cruel extermination. It is difficult at the present day to ascertain the precise amount of guilt which attached to them, considering they were the objects of the animosity of so unscrupulous and determined a monarch as Philippe-le-Bel. The result, however, was that the order was suppressed in 1312.

A third military order, that of St. Mary of the Teutons,

remained but a short time at Acre, the place of its origin;
it soon removed to the north of Europe, to war against the
still heathen population of Prussia and Poland. There they
acquired large possessions; and at length Albert of Brandenburg, one of the grand masters, secularised those possessions
and rendered them hereditary in his family, having first taken
the precaution to become a Protestant. This is the origin
of the monarchy of Prussia.

With the aid of these three military orders, the kingdom
of Jerusalem endured for some time, and even attained a
high degree of consequence and prosperity by the conquest
of the adjacent countries. But this career of success was
closed by the death of Baldwin II. in 1131; the infidels,
recovering from their panic, made their appearance with a
fresh generation of troops. They besieged Edessa and took
it by assault; overthrew the churches, and massacred the
Christian population. Tidings of this disaster reached Europe, and called forth the second Crusade.

§ 2. Foundation of new Orders: the Premonstrants, Cistercians,
Trinitarians.

While the prolific vigour of the Church was thus mani-
festing itself in the East, other orders of a more pacific character were rising up in Europe; orders destined to effect
much and lasting good. St. Norbert was raised up to exhibit
to the clergy an example of the virtues which befit their
sacred office by instituting the canons regular. This great
saint was born of a noble family in the duchy of Cleves. Remarkable for piety in his early youth, his life, after his admission into holy orders, was little in accordance with the
sanctity of his calling. He squandered in luxury and vanity
the revenues of many valuable benefices, until it pleased God
to arrest him in his mad course, and to cast him down in
order to raise him the more gloriously. One day when he
was riding through a pleasant meadow, there came on a
terrific storm; the lightning struck the ground immediately
before the horse's head, and Norbert was thrown half dead
to the ground. He remained for an hour in a state of un-
consciousness; and on recovering his senses, he exclaimed,
with Saul of Tarsus: *" Lord, what wilt Thou that I should
do?"* He felt the answer to his question—he must begin to
lead a life conformable with his sacred vocation. He returned

home, disposed of all his costly apparel, and, assuming a rough hair-shirt, became in his own person a perfect exam-ple of the penance which he now began most strenuously to preach. Summoned before a council, and rebuked for preaching without mission, and for affecting a life of aus-terity before he had himself renounced the goods of this life, he resigned his benefices, sold his patrimony, and departed barefoot to seek Pope Gelasius, who, struck with his simpli-city and zeal, granted him the permission he solicited. Armed with these extraordinary powers, he continued his evangelical labours with wonderful success. The Bishop of Laon was anxious to secure the services of such a man for the benefit of his people; and as Norbert repeatedly expressed his wish to retire into solitude, the bishop led him from place to place in his diocese, hoping thus to retain him within it. The saint fixed on a very lonely spot, called Prémontré, and there established his cell. His preaching and the fame of his sanctity drew around him a number of disciples; and in a short time he had with him forty ecclesiastics and a number of laymen, all imbued with his spirit, and eager to imitate his virtues. St. Norbert, after long deliberation, fixed on the rule of St. Augustine; and his disciples made solemn profession of it. The holy founder then went to Rome, to solicit from the Pope the confirmation of his order. Pope Honorius granted him all he requested; and the institute spread rapidly throughout Christendom. Thibaut, Count of Champagne, was so impressed with the discourses and virtues of the saint, that he came and offered to place himself and all his posses-sions unreservedly in his hands; but Norbert counselled him to remain in the world, and to glorify God by discharging with the utmost perfection the duties of his high station. In their origin these several bodies were full of disinterestedness and self-sacrifice, and refused wealthy endowments and large donations. Their astonishing labours in clearing and cultivat-ing waste lands, and their prudent administration of the funds thus placed at their disposal, were the chief source of their wealth.

God, who had raised St. Norbert to so high a degree of sanctity, had destined him to govern a great people, and to be a light and the source of edification to all Germany. Being on a journey, he reached Spires while the election of an archbishop for the vacant see of Magdeburg was going on. Norbert was invited to preach; and, unknown to himself, was named as one of three who were deemed eligible to so high a dignity. He was sitting apart in the assembly absorbed in prayer, when suddenly the second candidate on the list, as if moved by a Divine inspiration, exclaimed, pointing to the saint, that the humblest was most worthy of being exalted. Immediately the deputies of the church of Magdeburg set up the cry, "Norbert is our bishop! Norbert is our father!" The choice was hailed with universal acclamations. After the confirmation of his election by the Papal legates who were present, the new bishop was borne off to his see. When they came in sight of Magdeburg, Norbert insisted on completing his journey barefoot; and so he proceeded, meanly clothed, and with a modèst and mortified demeanour, towards the town. The concourse of people was enormous. When he presented himself at the gate of his palace, the porter thrust him back, saying: "You ought to have come when the other poor came; be off now, and don't stand in the way." The crowd exclaimed: "It is the archbishop; it is your master whom you are repelling!" The unlucky porter would have run away, but the archbishop stopped him and said: "Be not alarmed, my friend; I am not angry with you: you know me much better than do they who compel me to live in a palace." He administered his diocese with unwearied zeal, but not without much trial and suffering. The church of Magdeburg had fallen into great disorder and confusion, and he resolved on a thorough reform. With many his efforts were successful; but many also became his enemies, because he would have them fulfil the duties of their office. "Why," said they, "did we bring in this foreigner, whose ways are so different from ours?" They not only insulted and calumniated him, but even sought to take away his life. Norbert suffered with unvarying patience, and said to his friends: "Is it strange that the devil should be enraged against me, since he assailed the life of Jesus Christ, our Example and Head?" His charity, his mildness, and his perseverance, at length triumphed, and he died worn out by toils and austerities.

The Cistercian Order was established about the same time, in 1098, and became equally celebrated and equally useful to the Church. St. Robert of Molesme, its founder, had embraced the religious life at the early age of fifteen. As he wished to secure a more secluded retreat, and to practise the rule of St. Benedict without any relaxation, he went with a few companions into the forest of Citeaux, about five miles from Dijon. It was a wilderness, tenanted only by wild beasts; but they deemed it the more suited to their purpose. They set about clearing the ground, and built a few wooden cells for themselves; it was rather a collection of huts than a monastery. There they practised the most rigorous and unrelenting penance, and lived in almost unceasing prayer. Often their provisions failed them, because their toil was inadequate to supply their wants; and yet, in their desire to preserve holy poverty, they refused the costly presents offered them by the Duke of Burgundy. The new institute, though destined to wide and lasting renown, remained for many years without visible progress. Still it was obviously a plant which the Lord was secretly watering and blessing. Amongst others, a young noble named Bernard presented himself one day with thirty companions whom he had induced to share his retreat. Bernard was born at the *château* of Fontaine, in Burgundy. The graces of his person and the vigour of his intellect encouraged in his parents the highest hopes. The world lay bright and smiling before him, when he renounced it for ever. His brothers, his friends, all endeavoured to dissuade him, but in vain; he even succeeded in leading some of them to follow his example. He was followed to Citeaux by all his brothers, except Nivard, the youngest, whom he left to be the consolation of his father in his old age. When they were taking their departure, the eldest said to Nivard, who was playing with some other children : " You will be the sole heir of all our possessions; we leave all to you." " Yes," replied the boy ; " you leave me earth, and keep heaven for yourselves; the division is not fair." After a while, he too forsook the world and joined his brothers at Citeaux. Bernard soon became distinguished for his obedience, his mortification, his deep spirituality, and his eloquence. So great was his power of abstracting himself from outward things, that when he left the rooms occupied by the novices, he knew nothing of their shape or material. He kept alive the flame of devotion, by repeatedly asking himself, " Bernard, to what end didst thou come hither?" and the words were always a stimulus to renewed fervour and zeal.

His example attracted so many novices, that it was found

necessary to erect several other monasteries, and amongst
them that of Clairvaux. It was built in a desert place, the
resort of robbers, and named the Vale of Wormwood. Bernard was appointed its abbot, with twelve monks, whose
number increased with wonderful rapidity. It was the habit
of St. Bernard to say to those whom he received as novices :
" If you desire to enter here, leave at the threshold the body
you have brought with you from the world; here there is
room only for your soul." His rule was rigorously austere.
As the monastery was very poor, the food of the monks consisted of coarse bread, and a soup made from beech leaves.
Yet the love of penance made this wretched diet a luxury.
Toil and prayer succeeded each other, and silence was always
observed. Nothing so impressed the secular persons who
came to the monastery, as the deep unbroken silence. Yet
these were men who had been wealthy and famous in their
day, who now gloried in their conformity to the poverty of
Jesus Christ; for His sake gladly enduring hunger and thirst
and cold, and submitting to every humiliation. Their holy
abbot surpassed them all in the severity of his life. So lofty
was his ideal of the religious life, that at first he expected too
much from his monks, and was so severe in his chastisements
for the smallest faults, as to discourage them in their efforts
after holiness. But he was soon made sensible of his error;
and by the sweetness of his corrections and the mildness of his
rule, led forward his religious with wonderful success in the
ways of spiritual perfection. His influence on his family was
remarkable. He now had with him all his brothers; and at
length, Tescelin, his father, came in his old age to exchange
wealth and honour for the poor and austere garb of a monk
of Clairvaux. One only sister remained behind; she was
married, and loved the world and its pleasures. On one
occasion she wished to see her brother, and came to the
monastery magnificently dressed, and with a splendid retinue. The holy abbot refused to see her, surrounded by such
worldly pomp. His refusal touched her heart with shame
and compunction. " Although I am but a poor sinner," she
said, " yet Jesus Christ died for me. If, as my brother, you
despise my outward show, yet, as a minister of Christ, despise not my soul. Come, command; I am prepared to obey
in all things." Then St. Bernard consented to receive her
visit. She was so touched with his advice, that she forsook

her vanity; and two years later, with the consent of her husband, she entered the convent of Jully, and died with the reputation of sanctity.

The fame of the talents and virtues of Bernard was diffused far and wide; and at length he received of God the gift of miracles. The first of these was wrought in favour of a gentleman, a distant relative of the saint. The gentleman was suddenly seized with illness, and lost all consciousness. His family was in poignant distress, as he had led a worldly life. They sent for St. Bernard, who assured them that the sick man would recover his senses if they repaired the wrongs he had done. They did so, while the abbot went to offer the holy sacrifice. Before the Mass was over, the sick man recovered his senses, and asked for a confessor. He made his confession with every mark of true contrition, and three days afterwards died in peace.—One day a poor woman brought to the saint her child, whose arm had been withered from his birth. He had compassion on her, and told her to lay her child on the ground; he then prayed for a few moments with great fervour, made the sign of the cross over the disabled limb, and it was healed immediately. At the report of these miracles, there were brought to him from afar sick persons of all kinds—deaf and blind and paralytic; and he healed them all. But his greatest miracle was his power in effecting conversions. It was impossible to resist the unction of his words, or rather of the Holy Spirit who spoke by his mouth. A party of young nobles set out, in a spirit of levity and curiosity, to pay a visit to the house of Clairvaux. The abbot received them courteously, and invited them to remain a few days, but they declined. "I hope," he said, "that God will grant me what you refuse." He set refreshments before them, and bade them drink to the health of their souls; they did so with a smile, and went their way. Ere they had gone far, they felt themselves drawn to return; they obeyed the call, and all became fervent religious.

It was natural that virtues and gifts so rare should have led many churches to covet St. Bernard as their bishop. Milan, Rheims, Langres, Châlons, and others, were offered to him; but he steadily refused; and the regard which the Pope cherished for him prevented his insisting on doing violence to his humility. The saint desired only to continue in his quiet retreat, and to advance, in company with his religious, in the way of perfection; but he could not be hid,—his retirement was broken in upon continually. He was the refuge of the unfortunate, the defender of the oppressed, the scourge of heretics, the beloved adviser of popes, the oracle of bishops and kings,—in one word, a genuine churchman, ever ready to defend the Church's rights, to preserve her unity, to confound her enemies, to advance her empire, to teach her doctrines, to minister her sacraments. His writings are amongst the most precious treasures of the Church; they have procured for him the title of the Last of the Fathers.

Somewhat later there arose a new and striking institution. During the Crusades many Christians had been taken prisoners by the infidels; they were loaded with chains, and exposed to the severest trials, without prospect of release or mitigation of their sufferings. John de Matha, a native of Provence, conceived the design of rescuing them from their unhappy condition. He was a holy and learned man, whom the Archbishop of Paris had recently ordained priest. It was while offering for the first time the Adorable Sacrifice, that he was inspired with the idea. After preparing himself by retirement and penance, he felt drawn to go and impart his plans to a monk named Felix de Valois, in the diocese of Meaux. Together they devised a scheme for the redemption of Christian captives from the infidels. They went to Rome, and Pope Innocent III. approved their scheme in a bull, and sanctioned the foundation of a new order, that of the Holy Trinity, for the Redemption of Captives. Their first house was that in which Felix de Valois had lived. The holiness of their lives, and the noble object of their institute, procured them many novices; so that they were obliged to construct new monasteries. Money also flowed in on all sides. Then they began their work. Two of the monks were sent to Africa, and ransomed 186 Christian slaves. John himself went to Spain and to Barbary, and released 120 captives. Neither storms nor peril of death could arrest his intrepid zeal. Meanwhile he would not abate his customary austerities, and was at length obliged to retire to Rome, where he passed the last two years of his life in visiting the prisoners and the sick.

Only the religion of Christ can furnish examples of that generous charity which embraces every form of human sufferings, and sacrifices health and rest and life to its alleviation.

Mere natural sensibility, ordinary benevolence, will impel men
to isolated acts of self-devotion : such motives, however, have
but an intermittent and desultory influence ; they are incapable of inspiring a life-long heroism.　That religion alone
can permanently sustain our feeble nature in a course of such
continual self-sacrifice, which furnishes it with supernatural
motives and supernatural aids.

§ 3. The Church in England.

The conquest of England by William of Normandy had
produced a great effect on the Church.　It was his object to
depress the native English, and to exalt his own followers ;
and by degrees every episcopal see and every ecclesiastical
dignity was intrusted to a foreigner.　In the first flush of
victory the monasteries were ravaged, and their sacred vessels,
ornaments, and treasures carried off.　Pope Alexander had
sent legates into England at the king's request, ostensibly
for the reformation of the clergy.　Councils were held at
Winchester and Windsor ; and William easily contrived to
inculpate most of the native bishops and abbots, and to obtain their deposition.　It should be observed, however, that
while William too often bestowed the inferior preferments of
the Church on unworthy ecclesiastics, the higher dignities
were filled with prelates of learning and unblemished life ;
and that the change, though violent and unjust, was really
a national benefit.　The infusion of a new element roused
the Church from its torpor, and learning and science followed
in the train of reviving zeal.

The most illustrious of these new prelates was Lanfranc,
an Italian by birth, and for many years professor of laws at
Pavia.　Thence he came to France, and established a school
at Avranches, which had great success.　In 1042 his growing
desire after perfection led him to retire to the poor and lonely
abbey of Bec.　There he was compelled to exercise his wonderful gift of teaching, and more than a hundred scholars
attended his lectures.　In 1063 William made him abbot of
his newly-founded monastery of St. Stephen at Caen ; and in
1070 removed him to the archiepiscopal see of Canterbury.
His zeal and piety edified the Church ; while his firmness and
perseverance preserved much of its property from spoliation.
He rebuilt the cathedral of Canterbury, which had been de-

stroyed by fire, and founded two hospitals in the city, one for lepers, and one for the poor and infirm. He died in 1079, at a very advanced age. William's reign was, on the whole, favourable to the Church. "He was mild to good men who loved God," says the Saxon chronicle; "he had a strong sense of religion, and a great regard for its institutions."

His son and successor, William Rufus, was the fierce oppressor of the Church during his whole reign. He reduced the prelates to poverty, by seizing on the revenues of their sees; and kept bishoprics and abbeys vacant for years, in order to appropriate their temporalities. In 1095 a dangerous illness induced him to appoint to the see of Canterbury the celebrated St. Anselm, abbot of Bec. He had previously declared that he would never part with the temporalities of Canterbury until his death; but in the anguish of his soul, William yielded to the remonstrances of the bishops. St. Anselm had so clear a foresight of the inevitable conflict that awaited him, that he repeatedly refused the proffered see; but he was compelled by his superiors to accept it. His presentiments were but too well founded. When William recovered, he felt ashamed and mortified at his weakness, and relapsed into all his former habits of rapacity and vice. The conflict began; Anselm was driven to seek refuge at Rome; and the sacrilegious king was killed by an arrow from an unknown hand while hunting in the New Forest.

St. Anselm returned only to engage in a more dignified but equally painful conflict with Henry I., on the matter of investitures. When the nomination of bishops passed into the hands of the king, he required the prelate-elect to swear fealty and do homage to him as superior temporal lord. The monarch now extended his pretensions, and claimed the right to invest the new bishop with the ring and crosier, the symbols of spiritual jurisdiction. On this point the king and the archbishop were brought into collision. It would lead us too far to detail the vicissitudes of a conflict which continued for many years. In 1108 a kind of concordat was made. Fealty and homage, which were civil duties, were to be paid by the prelate-elect; the ring and crosier were to be bestowed by the archbishop. St. Anselm was a man conspicuous in an age of great ecclesiastics. In theology, in metaphysics, and in science, he had few equals, and no superior. When he was expelled by Rufus, and had taken refuge in

Rome, he was received with singular honours; and in the council of Bari he was deputed to defend the Catholic Church against the Greek schismatics on the doctrine of the Procession of the Holy Ghost. He was a man of great spirituality, and austere in his treatment of himself. Troubled as was his life, it was one of almost continuous prayer; frequently a day of harassing fatigue was followed by a night of watching and communing with God; and while his theological writings place him in the first rank of the Church's doctors, his meditations and other devotional works distinguish him amongst her ascetic divines.

Many holy bishops ruled the Church in England; but the record of their deeds lies beyond the scope of this manual. The next great name which claims attention is that of St. Thomas of Canterbury. This celebrated man was born in London in 1119; and his many great qualities had raised him to the chancellorship of England. When the see of Canterbury fell vacant, Henry II., anxious to place in it some one who would be supple to his will, fixed upon his chancellor, a layman. Thomas resisted; and told the king, that as archbishop he should certainly incur the royal displeasure, because he should feel it a duty to correct and reform all abuses. Henry would not listen to any objections; and Thomas à Becket was accordingly elected and consecrated Archbishop of Canterbury. He kept his word. The king, like the wretched Rufus, habitually held the bishoprics vacant, that he might enjoy their revenues. Against this, and all other derogations from the rights of the Church, the new archbishop offered the most persevering opposition. Henry was surprised and annoyed; he required the bishops to take an oath to maintain the customs of the realm. The archbishop knew how great a latitude of interpretation such a formula would admit, and how many sacrilegious abuses would find shelter under the term " customs of the realm;" and he refused the oath. Thenceforward his life was one long endurance of provocation and persecution; and he was obliged to seek refuge in France. He sent two of the companions of his flight to Louis VII. to beg for an asylum; the king granted him his protection, and strove to bring about a reconciliation between the archbishop and the misguided king. On the faith of promises made by Henry, Thomas returned to England, only to renew his combat and his sufferings. Some words which fell from the king in a moment of irritation were caught up by some of his courtiers. Four of them proceeded on the instant to Canterbury, broke into the cathedral, and killed the archbishop before the high altar. When tidings of this sacrilegious murder reached the king, he protested that he had not commanded it; and he remained three days in his room fasting, and in despair. He knew well the gravity of his sin; and he performed the humiliating penance imposed on him with apparent contrition. It pleased God to attest the sanctity of His martyr by numerous miracles wrought at his tomb; the shrine of St. Thomas became the resort of vast crowds of pilgrims, and was renowned for the many rare and precious offerings with which it was enriched, until it was despoiled by the rapacious revolters of the sixteenth century. Like his Lord and Master, St. Thomas had conquered by his seeming defeat. That which his life could not wrest from the king, was won for the Church by his martyrdom. Henry abolished the abuses which, under the name of customs of the realm, he had endeavoured to confirm; and restored to the Church all the lands and revenues he had sacrilegiously usurped.

§ 4. The Crusades, 1147-1229.

The cruelties practised by the infidels after their capture of Edessa, which we have already mentioned, excited the indignation of the Latins, and their sympathy for the sufferers. The Holy Land seemed about to fall again under the sway of the unbeliever, when Pope Eugenius II. undertook to rekindle in the hearts of Christians the ardour which Urban II. had aroused fifty years before. He wrote a letter to the king of France, in which he exhorted him to arm in defence of religion. St. Bernard was charged to preach the Crusade.

Then took place throughout France and Germany a movement without parallel. The preaching of St. Bernard was accompanied with miracles; and crowds of nobles rushed to assume the cross with an ardour which threatened to precipitate the whole European population upon Asia. King Louis set the example to his subjects, and prepared to put himself at the head of his army. The emperor, Conrad III., left Germany about the festival of the Ascension, 1147. His troops were composed of 66,000 mailed horsemen, besides infantry and light cavalry; nor was the French army much inferior in number. But the greater part of this enormous host perished from its unwieldiness and want of discipline. When they reached the territory of the Eastern Empire, they perpetrated enormities which excited the hostility of Manuel Comnenus, who then occupied the throne of Constantinople. He resolved to lead them on to their destruction; and intrusted them to guides who conducted them into the deserts of Asia Minor, where they fell into the hands of the infidels. It was with great difficulty that Louis and Conrad effected their escape into Syria with the wreck of their armies. There they invested the city of Damascus; but they were compelled to raise the siege, and to return hastily to Europe. Such was the end of this disastrous expedition, in which two magnificent armies utterly perished. In the agony of their sorrow and shame, the survivors laid the blame on St. Bernard, who had preached the Crusade, and had prognosticated its success; the saint exculpated himself by saying that the Crusaders had drawn down on themselves the anger of God by their disorders and excesses, and had thus, like the Israelites of old, forfeited the protection and the promises of God. Worn out by fatigues of body and mind, St. Bernard did not long survive the melancholy catastrophe. He died in 1153.

Third Crusade, 1189–1193.—Henry II., king of England, had resolved to undertake a new crusade in expiation of the crime he had committed in occasioning the death of St. Thomas of Canterbury. He died before his preparations were complete, and was succeeded, in 1189, by his son, Richard Cœur-de-Lion. The Holy Land was then in a most wretched condition. Saladin, sultan of Egypt, had invaded it with 50,000 men; he had defeated the Christians in an important battle, and had taken prisoners Guy de Lusignan, the king of Jerusalem; Renaud de Châtillon, the grand master of the Knights of St. John; and many other distinguished nobles. But the saddest loss of all was that of the true Cross, which had been carried forth with the army, and was now in the hands of the infidel. This victory opened the whole of the Holy Land to the conquering Saladin. Jerusalem, which had been free for eighty-eight years, submitted after a very brief siege. The Christians retained only three cities in Palestine—Antioch, Tyre, and Tripoli.

The tidings of this disaster filled the Western world with consternation. Pope Urban III. died of grief. Richard and Philip Augustus, the kings of England and France, who

were then at war, were so affected that they forgot their
private contentions, and thought only of the war with the
infidel. To provide the requisite funds, a tax, named Saladin's tithe, was laid on all ecclesiastical property. The two
kings embarked, each with a magnificent army. Philip was
the first to reach Palestine, and he joined the Christians, who
had been engaged for two years in the siege of Acre. This re-
inforcement enabled the besiegers to attempt an assault; but
Philip generously awaited the arrival of Richard, that the
English king might share the triumph and the honour.
Acre capitulated; the holy Cross was restored untouched; and
every thing seemed to announce a series of brilliant successes.
But Philip's health failed; he thought he had reason to com-
plain of Richard's conduct; and he resolved to return to
France, leaving with his ally 10,000 foot-soldiers and 500
cavalry, with money enough for three years' pay. Richard
gained an important victory over Saladin, and if he had
marched at once on Jerusalem, its fall would have been certain. His delay allowed the enemy to fortify the city; and
finding it impregnable, he made a truce with Saladin for three
years, and returned to Europe. Thus, the sole fruit of this
grand expedition was the capture of Acre, which became
a refuge and shelter for the Christians of the East, from
which they cast, during long years, wistful looks towards their
revered and beloved Jerusalem; but in vain. Richard meanwhile was thrown by a storm on the Adriatic coast, whence
he endeavoured to make his way in disguise through Austria.
He was discovered; and, in revenge for an affront put upon
Leopold at the siege of Acre, was detained a prisoner by the
duke until he was ransomed at an enormous sum.

The failure of the third Crusade did not discourage the
Christians. Shortly after the return of Philip Augustus, a
new expedition was undertaken by some French and Italians,
commanded by the Marquis of Montferrat, and Baldwin
Count of Flanders. It was agreed that they should meet at
Venice, whence the republic promised to convey them to the
Holy Land. The Venetians not only kept their word, they
equipped, besides, fifty galleys, and 500 of their noble youth
joined the Crusaders. While they were awaiting the proper
season for their voyage, the youthful Alexis, son of the emperor of Constantinople, came to implore their aid in behalf of
his father, whom a usurper had dethroned and thrown into

prison, after having plucked out his eyes. His promises were captivating—the extinction of the Greek schism; 200,000 marks of silver, and provisions for one year; and aid in the conquest of the Holy Land, where he engaged to maintain every year 500 knights for its defence. These offers were irresistible, although an acceptance of them involved a temporary abandonment of their great enterprise; and the Crusaders set sail for Constantinople. In six days they had taken the city; the usurper fled, and the youthful Alexis ascended the throne. Within a short time the new emperor was strangled by one of his officers, and the crown was usurped by the murderer. The Crusaders took counsel together, and deemed themselves authorised to avenge the death of Alexis; accordingly they captured the city a second time, and gave it up to pillage. In their capacity of masters of Constantinople, they now resolved to appoint one of their number as emperor; and their choice fell on Baldwin, Count of Flanders, whose virtues were reverenced and extolled by the Greeks themselves. Baldwin was crowned in the church of St. Sophia, and assumed the title and insignia of Emperor of the East.* This was in 1204. The Crusaders then divided amongst themselves the fairer parts of the European provinces, and abandoned their expedition to the Holy Land, in order to attend to these new possessions. Thus began the empire of the Latins at Constantinople, which lasted until the Greeks placed on the throne Michael Palæologus, a descendant of their ancient emperors.

Pope Innocent III., grieved and indignant that other and private interests had supplanted those with which the Crusaders had left Venice, besought the princes of Christendom to make one further effort; and the fifth Crusade was decreed at the fourth Lateran Council, in 1215. His successor, Honorius III., appointed Andrew II., king of Hungary, to lead the expedition; and his standard was followed by a great number of knights from Germany and France, amongst whom was John de Brienne, the destined King of Jerusalem. Andrew returned home when the Crusaders reached Acre.

---

* At this time was founded what historians call the Empire of Trebizond, on the Black Sea. The ancient masters of Constantinople took refuge there, to wait for better days. They regained their crown in 1261. The Empire of Trebizond, where many members of the imperial family continued to reside, was destroyed by Mahomet II. in 1461.

Damietta was captured; but a wasting sickness weakened the troops, incurable divisions arose among their leaders, and the Crusaders were reduced to a disgraceful capitulation. They retreated from Egypt, leaving John de Brienne as a hostage in the hands of the infidels.

The sixth Crusade was undertaken by the Emperor Frederick II., in accomplishment of a vow. He set forth under a ban of excommunication, on account of his systematic violation of his oaths, vows, and promises, and treated with the Sultan Meleden for the possession of Jerusalem. He wished to be crowned king of the Holy City; but no bishop would give the royal unction to a prince lying under the censure of the Church. Sixteen years later, Jerusalem was retaken by the infidels; and it was reserved for St. Louis to make one last great effort to wrest it from their polluting grasp.

§ 5. St. Francis of Assisi, St. Dominic, 1204-1221.

Of far greater interest and importance than the conquest of Byzantium was the contemporary origin of two of the most celebrated orders in the Church—the Franciscans and the Dominicans. The founder of the former was St. Francis, a native of Assisi, a small town in Italy. His father, who was a wealthy merchant, destined him for business, and gave him an education suited to his prospects. Although, in his youth, Francis took more interest in vain pleasures than in religion, he was, from his earliest years, remarkable for his tenderness and charity towards the poor. Once he refused an alms; and his regret was so keen, that he resolved never again to deny relief to any one who asked it for the love of God. A dangerous illness, for the time, disenchanted his soul of its illusions; but he again returned to the world and its vanities. His charity to the poor, however, daily increased. Meeting a poor gentleman shabbily dressed, he was so moved to pity, that he took off a new suit of clothes he wore, and made him put them on. At length, in obedience to the Divine inspiration with which he was favoured, he resolved to renounce the world, and to devote himself exclusively to the glory of God. On one occasion, he saw a leper, so disfigured as to excite disgust and horror. He reflected that the first step in the service of Christ is self-conquest; he dismounted from his horse, and kissed the leper as he gave him relief. Francis grew rapidly in grace, and became a new man; his

greatest enjoyment now was solitude, that he might meditate
undisturbed on the sufferings of our Lord Jesus Christ. His
contempt of the world, and his singular love of poverty,
greatly displeased his father, who ill-treated, and at length
disinherited him. Francis deemed himself richer than he had
ever been: "I am cast off by my father on earth," he said;
"I will commend myself to my Father in heaven." He then
withdrew to a little church called Portiuncula, or Our Lady
of the Angels, and devoted himself to the care of lepers, and
to the most repulsive works of mercy and humility. Having
heard in the Gospel one day the words addressed by our
Divine Lord to His Apostles: "*Do not possess gold, nor
silver, nor money in your purses: nor two coats, nor shoes,
nor a staff,*" a new light broke in upon his soul. He left
off shoes, threw away his staff, distributed his money among
the poor, and kept only a long cloak tied round his waist with
a girdle. He then began to preach, and to call the multitudes
to repentance, in words most simple, but remarkable for their
solidity and unction.

He soon found himself surrounded with disciples, who
imitated him in his penances and in his zeal; they preached
the Word of God, exhorting all whom they met to fear God
and to love Him, and to keep His commandments. Some listened with reverent attention; others ridiculed their uncouth
dress and their austerity of life. They were asked whence
they came, and what they were; often they were refused admission into houses, and were obliged to pass the night on
the steps of the churches. Sometimes they were injured as
well as insulted; children were taught to throw stones and
mud at them; but they rejoiced to be permitted to suffer for
the sake and in the cause of their Master. At length, their
disinterestedness and their patience dispersed all prejudices,
and they were every where venerated and welcomed.

When St. Francis saw the increasing number of his followers, he drew up for them a rule of life, which was, in reality, only a carrying out of the counsels of the Gospel; he
added a few lesser things, to insure uniformity in their mode
of life. He went to Rome, and his rule was approved by
Innocent III. The servant of God then led his little congregation to the church of Portiuncula, which was given to
them by the Benedictines; and there he formed his first
community. He then devoted himself to the training of

his disciples for their apostolate; he instructed them how
to grow in grace, and how to win souls to Christ; above all,
he recommended them to adhere firmly to the faith of the
Holy Roman Church. After having spoken much to them
on the kingdom of God, the contempt of the world, the renunciation of their own wills, and the mortification of their
bodies, he added: "Fear not because we are despised and
scorned of men; put your trust in God, who hath overcome
the world. You will meet with rude men who will ill-treat
you; learn to suffer with perfect patience." He then sent
them abroad into different countries, reserving for himself
the mission of Syria and Egypt, hoping to win there the
crown of martyrdom. He set sail with one chosen companion, and landed at Damietta, where Sultan Meledin then
lived. The sultan asked him, by whom he had been sent.
"The Most High God has sent me to show the way to heaven to you and to your people," was the intrepid answer.
The astonished sultan invited him to remain. "Willingly,"
answered the saint, "if you and your people will be converted.
And that you may feel no hesitation in forsaking the law of
Mahomet for that of Jesus Christ, kindle a large fire: I will
walk into the midst of it with your priests, that you may
know which of us is sheltered by the protection of God." "I
hardly think," said the sultan, with a smile, "that any of our
imaums will be eager to embrace your offer; besides, there
would be reason to dread some tumult." Nevertheless, Meledin was pleased with the discourse of the saint, and astonished at his refusal of the costly presents offered to him.
On his departure, the sultan said: "Pray for me, father, that
God may show me the religion which is most agreeable to
Him, and give me the courage to embrace it."

On his return from Egypt, Francis convoked a general
chapter of his order at Assisi. Five thousand religious obeyed
his summons. When some of them urged him to obtain from
the Pope the privilege of preaching wherever they pleased,
even without permission from the local bishops, he replied,
with warmth: "What! my brethren, do you not know the
will of God? It is His will that we should conciliate our
superiors by our humility and respect, that we may gain their
flocks by our teaching and our good example. When the
bishops see that you live holy lives, and that you do not wish
to weaken their just authority, they will implore you to la-

bour for the salvation of the souls committed to their charge. Let it be our singular privilege to have no privilege at all." When he felt his last hour approaching, St. Francis redoubled his penitential fervour. On the day of his death, he had the Passion of our Lord read to him; he then repeated the 141st Psalm, and expired as he uttered the words: "*The just wait for me, until Thou reward me.*" To this saint was granted the rare privilege of "bearing in his body," literally, the *stigmata*, or "marks of the Lord Jesus." His order assumed the name of Friars Minor.

St. Dominic was born of an illustrious family of Spain. From his earliest youth, he felt himself urged to labour for the salvation of souls, and especially for the conversion of those who were plunged into the thick darkness of error and heresy. He soon found an opportunity for exercising his zeal. He was canon-regular of the church of Osma, where Don Diego, the bishop, was charged by Innocent III. with a mission to instruct and bring back to the faith the Albigenses, who were then spreading their pestilential errors throughout Provence. Dominic accompanied his bishop in this apostolic mission, and laboured with characteristic ardour for the conversion of these heretics. The Albigenses were split into many sections; but all agreed in rejecting the authority and sacraments of the Church, and in opposing all her holy discipline. These fanatics were accustomed to assemble in large bodies, and pillage towns as well as villages, murder the priests who fell into their hands, desecrate the churches, and destroy the sacred vessels. The missionaries knew well the danger, as well as the difficulty, of their undertaking; but they had counted the cost, and were prepared to sacrifice their lives for the Gospel. God preserved them in a wonderful manner, amidst strange and manifold perils. Assassins once lay in wait for Dominic himself; but he escaped their hands. When he was asked, what he would have done if he had fallen into their hands, he said: "I should have given thanks to God, and besought Him to increase my torments, that my crown might be the more glorious." The missionaries held several conferences with the heretics, and not a day passed without some remarkable conversions; but the great body of the Albigenses became only the more enraged, and, supported by Raymond, Count of Toulouse, indulged in the most brutal violence and cruelty. A crusade was accordingly published against them; not so much by reason of their heresy, as because they disturbed the public peace, and violated the fundamental laws of society. Simon de Montfort was the leader of the army appointed to chastise and repress the seditious heretics; and although the cruelties committed by his troops cannot be justified, they may be explained, and even palliated, by the ferocity of the sectaries, and the horror and hatred which their enormities had inspired. In this military expedition Dominic had no part; either in advising, or in conducting it. The only arms he employed were, gentleness and patience, and the Word of God. He endeavoured to avert the terrible chastisement from the obstinate people; and, as he found that a large number of the crusaders were actuated only by the desire of pillage and the love of license, he laboured for their conversion as earnestly as he had done for that of the Albigenses.

Dominic now felt himself incited to found a society of apostolical men, who were first to sanctify themselves by the various practices of the religious life, and then to labour unweariedly for the diffusion of the faith, and the sanctification of their brethren. With this object, he attached to himself a few companions who were willing to follow the plan he had designed. The Bishop of Toulouse favoured the execution of the project with all his influence, and took Dominic with him to Rome in order to obtain the approbation of the Sovereign Pontiff. After some slight delay, the new institute was approved, and its constitutions confirmed. The bishop then gave the saint and his followers the first church they possessed, that of St. Romain, in Toulouse; and the pious citizens contributed largely towards this establishment. Their example was followed by the whole province; and soon Montpellier, Bayonne, Lyons, and other cities, possessed houses of the new order. The Friars Preachers, as they called themselves, soon became renowned far and wide, and many men of distinguished merit sought to enter the order. The holy patriarch then sent a number of his disciples into other lands, to preach repentance, and to defend the purity of the faith against heretics. Seven of them came to Paris, and through the exertions of the dean of St. Quentin, obtained a grant of the house of St. James. The little community, which was known as the Jacobins, from the name of their house, numbered thirty religious when St. Dominic visited it in 1219.

The holy founder had the consolation of seeing his work flourish, and longed to preach the gospel amongst the barbarians, and to shed his blood for Jesus Christ. He made preaching the primary object of his order; and prepared his disciples by imbuing them with an ardent charity for heretics and sinners, as well as exercising them in learning and the study of eloquence. He was asked one day in what book he had studied a sermon which he had just preached. "The book I used," said he in reply, "is the book of charity." Long before his death, he predicted the day and hour at which it would take place. Towards the end of July 1221, he said to some friends: "You see me now in perfect health, and yet ere the Assumption I shall have quitted this world." He was seized with a violent fever, and after exhorting his disciples to practise humility and the love of God, was laid, at his own request, on a bed of ashes, and peacefully surrendered his soul to God.

§ 6. The seventh and eighth Crusades, St. Louis, king of France, 1215-1270.

The thirteenth century was illustrated by the virtues of the king of one of the greatest nations of Europe. Louis IX. was scarcely twelve years of age when his father, Louis VIII., died. He was educated under the care of his mother, Blanche of Castile, who governed the kingdom as regent. This admirable queen instilled into her son the love of virtue; she often said to him, in words worthy of a Christian mother, "My son, dearly though I love you, I would rather see you lose your throne and your life, than stained with the guilt of one mortal sin." Louis never forgot the wise and holy teaching of his mother, followed up as it was by that of pious and able instructors. Throughout his life, he attested the value he placed on the grace of baptism, by the affection with which he regarded the place where he had received it. He sometimes signed his name "Louis de Poissy," as if to show that he preferred the common title of Christian to that of king. He was crowned at Rheims, on the first Sunday in Advent, 1226. In the esteem of the youthful king, it was no mere ceremony; he regarded it as a solemn engagement to labour for the welfare of his people. He prepared for it with great care, beseeching God to shed upon his soul the unction of His grace. His education had been as solid as it was appropriate;

he had learned the arts of government and war; he had deeply
studied history, that best school for princes; and, in short, he
was furnished with every kind of knowledge that befits and
adorns a king. He had also read many of the writings of the
Fathers, in order to sanctify his other studies. His aim was,
to discharge all his duties with scrupulous fidelity. Though
he could assume magnificence when it was necessary, he loved
simplicity and economy; his dress, his table, his court,—all
showed that he was opposed to pomp and display. He devoted several hours a-day to the exercises of religion; and
when some of his courtiers found fault with him for being
needlessly pious, he replied: "Men are strange beings; they
blame me for being attentive to prayer, and they would not
say a word if I were to waste whole days in games of chance,
or in hunting and shooting."

But the name of St. Louis is inseparably connected with
the Holy Land. Baldwin III., the Latin emperor of Constantinople, had come to France, to beg for aid and support
for his tottering throne. That throne, from the first, had
never been stable; and it was now vigorously assailed by
the Greeks. In gratitude for the kindness of St. Louis, Baldwin presented to him the crown of thorns of our Divine Lord,
which had been preserved from time immemorial in the chapel
of the palace of Constantinople. The pious prince received
this gift with indescribable joy and emotion. He went forth
to meet it as far as Villeneuve, accompanied by his court and
a numerous body of clergy. At sight of the sacred crown,
he burst into tears; and receiving it at the hands of those
who bore it, he carried it barefoot from the gates of Sens to
the church of St. Stephen. Some years later, he collected
other precious memorials of the Passion, and built for their
reception the exquisite chapel known as the Sainte Chapelle.
There he passed whole nights in prayer, absorbed in meditation on the sufferings of our Redeemer. But his piety did
not prejudice his royal duty. The monuments of his reign,
the noble establishments he founded, the wise and just laws
he enacted, show that his attention was directed to every de-
partment of his office.

It was during a dangerous illness that he resolved to undertake another crusade. His sickness had brought him to
the gate of death, when the application of a fragment of the
true Cross restored him to consciousness. The first words he

uttered expressed his desire to see the Bishop of Paris. On the arrival of the prelate, the king asked him for the Cross, as he purposed going to the rescue of the Holy Land. As he persisted in spite of every remonstrance, his request was granted; he kissed the Cross with joyful emotion, and declared that he felt himself perfectly cured of his disorder. The majority of his nobles, and a large proportion of the people, prepared to follow him to the Holy Land. The king's intention was, to carry the war into Egypt, into the heart of the enemy's country. They reached Damietta in safety, and found that strong city defended by a numerous army. The king then addressed his nobles in the following words: "My friends, it is by a special providence that we have undertaken this expedition; we cannot doubt that God has some great design to accomplish by us; we shall be invincible if we remain united; but whatever be the issue, it cannot fail to be of advantage to us. If we die, we secure the unfading crown of martyrdom; if we conquer, God will be glorified in our victory. Let us combat for Him, and He will triumph in us and for us. Do not be anxious about me; regard me only as a man whose life is in the hands of God." These words, and the air of intrepid resolution with which they were uttered, excited the enthusiasm of the troops to the highest pitch, and they advanced boldly towards the shore. The king leaped first into the water to gain the land, and was followed by all the Christian army. The impetuosity of the assailants was proof against the shower of arrows with which they were received, and soon the infidels took flight in terror and disorder. St. Louis entered the abandoned city, not with the pomp and pride of a conqueror, but with the humility of a truly Christian king—barefoot, and in a solemn procession of the nobles and clergy. His first care was, to render thanks to the God of victories; a mosque was purified and blessed, and in it Mass was said by the Papal legate.

The next step was to take Cairo, the capital of Egypt; but it was necessary first to defeat and dislodge a large body of infidels posted on the opposite side of the Ashmoum canal. The assault and the defence were equally spirited; but the temerity of the Count d'Artois, and his disobedience of orders, drew down on himself and on the Christian army a disastrous defeat. The result of the battle was, indeed, indecisive; but the enemy, being on his own territory, could easily repair his losses; whereas the Crusaders had no reinforcements on which to fall back. To make their position more desperate, a contagious disease broke forth in the camp, and prevented their moving for several months. In the train of pestilence followed famine; and the reduced army was compelled to retreat upon Damietta, followed by the enemy, and cruelly harassed on the march. The good king used every effort to secure a safe retreat, but all was in vain; he was taken prisoner, together with two of his brothers, and the greater part of his forces. St. Louis in prison was as much a king as when he sat in safety and peace on his throne; the very barbarians were awed by the majesty of his demeanour, and in their astonishment declared that he was the proudest Christian they had ever seen. Though treated with contumely and insult, he behaved always as a king whose grandeur does not depend on outward circumstances; as a Christian to whose heart God alone is all in all; as a hero whose soul is superior to every reverse. "You are in chains," said the barbarians, "and yet you treat us as if we were your captives." The sultan was so impressed by the dignity and patience of Louis, that he offered him his liberty, on payment of a considerable ransom for himself and his soldiers. "The person of a king of France can be neither bought nor sold for money," replied the king; "I will give for myself the city of Damietta, and for my subjects the sum you have mentioned." The sultan acceded to this offer, and, to testify his admiration, abated one-fifth of his demand. Before the treaty could be carried into effect, the sultan was killed by his emirs, and the king found himself involved in new and increased perplexities. Some of the infidels rushed madly into his prison, and would have slain him, but that they quailed before the intrepid king. They ratified the treaty anew, and even debated whether they should not make Louis their sultan. At length he was set at liberty, and performed the conditions of the treaty with perfect good faith.

Nevertheless, the infidels persisted in detaining a great number of French prisoners, whom they attempted to frighten and to torture into apostasy. St. Louis would not return to France until he had rescued those helpless prisoners; and in order to aid them, he sailed to Acre, where he was received with enthusiastic joy. Although he had but 6000 men, he would not relinquish his attempt, but remained for some time

in the Holy Land, to watch the course of events. He visited
the holy places with profound veneration. Having reached
Nazareth on the festival of the Annunciation, he alighted
from his horse and knelt in adoration; he then performed
the remainder of his journey on foot, and fasting. He used
every effort to improve the position of the Christians of
Palestine, and restored and fortified the few places which
still remained in their power. While thus occupied, he received tidings of the death of his mother, the Queen Blanche.
He was deeply affected by this bereavement, and kneeling
before the altar, he said: "O Lord, I bless Thee and give
Thee thanks that Thou hast so long spared me a mother so
worthy of my love; it was a gift of Thy mere mercy and
bounty; and now Thou hast resumed it, I do not murmur
or repine. It is true, she was dear to me beyond words; but
since Thou hast been pleased to take her to Thyself, blessed
be Thy holy name for ever." This loss hastened the king's
return to France, from which he had been six years absent.
One of his first acts was, to return public thanks to God in
the cathedral of St. Denis, which he enriched with many
costly gifts.

St. Louis would not abandon his hope, and regarded
himself still as a crusader. He was confirmed in his desire
to undertake a second expedition by the tidings which came
to him from Palestine. The infidels had captured many of
the towns which he had fortified, and were exercising the
most barbarous cruelties upon the Christians who refused to
apostatise. His appeal to his nobles was so successful, that
he soon found himself at the head of a numerous army, and
embarked for Tunis in July 1270. He had been led to hope
that the monarch of that country was prepared to become a
Christian; but his hope was vain; and he found himself obliged
to wait for reinforcements before undertaking the siege of a
city so well fortified and defended. But soon malignant fever
and dysentery made their appearance in his camp, and more
than half the army perished. The king himself was seized
with illness, and knew that his end was at hand. Yet never
did he appear more dignified than in these painful moments.
Notwithstanding his suffering and his weakness, he would not
remit his exertions; from his dying bed he issued his orders,
and testified his desire to soothe and mitigate the distresses
of his soldiers. He summoned all his remaining strength to

exhort and counsel his eldest son and successor, in words of singular and touching beauty. "My son," said the dying saint, "the first thing I commend to you is, to love God with all your heart, and to resolve to suffer any thing rather than commit a mortal sin." It is the echo of the earliest admonition of his sainted mother—the rule of all his own life. He then asked for the last sacraments, and received them with a fervour which moved those about him to tears. When he felt his last moment approaching, he ordered the attendants to lay him on a bed of ashes; and then, crossing his hands on his breast, he fixed his eyes on heaven, and said : "In the multitude of Thy mercy, I will come into Thine house; I will worship towards Thy holy temple." They were the last words of St. Louis.

REFLECTIONS ON THE CRUSADES.

It was the fashion during the last century—it is so still— to sneer at the Crusades. They were attributed to a gross fanaticism, to the ignorance of our ancestors; and their disasters were exaggerated, while their benefits were depreciated. Yet these expeditions were certainly beneficial, not only to the religion, but to the civilisation of the twelfth and thirteenth centuries. They were lawful in principle, since they were undertaken to rescue Christians from the outrages and persecutions of an infidel power; to free the sepulchre of our Lord from their profanation; and to arrest the tide of Arab invasion. They were mainly instrumental in liberating the serfs of Europe, and in laying the foundation of our civil liberties. The nobles were obliged to sell their estates and privileges, in order to provide for the expense of a distant and protracted war; and to this may be referred, in many instances, the origin of municipal rights. The Crusades likewise partially suspended those intestine dissensions and wars, which were sapping the strength of Europe; while they gave a new direction to the superfluous valour of the nobles. Commerce received a great impetus; navigation was brought to a greater perfection; new branches of industry were created. Sciences, letters, and arts acquired a higher value. The treasures of art in Constantinople were not lost upon the Crusaders; the languages of Europe acquired form and solidity; and the nations of Christendom were taught to feel their unity, by being

associated for a common object. Had they been as ably conducted as they were wisely planned, their effect would doubtless have been to reunite the East and the West; and Egypt,
Syria, and Greece would have become Christian colonies.
Then would have been renewed, under the influence of the
Gospel, the state of the world such as it was under Augustus:
all the seas would have been free; the cities would have exchanged their arts and their industry, and the nations their
productions and their knowledge.   But without pursuing
these considerations further, let us observe that, simply in
their religious aspect, the Crusades did, as a matter of fact,
bring back to God multitudes of sinners and of lukewarm
Christians.   Proud nobles joined them in expiation of their
crimes, and returned humbled and reformed—the examples
and the benefactors of their people, instead of their tyrants
and oppressors.   But their greatest effect was doubtless the
preservation of the faith in the West.   The Arabs and Turks
threatened Europe with desolation; and, but for the terror
inspired by the Crusaders, Germany and France, Italy and
England, might have been crushed, as Greece and Palestine
were crushed, under the heel of a polluting and barbarous
power.   The fall of the Greek empire was retarded for at
least two centuries; and it is easy to see how much more
might have been effected, could the monarchs of Europe have
been persuaded, by the constant and earnest entreaties of the
Sovereign Pontiff, to lay aside their selfish animosities and
ambitious designs, and unite for the defence of Christendom,
and the liberation of the East.   The Christian will reflect
further, that the Crusades were approved by the best and
wisest men of their times; that they were authorised and
blessed by the Church; and that they failed not of their end
in the counsels of God, although their results did not fulfil
the sanguine expectations of their promoters.   That they did
not accomplish all that the Church desired, should not lead
us to imagine that they did not accomplish the end for which
God permitted them.   Anyhow, they were an outburst of
love for His Incarnate Son, whose majesty had been insulted,
and whose humiliations had been derided, in the profanation
of the holy places in which His divine footsteps had trod
and His blood had been shed for the redemption of mankind;
and as such they were acceptable to Heaven, and the occasion
of untold merit to many thousands of souls.

CHAPTER VII.

FROM THE DEATH OF ST. LOUIS, 1270, TO THE FALL OF THE EASTERN EMPIRE, 1454.

§ 1. St. Thomas Aquinas, St. Bonaventura, 1227-1274.

Four years after the death of St. Louis, the Church bewailed the loss of two of her profoundest and most illustrious doctors, who had been the consolation and the guide of the new orders founded by St. Dominic and St. Francis. If we weigh well the services which the religious orders have rendered to the Church,—their influence on the conversion, instruction, and civilisation of the nations; the aid they have given to the pastor in the care of his flock; the noble vindications and expositions of the faith they have produced,—we must allow that they have been the most fruitful sources of benediction to the Church and to the world. So felt St. Louis. He had a special regard for the Friars Minors and the Friars Preachers —the Dominicans and the Franciscans. He admired, as every Christian must admire, their zeal for the salvation of souls, their profound humility, their penitential and mortified mode of life, and their perfect disinterestedness. He often said, that if he could divide himself into two parts, he would give one to the sons of St. Francis, and the other to those of St. Dominic.

St. Thomas Aquinas, the ornament and glory of the Dominicans, was born of a noble family in the kingdom of Naples. He received an education suited to his birth, and to the brilliant prospects which lay before him. He was sent to the most celebrated schools of Italy, to Monte Casino, and to the then renowned university of Naples. There he manifested the most brilliant talents and the purest virtue. Some conversations he had with a Dominican of singular holiness, inspired him with a strong desire to join that order; and he assumed its habit in his seventeenth year. His family tried every means to shake his resolution; but in vain. At last they shut him up, and treated him with great severity, and even endeavoured to lead him into grievous sin; but Thomas continued firm, and resisted every inducement and every

temptation.   He renewed the dedication of himself to God,
and besought Him to grant him grace according to his need.
God heard his prayer; he was soon set at liberty to follow his
vocation.   His superiors then sent him to Cologne, to study
theology in the school of Albert the Great.   Under a master
so learned, he soon made wonderful progress; but, lest he
should be tempted to pride, he concealed his learning, and
seldom uttered a word.   His silence was taken as an indication of stupidity, and he was called by his fellow-students in
derision "the Dumb Ox."   His master, who had taken a more
accurate measure of his capacity, reproved them for their un-
mannerly conduct; telling them that the bellowing of that ox
would one day echo from one end of the earth to the other;
nor was he deceived in his estimate of Thomas's powers.
After having finished his studies and received the degree of
doctor, Thomas went to Paris, where he taught for some time
with brilliant success; his numerous writings spread his fame
far and wide; but the holy doctor attributed his learning far
less to study than to prayer.   He always invoked the aid of
the Holy Spirit before study or composition; and his prayers
were increased whenever the subjects of his investigations
were unusually recondite.   Clement IV. offered him the archbishopric of Naples, which the holy doctor declined.   The
Pope yielded to his earnest entreaties, but commanded him to
attend a council which was summoned at Lyons.   Thomas
obeyed, although he was then ill of a fever.   His illness increased during the journey, so that he was obliged to stop at
a monastery of the diocese of Terracina, where he died in the
year 1274.   When the ambassadors of the king of Naples
came to solicit his canonisation, the Pope declared that
Thomas alone had done more to enlighten the Church than
all her doctors together.   But the most magnificent and
decisive testimony to his merit was given by the Council of
Trent.   On a table in the middle of the hall in which the
sessions of the council were held, were placed the Holy Scriptures, the decrees of the Popes, and the *Summa* of St. Thomas.
His theological writings were not his only labours.   He was
an indefatigable teacher of the young, who thronged to his
lectures with avidity; he was frequently consulted by St.
Louis on temporal matters; he preached constantly; and his
journeys were numerous and long.   He is said to have kept
three or four amanuenses, to whom he dictated on different

subjects at the same time. On one occasion, when dining at the table of St. Louis, he seemed wrapped in thought, and suddenly striking the table with his clenched fist, he exclaimed, "There; the Manichæans are done for!" He had solved his problem, and had utterly forgotten where he was, until recalled to himself by the merriment of the pious king. On his merits, and on those of his contemporaries and successors in the schools, it may suffice to quote the words of the Protestant historian Neander. "The whole systematic theology of these centuries," says that writer, "we see interpenetrated and quickened by that which St. Augustine has represented as the principle of living Christianity. Very far indeed were these theologians from substituting any form of legality for living Christianity. .... On this foundation proceeded also the schoolmen of the thirteenth century; and new and profound explanations of the progressive development of the Christian life were added by them."

St. Bonaventura conferred on the Franciscan order scarcely less honour than St. Thomas had conferred on the Dominicans. His original name, like that of his father, was John of Fidenza; and he was born in 1238 at Bagnarea, not far from Viterbo, in Italy. He obtained the name of Bonaventura in consequence of St. Francis of Assisi exclaiming, as he foresaw the extraordinary graces which God had prepared for the child, *O buona ventura!* "O good fortune!" When only four years old, he was seized with a dangerous illness. His distracted mother went to St. Francis; and the saint obtained, by his prayers, the recovery of her child. Bonaventura never forgot this great favour granted him by God; and at the age of twenty-two he entered the order of the Friars Minors. Shortly afterwards he was sent to Paris to complete his studies under the celebrated Alexander of Hales, one of the most learned members of the Franciscan order. There Bonaventura became acquainted with St. Thomas, and the friends received the degree of doctor at the same time. Their friendship deepened throughout life. One day St. Thomas, going to visit his friend, saw him through the door of his cell miraculously raised above the ground while employed in writing the life of St. Francis. "Let us not interrupt him," said he; "let us leave a saint to write the life of a saint." St. Bonaventura occupied the chair of theology at Paris for many years with great distinction. In his lectures he showed that he was

less anxious to form learned scholars than to train humble
and reverent Christians; and while he taught them what they
were to believe, his example showed them what they ought to
do. He was only thirty-five years of age when he was placed,
in spite of his remonstrances, at the head of his order; and he
governed it with equal prudence and ability. Pope Gregory X.
conceived such an esteem for him, that he resolved to make
him a cardinal; the holy doctor quietly made his escape from
Italy; but the Pope sent him a summons to repair to Rome.
On his way he stopped for a while to repose himself at a convent of his order near Florence; and there two Papal nuncios,
who were sent to meet him with the cardinal's hat, found him
in the act of washing the dishes. The saint desired them to
hang the hat on a bush that was near, as his hands were not
in a fit condition to receive it, and to take a walk in the garden until he had finished what he was about. Then taking
up the hat with unfeigned sorrow, he joined the nuncios, and
paid them the respect due to their character. Shortly afterwards the Pope consecrated him with his own hands Bishop
of Albano, and commanded him to assist at the approaching
Council of Lyons. St. Bonaventura obeyed, and preached at
the second and third sessions. Then his strength failed him,
and he died before the council had closed its deliberations.
He has left a great number of writings, remarkable for their
combination of mystical with dialectical theology. They
breathe a piety at once deep and fervent; and they have de-
servedly placed him at the head of the great masters of the
spiritual life.

Nor should we omit honourable mention of the Dominican
Albert the Great, the master of St. Thomas at Cologne. He
was descended from an ancient family of princely rank, and
was born at Lawingen in 1193; entered the Dominican order
in 1223; studied at Paris, Padua, and Bologna; and taught at
Hildesheim, Freiburg, Ratisbon, Strasburg, Paris, and Cologne. The last-named city especially was the scene of his
wonderful activity as a teacher. In 1260 he was compelled
by the Pope to accept the bishopric of Ratisbon; but, at the
expiration of two years, he implored the Holy Father to allow
him to resign his see, that he might return to Cologne and
resume his duties as a teacher and writer. He was present
at the Council of Lyons, and died in 1280. His capacious
mind was stored with all the whole compass of knowledge

accessible in his day.   He is said to have been possessed of
extraordinary faculties for the investigation of truth, and to
have abounded in profound and suggestive ideas, which stimulated the minds of his scholars.   It is a sufficient glory to
have moulded the mind of his great disciple, St. Thomas.

§ 2. General Council of Lyons, Reunion of the separated Greeks, 1274.

The Council of Lyons, to which Pope Gregory X. had
summoned the celebrated men already enumerated, was called
for the special purpose of reuniting the Greeks to the Catholic
Church, from which they had been so long severed.   It was
opened on the 27th May 1274, and closed on July 17th in the
same year.   There were present 500 bishops and 70 mitred
abbots.   James, king of Arragon, and many other princes
and ambassadors, attended the sessions of the council, and took
a lively interest in its deliberations.   Michael Palæologus, the
emperor of Constantinople, greatly desired this union from
motives of temporal policy ; he dreaded lest the Latin princes
should combine to restore Baldwin III., whom he had just
driven from the imperial throne; and, in order to avert the
threatening storm, he applied to the Pope, and promised to
exert his authority to heal the schism.   The Pope was delighted at the prospect, and deemed the circumstances favourable to the accomplishment of an object for which his predecessors had never ceased to labour.   Michael solicited Gregory to summon the council, and sent thither, with four other
ambassadors, Germanus, formerly patriarch of Constantinople,
and Theophanes, the metropolitan of Nicæa.   They were intrusted with a letter to the Pope, in which he was styled the
First and Supreme Pontiff, the common Father of all Christians.
They were bearers also of another letter, written in the name
of thirty-five Greek archbishops and their suffragans, and expressive of their cordial concurrence in the project of a reunion.
The ambassadors were met on their arrival by all the Latin
fathers of the council, and conducted into the presence of the
Pope, who received them standing, and gave them the kiss of
peace with every token of fatherly affection.   The ambassadors, on their part, paid to the Sovereign Pontiff the respect
due to the Vicar of Jesus Christ, and head of the universal
Church.   They declared that they came, in the name of the
emperor and bishops of the East, to pay their tribute of alle-

giance and obedience to the Roman Church, and to profess one and the same faith with it; a declaration which diffused universal joy. On St. Peter's day, the Pope celebrated Mass in the cathedral, in presence of the council. When the Creed had been said in Latin, the Greek bishops repeated it in Greek, to attest their unity of faith with the Sovereign Pontiff. In the council they sat on the Pope's right hand, immediately below the cardinals. The letters they had brought were read; and George Acropolites, high-treasurer of the empire, in the name of his countrymen, abjured the schism, accepted the faith of the Roman Church, and confessed the supremacy of the Holy See. After a few words, in which the Pope, with tears in his eyes, expressed the Church's joy in pressing once more all her children to her maternal bosom, he intoned the *Te Deum*, and the council gave hearty thanks to God. Every thing seemed to promise a durable union of the East and West; it lasted throughout the reign of Michael Palæologus; but the newly-healed schism was opened afresh by his successor.

And now the end of the thirteenth century was at hand. Pope Boniface VIII., wishing to show his favour to the numerous pilgrims who flocked to Rome at the close of each century, promulgated a jubilee,—that is, a plenary indulgence granted to all those who, being truly contrite, and having confessed their sins, should visit for thirty successive days, if they were inhabitants of Rome,—and for fifteen days, if they were only visitors,—the churches of the Apostles St. Peter and St. Paul, and should pray for the welfare of the holy Catholic Church. This was the first secular jubilee, or jubilee marking the close of a century. Succeeding Popes extended the conditions of the indulgence; allowing it to be gained by those who could not visit Rome, on condition of their complying with the other conditions. Clement VI., in 1350, appointed the jubilee to be held every fifty years, after the manner of the jubilees of the Jews. Lastly, Pope Urban VI., reflecting on the small number of those who could avail themselves of this boon, decreed a jubilee every twenty-fifth year; and this is the rule in our own day.

§ 3. The great Schism of the West, Council of Constance, 1378-1449.

Towards the end of the fourteenth century, a schism, more scandalous even than that of the Greeks, harassed and laid waste the Church. Pope Clement V., who was a native of France, was driven by the violence of the Italian nobles to fix his abode at Avignon, in 1309; and his successors followed his example. Italy suffered greatly from the absence of the Popes; and Rome, in particular, was torn by contending factions. There was one universal and eager cry for the return of the Sovereign Pontiff to his own see. At length, in 1377, Gregory XI. yielded to the entreaties of the people, and was welcomed at Rome with extraordinary enthusiasm. After his death, the Roman people, apprehending that if the new Pope were a Frenchman he would return to Avignon, collected round the building in which the cardinals were assembled, and shouted, " We will have a Roman Pope!" They threatened the conclave that, if their request were not granted, they would make their heads as red as their hats. The terrified cardinals hastily elected the Archbishop of Bari, who took the name of Urban VI. They shortly afterwards deliberately confirmed the election, and were all present at the Pope's enthronisation. Urban, though remarkable for the piety and austerity of his life, and his zeal against abuses, was unhappily a man of a stern and inflexible character; and his severity soon alienated the majority of those who had elected him. All the cardinals, with the exception of four who were natives of Italy, retired from Rome; they declared that their election was null and void, as having been made under compulsion, and chose another Pope under the name of Clement VII. This unhappy event threw the Church into confusion. Christendom was divided between the two Popes. Clement was recognised in France, Spain, Scotland, and Sicily; while Urban was supported and obeyed by England, Hungary, Bohemia, and a part of Germany. Excommunications were pronounced on both sides, and dissensions were increased, and men's minds exasperated by deeds of deplorable violence. The schism was perpetuated by the adherents of each Pontiff electing a successor on the death of the respective claimants of the Papal throne. At length the cardinals and prelates of both parties met in synod at Pisa, with the hope of extinguishing the schism. They took upon themselves to depose both the existing claims, without, however, deciding on their respective pretensions, and by the same assumed authority elected Alexander V. as Pope. Their motive was good, but the act was irregular; and the effect was merely to increase the confusion that prevailed. Instead of two, there were now three claimants of the Papacy, each of whom was regarded by his own party as the only lawful Pontiff. The jealousy of the cardinals of the several obedi- ences, the conflicting interests of temporal princes, the ani- mosity of the people, seemed to threaten the continuance of the schism; but the promise of Jesus Christ was accom- plished, and the danger was dissipated. All the obstacles in- terposed by human passion or policy were removed by a coun- cil held, with the concurrence of all three claimants, at Con- stance, in 1414, at which Gregory XII., Urban's successor, and therefore lawful Pope, voluntarily resigned; the two anti-Popes, John XXII. and Benedict XIII., were deposed; and a new Pope was elected, who took the name of Martin V. Benedict obstinately persisted to the last in asserting his unlawful claims, and died in schism.

It is worthy of notice that the Council of Constance be- came a really general council, and not a mere assembly of cardinals and bishops, only by the act of Gregory convok- ing it, and authorising its proceedings before resigning the Papacy. It should be observed also, that although opin- ions differed as to the right of the several claimants, there was but one belief as to the authority of the Apostolic See, and the necessity of union with it. Hence this disastrous schism was less injurious to individual Christians than many lesser scandals. And this is noticed by St. Antoninus, Arch- bishop of Florence, who wrote about the middle of the following century. "It is conceivable," he says, "that a person might belong to one or the other party in perfect sincerity, and with a safe conscience; for, although it is ne- cessary to believe that there is, and can be, but one visible head of the Church, it is not necessary to believe that this or that rival claimant is the legitimate Pope. All that is necessary to be believed is, that the true and lawful Pope is he who has been canonically elected; and an ordinary Christian is not obliged to discover which election has been canonical. He may safely follow the opinion and the conduct of his pas- tor." The great design of God in the sanctification of His elect was not frustrated by these scandals; and on both sides there were persons whom the Church now numbers amongst her saints.

Besides the healing of this schism, the Council of Constance was summoned to condemn the heresies which had been spread throughout Germany, in consequence of the relaxation of discipline. The originator of these heresies was John Wickliff, a doctor of the University of Oxford, whose wild and fanatical opinions were condemned by Pope Urban V., as well as by the bishops of England. The heresiarch then pushed his conclusions further still, and assailed the whole ecclesiastical hierarchy. He taught that the Pope is not the head of the Church, that bishops have no pre-eminence over simple priests, that all ecclesiastical powers are forfeited or in abeyance during mortal sin, and that confession is utterly useless. These errors produced at that time but little effect in England; and on the death of Wickliff, his few followers were scattered and came to nothing; but he had left many writings infected with the venom of his heresies. These writings were taken to Prague by a gentleman of Bohemia, who had been studying at Oxford, and by him communicated to John Huss, rector of the University of Prague. This unhappy man imbibed the pernicious teaching of Wickliff, and began to preach his doctrines with extraordinary zeal. He added some new errors of his own, and drew to him a number of disciples, among whom Jerome of Prague was the most violent. The new sect began to spread in Bohemia, and the efforts of the bishop, though seconded by the Pope, were unable to repress it. John Huss meanwhile continued to preach with great success in the towns and villages of Bohemia. Things were in this state when the Council of Constance met. John Huss came to defend his heresy in person. Before leaving Prague, he had affixed to the doors of the church an insolent notice, in which he declared himself ready to undergo the punishments decreed against heretics if he could be convicted of any error contrary to the faith. After this declaration, the Emperor Sigismund gave him a safe-conduct, not to shelter him from the punishment to which he professed his readiness to submit, but to protect him during his journey, and to procure him an opportunity of vindicating himself from the charges brought against him. He had no sooner reached Constance than he began to teach, without awaiting the decision of the council on his doctrine. He was then seized, and his writings were examined by commissioners appointed by the council. They were found replete with errors; he was urged to retract; but in vain. He

was present at the session of the 5th June, and many of the
errors he had adopted from Wickliff were produced. He
was allowed time to explain his meaning in regard to each
article, and then urged to submit to the judgment of the
council. A form of retractation was set before him, but he
obstinately refused to sign it. The council repeated the attempt several times; they first condemned his writings to
the flames, hoping that this step would intimidate him. As
he persisted in his obstinacy, he was solemnly degraded and
given up to the magistrates of Constance, who, in accordance
with the laws of the empire, condemned him to be burnt.
Jerome, his disciple, suffered the same punishment. The
council did not urge his death, but simply allowed the civil
law to take its course; and that law regarded him as one
who disturbed social order, by preaching doctrines which
were anarchical and revolutionary as well as heretical.

The Council of Constance closed the schism by establishing Martin V. in the chair of St. Peter. The Pope had summoned another council at Basle, for the year 1431, but he
died before it was assembled. His successor, Eugenius IV.,
sent a legate as his representative; but the council cited the
Pope to appear in person, and on his refusal deposed him.
Eugenius then dissolved the council, and convoked another
at Florence, to treat of the reunion of the Greek schismatics.
The Council of Basle retorted by anathematising the Pontiff,
and opposing to him an anti-pope, Amadeus, duke of Savoy,
who took the name of Felix V. This schism was, mercifully,
of brief duration. The Council of Basle was discredited every
where, and ended by submitting to the Pope in 1449. Thus
the Church regained the blessing of peace after a discord of
seventy years.

§ 4. Council of Florence for the second reunion of the Greeks, Capture of Constantinople, 1439-1453.

The Council of Florence, of which mention has just been
made, was held in 1439, and its occasion was as follows.
Since the relapse of the Greeks into schism, the sovereign
Pontiffs had made many fruitless attempts to bring them
to a better mind. At length, in 1437, the Greek emperor,
John Palæologus II., and Pope Eugenius IV., renewed negotiations, and agreed that a general council should be held in

the West, composed of Greeks and Latins alike. In virtue of this agreement, the council was opened by the Pope in person at Ferrara, in Italy; the emperor and the aged patriarch of Constantinople attended it, with twenty archbishops of the East, and a large number of subordinate clergy. The patriarchs of Alexandria, Antioch, and Jerusalem also sent their representatives. As Ferrara was found inconvenient, the council was transferred to Florence, with the full consent of the Greeks. After all the difficulties had been discussed and settled, the emperor, the patriarch, and all the Greek prelates adopted the Roman confession of faith, recognising fully the procession of the Holy Spirit from the Father and the Son, and the universal primacy of the Pope. Thereupon the reunion was decided on; a decree was drawn up rehearsing the points which the Greeks had formerly contested, and was signed by the Pope and all the oriental bishops except the bishop of Ephesus, who persisted in his refusal. Thus this important affair was brought to a termination, which occasioned great joy throughout the Church; but it was a joy of brief duration. On their return to Constantinople, the Greeks found the people and the inferior clergy irritated and prejudiced against the union. They loaded with insults all who had signed the decree; and exalted to the skies the bishop of Ephesus, the one solitary recusant. Thereupon several of the bishops retracted their assent to the decrees of the council; the patriarch Joseph had died at Florence; his successors laboured in vain to bring the Greeks to reason; and at length, in spite of the efforts of the emperor to the contrary, the three patriarchs of Alexandria, Antioch, and Jerusalem annulled all that had been effected; the monks, the clergy, and the people rose in open revolt, and proclaimed the union entirely and for ever at an end. Some years later, Nicolas V., a pontiff of great piety, reflecting on the inefficacy of the means which had been employed to convert the Greeks, wrote them a letter, in which he expatiated on the gigantic preparations of the Turks, and exhorted them to open their eyes to the results of their obstinacy ere it was too late. " Long time," wrote the holy Pope, " have you abused the patience of God by persisting in your schism. God is waiting, as in the parable, to see whether the fig-tree which has been tended with such care will at last yield its fruit; but if within three years it shall bear none, the tree will be hewn down, and the Greeks will be overwhelmed by the justice of God." We shall see how exactly this prediction was fulfilled.

Mahomet II., having resolved to reduce Constantinople, began the siege, in 1453, with an army of 250,000 men, and 150 galleys of the first class, having on board 24,000 soldiers. The garrison of the ill-fated city consisted only of 7000 Greeks and 2000 foreigners, under Giustiniani, a Genoese officer of great skill and experience. Nothing had been neglected that could strengthen the fortifications. As the city was surrounded by a double wall, Mahomet prepared fourteen batteries, in which were cannon of prodigious size; some of them could discharge blocks of stone weighing two hundred weight. These batteries played day and night on the city, and soon effected several large breaches in the walls. The besieged resisted valiantly, repairing the breaches as they were formed, and making impetuous sallies, in which they killed many Turks, and destroyed their works. The infidels were discouraged, and would have abandoned the siege; but Mahomet stimulated them to fresh exertions, by promising them the pillage of the city, and led them on to a general assault by land and by sea. The defence of the Greeks was heroic and protracted until Giustiniani was obliged to leave his post, dangerously wounded. They then lost courage and gave way. The Turks poured through the breach, pursued the fugitives, and put the greater part of them to the sword. The emperor, whose valour deserved a happier fate, had taken his stand in the breach; he was hurried along by the impetuous throng, and perished in the confusion. After the death of the emperor, the Turks met no resistance; they took possession of the city, and nothing escaped the ravages of the conquerors. The greater part of the inhabitants were slain or sold into slavery; and the great church of Santa Sophia was desecrated and converted into a Turkish mosque.

Thus fell the empire of Constantinople after a duration of 1123 years. Its fate was regarded as a manifest judgment on the Greeks for their perverse and obstinate schism. God had borne long time with them, and they had refused to hear His voice. They would not submit to the paternal sway of the successor of St. Peter; they fell into the hands of the infidel, and " they that hated them have dominion over them."

Thus every nation and kingdom which opposes the kingdom of God is threatened with the divine malediction, and shall perish and come to naught.

CHAPTER VIII.

FROM THE TAKING OF CONSTANTINOPLE BY THE TURKS
TO THE CLOSE OF THE COUNCIL OF TRENT, 1453-1563.

THE grief and indignation of Christendom at the success of the infidels, and the overthrow of the eastern empire, were so great, that it seemed as though the princes of Europe were about to unite and march against the conquerors. Pope Pius II. used every effort to inaugurate another Crusade, and would have accompanied the army in person, but he died on the eve of its departure, and with him vanished the last faint hope of the Greeks. Their only remaining consolation was, that Mahomet II. used his victory with moderation; he tolerated the Christian religion, and even appointed a patriarch to the vacant see of Constantinople.

At this time the Church was edified by the conspicuous holiness of St. Francis of Paula, whom God raised up to found a new religious order, specially consecrated to penitence and humility. St. Francis was born in 1416, in the little town of Paula, from which his name is derived. He was carefully educated by his pious parents; and at an early age felt himself drawn towards an austere and mortified life. He ate neither meat, nor fish, nor eggs; nor would he drink milk; and to this rule he adhered throughout his life. Urged by a strong religious instinct, he withdrew into a cave near the sea, and devoted himself to a life of contemplation. His bed was the rocky floor of his cave; the herbs which grew near it were his only food; and beneath a worn and tattered cloak he wore a shirt of hair. Soon many young men besought that they might be allowed to share his retreat, and place themselves under his rule. He received them; and a few cells, with an oratory, were built near his cave. This was the lowly cradle of the new order. The rapid increase of his community compelled him ere long to build a monastery and a church, the funds for which were furnished by the people of the neighbourhood. The rule he prescribed was, to keep a perpetual Lent; and he gave his disciples the name of *Minims*, to show them that they were to regard themselves as the least and lowest of the monastic orders. His institute was approved by Sixtus IV. in 1474. Louis XI., king of France, having heard of the extraordinary sanctity of Francis, sent for him, hoping to obtain through his prayers the cure of an inveterate disease. The Pope commanded Francis to comply with the king's summons; the saint obeyed, and was received with every mark of veneration. Louis threw himself at his feet, and implored him to obtain from God the restoration of his health; but Francis strove rather to lead the monarch to submit to the will of God, and to prepare to offer his life as a sacrifice to Him. Throughout the court he was known as "the holy man," "the man of God." The successors of Louis lavished their favours on him; and his order extended not only throughout Italy and France, but into Spain and Germany. He was taken ill in the convent of Plessis-le-Tours, on Palm Sunday 1507; on Holy Thursday, after collecting his religious in the church, he received the Holy Eucharist, as prescribed by his rule for that day, barefoot, and with a cord round his neck; and died on Good Friday, exhorting his disciples to adhere strictly to their rule, and to love one another.

§ 1. The pretended Reformation in Germany, 1517-1545.

The Church of Christ on earth is ever militant,—that is to say, ever in conflict. That which Luther occasioned in the beginning of the sixteenth century, was the most fearful and the most deadly she had known since the downfall of Arianism: Luther, by birth a Saxon, was a monk of the order of St. Augustine, and professor in the University of Wittenberg. He possessed great natural powers, but they were perverted by a proud and restless disposition and a refractory will. In the solitude of the cloister he had adopted heretical theories on the subject of faith, which he also covertly taught from his professorial chair. But the pretext he seized upon for the first public manifestation of his errors, was the promulgation of a plenary indulgence by Leo X. He openly assailed, not only the doctrine of indulgences, but the very first principles of the Catholic religion on which that doctrine is founded.

He then went rapidly forward in the career of innovation, and impugned the teaching of the Church on original sin and predestination, on justification and the sacraments. When his impious novelties were condemned by the Pope, the impetuous heresiarch attacked the supremacy of the see of St. Peter; and pushed his errors further and further to their logical consequences, until he revived the heresies and the seditious principles of the Albigenses, of Wickliff, and of John Huss. He wrote, in coarse and insolent style, against purgatory, freewill, the merit of good works, and, in short, against almost every article of the Christian faith. This was the beginning of that melancholy apostasy which he ventured to call a *Reformation.** To obtain the support of the world, Luther exhorted the princes of Germany to confiscate the property of the Church. It was a tempting bait; and the hope of a share in the magnificent spoils drew to his party a great number of powerful nobles. Frederic, the elector of Saxony, and Philip, landgrave of Hesse, openly espoused his cause. The favour of the latter prince was secured by other means still more shameful. Philip wished to contract a second marriage, his first wife being still alive. He applied to Luther, who assembled the leaders of the religious revolt, and procured from them a permission to the landgrave to have two wives at the same time. He assailed also the monastic institute and the celibacy of the clergy; and to give the more effect to his assault, he did not scruple to commit the double sacrilege of taking as his wife a young nun, whom he had enticed from her convent. Lessons such as these, enforced by such examples, were too acceptable to the corrupt heart of man to be neglected; and the new sect made rapid progress. From Upper Saxony it spread into the south, into the duchies of Brunswick, Mecklenburg, Pomerania, and Prussia, where Albert of Brandenburg, grand master of the Teutonic order, became a Lutheran, and appropriated the property of his community. When Luther thus found himself at the head of a powerful party, he abandoned all reserve, and poured out a torrent of invectives against the Pope, the Church, and the doctrines of the faith. It is a melancholy task to peruse the

* The followers of Luther were called *Protestants*, because of their protest against a decree of the Emperor Charles V., in the diet of Spires, in 1529. This decree was to the effect that Lutheranism should be excluded from all those countries which it had not yet infected, but that it should be tolerated wherever it had already established itself.

coarse jests, the low and disgusting buffoonery, the vile indecencies, with which his books are filled; and it is difficult to conceive how such a leader could have found followers. The relaxation of all restraints, the love of money and of pleasure, must have deeply corrupted the hearts of both clergy and people ere they could have stooped to such degradation.

When Luther had once set the example of innovation and revolt, there rose up a great number of pretended reformers, whose views accorded more or less with his own. Calvin, who is regarded as second only to Luther, was born at Noyon, and studied at Paris, Orleans, and Bourges. His teacher at this last place was a German professor, who had adopted the Protestant errors. Calvin imbibed the pernicious novelties of his master with eagerness, and expressed his sentiments with characteristic vehemence. When Francis I. of France had resolved to check the progress of Lutheranism within his dominions, Calvin retired to Basle, and during his sojourn in that city published his *Institutes*, which contain a compendious account of his doctrine. He differed from Luther especially on the article of the Eucharist; he taught that free-will was entirely destroyed by the fall; that the reprobate were damned by God's absolute decree; he rejected the invocation of the saints, purgatory, and indulgences; he renounced, not only the Pope, but bishops and priests; and abolished festivals and sacred ceremonies, and all those sensible means by which the minds and hearts of men are raised to the contemplation and worship of God. Luther never succeeded in ridding himself of the conviction of our Lord's real presence in the Blessed Sacrament; but the logic of Calvin was more consecutive and daring; he rejected it utterly. Yet his works show that he was unable to accept with comfort the express words of Jesus Christ; and that he was irritated by the constant and universal belief of the mystery they reveal. The innovator travelled far and wide to spread his opinions; and at last settled at Geneva, which had expelled its bishop some years before, and embraced the doctrines of Luther. At Geneva he taught theology, and preached constantly. He made it the centre and pivot of his operations upon France and the rest of Europe. His power was absolute, and was used with extreme rigour. No one dared to oppose him; and he who taught that it was sinful to hear and to obey the Church, exacted from all around him the blindest submission to his doctrines and his will. A physician of Geneva, Michael Servetus by name, carried out Calvin's theory of private judgment somewhat further than his master, and advanced some errors on the mystery of the Holy Trinity. He was burnt by Calvin's direction; and yet the same Calvin declaimed with intense bitterness against the severity with which heretics were treated in France. He assailed with revolting abuse those whom he could reach with no other weapons; his adversaries were described as swine, as wild-beasts, as asses, as dogs, &c. We need only compare this gross and violent language with that employed by the Pope, or by any Catholic controversialist of the day, to feel the infinite difference between the accredited messengers of God, and the teachers of impious novelties.

Although heresy is based upon the principle, that every man may form his own religious opinions for himself, it has always shown itself in practice to be overbearing and merciless. Itself the enemy of all subordination, it is intolerant of opposition. The temporal as well as the spiritual power was denounced, if it did not at once accept the dogmas of the new teachers. "If I am at liberty," said Luther to his sovereign, "to trample under my feet with contempt the decrees of Popes and the canons of councils, in my zeal for Christian freedom, do you think that I shall yield obedience to your commands?" The teaching of this heresiarch relaxed the bonds of social as well as of religious obligation. It plunged Europe into a war which is almost without parallel for ferocity. In Germany the peasants, acting on Luther's teaching, took up arms and ravaged the provinces of Suabia, Franconia, and Alsace; they pillaged and then burnt the churches, destroyed alike monasteries and castles, and slaughtered the priests and the monks. They numbered 72,000 men, and Charles V. had great difficulty in reducing them to submission. The saints were to possess the earth; *they* were the saints; why should they not take their own inheritance? Thus also France was a prey, during three consecutive reigns, to all the ravages and miseries of civil war. The history of the new heresy is its best refutation. During the wars of religion, the fanatics destroyed more than 20,000 churches; in the single province of Dauphiny, they put to death 256 priests and 112 monks, and laid waste 900 towns and villages. Their rage even vented itself on the remains of the dead; they profaned, with sacrilegious hands, the relics of the martyrs and confessors of Jesus Christ; they burnt their bones, and scattered the ashes to the winds. Thus, for instance, in 1562, they broke up the shrine of St. Francis of Paula, at Plessis-le-Tours; and finding his body incorrupt, they dragged it through the streets and burnt it in a fire, the flames of which they fed with fragments of the crucifix. In the same year they seized at Lyons the shrine of St. Bonaventura; burnt the precious relics of the saint, and threw them into the Saône. They seemed to be seized with a demoniacal fury against the holiest servants of God, and the greatest benefactors of the human race.

Another invariable note of heresy is its restlessness, its tendency to split into sects, and to change and alter its dogmas. As the heresiarch fashions his doctrine by his own unaided judgment, so every one of his followers may vary and modify it according to his own individual will; he is not bound to an implicit faith in any authority; he has just as much right to innovate as his teacher. We have had occasion to remark this shifting character in the Arians, Pelagians, and others; it has been even more conspicuous amongst Protestants. Neither Luther nor Calvin could keep his disciples within the limits he prescribed; for the fundamental maxim of Protestantism is, that there are no limits to change; that it is part of the liberty of the Gospel that every one should form his own opinions for himself. What could be expected from such a maxim, but the strangest medley of dogmas and perpetual variation? "Those who have rejected one doctrine," said the celebrated Vincent of Lerins in the fifth century, "will soon attack the rest; and what can follow from this method of reforming the Divine religion, but that its promoters will be ever on the move, changing continually, until every trace of their original belief is destroyed?" The progress of the so-called Reformation has attested the wisdom of this remark: having shaken off the salutary yoke of the authority of the Church, it no longer possessed any principle of unity; for nothing but an authority recognised as divine can restrain the licentious tendency of the human mind. The new reform, surrendered to the examination and judgment of every individual amongst its adherents, has undergone a thousand changes, and assumed a thousand different forms; Episcopalian and Presbyterian, Calvinist and Arminian, Puritan and Socinian,

Baptist and Quaker, &c. &c.,—all of which sects hold different doctrines, and agree only in their common hatred of the ancient faith, and their rejection of all authority. At the crisis of the revolt, new teachers were continually heard broaching new opinions, and confuting those of their masters. New confessions of faith were continually appearing; the builders upon the shifting sand of private opinion were seen busily destroying to-day what they had but yesterday erected. So that the words directed by St. Hilary against the Arians find here also a melancholy application : " You are like unskilful architects, who are never satisfied with their work; you do nothing but build and demol'sh. There are now as many confessions of faith as there are individuals amongst you; and as many doctrines as there are minds. Every year, every month, witnesses the pompous introduction of a new confession; you grow ashamed of the old ones; you throw them away, and fabricate new ones, to be also discarded in their turn." One of their own teachers thus laments their inconstancy of opinion : " What manner of men are our Protestants; going astray every moment, and then retracing their steps, and carried about with every wind of doctrine; now on this side and now on that? You may with some difficulty get at their views of religion to-day; but no wit of man can conjecture what they will be to-morrow. On what article of faith do those churches agree which have cut themselves off from communion with Rome? Examine the points of their belief : you will not find a single article affirmed by one self-appointed teacher, which is not flatly contradicted by another, and condemned as something impious." It is not astonishing that men should wander thus, when they disdain all guidance; they have rejected the Church which Jesus Christ commands us to hear; alone and undirected, they lose themselves on the trackless field of investigation : the truth is but one; the by-paths of error which lead from it are infinite in number. Not thus has it been with the Church Catholic. Her government and her conduct have never known change. Her doctrine is ever one and the same. She received it from her Divine Head, and she has kept the precious deposit inviolate. She develops her definitions to meet heresies as they arise; but her faith has known neither addition or diminution,—she is " the pillar and ground of the truth."

§ 2. The Schism in England, 1533-1560.

The Church had now existed in England for thirteen hundred years. Under its influence the nation had won for itself a high and honourable position among the commonwealths of Europe, and had become possessed of free institutions, which to this day are the glory of its people, and the envy of less fortunate countries; though it is too apt to forget that it owes these advantages mainly to the free spirit of Catholicism and the patriotic exertions of Catholic prelates. Before we enter on the sad story of the severance of the "island of saints" from the unity of the faith and the obedience of the Apostolic See, let us cast a glance backwards on the glories which then passed away from our beloved country. "When Protestantism appeared," says M. Nicolas, "Christian art and Christian science had reached their culminating point. All the great sources of civilisation were opened wide. Our mightiest and purest architectural creations had been standing for centuries; and they help us to form some notion of the society which could raise and appreciate them. Now that our reawakening taste permits us to contemplate them, we are lost in admiration of the buildings themselves, and of all that they imply: the science, the taste, the feeling, the life, the resources, the self-sacrifice, the faith, of the ages which produced them. They are an exposition of the arts, sciences, and industry of their times. Mechanics, optics, acoustics, chemistry, metallurgy; painting, mosaics, statuary;—all the arts and sciences combine in our sanctuaries. . . . . And all this is but the letter and the form. There is nothing capricious or accidental in this: it is but the simple expression of the idea of those times. They are poems which tell the glory of Jesus Christ, and reproduce the miracle of the Incarnation, by showing us matter in all its elements, and nature in its several kingdoms, christianised and animated by the faith. They are at once the profoundest treatises of historical, dogmatic, and moral theology, the synthesis and combination of all the truths which bind in one the natural and the supernatural order. . . . They date from the time when St. Anselm was writing meditations, whose fulness and depth Descartes has ill understood, and from fragments of which he has created his fame; when St. Bernard was shaking Europe with his eloquence, and charming it with his incomparable grace and sweetness; when St. Bonaventura was perfecting the alliance between mysticism and scholasticism, and harmonising all the sciences with theology; when Gerson and à Kempis were enlightening and consoling the humble in heart, and St. Thomas was inditing those works in which mortal genius soars on angel's wings to penetrate the mysterious deeps of things human and divine; when Dante was succeeded by Petrarch, Tasso, and Ariosto; and Michael Angelo and Raphael were following in the steps of Giotto, Massaccio, and Fra Angelico; when Robert Agricola in Germany, Louis Vivès in Spain, Bordæus in France, Picus of Mirandola in Italy, Fisher, Colet, and Lilly in England, were extending the limits of science and literature. . . . Then flourished the great Catholic universities: Oxford, established in 895; Cambridge in 915; Padua in 1179; Salamanca in 1200; Aberdeen in 1213; Vienna in 1237; Glasgow in 1453; without enumerating those of Paris, Bologna, and Ferrara, whose antiquity is still greater, or the numberless contemporary foundations in every state of Europe." England had largely contributed to this enlightenment, and fully shared in its blessings. Its liberties were founded, extended, and defended by Catholics, who were penetrated with the grand definition of law given by St. Thomas: " A certain regulation dictated by reason, for the common good, and promulgated by him to whom the care of the commonwealth is intrusted."*

The Catholic religion had covered England with churches and with schools. Six hundred and sixteen religious houses were so many centres of civilisation, charity, and blessing. It amalgamated the various races which inhabited our island; it abolished villanage; it opened a free career to genius and ability; it inspired the men who covered our arms with glory; it gave us the Great Charter; it ever stood between the people and their oppressors. It would have effected even more, but for the avarice and tyranny of the secular power, and its jealousy of the rights of the Holy See. To say that there were abuses among its children, is but to assert the Catholic doctrine that scandals must arise, that the cockle will ever be min-

* 1, 2 quæst. 90, art. 4 : " The doctrines of St. Thomas, laid down in this part of his writings, are those of all theologians. They are the most explicit protest against despotism, the most explicit declaration of the limits of the civil power, the noblest assertion of the rights of man." *Balmes.*

gled with the wheat, that the enemy of God and of man is ever going about to ruin or to sully the noblest works of God.

The passions of one man overthrew this magnificent fabric, and left us the ruins, on which, like the returning Jews, we are beginning to rebuild the house of our God.

Few kings have ever begun to reign under more favourable circumstances, few with so much of promise, as Henry VIII. His able and thrifty father had bequeathed to him a noble heritage, and his reign might have been one of unparalleled glory. Although, as we have said, the jealousy of the secular power had proceeded to the utmost limits compatible with a recognition of the supreme authority of the Holy See, in throwing impediments in the way of a free and unrestricted intercourse between the head of the Church and the members; and although even heresy itself had received encouragement in high places, the English were still profoundly Catholic. Wycliff, Occam, and others, had recanted their errors, and died in obscurity. Henry himself undertook the defence of the Church against Luther; and it is curious to read at the present day the words of one destined to sever his land from the obedience of Rome. " I will not so far wrong the Bishop of Rome as to argue his right, as if it were a matter which admitted of doubt. The enemy (Luther) cannot deny that all the faithful honour and acknowledge the Holy Roman See as their mother and mistress. . . . . I would fain know of him *when* the Pope acquired so great power, for it cannot have an obscure origin. . . . Truly, if any one will look at ancient monuments, or read the histories of former times, he will find that since the conversion of the world all churches in Christendom have been obedient to the See of Rome. . . . St. Jerome openly declares, though himself not a Roman, that it was sufficient for him that the Pope of Rome did approve his faith, whoever else did disapprove of it." Henry's work* was learned and able; he had been destined to eminence in the Church, while his elder brother Arthur was alive, and had consequently received a theological education. The Pope was so pleased with his book, that he bestowed on Henry the title of *Defender of the Faith*, which is still borne by the sovereigns of England.

The king had married Catherine of Aragon, the widow of

---

* It is generally believed, however, that Fisher, the holy Bishop of Rochester, and subsequently one of Henry's most celebrated victims, had the chief hand in its composition.

his brother Arthur, in virtue of a dispensation from the Pope. They had been united eighteen years, when he conceived a passion for one of the queen's maids of honour. He wished to raise her to the throne; but his marriage presented an insurmountable obstacle, unless he could establish its original unlawfulness. He therefore affected scruples of conscience, and applied to Rome for permission to put away Catherine, and marry Anne Boleyn. Pope Clement VII. examined the case, and decided that there were no valid grounds for dissolving a marriage which had been solemnly contracted. He refused to separate what God had made one; and commanded Henry to take back his lawful wife. Henry would not yield. With the sanction of the subservient Cranmer, whom he had made Archbishop of Canterbury, he privately married Anne Boleyn, * in 1532; and the servile convocation of England declared his former marriage null, and approved that which he had just contracted. In the two years following his marriage, Henry abolished many ancient prerogatives and privileges of the Holy See in England. He forbade application to be made for the pallium, or for bulls of institution; all prelates were to be chosen and consecrated and empowered in England alone. He rendered appeals to Rome illegal; and thus denied the Holy See to be the source of jurisdiction. On the 30th March 1534, he took the final step, and severed England from the unity of the Church. He assumed "all authority of jurisdictions, spiritual and temporal, to be derived and deduced from the king's majesty." In later times some members of the establishment have endeavoured to evade the meaning of the royal supremacy. That meaning is to be sought in the law-books, and in experience. "What the king and his favourite counsellors meant, at one time, by the supremacy, was certainly nothing less than the whole power of the keys. The king was to be the pope of his kingdom, the vicar of God, the expositor of Catholic unity, the channel* of sacramental graces. He arrogated to himself the right of deciding dogmatically what was orthodox doctrine, and what was heresy; of drawing up and imposing confessions of faith. He proclaimed that all jurisdiction, spiritual and temporal, was derived from him alone; and that it was in his power to confer episcopal authority, and to take it away. He ordered his seal to be put to commissions by which bishops were appointed, who were

---

* That is to say, by virtue of his supreme jurisdiction.

to exercise their functions as his deputies during his pleasure. According to this system, as expounded by Cranmer, the king was the spiritual as well as the temporal chief of the nation. As he appointed civil officers to keep his seal, to collect his revenues, and to dispense justice in his name, so he appointed divines of various ranks to preach the Gospel and to administer the Sacraments. It was unnecessary that there should be any imposition of hands. The king, says Cranmer, might make a priest; and the priest so made needed no ordination whatever."* If we turn to the practice of the king, we see that Thomas Cromwell was appointed his vicar-general, with full spiritual powers. He was to visit the Church, to punish with spiritual censures, &c.; and during his visitation all episcopal powers were held in abeyance. Bishops were appointed in just the same terms as civil magistrates : "We name, make, create, constitute, and declare N. bishop of N., to have and to hold to himself the said bishopric during the time of his natural life, if for so long a time he behave himself well therein; and we empower him to confer orders, &c. in place of us, in our name, and by our royal authority."

Still the king would allow no innovation in doctrine. Those who denied the Real Presence were to be burnt as heretics. Those who impugned clerical celibacy, or denied the necessity of confession, &c. were to be punished as guilty of heresy; while those who refused to acknowledge his preposterous and unprecedented lay supremacy, were punished as traitors. The secular clergy submitted, with reluctance indeed, but with shameful servility. Fisher, Bishop of Rochester, stood alone in his fidelity to God and His Church; and was beheaded. Sir Thomas More, a profound lawyer, as well as a great and holy man, met the same fate. When asked what he had to say why sentence should not be pronounced upon him for refusing to take the oath of supremacy, he replied, "Forasmuch, my lords, as this indictment is grounded upon an act of parliament directly repugnant to the laws of God and of His holy Church, the supreme government of which, or of any part thereof, no temporal prince may, by any law, presume to take upon him, as rightfully belonging to the See of Rome, as a special prerogative granted by the mouth of Christ Himself to St. Peter and the Bishops of Rome his successors, it is, therefore, among Catholic Chris-

* Macaulay, *History of England,* i. 55.

tians insufficient in law to charge any Christian man to obey
it." When the savage sentence had been pronounced, Sir
Thomas More spoke out more plainly still in words which
sum up the whole question and controversy : "When I perceived that the king's pleasure was to sift out from whence
the Pope's authority was derived, I confess I studied seven
years together to find out the truth thereof. But I could
not read in any one doctor's writings, approved by the
Church, any one saying that avoucheth that a layman was,
or ever could be, head of the Church. And as the city of
London could not make a law against an act of parliament
which bound the whole realm, neither could this realm make
a particular law incompatible with the general law of Christ's
Universal Catholic Church." He suffered martyrdom on the
6th July 1535. Many executions followed. The same cart
conveyed to death Catholics who denied the king's supremacy, and heretics who denied the Real Presence of Christ in
the Blessed Sacrament.

Meanwhile the monasteries were suppressed, and their revenues squandered upon the king's needy favourites. The
king soon wearied of Anne Boleyn, the guilty occasion of so
many troubles and so much evil. With the aid of his com-
plaisant tool, Cranmer, he caused the marriage to be dissolved,
and the unhappy woman to be beheaded. Henry took in
succession four other wives ; one of whom shared the fate of
Anne Boleyn, and another was divorced. The king seemed
utterly given up to the lawless impulses of his own depraved
heart, and died in 1547, leaving a name execrated by posterity.

Under Edward VI., his youthful successor, the foreign
"reformers" exercised great influence, and many important
changes were made in the state religion. Schism leads naturally to heresy ; every form of error has free course where
the very principle of Divine authority is rejected. Even in
Henry's time, and in spite of his terrible measures of suppression, Lutheranism had made great progress in England.
Edward suppressed the Catholic religion entirely, and established in its stead the pretended Reformation. The Holy Sacrifice of the Mass was abolished ; images and altars were
thrown down ; churches were pillaged and profaned ; and the
pulpits were occupied by declaimers, who heaped every kind
of insult on the faith and holy ceremonies of religion. Still a

large number remained true to the proscribed creed; and the great body of the people, though not ardent in its defence of the ancient faith, was yet slow to feel any attraction for the new religion.   On the death of Edward in 1553, Mary, daughter of Henry and Catherine of Aragon, and the only legitimate heir whom the king had left, succeeded in bringing back the kingdom to its obedience to the Holy See.   The parliament entered into her designs as readily as it had concurred with those of Henry and Edward.   Cardinal Pole absolved the nation from the censures incurred by schism and sacrilege; and there was every reason to hope that the storm had passed away.   But unhappily the counsellors of Mary forgot the laws of meekness and charity in their treatment of the refractory Protestants, many of whom were burnt for heresy; and a further cause of alienation was given in the marriage of the queen with Philip of Spain.   The Catholic religion became identified in the mind of the nation with foreign domination; and thus lost ground among a people ever sensitive to aggression on their independence and liberties.

Mary's reign was of short duration.   She died in 1558, and was succeeded by Elizabeth, daughter of Anne Boleyn. The new queen was crowned according to the Roman ritual, but speedily adopted Protestantism, purely from motives of policy and self-interest.   Being illegitimate by birth, she had no hereditary title to the throne; moreover, another rightful claimant to the crown existed in the person of Mary Queen of Scots, who, having thrown herself on Elizabeth's protection from her own rebellious subjects, was detained in a cruel imprisonment, and at length barbarously put to death.   Fearing, therefore, that her claims would not be recognised by the Pope and her Catholic subjects, Elizabeth resolved to identify her own cause with that of the new opinions.   Accordingly, after taking the accustomed oath to maintain inviolate the faith and the privileges of the Catholic Church, she hesitated not to renounce all communion with and obedience to the Holy See.   Nor was she slow in exercising the supremacy she had usurped; and the Christian world stood amazed at the unprecedented spectacle of a female pope swaying the religious destinies of England.   Elizabeth may be regarded as the real founder of the National Church as it now exists.   In her reign was given the final touch to the constitution of the established religion; and it remains an awkward compromise of contradictory doctrines and usages.   It is worth observing how purely political were the motives of so fearful a change. In spite of the subservience of many of the clergy, Jewel tells us that there were not two persons in Oxford who thought with the reformers;* the change was the work of that able and unscrupulous body of men who upheld the throne of Elizabeth, and who, in the words of a great Protestant author, "were not restrained by any scruples of conscience from professing, as they had before professed, the Catholic faith of Mary, the Protestant faith of Edward, or any of the numerous intermediate combinations which the caprice of Henry and the servile policy of Cranmer had formed out of the doctrines of both the hostile parties.   They took a deliberate view of the state of their own country and of the continent; they satisfied themselves as to the leaning of the public mind; and they chose their side.   They placed themselves at the head of the Protestants of Europe, and staked all their fame and fortunes on the success of their party."

After Elizabeth had made herself supreme governor of the Church in England, an oath was tendered for the acceptance not only of the clergy but of the civil magistracy, by which they were to acknowledge the queen's supremacy, and renounce that of the Pope.   The bishops, together with the greatest portion of the clergy, refused compliance; and the whole hierarchy was accordingly suppressed.   One only of the Catholic prelates was flattered or frightened into submission; and he was one, says a Protestant, "who had always believed according to the last act of parliament."   Thus perished the Catholic Episcopate for that time.   Those who assumed the name of bishops in the state Church had neither jurisdiction nor orders, and were as merely civil officers as their parish clerks.   The great majority of the higher clergy were deprived; and such was the deficiency of ministers, that, as Hallam informs us, laymen and even mechanics were set to read the service.   For months together there was neither prayer nor preaching in many places.   Dr. Heylin, another Protestant writer, tells us that the new clergy "was made up of cobblers, weavers, tinkers, tanners, fiddlers, tailors, bagpipers, &c."   In the year 1560, one hundred parishes in the

* As late as 1578, Strype tells us there were only four Protestants at Exeter College out of eighty members,—"all the rest being secret or open Roman affectionaries."

diocese of Ely had no ministers. The Catholic priesthood would have died out with those who had apostatised, but for the establishment of a seminary in Flanders, from whence English students, after receiving holy orders, came over at the risk of their lives to minister to their persecuted countrymen.

Every means was now employed to coerce the people into submission. All official persons were compelled to take the oath of supremacy. Those who wrote in defence of the old religion forfeited all their goods for the first offence, were imprisoned for life for the second, and hanged, drawn, and quartered for the third. Ruinous fines were levied on all who did not attend the state prayers. In 1563 the oath of supremacy might be tendered to any one; and on a second refusal, the penalty was death by hanging, drawing, and quartering. Thus, throughout Elizabeth's reign, the penal laws became more and more stringent and cruel. It was death to be reconciled to the Catholic Church, or to reconcile another to it; death to be a Jesuit or a seminary priest; death to harbour, or conceal, or relieve a Jesuit or seminary priest; death to be a student in a foreign seminary. And all the while, Parker, who is called Archbishop of Canterbury, gently blames the queen for her leniency, and urges her to root out Catholics with greater rigour.

A persecution, which almost rivalled in atrocity those that had taken place in the reigns of the heathen emperors, raged throughout England. Many holy priests suffered martyrdom; many laymen died the horrible death of traitors for receiving their hunted clergy into their houses; the mansions of the gentry were searched with every circumstance of violence and insult for priests supposed to be concealed; numbers were thrown into prison; many families in the middle as well as the higher classes were ruined by the heavy fines that were levied on them; and the whole Catholic community was harassed in every possible way, because they would not accept a new and false religion at the dictation of a Protestant government.[*]

Nor was this all. There were many fervid Protestants who detected the remains of what they called "Popery" in

---

[*] See Challoner's *Missionary Priests.* A short and accurate summary of the religious transactions of Elizabeth's reign, as well as of Mary's, is given in the *Clifton Tracts.*

the state religion, and who agreed with Calvin in styling the royal supremacy a blasphemy. They were the most logically consistent of the so-called reformers; the reform, as established, was not searching and extensive enough for them. They had dethroned the Pope; they had no wish to replace him by a more cruel master. Why should they, whose watchword was liberty to believe what they pleased, submit to any authority? Why should they fear to rebel against those who had so recently rebelled against that authority hitherto regarded as the most sacred? Elizabeth's government replied by persecution, and thus excited an animosity against the crown in addition to a hatred of the state Church. These views spread widely among the middle classes, and eventually led to the rebellion against Charles I. When, somewhat later, a new body of divines strove to create a reaction against the levelling tendencies of the Reformation, the descendants of these Puritans, as they were called, forsook the Church, and split up into the various sects we see around us. And about the middle of the eighteenth century John Wesley founded the large and influential body which bears his name.

The Irish alone, of the northern nations, remained true to their religion. All efforts failed to pervert them. After exhausting all the resources of a most savage persecution, "the government," says a Protestant historian, "contented itself with setting up a vast hierarchy of Protestant archbishops, bishops, and rectors, who did nothing, and who, for doing nothing, were paid out of the spoils of a Church loved and revered by the great body of the people."

In Scotland the Reformation was accepted in its extremest form. Political events combined with peculiarities of national character to give the new religion this particular shape. "In no part of Europe"—it is still a Protestant writer we are quoting—"has the Calvinistic doctrine and discipline taken so strong a hold on the public mind. The Church of Rome was regarded by the great body of the people with a hatred which might justly be called ferocious; and the established Church of England was an object of scarcely less aversion." ·

Such is a very brief and imperfect account of this deplorable change;—a change which undid the work of ages, and which substituted in these islands the license of human opinion for the divine authority of the Church.

§ 3. St. Ignatius Loyola, St. Francis Xavier, 1521-1552.

The mercy of God did not abandon His Church in this her great trial. At no time was she so prolific of illustrious saints as at this crisis, when she was torn by heresies and schisms, and to human eyes threatened with dissolution. Reforms were needed in many quarters; and it pleased God to raise up reformers after His own heart. Among these holy and great men our attention is arrested in an especial manner by St. Ignatius Loyola and St. Francis Xavier. Ignatius was a Spaniard by birth, and belonged to a distinguished family in the province of Biscay. He was born in the year 1491, and chosen of God to defend and sustain the Church against the assaults of Luther, Calvin, and other heresiarchs of the time. Ignatius was converted in the year 1521; in that very year Luther began his open revolt; and Calvin and Ignatius were both at the same time in Paris, preparing, as it were, each in his place, for the momentous conflict. In 1534 Henry VIII. severed England from the obedience of the Pope; and in that same year Ignatius laid the foundation of his order at Paris. With the disease came the divinely-appointed remedy. Ignatius was early introduced into the service of King Ferdinand, and trained in the exercises of chivalry and of warfare, the love of which captivated his ardent mind, notwithstanding the deep religious impressions it had received.

In 1521, he assisted in the defence of Pampeluna against Francis I. of France; and while defending with heroic bravery a breach in the walls, he was struck down by a cannon-ball which shattered one of his legs. The French were so impressed by his gallantry that, after attending to his wound, they sent him home to the castle of Loyola with all the honour due to a noble and valiant enemy. The fracture was so imperfectly set, that it was found necessary to break the bone again; a long fever followed, and the life of Ignatius was for some time in great danger. This was the time that God chose for speaking to his heart, and for preparing him for his wonderful work. Ignatius was passionately fond of the romances of chivalry; there were none to be found in the castle of Loyola, and he was obliged to substitute for them the Lives of the Saints. He began perusing them with great repugnance; but he had no other means of beguiling the weary days of his convalescence. Soon he began to feel a deep interest in these lives; he read them again and again. They gave him an idea of a loftier heroism than he had hitherto dreamed of; he began to compare his own life with those of the saints—how different! and yet to him, as well as to them, the salvation of his soul was the main end of existence. These reflections were divinely blessed to his conversion; he resolved to change his life, and to consecrate himself entirely to God. When he arose from his bed of sickness, he went on pilgrimage to our Lady of Montserrat, and then retired to Manresa, where he applied himself to practices of the most austere penitence. His diet was bread and water; the earth was his bed; and he passed seven hours daily in mental prayer. From Manresa he betook himself to a lone cavern, where he increased the rigour of his penances. He came forth only to study for the ecclesiastical state, to which he had resolved to consecrate himself. He went to Paris, then the most renowned university in the world; and there he became acquainted with the fascinating Xavier, whom he succeeded in reclaiming from the world. Xavier was a young noble of the kingdom of Navarre; he was then teaching philosophy at Paris with great success; and though he possessed many noble and good qualities, he had no other ambition but to gain to himself an honourable name in the world. "What doth it profit a man if he gain the whole world, and suffer the loss of his own soul?" These words, incessantly repeated to him by Ignatius, opened his eyes to the vanity of all earthly objects and aims, and soon he attached himself to the saint, and devoted himself to the work of the ministry. Ignatius drew around him a few other noble spirits; and on the festival of the Assumption, 1534, they made their memorable vow in the crypt of the church of Montmartre, at Paris, where the apostle of France had received the crown of martyrdom. Besides Xavier, the little band, before which heresy was doomed to tremble and recede, contained Salmeron and Laynez, Bobadilla and Rodriguez. Such was the lowly beginning of the great Company of Jesus, which has given to the Church so many learned and eloquent defenders, so many masters and examples of the science of the saints, so many intrepid martyrs and confessors. Just as the so-called Reformation was beginning its desolating ravages, God raised up this barrier to its excesses and its triumphs. Hence never has a community been assailed with such unrelenting malice, or suffered such continued persecution. The order was solemnly approved by Paul III., in 1540. To the usual vows of poverty, chastity, and obedience, the new religious added that of a special obedience and devotion to the successor of St. Peter, and dedicated themselves to the propagation of the faith in pagan and heretical countries as well as in those which were still Catholic. They took also on themselves a vow which precluded them from all ecclesiastical dignities. Their order grew and spread, and did the work for which it was raised up; and it still survives, after many storms, its gigantic strength unabated, its devotion as fervent, its labours and sacrifices as magnanimous and successful as ever.

St. Francis Xavier was chosen to bear the Gospel to the East, where the Portuguese had founded colonies. He embarked at Lisbon in 1541, and after a long voyage reached Goa, the chief seat of the Portuguese dominion in India. The deplorable state in which he found religion filled his soul with grief, and kindled in it an ardent zeal. As the scandalous lives of the nominally Christian Portuguese were the chief obstacles to the conversion of the idolaters in the midst of whom they lived, he began his apostolical labours amongst his own countrymen. He applied himself especially to the instruction of the young, gathering them in the church, and explaining to them the Creed, the Commandments of God, and the practices of the Christian life. The piety of these children had its effect. Sinners began to blush at their sins, and to resort to Xavier for counsel and aid. He received them with great kindness, instructed and exhorted them, and won their hearts by his gentleness and charity. He then betook himself to the pearl-fisheries of the straits of Manaar, where persons who had been baptised were living amidst the superstitions and vices of paganism. He lived amongst the poor fishermen, shared their coarse food, and allowed himself three hours of the twenty-four for sleep. He studied their language, and translated into it the Creed, the Lord's Prayer, and all the Catechism. He went from village to village with a small bell, with which he summoned the fishermen to his preaching. His labours had incredible success. The fervour of these converted Christians was wonderful; a tribe of abandoned profligates became a community of saints. Moreover, so great was the number of pagans who implored baptism, that Xavier was worn out with fatigue. He extended his labours into all the adjacent countries, where the name of Jesus was unknown; and soon the idol-temples gave place to churches in which Jesus was worshipped. In the following year, he passed over to Travancore, where, in one month, he baptised about 10,000 pagans. Forty-five churches were raised in the province; and the fervour of the new converts is described by Xavier himself as most touching and edifying.

The reputation of the holy apostle was soon spread throughout the East; and he received from all sides entreaties to come and instruct and baptise. The harvest was great; and Francis sent to Rome and to Portugal for labourers to aid in gathering it in. He would have drained Europe of its doctors and preachers, in the transport of his zeal. It would be a long, and it is a needless, task to track his steps through all his apostolical journeys; Malabar, the Moluccas, Japan, were insufficient to satisfy the cravings of his soul. The number of converts was enormous; and wherever he went he left a church for the use of the new Christians. His labours almost surpass belief; the dangers he encountered were most formidable, and his sufferings often extreme; but a torrent of interior consolations refreshed his soul. "The perils to which I am exposed," he writes to St. Ignatius, "the labours I undergo for the cause of God, are of themselves springs of inexhaustible spiritual gladness; I never remember to have enjoyed such exquisite interior delight; and these consolations of my soul are so pure, so sweet, so continuous, that they take away all sense of suffering and weariness." So abundant were these favours, that he often besought the Lord to moderate them, lest they should incapacitate him for his daily toils.

It was in 1549 that Xavier embarked to visit the people of Japan: with the aid of a Japanese whom he had converted in India, he translated into their language the Creed, and an exposition of its several articles. He obtained an audience of the king, and received permission to preach the faith. His success was so rapid, that the bonzes, or native priests, took the alarm, and denounced him to the king, as a dangerous disturber and perverter of the people. He was obliged to leave the kingdom of Saxuma, and betook himself to Firando, the capital of another small kingdom. There he was received with much kindness, and permitted to preach Jesus Christ.

P

The fruit of his toil was abundant beyond measure; he made more converts in three weeks than he had made in Vaxuma during a whole year. He left this infant church under the care of one of his fellow-labourers, and set off for Meaco, the capital of Japan. On his way, he passed through Amanguchi, the capital of Nagoto, which was sunk in frightful corruption. His preaching was utterly fruitless. The inhabitants laughed at the western bonze, who, as they said, would allow them only one God and one wife; and they drove him out of the city with violence and insult. When he reached Meaco, he found, to his great grief, that the inhabitants were equally unfitted to receive the truth, and he was obliged to return to Amanguchi. As he had noticed that the poverty of his appearance shocked and repelled the people, and prevented his being presented at court, he so far humoured them, as to make his entry in a magnificent dress. He soon obtained access to the king, and by a few presents gained his protection, and was permitted to preach the Gospel. He baptised 3000 persons in the city, and then went onwards to Bongo, where the king was eagerly awaiting him. In several public disputations, he silenced the bonzes, who were anxious to discredit him with the king and people, and even succeeded in converting some of them. The effect produced on the inhabitants was very great, and they came in crowds to be instructed and baptised. The king himself was fully convinced of the truth of the Gospel; but an unlawful passion, which he would not relinquish, kept him from becoming a Christian. Subsequently he received grace to renounce his sin, and was baptised. At length, after a sojourn in Japan of more than two years, Xavier felt constrained to attempt to proclaim the Gospel in China. The entrance to this populous empire was most strictly closed against foreigners, and yet Xavier could not relinquish his hope. Obstacles and difficulties crowded about his path, but nothing could abate his ardour; and soon he reached the island of Sancian, near Macao, on the coast of China. The infinite wisdom of God seems at times to inspire the saints with designs they are never able to complete; and thus Xavier fell ill at the very moment when his long-cherished designs seemed on the point of being accomplished. He reached the borders of the land he so eagerly longed to convert, and, like Moses, he did but look and die. At his own

request he was removed to the shore; and there, in a state of
the greatest pain and weakness, he lay stretched on the beach,
amidst the cold of a Chinese winter. The fever gained ground
rapidly, and no aid was at hand. His last hours were cheered
with unspeakable consolations. He died almost alone, clasp-
ing his crucifix, and uttering the words : "In Thee, O Lord,
have I hoped; let me not be confounded for ever." He was
but forty-six years of age, and he had traversed oceans, con-
tinents, and islands, bearing the glad tidings of salvation to
the heathen. 700,000 converts are numbered as the fruits
of his zeal. He was buried where he died, on the lonely
island of Sancian; and the grave was filled with quicklime,
in order that the flesh might be speedily consumed and the
bones more easily transported to India. But when the grave
was opened at the expiration of two months, the body of the
saint was found untouched by corruption, and as fresh as
when he was alive. It was removed to Goa, and placed in
the church of St. Paul; and many miracles are ascribed to
this precious relic of the great apostle of the Indies.

Meanwhile St. Ignatius had been constrained to accept
the government of his order, and had taken up his abode at
Rome, where his sanctity and the effects of his inexhaustible
charity wrought wonders. He did not deem it beneath him
to perform the humblest offices for the sick in the hospitals,
or to catechise children in the churches. So great was his
skill in this latter work, that soon fathers and mothers, as
well as' crowds of persons distinguished for their rank and
learning, and even eminent theologians, thronged to his catechetical instructions. The success of his labours for the salvation of souls was very great, and the Company of Jesus
increased rapidly. It was limited at first to sixty members;
but soon it spread throughout Christendom, far away into
India, and even into the heretical kingdoms of the north of
Europe. It flourished with especial vigour in Spain, from
which its first members had been taken ; but its progress was
slow in France, where it was first formed, by reason of the
war between Francis I. and Charles V. The French king
looked with an evil eye on a society, the head and leading
members of which were Spaniards. St. Ignatius did not live
to witness the reaction, and the numerous establishments
of his order in France. He died in 1556, leaving to the
Church the memory of a life entirely devoted to the glory of

God, and to his society an organisation and rules of consummate wisdom.

§ 4. Council of Trent, 1545-1563.

The spread of the Protestant heresy in Germany, as well as the need that was felt of certain reforms of discipline, induced a universal desire that a council might be summoned to arrest the progress of the mischief, and to heal the wounds it had already inflicted on the Church. After many vexatious difficulties, which the jealousies and selfishness of the monarchs of Europe threw in the way, Pope Paul III. at length issued the bull of convocation. The city of Trent was selected, as uniting many advantages; but it was not until 1545 that all obstacles were surmounted, and the council held its first session. The proceedings opened by the prelates assisting at a solemn Mass of the Holy Ghost, and reading the Creed, as was done in the earlier councils, in order to show that they adhered stedfastly to the faith of the Church, and that their decrees would be only explanatory of that sacred deposit. They then laid down the points to be discussed, and the order in which they should be taken. After this, the question of the canon of Scripture was considered, inasmuch as it lies at the foundation of theological science; and it was unanimously decided that all the books of the Old and New Testaments were to be esteemed canonical. On this point, one of the legates spoke with wonderful clearness and force, and showed that all these books had been revered as sacred by the earlier councils, as well as by individual doctors of the Church, from the earliest ages. They treated also of tradition; that is, of the unwritten Word of God, which the Church preserves, and proposes to the faithful to be believed with the same certainty as the sacred Scriptures. On these two points a decree was drawn up in these words: "The holy, œcumenical, and general Council of Trent, lawfully assembled, under the guidance of the Holy Spirit, and presided over by the legates of the Apostolic See, considering that the doctrines of faith and the rules of morals are contained in the sacred writings, and in the unwritten traditions which were received from our Lord by the Apostles, or taught to the Apostles by the Holy Spirit, and by them handed down to us; the holy council, following the example of the orthodox fathers, receives all the books both of the Old and New Testaments, and also the traditions on faith and morals, with equal reverence and respect; and that no one may be in doubt which are the sacred books received by the council, it has resolved to insert a list of them in this decree." (Here follows a list of the canonical books contained in the Vulgate.) The council then adds: " If any one does not receive these books as a whole, and every part of each of them, or if he knowingly and deliberately contemns the traditions herein mentioned, let him be anathema." Then, in order to restrain turbulent spirits, the council decrees that, in all matters touching faith or morals, no one should so far presume on his own private judgment as to make the sacred books confirm it, in opposition to the interpretation given of them by Holy Church, to whom alone it pertains to judge of the true sense and interpretation of the sacred writings, or in opposition to the unanimous consent of the fathers. The council orders that all who pervert the words of Scripture to profane uses, as, to superstition, or jesting, or the like, should be punished as persons profaning the Word of God. The other sessions were devoted to the questions of original sin, which can be effaced only by the merits of Jesus Christ applied in holy baptism; of the justification of a sinner; of the seven sacraments instituted by our Lord, especially of the Divine Eucharist; of the sacrifice of the Mass; of penance, purgatory, indulgences, the *cultus* of the saints, &c. On all these subjects the errors of the Protestants were refuted and condemned.

The council was brought to a close, after many interruptions, in 1563, under the pontificate of Pius IV. During the eighteen years it lasted, many artifices were employed by those who were interested in maintaining abuses, to interfere with its deliberations, influence its decisions, and thwart its projected reforms. But the cause of truth triumphed gloriously, and God compelled the passions of men to subserve the glory of His Church. The twenty-fifth and last session was held on the 3d December; all the decrees were solemnly read and subscribed, and then this holy and illustrious assembly was dissolved. It was a solemn moment, and the fathers of the council were moved to tears. The Pope confirmed its decrees by a bull, and urged the faithful to accept them with religious submission. From that moment the definitions of Trent have been the faith of the Church. It may be regarded as the complement and compendium of all preceding councils. Never has any council embraced so many points of dogma and of discipline; never has any council expounded the doctrines of the faith with greater clearness and precision. The Protestants, who had so eagerly appealed to a general council, as that which would heal all dissensions, and to which they professed themselves willing to submit, rejected the Council of Trent, and disavowed its authority, because it condemned their heresy and schism. A creed was drawn up, in which were embodied the decisions of the assembled prelates; and it is known and revered by all Catholics as the creed of Pope Pius IV.

CHAPTER IX.

FROM THE COUNCIL OF TRENT TO THE BEGINNING OF THE EIGHTEENTH CENTURY.

§ 1. From the Council of Trent to the conversion of Henry IV. king of France, 1563-1593.

WHILE heresy was leading astray vast numbers of souls, it pleased God to confound its pretensions, not only by the real reforms decreed in the Council of Trent, but by raising up within the Church saints, whose endowments peculiarly fitted them to correct the evils of the day, and check the rising spirit of innovation. After toiling through the weary and repulsive history of the so-called reformers, it is a refreshment to turn our eyes towards St. Charles Borromeo, St. Theresa, and other saints, who, according to their several vocations, carried on the great work of reformation. Our Lord has taught us to discern the tree by its fruits; and this is a clear and infallible test for distinguishing the true Church from those which falsely assume its title and its office. To the Catholic Church alone belongs the glorious attribute of sanctity, as well as those of unity and apostolicity.

The most illustrious saint of the period at which we have now arrived was St. Charles Borromeo, the model of bishops, the great restorer of ecclesiastical discipline. He was born in the territory of Milan, of a family amongst the most distinguished of Italy. From his childhood he gave tokens of

the perfection which through life was his constant aim; and
his piety and application to study were alike remarkable.
His uncle, Pope Pius IV., summoned him to Rome to take
part in the administration of the Church's government; he
then named him cardinal and archbishop of Milan, at the
early age of twenty-two. The maturity of his intellect, and
the lustre of his holiness, supplied his lack of years; and he
was in every respect worthy of the high station in which the
providence of God had placed him. At that time the important and intricate business of the Council of Trent was in
progress. The archbishop exerted all his authority to further
the ends of the council; and he was the main instrument in
bringing it to a satisfactory conclusion. One of the chief
objects of the council was, as has been said, the reformation of the clergy; and the holy archbishop set an example of
perfect submission to its decrees. Having long most ardently
desired to resign the important offices he held at Rome, that
he might repair to his diocese, he now availed himself of
the canon which enjoins on all bishops the duty of residence,
to obtain from the Pope a reluctant permission to visit his
flock. The death of the Pontiff enabled him to resign the
charges which were incompatible with residence, and at the
same time he gave up to his natural heirs the whole of his
large paternal property. He reduced the number of his servants, with a liberal donation to those whom he felt it his
duty to dismiss; he left off wearing silk, cut off all expenses
which contributed only to state and magnificence, and began
a life of extraordinary mortification. He would not allow
himself even the most harmless gratification; prayer, preaching, the ministry of the Sacraments, the government of the
Church intrusted to him, divided and filled up all his time.
In his house he would have none but ecclesiastics, except
for the most menial offices; and he required from them the
austere life of cloistered monks. The hours of prayer were
fixed, and attendance was compulsory; their meals were in
common; and while they were at table some book of devotion was read. In addition to the ordinary abstinence of
Friday and Saturday, they ate no meat on Wednesdays,
nor during Advent. With his flock he was a living image of
the Good Shepherd, and the most tender father. Owing to
the long absence of their archbishops, not only the laity but
even the clergy were in a most deplorable condition, as to both

ignorance and immorality. Besides the provincial synods which he held regularly for the restoration of discipline, he resolved to procure for his diocese the benefit of seminaries, in which those who aspired to the solemn charge of the priesthood might be trained and prepared for their sacred duties. He founded five of these invaluable houses; and he drew up for their use a body of rules, which have served as the model for those of all seminaries. Nothing escaped his care or his zeal; he visited in person every corner of his vast diocese; penetrated the valleys of Switzerland, notwithstanding the hardships such journeys entailed; and at length succeeded in correcting the disorders, and rekindling the fervour of both clergy and people. Then too arose, under his inspiration, those magnificent churches which now adorn that part of Italy. Amidst this unwearied toil the saint devoted himself assiduously to his own interior perfection; his life was almost one continuous prayer; his penances were multiplied, and he confessed every day.[*]

A virtue so rare and perfect must needs be tested by trials and sufferings; and the saint had his full share of them. Those whose vices he repressed and punished, uttered the blackest calumnies against him; once they even attempted his life. He had undertaken to reform an order of religious called the Humiliati, founded in the twelfth century by some wealthy Milanese, who had escaped from the prisons into which they had been thrown in Germany. They separated themselves from the world and lived in community: but fervour and modesty had now ceased to be their characteristics; and their successors had fallen into scandalous disorders. The superiors would not be induced to live according to their rule; and when the archbishop persisted, three of their number entered into a conspiracy to murder him, that they might be rid of an enemy who threatened to disturb their pleasant and sinful course. The holy prelate was accustomed to admit many persons of the city to the evening prayers in his palace. One of these wretched monks disguised himself as a secular, slipped into the palace with those who usually attended the prayers, and discharged at the archbishop a loaded gun, at

---

[*] It is interesting to know that St. Charles's ordinary confessor was Mr. Gryffydb Roberts, a Welshman, who was canon of Milan. The saint kept with great respect a portrait of Bishop Fisher, martyred, as has been said above, under Henry VIII.; and received with most affectionate kindness many English priests who were voluntary exiles for their faith.

the moment when they were singing the words, " Let not your heart be troubled." The congregation sprang to their feet in alarm; but the saint bade them kneel down again, and finished the prayers with as much composure as if nothing had happened; so that the assassin was enabled to make his escape unobserved. The prelate had felt the ball; and, deeming himself mortally wounded, had commended his soul to God. But the ball, instead of penetrating his flesh, had stopped at the skin, and fallen down at his feet. When the supposed wound was examined, there was found only a slight contusion, which was not so much a wound as a monument of the special providence which had preserved a life so precious. The guilty monk was discovered some time afterwards and executed for his crime, notwithstanding the entreaties of the saint; and the Pope suppressed the order of the Humiliati, as being too deeply corrupted to admit of reform.

Another trial, and one demanding a rarer and more self-sacrificing courage, was soon laid upon the holy cardinal—the plague broke out in Milan. Those who were rich immediately took flight, and Charles was entreated to withdraw from the devoted city. He was told that it was his duty to preserve himself for the sake of his flock, and to send by the hands of others the succours and consolations of religion. But he rejected with indignation the unworthy suggestion, and quoted the words, " the good shepherd giveth his life for his sheep." He then devoted himself entirely to the care of those who were stricken with the plague: his charity knew no bounds; by day and by night he might be seen at the bedside of the sick and dying; speaking to them words of peace and resignation; soothing their anguish, sustaining their courage, and never leaving them until he had induced them to cleanse their souls by a sincere and contrite confession of their sins. When his resources failed him, he sold his property, his furniture, his very bed itself. At length the anger of God abated; and ere he died, the saint was permitted to rejoice in the peace and prosperity of his diocese. He seldom left it, and never but for some important object. He attended the death-bed of his uncle, Pius IV.,* and concurred in the election of a new Pontiff worthy to govern the Church of God. The choice of the conclave rested upon Pius V., whose virtues have ob-

---

* Pius IV. was also assisted in his last moments by St. Philip Neri, of whom some account will be given at p. 220.

tained for him a place among the saints. St. Charles Borromeo died on the 3d November 1584, to the grief of his flock,
who loved him as the most tender of fathers; of the Holy See,
which lost in him one of its ablest advisers; and of the whole
Church, which he had edified by his holy life.

St. Charles entertained an affectionate friendship for another
prelate who had distinguished himself by his ability and zeal
at the Council of Trent, Bartholomew de Martyribus, Archbishop of Braga in Portugal. He was the glory of the Portuguese church, and the instrument employed by God to
carry out in Portugal the reforms decreed by the Council of
Trent. Towards the close of his life he obtained, after repeated solicitations, permission to resign his see and to retire
into a monastery, where he insisted on being considered the
lowest of the monks. His charity towards the poor was immense. On one occasion, after he had become a monk, he
met a poor woman in extreme want and suffering; he gave
her his own bed, and slept in a wretched chair, the only one
in his cell. Several days elapsed before the superior knew
of this act of self-denial. The holy prelate died in 1590.

Meanwhile the Protestants were waging a fierce warfare
with the Catholics in every country into which they could
penetrate. These turbulent sectaries abandoned themselves
to the most fanatical excesses. In France the followers of
Calvin aimed at setting up a republic on the ruins of the
throne; and on three several occasions they made an attempt
to seize the person of the young king, Charles IX. The horrible profanations and cruelties committed by the Protestants
provoked the Catholic population to deplorable acts of retalia-
tion. France had become one vast battle-field, whereon raged
the most odious of wars—a civil war of religion. At Nîmes,
Alais, Sully, &c. the Protestants massacred a great number
of monks and priests, as well as of laity; at Orthez it is related that the streets literally ran with blood. On St. Bartholomew's day a large number of the Catholic nobility were
slaughtered at Pau, with circumstances of atrocious perfidy.
This outrage may have suggested the perpetration of a similar crime in that second massacre of St. Bartholomew's day
which has gained so infamous a celebrity. Its origin is still
to this day wrapt in obscurity. It has never been clearly
ascertained whether it was the result of a meditated plot, or
of a sudden alarm; neither is it certain who were its insti-

gators; though there seems little reason to doubt that it was perpetrated, with the consent of the king, at the instance of his mother, Catherine of Medicis, a crafty and wicked woman, who had favoured Protestantism so long as it suited her purposes, and was a Catholic only in name. There was peace between the Catholics and Protestants; and the latter were collected in great numbers in Paris on the occasion of a marriage between the young king of Navarre and the sister of Charles. On the 23d August 1572, the king hastily summoned a council, at which no ecclesiastic was present; he declared that a general rising of the Protestants was threatened; his life was in danger; the conspiracy must be frustrated by anticipating the attack. Accordingly it was resolved that a general massacre should take place that very night, the signal being given by ringing the bells of the palace. When the appointed hour was come, the soldiers, dispersed throughout the city, were joined by the citizens, whom the ferocity of the Protestants had goaded to madness. It was a fearful night; the chiefs of the Protestant party were murdered with all their domestics: then the popular fury turned against all who had taken arms in the cause of heresy; and not only soldiers, but mechanics and merchants, were stabbed, or shot, or drowned, without distinction of age, or rank, or sex. The Louvre itself afforded no sanctuary; and many Catholics perished in the general confusion. Similar scenes were enacted in some other cities of France; but the massacre was by no means general. The Catholic clergy displayed, on this frightful occasion, the utmost charity and humanity; and many heretics owed their preservation to the very men whom they had so long calumniated, and whose brethren they had every where slaughtered. We may mention in particular the Bishop of Lisieux, John Hennuyer, who opened his palace as an asylum for proscribed sectaries. At Lyons they were similarly sheltered; but the populace forced the house, and all who had taken refuge in it were slain.

Such was this terrible event, so memorable in the history of France. Whoever were its authors, and under whatever circumstances it took place, the Church was in no way implicated in it; although her enemies have attempted to make her a guilty accomplice in the crime. Immediately after its commission, the king sent an envoy to inform Pope Gregory XIII. that a plot against his person and his crown had been discovered; and that he had been delivered from death, and the realm from the horrors of civil war, by the destruction of the conspirators. The Pope, deceived by this report, ordered a *Te Deum* to be sung in thanksgiving to God, and a medal to be struck in commemoration of so great a deliverance; yet even before he was apprised of the real facts of the case, he is described as shedding tears over the fate of so many unhappy Christians, and exclaiming, "Alas, how can one be sure that many innocent souls have not suffered with the guilty!"

Meanwhile new congregations were being formed in the Church. The Theatines, founded by Pope Paul IV., were extending far and wide the blessings of their ministry; while the Barnabites devoted themselves to missions, to preaching, and to the instruction of youth. St. John of God instituted at Granada the Brothers of Charity, to tend the sick; the Recollets reformed the order of St. Francis, and observed his rule in all its original purity and rigour; while the Feuillants were set up by John de la Barrière in the abbey of Feuillant, near Toulouse. During this time also the celebrated St. Philip Neri formed the congregation of the Oratory, with which his children have made us familiar in England. Philip was born in 1515, and from his infancy gave signs of singular piety and recollection. He was one of the most learned men of his age; but he accounted every thing but loss in comparison with the knowledge and love of Jesus Christ. He was specially favoured by God, not only with interior consolations, but with the gift of miracles and of prophesy, and with a supernatural power of penetrating the hearts of all who came near him. His life was one astonishing miracle. It was the will of God that it should be spent in the Eternal City; and his various works of charity have justly procured for him the title of the Apostle of Rome. The congregation of the Oratorians was begun in 1551; they lived in community under rule, but without special vows. Amongst its earliest members was the celebrated Baronius, the author of the *Ecclesiastical Annals*, a man of singular sanctity and simplicity of character. Gregory XIII. approved the congregation in 1564, and bestowed on it the church of Our Lady in Vallicella. The saint lived to see many houses of his congregation erected at Florence, Naples, Lucca, Firmo, Padua, and many other cities of Italy. In our own times his sons have established themselves in London and Birmingham. The saint was beloved by a succession of Popes, and by other great and learned men; especially by St. Charles Borromeo. During his last illness his continual prayer was, " Increase my sufferings, but increase also my patience." In May 1595 he lay apparently at the point of death; Baronius gave him Extreme Unction; and Frederic Borromeo brought him the Holy Viaticum. He then recovered his health suddenly, and predicted the day of his death with perfect calmness. During the three last days of his life, he enjoyed more than his wonted amount of spiritual joy and love; and in the night of the 25th of May, while Baronius was reading the commendation of the soul to God, he tranquilly expired, in the eighty-second year of his age.

Of all the institutes which date from this period, the most remarkable, however, is that of St. Theresa. This wonderful servant of God was born at Avila in Spain, in the same year as St. Philip Neri. It was a pious custom of her family to read aloud the Lives of the Saints; and the little Theresa became passionately attached to these lives, and read them again and again when alone, or in company with her brother. The lives of the martyrs especially affected them, and they were wont to express to each other their eager desire to confess Jesus Christ, even to death. Their childish fervour led them to set off to seek the crown of martyrdom amongst the Moors; but they were met by one of their relatives, and taken back to their parents. As they could not become martyrs, they resolved that they would be hermits; and they made cells in the garden into which they frequently retired for prayer. These pious dispositions soon passed away from the heart of Theresa. Her mother died when she was but twelve years old; and being deprived of her ever-watchful guardian and guide, she abandoned herself to the reading of romances, and to a life of worldly frivolity and amusement, though she ever retained in her heart a great fear of offending God. Having been placed in a convent of the Augustinians, the good example of the nuns so affected her, that she resolved to escape from the perils of the world by renouncing it altogether. She then retired into the convent of the Incarnation at Avila, of the order of Mount Carmel, and took the habit in 1536, when she had reached her twenty-first year. She has herself described the celestial joy which inundated her soul when she had thus given herself to God. For some years she was afflicted with excruciating maladies, which she bore with admirable patience, and during which she was received with many heavenly favours; yet, looking back afterwards to the early period of her conventual life, she speaks of it as a time of tepidity and of want of correspondence with Divine grace. God had called her to the highest walks of sanctity. The signal favours bestowed upon her by her Divine Spouse inspired her with an ardent desire to correct all her faults, and overcome all her evil habits. Her progress in the spiritual life astonished the sisters, who had neither the courage nor the wish to follow her in her heavenward course; the convent in which she lived was one in which the wholesome severity of the rule had been mitigated, and it had declined greatly from its original fervour. Theresa earnestly hoped that her sisters would hail a reform which should bring them nearer the ideal of Christian perfection, and to the real spirit of their order. But when she mentioned her hopes and her plans, she was looked upon as a mere visionary, and became the laughing-stock of the community. Every possible impediment was thrown in her way; but she would not abandon her design, and seemed to derive an accession of strength and courage from the accumulated obstacles she encountered. At length she had the consolation of seeing the first convent of her reform founded at Avila in 1562, under the invocation of St. Joseph. The main points of her rule were the practice of mental prayer and the mortification of the senses; she insisted on the strictest observance of the rule which forbade intercourse with the world without; she closed the parlours, interdicted epistolary correspondence, and made all unavoidable conversations as brief and rare as possible; and above all, she endeavoured to provide her houses with holy and skilful confessors, from a conviction that wise and experienced guides are necessary for those who would aim at high degrees of perfection.

Her zeal was not contented with reforming the nuns of her order; she longed to extend the reform to its monks also. She knew all the difficulties of this task; but she had recourse to God, her refuge and strength, assured that He would bless and prosper an enterprise which He had Himself inspired for His own glory. She spoke to the provincial of the order, who at first treated her very discouragingly, but by degrees began to listen to her suggestions, and at length entered heartily into her projects. The first monk who took the habit of the reformed order was Father John, called John of the Cross; and his example was soon followed by many others. Those who have adopted St. Theresa's reform are styled the discalced or barefoot Carmelites, because they wear no shoes. St. John of the Cross, who was a humble, mortified, devout monk, one who loved sufferings and the Cross, sustained and encouraged Theresa in her attempt to bring back again the original spirit of the order of Mount Carmel;* and the holiness of his life and his many miracles have given him a place among the canonised saints of the Church. During the lifetime of St. Theresa, sixteen convents of nuns, and fourteen monasteries of friars, embraced her austere reform; and it was soon spread throughout Christendom. She died on the 4th of October 1582, thankful to have been permitted to toil and suffer for the glory of God. She left behind her many precious works on the spiritual life, together with her own life, written by herself at the command of her director. In those works we see the same ardent love of God, the same yearning desire for suffering, the same detestation of the world, and the same profound humility which marked her whole life. She was favoured with wonderful revelations and communings with God up to the very day of her death. Words often failed her to express the glowing fire which was consuming her, and she fell into ecstasies and raptures and trances, from which no human means could arouse her. Now and then, those who stood around her caught a few of the words which escaped her during these sacred seasons; they were: " Enlarge, O my God, enlarge the capacity of my heart, or abate the torrent of Thy graces !"

On the other hand, fresh and grievous trials awaited the Church. Whole kingdoms threw off her allegiance, and embraced the errors of Protestantism, renouncing and insulting the mother to whose care they had owed their faith, their civilisation, and their material prosperity. Scotland, Denmark, and Switzerland cast off the Catholic faith; and even France was for some time in danger of being ruled by an heretical king. Henry III., the brother of Charles IX., was assassinated at St. Cloud by the fanatic Jacques Clement; and as the race of Valois was extinguished by the death of this prince, the law of succession called to the throne Henry of Bourbon,

---

* The order of the Carmelites was instituted on Mount Carmel by John, Patriarch of Jerusalem, in the year 400. It was intended to perpetuate the spirit and power of Elias. St. Louis introduced it into Europe in 1238.

king of Navarre; but Henry was a Calvinist, a fact which
presented an insurmountable obstacle to his reigning over Catholic France. A league was accordingly formed to exclude
him from the succession, and to give the crown to one of the
house of Guise. Henry, however, had many partisans, and
was withal a brave and able soldier. War was waged with
doubtful success, when it was happily concluded by the young
king's consenting to abjure his errors and embrace the true
faith. Henry had been for some time studying the Catholic
religion; and there is every reason to believe that his conversion was sincere. One day he inquired of several Protestant
ministers whether they believed that he could obtain salvation in the Roman Church; and when they answered in the
affirmative, he asked, "Why, then, did you abandon it? Catholics maintain that you cannot be saved in your schism;
you allow that they may be saved in their religion: surely
common sense requires me to take the safer side, and to embrace a religion in which every one allows that I may obtain
salvation." Faithful to the engagements he had contracted,
Henry consulted in the main the interests of the Church;
though, like most other monarchs, they were frequently set
aside for objects of state policy. At the same time, he treated
his Protestant subjects with leniency; an edict, known as that
of Nantes, securing to them, under certain conditions, the
public exercise of their religion. His natural dispositions
were generous and good, and he had moments of apparently
genuine piety; but his moral conduct was little in accordance
with the principles of religion. He perished, like his predecessor, by the knife of an assassin, being murdered by Ra-
vaillac, in 1610.

§ 2. St. Francis de Sales, St. Vincent de Paul.

While heresy and schism were thus producing their natural
fruits, the Church was quietly reaping the harvest of the
reforms enjoined by the Council of Trent. From the so-called
Reformation arose numberless sects, each advocating doctrines
fundamentally opposed and contradictory to the other; turbulent and restless men fearlessly applied what professed to
be the great principle of the movement—the rejection of all
authority, and the right of every man to fashion his own
religion out of the materials provided by Holy Scripture; and

new professions of faith succeeded each other so rapidly, that
it was easy to predict men would in the end lose all percep-
tion of truth, and lapse into mere unbelief. Still the doctrine
commended itself to the natural inclinations of the human
heart; it was aided by the secular power; it offered as a prey
the confiscated property of the Church; and it spread apace.

   A large portion of Germany became infected with error;
the northern nations embraced it eagerly; Switzerland and
Savoy were welcoming it, when God raised up an apostle
to oppose its ravages. This wonderful man, whose name
has become proverbial for gentleness and holiness, was St.
Francis de Sales. He was born in 1567, near Annecy, in
Savoy, and received from his admirable mother a Christian
education, and the germs of those virtues which he practised
so faithfully throughout his life. His studies were begun at
Annecy; but the Count de Sales, his father, sent him to pro-
secute them in Paris. When he reached that dangerous city,
his first care was to seek out a wise and holy man to be his
director; and under his enlightened guidance, he was enabled
to escape the pollutions of a gay capital, and the snares which
encompass youth. During his sojourn in Paris, he lost nothing
of his tender and fervent piety. More than once he was exposed to critical temptations: one great trial was a frightful
suggestion of despair; he deemed himself rejected of God,
and doomed to everlasting punishment. During this be-
wildering delusion he passed whole nights in prayer, with
groanings and tears, and in protestations that he loved God
supremely, and would love Him always. Still nothing could
restore his confidence, or soothe his anguish, until one day,
as he was praying before an image of the Blessed Virgin, his
soul more than usually tortured by the apprehension of eternal perdition, he uttered these words: "My God, since I am
condemned to be cast forth from Thee, and to hate Thee
eternally, grant at least that so long as I remain on earth, I
may love Thee with all my heart." Scarcely had he uttered
these touching and heroic words, when a ray of sweet hope
penetrated the gloom of his soul, and soon dispersed the
clouds which darkened it.* Francis de Sales left Paris at

---

* St. Francis regarded this grace as the effect of the intercession of our
Blessed Lady. The image, before which he was praying when he received
this blessing of peace, is still preserved in the chapel of the Dames de St.
Thomas, Rue de Sèvres.

the age of seventeen, and proceeded to Padua, where, during several years, he studied jurisprudence and theology with great success. He then travelled throughout Italy, in compliance with the will of his father, who destined him to occupy in the world a position suited to his birth and his great attainments. He examined all its wonders attentively, and returned to his father's house with his simplicity and innocence unsullied. He had long desired to become a priest, and had privately taken a vow of chastity; but he had never, as yet, mentioned his wish to his father. When a proposition was made to him to marry very advantageously, he revealed his wish and his vow, and, after many difficulties and refusals, was allowed to be ordained priest in 1593. From the day of his ordination, he appeared like one imbued with the true apostolical spirit, glowing with zeal for the conversion and salvation of souls. He seldom preached in the towns, dreading the honour and the applause of men; but he went into the villages and hamlets, to instruct the poor country people, many of whom were living in ignorance and irreligion. But soon a wider field was thrown open to his zeal.

The Duke of Savoy, having regained possession of his states, which had been invaded by the Swiss Protestants, resolved to instruct his people carefully in their religion, to which the heretics had rendered them either hostile or indifferent. Every one shrank back in dismay from the perils and discomforts of so thankless a mission; but Francis volunteered to undertake it, and was accompanied by Louis de Sales, one of his relatives. When he drew near the scene of his labours, he threw himself on his knees and prayed fervently to God; he then tenderly embraced Louis de Sales, his companion, and said to him: "We are going amongst these people to do the work of Apostles; if we desire to succeed, let us follow the example of the first Evangelists; let us send back our horses, proceed on foot, and content ourselves with what is simply necessary to support life." They did so: Francis retained one small bag, containing the Holy Scriptures and his breviary; and, staff in hand, they walked forward through a rugged and almost impassable country. They endured during their mission toil and weariness, contradictions and persecutions; the inns were closed against them, and they were obliged to sleep in the open air; they were refused all the civilities of life, and treated as sorcerers and impostors. The rage of the Protestant ministers led them to attempt the life of Francis on several occasions. But nothing could abate his zeal or daunt his courage; and his mildness, his resolute perseverance, his holy example, accomplished by degrees what his sermons had failed in effecting. The most blinded and hardened heretics were gained over, and returned to the bosom of the Church; and in a few years an astonishing revival of religion was seen throughout the diocese of Geneva. The Catholic religion was almost every where restored; and many other labourers followed in the track of Francis, when once he had overcome the preliminary difficulties of the undertaking, and had proved the possibility of success.

The Bishop of Geneva was so struck by the resurrection of faith in his diocese, that he sought to obtain Francis as his coadjutor, and informed him of his wish. The holy priest refused for a long time the proffered dignity, but was at length constrained to yield to the combined entreaties of his bishop and of his sovereign, the Duke of Savoy. He was consecrated bishop in 1599; and his conduct in that high office showed that he regarded it only as an occasion for labouring more earnestly for the glory of God, and for the conversion of those who had wandered from the one fold into the wilderness of heresy and schism. He now directed his efforts to the country around the town of Gex; and in a very short time the entire population returned to the Catholic faith. He then set forth to visit his whole diocese. Through desert lands, over almost inaccessible mountains, he went on foot, climbing precipices where one false step would have hurled him to destruction, and sleeping on straw in the huts of the peasantry. His marvellous gentleness and sweetness of character won all hearts, and reclaimed a larger number of souls than the more vigorous and impassioned assaults of his missionaries. He was wont to say, that one drop of honey will attract more flies than a whole cask of vinegar; a maxim of controversy commended to our attention by its astonishing success. He established every where a regular system of catechetical exercises for the instruction of the young; and it was his wish that for them the truths of religion should be expounded with the greatest simplicity and clearness, and enforced with tenderness and unction. His zeal extended to every minutest detail; and was neither embarrassed by the multitude of its aims, nor impeded by the greatness of the obstacles it encountered. In concert with St. Jane Frances de Chantal, a woman of rare holiness, he founded the Order of the Visitation, which spread rapidly throughout France, Italy, and Spain. He reverenced the poor as the members and living representatives of Jesus Christ; and the abundance of his alms astonished those who knew how scanty were the revenues of his see. The Sovereign Pontiffs wrote to applaud and to bless his labours; and the kings of the earth were loud in the expressions of their esteem and admiration. Henry IV. offered him the bishopric of Paris; but Francis would not desert the portion of the Lord's vineyard intrusted to his care. He composed many works of piety, the merits of which are too well known to need mention. He died at Lyons in 1622, in the fifty-fifth year of his age, as he was returning from a mission to Louis XIII.

About the same time, another holy apostle was devoting himself to the instruction of the poor peasantry in the rude mountains of the Vivarais and Vélay. St. Francis Regis was born in Languedoc, and from his boyhood had felt drawn towards the religious state. As soon as he was master of his own actions, he entered the Company of Jesus, which was then so actively and beneficially labouring in every part of the world. He was employed in missions; and displayed a most wonderful zeal, courage, and activity for the glory of God. In order to succeed the more effectually with the rude inhabitants of the mountains, he chose the winter as the time for his retreats; and as the labours of the field were then over, the people came in crowds to receive his instructions. Days of painful toil were followed by whole nights passed in the confessional, and that during seasons of intense cold. He died in an obscure village, deprived of all succour, surrounded by the poor whom he had loved so well. His reputation was soon spread throughout France; and, even to this day, numerous pilgrims flock to the tomb of the sainted Francis Regis.

A saint still more illustrious was vouchsafed to France about this time, 1576-1660. St. Vincent de Paul, one of the greatest men the world has ever seen, was raised to the priesthood in 1600, after having passed his youth in watching his father's cattle. He came of an honourable but poor family, in the country of Dax or Acqs, in Gascony; and it was with great difficulty that he contrived to study for the priesthood. The Lord, who destined him for so great a work, smoothed all difficulties before him.   Shortly afterwards, in returning from Marseilles to Narbonne, he was taken by a Turkish corsair and carried prisoner to Tunis.   There he succeeded in converting his master, who was a Savoyard and an apostate; and they both contrived to escape from Tunis in a frail boat. Subsequently Vincent accompanied the vice-legate of Avignon to Rome, and was employed by Paul V. in a mission to Henry IV., which took him to Paris.   Instead of availing himself of the personal advantages to be derived from so favourable an introduction to the king, he went to lodge in the Hospital of Charity, and passed a part of every day in teaching and tending the sick.   But this was not enough to appease his eager thirst for the salvation of souls; and he accepted the cure of Clichy, near Paris, at the suggestion of the Cardinal de Bérulle.   The alms which he received in the capital, furnished him with the means to rebuild and adorn his church, and to support the poor of his parish.   After a year of successful toil, the cardinal induced him to undertake, in 1613, the education of the children of the Count de Joigny, who was then general superintendent of the galleys of France.   Vincent at first procured some mitigation of the lot of these unhappy men in Paris; he succeeded in having them all lodged in one building, and provided so effectually for their souls and bodies, by instituting an order for their relief, that Louis XIII. named him at once chief chaplain to the galleys.   He went to Marseilles, and found the slaves in a most deplorable condition.   Their bodily sufferings were aggravated by their ferocity, which found vent in frightful imprecations, and by their foul and shameless vices.   Vincent's zeal was stimulated to the utmost.   He went from rank to rank, listening to every complaint, commiserating and soothing their sufferings, ministering relief to their most pressing wants, and thus opening a sure way to their hearts. He induced the officers to adopt a more humane line of conduct towards wretches whose misery was already so extreme. The result was speedy and most satisfactory.   Increasing kindness on the one side induced increasing docility and submission on the other.   The aspect of the place was entirely changed; the most hardened criminals became penitents, and patiently endured the punishment of their crimes.   Amidst this unceasing work he found time to care for the instruction of the country people, in whose welfare he ever felt a lively interest.   He began to establish missions for them; and collected by degrees a body of priests, who devoted themselves to this important work with kindred zeal and energy.   In 1624, on the death of Madame de Gondy, he took up his abode with his priests in the College des Bons-Enfants, and drew up for them a code of rules, which were subsequently approved by the Holy See.   The canons regular of St. Victor gave up to Vincent the Priory of St. Lazarus, in 1632; and it was made the head-quarters of the congregation, which began to go by the designation of the Lazarist Fathers.   The name they gave themselves was that of Priests of the Missions, because they devoted themselves especially to missions, both in France and in foreign lands, especially in the East. They were much employed likewise in the education of those who were preparing for holy orders; and the seminaries of many dioceses of France are still under their direction.

Vincent de Paul now applied his energies to the foundation of the society which has become so celebrated throughout the world, that of the Sisters of Charity.   The vocation of these daughters of St. Vincent is, to tend the sick, to bring up children whose parents have abandoned them, to instruct young girls who are exposed to peculiar perils, to attend the hospitals and prisons: an admirable institute, which religion alone could have conceived, and which the Catholic Church alone has been able to carry into effect.

The heart of Vincent was touched particularly by the sad fate of so many children, the offspring of sin or of misery, who were abandoned in the streets and lanes of the capital. He gathered together a number of pious ladies, and committed to them the charge of these helpless foundlings; but the expense of their maintenance became so great, that he was on the point of abandoning the project, lest it should exhaust resources which were demanded for works of charity even still more pressing.   In this extremity, Vincent assembled these ladies, and proposed to them the question, Whether the work should be abandoned or continued?   He laid before them the reasons on both sides: hitherto they had rescued 500 or 600 of these children, who would have perished but for their care; many were now learning useful trades, others were almost ready to begin; all had been taught to know

God and to love Him. And then, raising his voice, he concluded with these striking words: "Moreover, ladies, compassion and charity have induced you to adopt these little creatures as your children; you are their mothers in the order of grace, since their parents in the order of nature have cast them off. Consider, now, whether you will forsake them. Cease for a moment to be their mothers, and be their judges; their life or death is in your hands. I am now going to collect your votes. The time is come to pronounce their sentence, and to declare whether or no you will still have pity on them." The whole meeting was melted to tears, and it was resolved unanimously that the work must go on, at all costs. The king interposed with his assistance; and the pious work was placed on a solid foundation, and has lasted to our own days, not only in Paris, but in the larger cities and towns of France. It is striking to observe the lasting fruitfulness accorded by God to the labours of His faithful servants, as contrasted with the barrenness of the casual efforts of those who have forsaken and rejected the Church of God. Time would fail us to recapitulate the numerous works of charity which this man of lowly birth and simple manners set on foot in Paris. He obtained endowments for the hospitals of Bicêtre, Salpetrière, and la Pitié; for the hospital at Marseilles erected for the galley-slaves, and that of the Holy Name of Jesus for infirm old men. He was a zealous protector and reformer of convents. He supported the establishment of the Daughters of Providence, of St. Geneviève, and of the Cross; and laboured much in the reform of Grammont, Prémontré, and the abbey of St. Geneviève. He aided Cardinal Richelieu in the selection of holy and zealous priests for the higher ecclesiastical dignities; and was nominated by Anne of Austria, when regent, one of four, called a Council of Conscience, whose duty it was to decide upon the qualifications of those who were recommended to important offices in the Church. It has been calculated that more than 1,600,000*l.* passed through his hands for works of charity in France and elsewhere. During the ravages of civil war, whole districts were almost maintained by him and by his priests; Lorraine and Picardy were especially the objects of his care. But in spite of this weath and influence, and the wonders he wrought, he was stil poor, humble, and detached from every thing earthly. He died in 1660, professing himself the lowest and most useless of men. One such priest is enough to prove the divinity of the religion which could form and inspire him, and which has since placed him on her altars.*

§ 3. The Seventeenth Century.

The seventeenth century, which had been ushered in by St. Francis de Sales and St. Vincent de Paul, was destined to produce a long succession of holy men, who should perpetuate and extend the noble works begun by these eminent leaders, and illustrate and gladden the Church by the splendour of their virtues. It was a century of great men; and the Church in her degree shared the general elevation. Governments, laws, institutions, tribunals,—all were as yet penetrated by the holy influence of the faith; and although human passion too largely qualified the good that was working in society at large, still the recognised principles and rules of action and conduct were religious and Catholic. It was in this respect as far above the two centuries which have followed it, as its great men were superior to those of later times.

While St. Vincent de Paul was still alive, Father Bernard was actively engaged in works of charity in Paris. Born of rich parents, he at first led a life of dissipation; but on his conversion, he took holy orders, and devoted himself to the service of the poor, the sick, and those who were condemned to death. For twenty years he continued his labours of charity at the Hôtel Dieu, a large hospital of Paris, then at the hospital of La Charité; and he expended in alms a fortune of nearly 20,000l.

The Cardinal de Bérulle, who has been already mentioned in connection with St. Vincent, had founded at Paris the Congregation of the Oratory,† the object of which was to honour the infancy, the life, and the death of our Lord, to instruct the young, to direct seminaries, and to give missions and retreats. The second superior of the congregation, Father Condren, a man of remarkable holiness, contributed largely to the establishment of another institution destined to exercise a wonderful influence upon the clergy. M. Olier, curé of St. Sulpice, had been giving missions in France and Auvergne;

---

* For the labours of St. Vincent's congregation in Ireland see Bedford's Life of the saint, ch. xxi. p. 177.

† See the note on the French Oratory, at the end of the life of St. Philip Neri, in Butler's *Lives of the Saints*.

and, on his return to Paris, he resolved to found a seminary for preparing young men for the priesthood. He was encouraged in his resolve by St. Vincent de Paul and Father Condren; and commenced his labours first at Vaugirard, a village near Paris, and afterwards in his own parish of St. Sulpice. The community he formed has retained its name of Priests of St. Sulpice. M. Olier was one of the holiest and most successful priests of his day. He reformed the suburb of St. Germain, which was a kind of sanctuary for all who wished to live in crime. He formed an association of nobles and gentlemen, who promised, in the face of the congregation of St. Sulpice, on Whitsunday, that they would neither send nor accept a challenge to fight a duel. The practice of duelling was then one of the most grievous and incurable plagues of society; M. Olier rendered it dishonourable, and so prepared the way for its almost entire suppression. The pious and learned congregation he founded has continued to discharge, in the spirit of its founder, that duty of which it is hardly possible to overrate the importance—the training for the priesthood those to whom God has granted a vocation. "I know nothing more truly apostolical than St. Sulpice," said Fénélon, on his deathbed; and the experience of the clergy and faithful of France and of America has confirmed this judgment.

Another society of priests, that of St. Nicolas-du-Chardonnet, was formed by M. Bourdoise, who died in 1655, in the odour of sanctity. He was a man eaten up with zeal for the house of God; his life was an almost uninterrupted series of catechisings, missions, and conferences. The *Frères de la Doctrine Chrétienne*, or Christian Brothers as they are commonly called in England, were first assembled and established at Rheims, in 1680, by the blessed John Baptist de la Salle. This holy priest was profoundly affected by the ignorance which was one of the primary causes of the vices of the poor; and he devoted his life and his substance to destroy these vices at their root, by establishing schools in which children might be taught from their infancy the pure doctrines of the Gospel, and the practice of all Christian virtues. He collected a few devoted men, who entered into his plans, established a novitiate at Rheims, and afterwards at Rouen; and had the consolation of beholding his institute spreading and consolidating itself before his death in 1719. His numerous children have drunk deeply of his spirit, and have sown in all parts of the world the seed of the Word of God. Their admirable schools are still the source of numerous blessings to the cities of France; affording instruction to the poor labourer who wishes to learn, and aiding the priest in his labours to prepare the younger members of his flock for confirmation and first communion.

While the Catholic Church was thus silently refuting the calumnies of heretics by her long array of devoted saints, God raised up for her other defenders in other departments of thought and action, men who came forth armed for the fight,—as were St. Augustine, St. Chrysostom, Origen, and St. Jerome,—with the sword of the Spirit—the word of God. Bossuet, the greatest man of an age which abounded in great men, was one of the most intrepid defenders of the faith. He was born in Burgundy, at a short distance from the village of Fontaine, which was the country of St. Bernard, his great model. From his childhood he gave indications of the magnificent future which was in store for him. He was but eight years old when he received the clerical tonsure; and never did he regret this early sacrifice of his liberty and life for the glory of God. The main object of his labours was the refutation and conversion of Protestants, numbers of whom he reclaimed from error and schism. His successes soon became known. Being summoned to Paris, he preached several times before the king, who was so struck with the genius and virtue of the youthful preacher, that he wrote to the father of Bossuet to congratulate him on a son who would immortalise his name. Louis XIV. soon gave a clearer proof of the esteem and confidence he felt for Bossuet, by intrusting to him the education of the dauphin, and by naming him Bishop of Condom; from which see he was translated to Meaux. His writings produced many conversions; and the celebrated Turenne was one of the fruits of his learning and skill. The life of Bossuet was worthy of his writings and of his fame; his time was employed either in study, or in the work of his ministry. He preached, catechised, and heard confessions constantly; in a word, he was a holy bishop, as well as an able defender and expositor of religion; and has won for himself a reputation which even the world cannot gainsay.

The Church of France glories almost equally in the memory of Fénélon, the learned and holy Archbishop of Cambray. He was educated at St. Sulpice, where his excellent

disposition, his gentleness, his vivacity, and ability, were
moulded and formed into a character of exquisite beauty.
In the earlier years of his priesthood, he undertook the missions of Poitou and of Saintonge. The simplicity of his character, joined to his extraordinary genius, the power of his
eloquence, and the suavity of his manner, enabled him to
bring back to the fold of Christ a great number of Protestants. In 1689, Louis XIV. appointed him tutor to his grand-
son, the Duke of Burgundy, and named him Archbishop of
Cambray. Fénélon was for a short time led astray by an
opinion which was afterwards condemned by the Holy See;
but he submitted with becoming and edifying humility to the
sentence, and devoted himself with increased zeal to good
works. His memory has ever been held in deserved veneration in the Church; and the writings he bequeathed to posterity have earned him a title to intellectual celebrity.

Louis XIV. was doubtless a great monarch. He raised
his nation to a high pitch of glory; but the faults of his
reign laid the foundation of the terrible miseries which were
in store for France less than a century later. His constant
wars—wars of ambition and aggression—exhausted the fin-
ances of the country; while his disregard for morality during
all the early years of his life—a disregard which was even
accompanied by a certain outward decorum and respect for
the ordinances of religion—had the worst effect in the way
of example on the nobility of the kingdom, who rendered him
a homage little short of idolatry. His faith never wavered;
and the piety which he had displayed by fits and starts during
his whole reign, became habitual in the latter and penitential
portion of his life, when he was assailed by adversities and family afflictions, which he bore with a noble and Christian spirit.
But his repentance came too late to repair the evil; vice was
but driven into concealment until the death of the king. In
common with most of the monarchs of his time, and as part
of that system of policy whereby the monarchy absorbed all
other powers into itself, he strove to loosen as far as possible
the connection between the Church in France and the Holy
See. He dreaded the power of the Pope, which had been of
late used against France; and he was jealous of that independence which could not be brought within the scope of his
personal government. Hence he came in collision with the
Sovereign Pontiff on various occasions, and his conduct was

overbearing and unseemly. In 1682 he convened an assembly of bishops, who drew up and signed the celebrated Four
Articles, the drift of which was to reduce the authority of the
Pope within the narrowest limits compatible with the preservation of unity. . They were an unsuccessful attempt to
determine the limit between the spiritual power and the temporal; they excited protracted and very injurious disputes,
which undoubtedly lessened the Church's influence over the
minds and morals of the people.

Louis XIV. likewise employed against his Protestant subjects measures of severity, the policy of which is very question-
able, while their injustice is manifest. Too easily persuaded
that his royal will would suffice to restore religious unity, and
irritated by the disloyal attitude of the Protestants, he revoked
the Edict of Nantes. The pacific policy of Henry the Fourth
was thus forsaken, and a solemn treaty violated. The result was
the expatriation of many thousands of sincere, though deluded
men, whom a more generous conduct might have won; and
the retention within the kingdom of a number of hypocrites.
It is true that a similar policy was elsewhere pursued against
Catholics, and that the opinion of the nation sustained the injustice of the government. The Church may well rejoice in
the great ecclesiastics who added such glory to his reign, and
award him her gratitude for his steady opposition to Jansenism;
while she regrets that she can render but a limited homage to
the memory of the great king of the seventeenth century.

§ 4. State of the Church in Europe at the beginning of the Eighteenth Century.

Among the illustrious Pontiffs who occupied the chair of
St. Peter, Innocent XI. and Innocent XII. deserve especial
mention for the zeal and prudence with which they sought
to carry out the decrees of the Council of Trent, by enforcing
a wise and holy discipline.

In the political world civilisation had largely advanced,
and all wore a fair appearance externally; but underneath
were fermenting those principles of atheism, immorality, and
anarchy which were soon to inundate Europe. The Catholic
faith, still respected by the temporal powers, had lost the
hold it had upon them during the middle ages. It was protected and upheld rather for state purposes than out of any
true zeal for the interests of religion. Spain and Portugal,

already deeply corrupted by the gold of the New World, were defended against the assaults of heresy by a formidable tribunal, called the Inquisition. This institution originated in France, during the war with the Albigenses, in the thirteenth century; but it did not gain a permanent footing in that country. It was introduced into Catalonia in 1232, and soon spread throughout the whole peninsula. It was directed, in the first instance, against the Jews and Moors, who, after embracing the faith, secretly returned to their former religion; but, in 1561, Philip II., the successor of Charles V., enlarged its powers and jurisdiction, and employed it with great effect to stay the progress of Lutheranism in Spain. It is to be observed, that the tribunal did not itself pass sentence of death; its function was simply to ascertain and declare the fact, whether the persons brought before it were either apostate Christians or heretics; the temporal power assigned the punishment, and executed it on the guilty. Rulers have an undoubted right, it is even their bounden duty, to maintain the peace and security of their dominions; and in the sixteenth century capital punishments were more common, and the administration of justice more severe, than in later times; nowhere was the judicial code more sanguinary than in our country, down to an almost recent date. No wonder, then, that the Protestant sectaries met with little mercy. They had contrived to set Europe in a flame; dissensions and civil wars followed hard on the steps of the new doctrine. They were consequently regarded by Catholic princes as innovators, whose teaching was as fatal to their own temporal authority as it is to the spiritual interests of mankind. Thus it was in Spain, heretics were punished as enemies of the state. But, inasmuch as the civil power is not competent to entertain questions of doctrine, it required the judgment of the Inquisition on the facts of the case. If a man was accused of heresy, the Inquisition was charged to examine him and decide on his innocence or guilt. If guilty, it reported that he had published, or that he held, doctrines opposed to the Church's teaching and subversive of public order. The civil power received the report, and dealt with the prisoner in its own fashion; the Church, as such, had nothing to do with the kind or measure of punishment awarded.

That the punishments inflicted were inordinately severe,

cannot be denied; but for this the Church was not responsible. The Inquisition was, as Ranke calls it, "a purely political institute," erected rather in opposition to the ecclesiastical power than in subserviency to it. The Popes continually re- monstrated against its proceedings; and when remonstrances were of no avail, offered the sufferers an asylum at Rome; thus rescuing, as it is recorded, in one year 230 persons, and 200 in another. Often, too, they set aside and annulled the judgments, and on more than one occasion censured and ex- communicated the Inquisitors. Moreover, we must judge the government of Spain by the peculiar circumstances of that time. Impartial history, while it laments the excessive cruelty which marked the Spanish government, will record that Spain was thus spared the horrors and ravages of the civil wars which the Protestants excited in Germany and in France; and, above all, will not fail to take into account the sufferings of Catholics in England, and in all countries where Protestantism was dominant, or where it was enabled to make head against the civil power.[*]

It is in England that we may study to best advantage the results and consequences of the great change in religion. The very principle of the falsely-called Reformation is inde- pendence, and revolt against authority. The ecclesiastical power was the first object of attack; the temporal, which had been exorbitantly increased under the Tudor sovereigns, was the second. The seventeenth century was, in England, one of rebellion, civil strife, and revolution. The unfortunate Charles I. lost his life on the scaffold. Cromwell, a bold and able usurper, seized the reins of government; the state church was swept away, and various religious factions contended for the possession of England. The restoration of Charles II. was a feeble and transitory reaction. This monarch, a slave to his own vices, suffered the Catholics to be persecuted, while in heart convinced of the truth of their religion, which he secretly embraced on his deathbed. His brother James II., already a convert, succeeded him. Had he been a better man, and had he followed the wise counsels of the Pope, his zeal for the faith might gradually have effected much to- wards restoring the Catholic religion. As it was, his impru- dence only excited against him the bigotry of his people,

---

[*] For some account of the Inquisition, see Balmez's *Protestantism and Catholicity compared*, chap. xxxv.-vii.; also *Clifton Tracts*, No. 58.

who, calling in his son-in-law, William of Orange, compelled the unhappy monarch to abdicate his throne. William and Mary were constituted joint sovereigns, on conditions which henceforth greatly restricted the royal authority. Complete liberty of conscience was solemnly guaranteed by William; but the Catholics benefited little by the engagement. Still, throughout this century, and under every form of government, even while the utmost license of opinion was claimed by such men as Milton, repressive measures of increasing rigour were employed against the professors of the ancient faith. Elizabeth had left the Catholics a feeble and depressed remnant, in consequence of the policy described in a former chapter; James I., son of the Catholic Mary, Queen of Scots, put in force a multitude of harassing and oppressive laws, the effect of which was even more discouraging than open persecution. No Catholic could travel more than five miles from his own home, or remain in London or within ten miles of it. Those who did not attend the services of the state church were fined 20l. for the first offence, 40l. for the second, 60l. for the third; and half the fine went to the informer. The zeal of churchwardens was stimulated by a reward of forty shillings for every "recusant" who absented himself from the Protestant church. At any moment the state bishops and justices of the peace might tender to Catholics the oath of supremacy. "Popish recusants" were forbidden to be counsellors, advocates, or attorneys, or to serve in the army or navy. Any one who betrayed a Catholic was rewarded with one-third of the convict's property. No Catholic could appear in a court of law, either as witness, plaintiff, or defendant. Those who did not take their children to be baptised at the Protestant church within a month after birth, were fined 100l. All beads, relics, Popish books, and crucifixes were to be defaced and burnt; and these are but specimens of the repressive laws of that unhappy time. Charles I. had married a Catholic princess, and was disposed to alleviate the sufferings of the oppressed race; but the high-church party of Laud combined with that of the Puritans to persecute and slander the adherents of the ancient faith. In the first nine years of this reign, 11,970 recusants were convicted and punished in England alone. In 1643, the lands of all "Papists," and of those who harboured any priest or Jesuit, or heard Mass, or did not publicly abjure the

"Bishop of Rome," were confiscated. The advocates of liberty of conscience expressly excepted from its privileges those who professed "Atheism, Popery, Prelacy, or any damnable heresy, to be enumerated by the parliament." In 1655, it was enacted, that no Catholic should vote for a member of parliament. It is a weary and a sickening task to follow the course of legislation and of popular violence during the Restoration; its spirit was aptly described by a noble peer in his place in parliament: "He would not have so much as a Popish dog at the palace; not so much as a Popish cat to purr or mew about the king." William III., the champion of civil and religious liberty, increased the rigour of the laws against Catholics. For example,—if any one apprehended a bishop or priest saying Mass, he was rewarded with 100*l.* Catholics were deprived of every thing but personal property; and this was reduced and drained by repeated and exorbitant fines. We have omitted mention of those who suffered death for religion during this century; it is enough to have shown the manner in which the theory of private judgment and liberty of conscience was understood by its advocates. Nevertheless, many Catholic families bore with unshrinking fortitude this vexatious and continuous persecution. Even Scotland, deprived of its priests and schools, contained many who preserved the true faith as a treasure more precious than property, or life itself. Towards the close of Cromwell's reign, some missionaries contrived to reach Scotland. In 1697, a bishop was sent; and religion has maintained itself in that Puritan country with singular success. Ireland, three-fourths of whose population continued Catholic, had preserved its bishops. The heretics had seized the churches, the houses, and the revenues of the lawful pastors of Christ's flock; but the succession of bishops and priests was continued in poverty and in sorrow; and the formidable schemes which Cromwell and William III. attempted to carry out with such revolting cruelty came to naught. Amidst persecutions and vexations the most oppressive and unrelenting, the true-hearted Irish have persisted in their allegiance to the faith; and the state establishment, forcibly imposed upon them, has never to this day become the church of the nation.

Germany was the cradle of Protestantism; and there it carried out its destructive principles to their legitimate con-

sequences. The House of Austria was its vigilant adversary;
and consequently the Lutherans directed their efforts against
the imperial authority. From schism to rebellion the step is
easy. Three sects contended for the mastery in Germany
during this century: the Lutherans, the Calvinists, and the
Sacramentaries—who, receiving the teaching of Luther in
other points, rejected his version of the doctrine of the real
presence in the Eucharist. Such elements of discord could
not long remain inoperative. Bohemia gave the signal of
war, and it was eagerly taken up by all the Protestant
princes; while the emperor and the Catholic princes formed
a league of resistance. This struggle, which entailed endless
wars and miseries on Germany, lasted for thirty years—from
1618 to 1648. The heretics were aided by the king of Denmark, and then by Gustavus Adolphus, king of Sweden, who
was killed at the battle of Lutzen, in 1632. Peace was restored in 1648; and a treaty was drawn up, which granted
special advantages to the Protestants. During the reign of
the Emperor Leopold I. (1658-1705), there were great hopes
of a reconciliation of the contending parties. Bossuet, the celebrated Bishop of Meaux, and Leibnitz, the eminent Protestant
philosopher, had a long correspondence on the subject; but it
led to no real result: the hour of mercy and of pardon for Germany was not yet come. Meanwhile, the Turks, emboldened
by lesser successes, advanced to the gates of Vienna, the out-
post and citadel of Christianity. God heard the prayers of
His servants, and raised up John Sobieski, king of Poland,
whose valour rescued the city and beat back the Turks for
ever from further aggression upon Europe.*

The pretended reform had left the Church to deplore the
loss of a large part of Switzerland. Seven cantons, among
which was Lucerne, the residence of the papal nuncio, preserved their fidelity to the Roman See; the rest were ravaged by the new heresy. The course of the so-called Reformation in Denmark and Sweden was, in most respects,
similar to that followed in England. It was brought about
by their respective monarchs, who, along with the greedy
nobility, coveted the wealth of the Church, and dominion in
ecclesiastical matters. Gustavus Vasa, celebrated in secular
history for the heroic bravery with which, in 1544, he freed
his country from the yoke of Denmark, is infamous in the

* See the *Knights of St. John,*—Relief of Vienna.

annals of the Church for the guilt of severing Sweden from Catholic unity. Still there remained many of the faithful in both kingdoms, governed by vicars apostolic, delegates of the Holy See. One of these deserves honourable mention for the ardour of his zeal, the holiness of his life, and the salutary effects of his ministrations in both these countries. He was a learned Danish anatomist, named Stenon, who relinquished his professional prospects and devoted himself to God in the priesthood (1638-1687). He was raised to the episcopate, and preached the Gospel in Hanover, Mecklenburg, and Denmark with great success. He died in the odour of sanctity.

We cannot but adore the mercy of God, in that, when He chastises a nation by allowing error to prevail, He still keeps open the fountains of salvation and sanctification for His elect. His protecting providence watches over those who are His; it will never allow any to perish for want of the needful succour of His grace.

CHAPTER X.

HISTORY OF MISSIONS AFTER THE DEATH OF ST. FRANCIS XAVIER, 1552.

§ 1. Missions of India, China, and Japan.

IT is a general tradition in the East, supported by many historical monuments, that the faith was first preached in India by St. Thomas the Apostle. About the sixth century, the Nestorians, retreating eastward, infested these primitive Churches with their errors, and intruded their patriarchs upon them. By degrees the people lapsed into extreme ignorance, and blended with their ancient faith and worship many dogmas and usages of paganism; they likewise fell into grievous sins, unchecked by their equally ignorant and corrupted pastors. In the twelfth and thirteenth centuries most of them yielded to the sway and religion of Mahomet; and there was still a large remnant attached to their original idolatry. When the Portuguese established settlements in India, the missionaries of the Catholic Church came in their train; an archbishopric was established at Goa, with suffragan sees at Cochin, St. Thomé, and elsewhere. Soon after this, St. Francis Xavier appeared, and wrought in this part of India the wondrous effects already recounted. He left religion in a flourishing state, the stream of conversions abundant, and the whole of society leavened with a wholesome and edifying morality. From that time to the present, the Jesuits and the French Congregation of Missions, established at Paris in 1663, have sent a constant supply of labourers into this part of the harvest.

The Apostle of India died, as we have seen, in sight of the Chinese empire; and, like Moses, beheld the good land he was not permitted to enter. Towards the close of the sixteenth century, Father Ricci and two other Jesuits were so eager to devote themselves to the conversion of the Chinese, that they found means to gain admission in the train of some Portuguese merchants. It seemed to them clear that Christianity had been already preached in this vast empire: a singular monument was discovered in 1625; a slab of stone, ten feet long, and five feet broad, on which was the sign of the cross, a list of seventy evangelists who had come from Judea to preach to the Chinese, and an abridgment of Christian doctrine,—all in Syriac characters. However this may be, it is certain that the name of Jesus Christ was utterly forgotten when the Jesuit fathers arrived. Father Ricci, who was profoundly versed in the language, laws, and customs of the country, began by gaining the admiration of the people for his mathematical and astronomical science. He obtained permission to establish himself in the first instance at Canton; then at Nankin, where he built an observatory. As the number of his admirers increased, so did the number of Christians; and his fame preceded him to the capital, whither he was summoned in 1600. The emperor was so much struck by his ability, that he permitted him to reside in Pekin; and even accepted and placed in his palace some paintings of our Lord and of the Blessed Virgin, which were presented to him by the missionary. The faith was soon preached every where; many of the great officers of the court were converted, and a large number of persons in all ranks of society; a church was erected; and at Father Ricci's death in 1617, he left this Christian community in a flourishing and hopeful condition. He was succeeded by Father Schall, who was summoned to court, placed at the head of the board of mathematical science, and created a mandarin. His period of court favour was, however, of brief duration; he soon found himself exposed to insults and persecution: was again restored to his dignities; disgraced a second time; and died in 1666, after having laboured and suffered as an apostle during forty-five years. Several Dominicans and secular priests came to the aid of the Jesuits, and their labours were followed by great success. The Pope divided the empire into districts; bishops and vicars apostolical were named for each province, except Pekin, where a titular bishop was located. This arrangement greatly furthered the propagation of the faith; and in 1698 new missions were established in spite of the opposition of mandarins and bonzes. Besides these persecutions, the Portuguese threw every obstacle in their way from motives of earthly policy; but the faith and fervour of the missionaries increased in the measure of their difficulties, and the work of conversion still proceeded. In 1644 a revolution placed a dynasty of Tartar princes on the throne, and by them the Church was protected and favoured during the remainder of the century. Throughout the empire, buildings were raised for the worship of the one true God; a magnificent church was erected even within the precincts of the imperial palace. A harvest so abundant attracted fresh labourers, who found themselves still unequal to gather-in the fruits which the grace of God was producing through their ministry. Their activity and devotedness supplied their deficiency in number, and the light of the faith penetrated to the remotest provinces of the empire.

Japan, which is contiguous to China, but totally different in its laws and customs, opened out a glorious prospect to the hopes of the Church. The Christian religion, which had been so energetically preached by St. Francis Xavier, had made such progress, that within sixty years of his death there were two millions of faithful. The greater number of the nobles were either Christians, or protectors and friends of the missionaries. Some of the reigning princes had renounced idolatry; and the sovereigns of Bongo, Arima, Fungo, and Omura, in particular, furthered the Gospel by their living faith and noble works of charity. They sent a solemn embassy to Pope Gregory XIII., in 1584, to convey to him their acknowledgment of his spiritual authority; and the ambassadors were welcomed in every city with public rejoicings. Their piety was the subject of wonder and admiration; and those who saw them could not but adore God for His mercy and grace towards a remote and idolatrous people. The change in Japan recalled to mind the primitive days of the Church: the new converts were remarkable for their docility and humility, with a most sensitive fear of sin; and so rigorous in their practices of penance, that it required all the authority of their directors to restrain them from injuring their health; they were more like an active body of religious than mere secular neophytes. Civandono, the king of Bongo, had long resisted the voice of God; and when at length he submitted, he swore, that if all the missionaries, and all the Christians in Europe, and the Pope himself, were to abandon the faith, he would still defend it to the last drop of his blood. He built a city, of which the population was exclusively Christian; meaning to retire to it after having abdicated the throne in favour of his son, that he might devote himself to the exercises of religion, and no longer behold any traces of idolatry. The other kings were similarly earnest and devoted. But meanwhile a terrific storm was slowly gathering. By one of those sudden revolutions so frequent in the East, and especially in Japan, a usurper, whose name was Teigo-Sama, seized the imperial throne. Having one day heard a Spanish pilot say, that his sovereign always began the conquest of a country by sending missionaries to prepare the way, he became alarmed at the presence of so many Jesuits and other religious in his dominions. His alarm was increased by intelligence that European ships, of strange forms and immense size, had appeared on the coast of China and among the adjacent islands. From that moment he resolved to sacrifice the new religion to his ambition and to the security of his usurped dominions. Many of his tributary kings either professed or protected Christianity; and for a time he was obliged to dissemble his intent; but in the provinces under his immediate rule, he soon commenced a general persecution. Then were renewed the glories of the primitive ages: fresh and horrible torments were invented to daunt the courage of the noble confessors of Jesus Christ; but in vain. They were arrested in great numbers and thrown into prison, where they were secured, not with chains and bonds, but with sharpened instruments, which pierced and lacerated their limbs. They were dragged along by the hair of their heads; thrown down and trampled upon amidst brutal mockeries. The legs of some were crushed and ground between beams of wood furnished with points of iron; others, deprived of their arms, their noses, their eyes, their ears, expired in lingering tortures. Among these victims of paganism were twenty-four whose sufferings attracted special attention. Three of them were Jesuits, and six were Franciscans; they were all crucified on a rising ground, since called the Martyrs' Mound or hill. As they were led to martyrdom, they sang hymns to God; and when they were stretched upon the fatal wood, they repeated together the canticle of Zachary, *Benedictus Dominus Deus Israel.* Among them were some in the first bloom of youth, whose holy fortitude edified the survivors, and sustained their failing courage.

Teigo-Sama died soon afterwards, in 1598. Although the number of Christians whom he put to death was comparatively small, he had set an example which his successors too faithfully followed, and transmitted to them a political prejudice which led to the total extermination of Christianity in Japan. Persecutions succeeded one another with great rapidity and unprecedented cruelty. Every ingenuity artifice could suggest was used to multiply and protract the torments of the martyrs. They were doubled together until their backs were broken; reeds and bones were thrust beneath their nails, which were then torn out with pincers; they were thrown into pits with venomous serpents; burning torches were applied to their limbs and bodies: but it is needless to multiply the horrible details. These manifold cruelties failed to abate their courage, or to extort one groan or tear; on the contrary, they sang praises to God amidst their torments. The calmness, the joyousness, the feeling of triumph with which they awaited death in its most appalling forms, attest the power of that grace which sustained them; nor were miracles wanting to convince the heathen that the Almighty hand of God was put forth to defend His suffering servants. A child, six years old, who at his baptism had received the name of Peter, was awakened early in the morning, and told that he was to be beheaded together with his father. The little confessor expressed his gladness with an air of sincerity which showed the power of Divine grace in him. He was dressed in his gayest clothing, and then took the hand of the soldier who had come to fetch him, and walked calmly forward to death. The first object which met his view on arriving at the place of execution, was the headless trunk of his father covered with blood. The child knelt down without betraying any emotion; said his simple prayer beside the corpse; and then loosened his collar and presented his neck to receive the fatal blow. The touching scene moved the crowd; the executioner himself threw down his sabre and fled. Several others were so affected that they too declined the murderous task; and it was found necessary to employ a brutal slave, whose trembling and inexperienced hand discharged a succession of blows on the head and shoulders of the tender lamb of Jesus, until he was hacked in pieces without uttering one single cry. Such was the might of the grace vouchsafed to infants and to sucklings; and thus did the enemy of souls renew, on this distant island, the bloody sacrifices which, in lands nearer our own, had marked the first spread of the Gospel of salvation. Nor were the martyrs of Japan inferior in courage and in fortitude to those of Rome, of Smyrna, of Carthage, or of Lyons. Their sufferings were even greater and more prolonged; whole volumes have been filled with their details. The son of the king of Tomba, who had been banished by the emperor for his faith, wrote to the persecuted Christians the following letter, not unworthy of Polycarp or Ignatius:

"I have learned with much sorrow, dearly beloved, that the persecution has led some few of you to apostatise; but I am consoled by the infinitely greater number of those whose resolution has remained firm and unbroken. O, how happy should I deem myself to be permitted to be amongst those glorious prisoners of Jesus Christ, whose blessedness it is to die the martyr's death! I would kiss the blood they shed for Jesus; I would implore them to pray that the same grace might be granted to me. And this is the prayer I wish you to offer for me, beloved brethren. I congratulate those who have relinquished every thing for their faith's sake. I admire them, but I am not astonished at them. How can any men be so void of sense as to throw away the pure gold for the mire of earth, to place its contemptible riches in comparison with everlasting rest and happiness? How great is the service that is rendered us, in depriving us of the worthless things we must one day forsake, and which meanwhile are the most formidable obstacle to our salvation! It does not beseem me, the lowest of you all, to give you advice; but I

conjure you, as my dear brethren in the faith, to trample beneath your feet every thing that is of this perishing earth.
Remember that we have now reached the time and the crisis
of our trial. It is by many rude and sharp strokes that the
shapeless stone is fashioned into the base or the capital of some
stately pillar; it is by fire and by blows that iron takes the
form designed for it by the artificer; it is by the fire and the
smart of many tribulations that Jesus Christ purifies and
sanctifies those whom He chooses to be living stones in the
spiritual and everlasting temple of His Church. Let us show
ourselves worthy of the honour thus laid upon us. The Lord
would never have allowed us to be assailed, did He not wish
and intend to crown us. Few could have borne more than
I have been and am compelled to bear; but God has so sustained my weakness, that my wearied persecutors now let me
alone, in sheer despair of overcoming me. Still it is not
enough to come forth the victor from a thousand combats;·
the reward is given to him alone who perseveres unto the end.
Cease not, then, to implore, for yourselves and for me, this
inestimable grace of perseverance."

These persecutions were encouraged and rendered still
more cruel by some wretched Dutchmen who had come to
Japan for purposes of commerce. Their jealousy as merchants was excited by finding Spanish vessels in the ports of
the empire; their zeal as Protestants was kindled against
their Catholic rivals; and they succeeded in persuading the
Japanese that the Jesuits were a detestable race of men who
had been ignominiously expelled from Germany, Sweden, and
England, for attempting to make those countries tributary to
Spain; and that their real object in Japan was to bring it
under the rule of European sovereigns. The guardian of the
youthful emperor—it was in 1613—had long plotted the
death of his ward and his own elevation to the throne; but as
religion is ever the surest warrant of the fidelity of subjects,
he had been deterred by a fear that the Christians would rise
in support of their legitimate sovereign. He resolved to exterminate these dangerous opponents by a sudden and sharp
persecution. An edict appeared, proscribing Christianity at
once and for ever. In the neighbourhood of Nangasaki is a
volcanic mountain, which vomits forth flame and smoke, while
streams of lava, and of boiling water impregnated with sul-
phur, pour down its sides. No animal found his lair there;

nor would the birds of the air cross it in their flight. Many Christians were thrown into the crater of this volcano; others were dipped partially into the lava or the boiling water, and then withdrawn, in the hope that the agony they suffered would induce them to apostatise. Some were laid on the brink of the crater and sprinkled with the water; and their torments were thus prolonged for ten, twelve, or fifteen days. Many were hung over pits full of loathsome matter, with their heads downwards. As we read these and other equally horrible details, we cannot but admire the might of that grace which can impart to weak man fortitude to endure, without shrinking and without complaint, torments the mere recital of which makes us shudder. The Dutchmen themselves were constrained to avow, that they had never witnessed or read of a persecution so unrelenting, cruelties more revolting, or martyrs more courageous. Tidings of these horrors were soon spread throughout India, and at length reached the West. The Popes sent letters of consolation to the oppressed Christians, and ordered public prayers in their behalf; the jubilee was even anticipated by three years, in order to obtain for these glorious martyrs grace proportioned to the severity of their conflict.

All the European missionaries employed in Japan were soon exterminated. The Society of Jesus lost more than 150 of its members; and to these were added a large number of the sons of St. Augustine, St. Dominic, and St. Francis. By a dispensation to us inscrutable, it was allowed that this persecution should attain its end. The Christians of Japan ceased to exist, and the Gospel was banished from the land it had so gloriously illumined. The penalty of death was decreed against every foreigner, not being a Dutchman, who should approach the isles of Japan. The Dutch were tolerated only for purposes of commerce; and even they had to pass into the single place at which they were permitted to land, over a prostrate crucifix. It is a dark and mysterious event, that the light of faith should be extinguished in a land so fruitful in the graces of the Spirit, moistened with the sweat of apostles and the blood of martyrs. Still the Christian can never cease to hope that it may once more shine upon this unhappy people; already has the attention of the civilised world been turned towards this remote island, and the missionaries of the Church have long been watching their opportunity to set foot again

upon its shores. May God prosper the counsels which tend to
an enterprise so glorious, and turn again the hearts of the
once promising Japanese!

§ 2. Missions of Africa and America.

The north of Africa, once the seat of so flourishing a
Church, had been overrun by the Mahometan conquerors, and
but a few insignificant missions were left within it. The few
Catholics of that territory were in a most wretched and deplorable condition. The great and noble work of the redemption of Christian captives was continued by zealous and cha-
ritable men, inheritors of the virtue of their holy founder, St.
John de Matha. At Algiers was a house of Lazarist priests,
sons of St. Vincent de Paul; the Spaniards had a bishop at
Ceuta, in Morocco, opposite Gibraltar; and episcopal sees were
scattered here and there along the coast, and even in the
capital of Congo, whose king was a Catholic. Many of the
petty chieftains afforded their protection to the missionaries;
and Pope Clement XI. addressed to them a letter expressive
of his satisfaction and his gratitude. When Louis XIV.
sheltered the apostles of the East, under the title of French
consuls and envoys of the most Christian king, he likewise
sent missionaries to Senegal. The islands of Madeira and
Cape de Verde, as well as the Canary Islands, were inhabited
then as now by Catholics; there was an episcopal see at Ten-
eriffe, and another at St. James, one of the Cape de Verde
islands. Eastward, in Ethiopia, the missionaries were often
welcomed with gratitude by the inhabitants, who came origin-
ally from Arabia Felix. Their capital was called Saba; and
their tradition is not without some degree of probability, that
it was one of their queens who went to admire the wisdom of
Solomon. They add that their present race of kings descends
directly from her; and it is well known that the Abyssinians
and Ethiopians did actually profess the Jewish religion before
their conversion to Christianity. Towards the ninth century
they followed the Alexandrian Church in its adoption of the
errors of the Oriental sects. In order to bring them back
to the true faith, the Franciscans had established a mission,
which had great success, notwithstanding persecution and
other obstacles. The blessed work was destroyed here, as in
Japan, by an usurper. He summoned the missionaries; and
having learnt that they desired the conversion of the Ethio-

pians, he said : "What! then you do not regard my people or myself as Christians?" They were sentenced to be stoned to death; but long experience has taught the Church that the blood of her martyrs is her richest and most fruitful seed.

America had been discovered in 1492 by Christopher Columbus. The wealth of this new world, especially its mines of gold and silver, attracted numberless adventurers, mostly Spaniards, men devoid of all religion and humanity, who perpetrated the most revolting cruelties. On their traces came the ministers of the Gospel of peace, who taught the idolatrous inhabitants to know the God who had created them, and to worship Him alone. But so fatal was the impression produced on the minds of the Indians by the cruelty of their conquerors, that, when they heard the Christian religion was that professed by their oppressors, they refused to listen to those who preached it. These difficulties were aggravated by the character of the country, the severity of the climate, and the multitude of strange and unwritten languages. The missionaries were often obliged to undertake journeys of eighty or a hundred miles, through tracts of country untrodden by foot of man, through forests so dense that their way had to be cleared with the axe, with no other guides than the sun and stars and the compass, amidst vast and shifting bogs, or over rugged and precipitous rocks; sometimes on the ridge of a lofty mountain, pierced with cold and rain and frost, always exposed to venomous reptiles, to wolves and other ferocious animals; unable to carry other food than a little maize, varied with such roots or wild fruit as the season might enable them to collect. If they found it necessary to cross a river or a lake, their frail canoes ran the risk of being swept down unobserved rapids, or coming into collision with floating trunks of trees, or being overturned by voracious crocodiles. Then the Indians were savages of almost incredible ferocity. Still no obstacles could arrest the course of the holy missionaries; many were cruelly murdered by the natives; many perished from other causes; but still fresh volunteers came forward to take the place of those who had fallen in this glorious enterprise. And God gave His abundant blessing. In a few years many of the tribes of Indians, both in North and in South America, submitted to the Gospel; a native priesthood was formed, and many sees were created and filled by holy and zealous pastors. They laboured also for the conversion of the conquerors of the New World; and many Spaniards were converted by their missions, and ceased to be a scandal to the Christian religion by their cruelty and the licentiousness of their lives. These converts were exposed for many years to much vexation and oppression; but they found an intrepid protector in the Bishop of Chiappa, in the republic of Guatemala, a prelate well known to history as Bartholomew de Las Casas. He was a Spanish monk of the Dominican order, and came to America with Christopher Columbus; there he passed fifty years of apostolic labour, remedying, as far as it was possible, the evils of war, and protecting the Indians from the tyranny of the Europeans. His memory is held in deserved veneration by the Church.

Towards the south of America extends a vast country named Paraguay, watered by numerous and mighty rivers, and covered with dense forests. About 1555, the Jesuits penetrated into this country, and converted some of the wandering tribes by whom it was inhabited; they then undertook to civilise their converts by forming them into one nation, and providing them with laws and all the benefits of social life. Few records of history are more interesting than the narration of this noble attempt. It was perfectly successful. The dream of ancient sages and modern economists was realised at the extremities of the earth by the exertions of a body of religious unversed in political science. But no science can equal the inspirations of sincere devoted piety. The converts were distributed into villages, which were called *reductions*. "Each hamlet or village," says the illustrious Chateaubriand,* "was governed by two missionaries, who directed both the temporal and spiritual affairs of the Indians. No stranger was suffered to remain longer than three days; and, in order to seclude them from evil influence, they were not allowed to speak Spanish, although many of the converts could read and write it correctly. In each reduction were two schools; one for elementary instruction, the other for music and dancing. When a child had attained the age of seven, the fathers carefully studied his character: if he seemed fitted for mechanical labour, he was placed in the workshops of the reduction, and taught the trade for which he was judged to be qualified. The masters in these workshops were the Jesuits themselves, who had learnt all kinds of handicraft in order to be able to

* *Génie du Christianisme*, part iv. ch. 5.

instruct their converts without extraneous aid. Those who
seemed fitted for agriculture were enrolled among the labourers; and those who still retained the habits of their wandering life were set to keep the flocks. The hours of work
were fixed by the sound of a large bell. At the first peep of
dawn it was rung; the whole population flocked to the church,
said their prayers, sang hymns, and heard Mass. At night-
fall they assembled again, to recite their evening prayers, and
to sing with musical accompaniment." The Indians were passionately fond of music, and, as they possessed good voices,
they were soon taught to excel in harmonised singing; many
of them learned to play the organ, the violin, harp, trumpet,
and other instruments. They were taught moreover to make
their own musical instruments. "The soil was divided into
lots, one of which was assigned to each family. A large public field was called *the Lord's portion*; and the produce of
this common was applied to supply the accidental defects
of harvest, and to maintain the widows, orphans, and infirm;
some part also was kept in reserve for the exigencies of war."
For the Portuguese of Brazil treated Paraguay much as the
Highlanders of Scotland treated the Low Country; they made
continual forages, carrying off cattle and corn, and even the
hapless Indians themselves, whom they sold into slavery.
Hence a militia was organised by the Jesuits; cannon were
cast, and powder manufactured; so that when the Portuguese
came down on the plain, they found, instead of a few timid
and scattered labourers, disciplined bands, who drove them
back defeated and crestfallen. "The missionaries enforced
the utmost simplicity of life; no luxuries were admitted into
the infant community. Those children who were gifted with
more than ordinary talent, were set apart and initiated into
science and literature. They were known as the *Congregation*, and were trained in a seminary, where they gave themselves to retirement and assiduous study. So keen was the
spirit of emulation among them, that the simple threat of
being sent back to the common school, was enough to quell
all disorder or disobedience. From these seminaries issued the
future priests, magistrates, and warriors of the country. The
hamlets were very extensive, and were generally located on
the margin of a river, or some other eligible site. The houses
were uniformly built of stone, of one story; and the streets
were broad and straight. In the centre was a public square,

the sides of which were formed by the church, the home of the Jesuit fathers, the arsenal, the granary, the hospital, and the building set apart for strangers. The churches were spacious and much adorned; the walls were covered with paintings, separated from each other by festoons of living foliage. On feast-days the floor was decorated with flowers, and sprinkled with odoriferous essences. Behind the church was the burial-ground, a long parallelogram, enclosed by a wall. Palm-trees, cypresses, lemon and orange trees, formed avenues converging from all directions to a central chapel, in which a Mass was said every Monday, for the repose of their departed brethren. Avenues of noble trees led away from the hamlet to rustic chapels, towards which the procession moved on days of great solemnity. On Sundays, after Mass, marriages were celebrated; and in the evening, children and catechumens were baptised. The Sacrament of Baptism was administered as in the primitive Church; the candidate was clothed in white linen, and immersed thrice. The great feasts were kept with extraordinary pomp. Bonfires and illuminations ushered in their eves; after the High Mass, there was a review of the military force; then a grand public feast, at which a little wine was allowed. The afternoon was devoted to various athletic exercises, and the fathers crowned the successful candidates. The festival of Corpus Christi offered a singular spectacle amidst these ancient forests and this primitive race of men. Arches were erected at intervals, adorned with luxuriant flowers, and numberless birds of brilliant plumage were tied to the branches which composed the arches, by threads so fine as to be almost invisible. Tigers and lions were collected at different points of the procession, and fish of various hues sported in large tanks of water. It seemed as though all creation were assisting at the glorious feast, and doing homage to the incarnate God in His August Sacrament. The first-fruits of the harvest were waved before the Lord, and the seed of the coming year was presented to receive His benediction. Fireworks and other tokens of public rejoicing closed this triumphant day. With a government so paternal, these new Christians seemed to realise the dream of a golden age. Their cruelty and thirst of vengeance were gone, with all their grovelling and degrading vices; and they were now gentle, patient, loving, and chaste. The Bishop of Buenos Ayres writes of them to Philip V. of Spain in these words:

" Sire, throughout these numerous tribes, composed of Indians
naturally addicted to all kinds of vice, there now prevails such
a spirit of innocence and purity, that I doubt whether a mortal
sin is ever committed amongst them."

There were neither lawyers, nor lawsuits, nor disputes.
The words *mine* and *thine* were scarcely known; for, as
Father Charlevoix said, those who are ever ready to share
what they have with those who need, may be said to have
nothing at all. Sufficiently provided with the necessaries of
life, governed by those who had drawn them out of the depth
of barbarism, possessing in the wilderness the purest blessings
of civilised life, these Indians enjoyed a happiness without
counterpart on the earth.

But, alas, all these wonders of grace vanished at the
breath of impiety, hatred, and intrigue. The enemies of the
Jesuits, jealous of their success, and eager to smite down the
foremost champions of the Church, succeeded in inducing the
king of Spain to recall them; and they were compelled to
leave the reductions in 1767. Their hapless flock relapsed
by degrees into barbarism; and now they retain nothing of
their transitory bliss but a faint and regretful remembrance.
This is one of the effects of the so-called liberal philosophy of
the eighteenth century, which was valiant in destroying good
and noble works, and powerless for good.*

Beneath the cold sky of Labrador and Canada, the Gospel
produced wonderful fruits. Converts were made, and churches
founded, among the Hurons, the Esquimaux, the Algonkins,
and numberless other tribes, whose names are scarcely now
remembered. These men, who, before their conversion, had
nothing of man but the outward shape, who lived in vices
which sank them below the level of the brutes, were no sooner
baptised than they became good citizens and men of blame-
less innocence. The Illinois, in particular, were remarkable
for a degree of general as well as religious instruction not
often attained by our European peasantry. The wild and ferocious Iroquois became fervent Christians by the power of
Divine grace. A young virgin of this tribe, named Catherine
Tehgahkwita, died, as she had lived, in the odour of sanctity.
It pleased God to grant her the gift of miracles; and so numerous were the prodigies wrought at her tomb and ascribed

* See *A History of the Missions of Japan and Paraguay*, by Cecilia
Mary Caddell.

to her intercession, that she was named the St. Geneviève of America. Her father was an unbeliever; and her mother, who was a zealous Christian, died before her daughter had attained her fourth year, and ere she could obtain for her the grace of baptism from the hands of a priest. The little orphan was now abandoned to the care of unbelievers. The small-pox so weakened her eyes, that she was for several years unable to bear the light of day; and this was the remote cause of her conversion. As she was obliged to live day after day in her hut, she acquired a love of retirement and silence, and preserved her innocence unsullied by the vices around her. When the missionaries arrived, her simple heart eagerly embraced their holy teaching; and from that moment she lived for God alone. Nothing could induce her to marry; she had resolved that no earthly affection should share her heart with God. Her relatives now began to treat her with great cruelty; and she suffered the most humiliating and painful treatment with invincible patience. Without murmuring or remonstrance, she suffered all with a submission, sweetness, and perseverance which at length won their admiration. This was in 1676. The same grace which had brought her the gift of faith, continued to lead her along the lonely path and up the rugged heights of perfection. Vain were all the snares spread to destroy her innocence and purity; her horror of sin was extreme; and she escaped all perils by prayer and vigilance, by the love of penance, and of the Cross. At length she was constrained to escape from the unrelenting cruelty of her relatives, and took refuge in a distant mission, where she was gladly welcomed. There she made rapid progress in the spiritual life. She passed her days before the altar or in perfect solitude. No conversation pleased her unless God were its subject. She saw Him every where, heard Him in every sound, and held uninterrupted converse and communion with Him. She prayed without ceasing; and the hours of the night were devoted to meditation. Her fasts and austerities increased from day to day. In the winter she would take off her shoes and walk barefoot through the snow and ice. She strewed the mat on which she slept with thorns, and sought in every way to mortify the flesh. A slow fever brought her to the grave at the early age of twenty-four. Her wasted features were suffused with a lustre so ravishing that the spectators cried out, "The

saint is dead! the saint has passed away to heaven!" Her
example had many followers throughout America, and especially in the mission she had edified by her sanctity. The
spirit of rigid penance, hatred of the flesh, the love of the
Cross and of mortification, spread far and wide. Rigorous
fasts, the use of the discipline, all the macerations of the severest religious orders, were common practices.*

    While most of the American missionaries were trying to
reclaim and convert the Indians, one of their brethren, Father
Peter Claver, of the Company of Jesus, devoted himself to
the negroes, the most degraded and despised part of the population. These negroes were brought from Africa and sold
into slavery; and this abominable traffic was a regular branch
of commercial enterprise. In the seventeenth century, Cartha-
gena, in the Gulf of Mexico, was the principal slave-mar-
ket. Vessels were daily arriving, in which those wretched
creatures were heaped together, without beds or clothing,
loaded with chains, and in a state too loathsome to be detailed. No care was taken of their souls; they were regarded
only as so many marketable animals. Father Claver's heart
was touched with pity; and when he made his vows of profession, he added these words: " Peter Claver, servant of the
negroes for his life." Never, perhaps, was vow more difficult
to keep; never was vow more faithfully kept. As soon as a
vessel arrived with its cargo of slaves, the good missionary
ran, laden with brandy, biscuits, fruit and preserves, and other
delicacies, to refresh the new-comers, and to soothe their grief,
as a mother soothes her helpless infant. His tenderness and
affection won the hearts of these poor wretches; their whole
soul opened to one in whom they recognised a true friend and
protector. Father Claver was well seconded by many pious
persons, who supplied him with all that he needed for his beloved negroes. He first baptised all the children; then he
visited those who were in danger of death; tended their
wounds, fed them, and left them at ease, and with every
comfort their state admitted. Besides his wallet of provisions, Father Claver carried always a little bag with a sur-
plice and stole, and wore a crucifix on his breast. He would
enter the damp stalls in which they were huddled together,
and the atmosphere of which was almost insupportable to an

* See Shea's most useful and interesting *History of the Catholic Missions among the Indian Tribes of the United States.*

European; there he would put together a sort of altar, and place on it a few striking pictures of the crucifixion, or heaven, or hell, or any thing which might attract the curiosity of these untaught savages. He would then arrange mats and benches for them to sit down upon, and the poor slaves would stare at him and marvel at his goodness. Intractable towards their owners, they were docile in the presence of one who thus tenderly cared for them; and there were few who held out against the good father's entreaties. He was not contented with making them nominal Christians only; he trained them to the faithful practice of their religious duties; and from this degraded portion of our race he extracted men who were patterns of all virtue, and who might put the best-instructed Europeans to shame. The very appearance of Father Claver would instantly hush all insubordination or disorder. The wildest savage bowed before the gentle priest of God. Father Claver had received a brilliant education, and belonged to a wealthy and distinguished Spanish family; and what must have been the constraining power of that grace which could lead him to relinquish the bright prospects of life for a ministry so toilsome and so repulsive!*

Like instances of heroic self-devotion were presented in the Levant, at Constantinople, Smyrna, and other places, by missionaries who were content to be shut up in the common prisons, that they might minister to the Christian slaves. One of them writes: "The greatest peril I ever encountered was in the hold of a Turkish ship. The slaves had arranged that I should come among them in the night to confess them, and say Mass for them in the early morning. We were shut in, and the door was secured by a double lock. Out of fifty-two slaves, whom I confessed, twelve were ill, and three died before the morning; you can fancy what sort of atmosphere I had to breathe in such a place. God, who saved me in that great danger, will, I trust, save me from many more." Surely it is the Spirit of God which inspires the Church. Where else shall we find such heroic charity?

* A Life of the Blessed Father Claver is included in the volumes published by the Fathers of the Oratory.

CHAPTER XI.

THE EIGHTEENTH CENTURY.

§ 1. The Jansenists.

WHILE the inhabitants of the new world were thus being evangelised, and were bringing forth such glorious fruit, the old world was exposed to fresh assaults from the restless spirit of heresy and unbelief. The Jansenist errors, which were destined to produce so much evil in France, did not originate in that country. A doctor of Louvain was the first to broach them, without, however, asserting them in a positive manner. Baius was anxious to bring about a better understanding between Catholics and Protestants, and in his eagerness to attain his object, contravened certain dogmas of the Catholic faith; he taught the gravest errors regarding grace and free-will, original sin and justification. In his system the indeliberate, involuntary movements of concupiscence, in which neither the heart nor the will has part, are sins; man is laid under a law of necessity, and yet is free in his actions, &c. Eighteen propositions, extracted from his writings, were censured by the faculty of theology at Paris in 1560; and, a few years later, Pope Pius V. condemned seventy-six erroneous statements detected in them. Baius seemed, at first, to submit to this condemnation; but afterwards he published a long apology for his teaching, and asserted that his doctrine was that of the Fathers, all of whom, therefore, he contended, were implicitly condemned by the Pope's Bull. The question was examined anew at Rome under the successor of Pius V., and the teaching of Baius was again condemned. After many hesitations and equivocations, Baius ended by condemning his own tenets with his dying breath in 1589. But his pernicious doctrine did not die with him; he left several disciples, who undertook to reduce it to system, to defend and to propagate it. Their success was but too great; in many of the schools this fatal heresy was covertly insinuated; but Jansenius, whose name it was henceforth to bear, brought it formally and publicly to the light.

Jansenius was a Dutchman, and had studied theology at Louvain and Paris. While at Louvain he had ardently espoused the novelties which were there taught him as most conformable with the doctrine of the great St. Augustine. He devoted twenty years of his life to a laborious collection of passages from the writings of that saint, in whose strong expressions on the subject of grace employed in refutation of the Pelagian heresy, he persuaded himself that he found support for the teaching of his master Baius; and the result of his labours was a large work which he entitled *Augustinus*, as though it contained nothing but the pure doctrine of the Bishop of Hippo. He had completed it in 1638, and was about to publish it, when he died of the plague during a visitation of the diocese of Ypres, which he had occupied two years. The book was published by his friends; it contained a protestation of submission to the Holy See, which it was difficult to reconcile with the author's knowledge that the errors of Baius had been thrice condemned. The *Augustinus* was censured by Urban VIII. two years after its publication; but this solemn condemnation failed to arrest the progress of the heresy; it served only to irritate the pride of its adherents, and to make them more obstinate than ever. What had been but a smouldering fire was fanned into a terrific conflagration.

During his stay in Paris, Jansenius had contracted friendships with several priests and doctors of the Sorbonne, and had infected them with his errors. The new opinions made great progress in that city; and when the syndic of the theological faculty obtained from the Sorbonne a condemnation of five propositions extracted from the *Augustinus*, seventy doctors protested against the censure and refused submission. The question being referred to the Pope, he condemned the five propositions, after an examination which lasted two years. The heretics now pretended that the propositions had not been condemned in the sense in which Jansenius had used them; and that the sentence of the Pope was sufficiently satisfied by a respectful silence, unaccompanied by an interior assent. This subterfuge was likewise exposed and authoritatively condemned; but they ceased not to have recourse to fresh evasions, refusing to recognise the voice of the Holy Ghost speaking to them through the Church. The plausibility of their system misled many men of great powers, such as Arnauld, Nicole, Pascal, and other learned writers; and the innovators gained credit with the multitude by the austerity of their theories and of their lives. People believed that those who taught and lived so rigidly could not be wrong. But their virtues, however apparently real in many respects, lacked one thing—that obedience, without which all else is vain and factitious. Our Divine Lord has said to His Church, "He that heareth you, heareth Me; and he that despiseth you, despiseth Me." Out of an affected respect for the Sacraments, they induced their disciples to abstain from communicating even at those special times required by the Church. Their teaching was of the most gloomy and discouraging description; and it is not easy to understand its temporary popularity, except that it is impossible to predict the course of the human mind when once it has thrown off the restraint of authority. The Jansenists taught that all the good works of unbelievers are but splendid sins, because they have not faith for their principle and motive; that all the good works of the faithful are purely gratuitous gifts of God, and are bestowed without any regard to the inner disposition of the soul; so that the sinner is punished for not having gifts which all his efforts could never have obtained. God imputes to us even those faults and sins which we cannot avoid, and will punish us for not practising virtues which were not in our power. Jesus Christ died on the cross to save only a few privileged and elect souls, and not the whole race of man. Such teaching was enough to destroy all confidence in God, and to drive men to despair, even if it did not lead them to cast off religion altogether; and yet this melancholy doctrine was for a time so popular in France, that it threatened the very existence of the orthodox faith. By a singular inconsistency, these men clung to the Church in spite of her condemnation of their teaching, and even while they were openly despising her authority; and this profession of union with the Catholic Church increased their power of doing mischief, by imposing on simple and ignorant persons.

In the Society of Jesus, that ever watchful guardian of the Lord's heritage, they found unwearied opponents; or rather devoted brethren, who employed every argument reason could suggest to bring them back to the truth, but without success. One of their most ardent disciples, who died in 1727, was raised by the sect to the honour of sanctity, and the tomb of the Abbé Paris became the resort of a misguided and fanatical multitude, and the scene of the most indecent and blasphemous exhibitions. The parliament itself, many of whose decrees at this time prove how deeply it was affected with the spirit of Jansenism, was staggered at this outburst of popular delusion. But the chief defender of the faith was Christopher de Beaumont, archbishop of Paris (1746-1781), whose virtues and exertions did much to repress the heresy. He earned the honour of being persecuted by the schismatics with unrelenting animosity; he was several times banished from his see, but he never ceased his efforts to unmask their dangerous delusion. The heresy, defeated in the field of argument and condemned by the Holy See, was crushed amidst the general destruction of the revolution, and, except in Holland, where it still numbers a few scanty adherents, has ceased to have a separate existence.

§ 2. Philosophism of the Eighteenth Century, Secret Societies.

On the death of Louis XIV., the crown of France reverted to his great-grandson, a boy five years of age, who took the name of Louis XV., and was proclaimed king under the regency of Philip, duke of Orleans (1715). Infidelity, which had been discountenanced and repressed by Louis XIV., now boldly reared its head, and assailed every thing which Christianity held most sacred. The regent had many brilliant qualities, and much real ability; but being utterly void of religion, he abandoned himself to the most degrading vices, and his palace became a sink of iniquity. The contempt of morality, as well as of religion, became fashionable, and spread throughout all classes of society. Around him was gathered a group of free-thinkers, who, confiding in his protection, declared against Christianity a war which lasted throughout the eighteenth century, and eventually led to one of the most cruel and bloody persecutions the Church has ever known. In 1723, the regent died; but the evil had attained too strong a growth to be stayed. At first anonymous pamphlets were circulated by stealth; no one as yet ventured to attach his name to any work which directly assailed religion or morality; public opinion was as yet untainted. By degrees *the philosophers*, as they affected to call themselves, threw off all restraint, and engaged in open and deadly strife with revelation.

At the head of this movement was a man of sad celebrity,

—a man as remarkable for his talents as for their abuse. Voltaire was born at Paris in 1694, and educated by the Jesuits, who predicted in part the evil he would attempt to do. He devoted himself to literature and poetry; and his success was so immediate and so great, that he became as vain as he was gifted. Being condemned and imprisoned by the parliament on account of his irreligious and seditious writings, he left France, and passed some time in England, where many able men had already found that Protestantism, pursued to its legitimate conclusions, resulted, as its last analysis, in blank unbelief. He then passed into Germany, where he was gladly welcomed by Frederick of Prussia, surnamed the Great; and it is hard to say which of these two agents of evil hated Jesus Christ and His Gospel with the greater virulence, and which was the more furious in assailing that Kingdom which can never be overthrown. Voltaire passed the last twenty years of his life at Ferney, and died at Paris in 1778. He was the leader and the soul of the infidel movement in Europe. He hated the Person and Name of our Divine Lord with dire infatuation; he applied to Him the most degrading epithets, and swore that he would devote his life to the overthrow of His religion. "In twenty years," said he one day, "the Galilæan will be no more." Twenty years passed, and the enemy of Jesus died a miserable death. His character and conduct were in mournful keeping with his impiety: a bad son, a bad citizen, a base flatterer of the great, —such was the patriarch of infidelity. His letters are filled with revolting but instructive passages: "Lie on, lie boldly, my friends!" he says in one of them; "something is sure to stick. I want to be read; I do not care about being believed." Such were the weapons of his warfare. His genius was as rich and fertile as the purposes to which he devoted it were vile and infamous.

Another writer, whose style possessed a fatal beauty of fascination, and whose character was equally in harmony with his teaching, joined in the reckless onslaught on religion. Jean Jacques Rousseau was a man without any solid convictions, who had become a Catholic and then relapsed into Protestantism, and had finally ended in becoming an avowed unbeliever. For twenty-five years this teacher of sentimental virtue lived in avowed libertinism; he wrote a treatise on education, and sent his own children to the Foundling Hos-

pital. While co-operating with Voltaire in seeking the destruction of Christianity, he speaks of him as an "abject soul,
whose melancholy philosophy reduced him to a level with the
brutes ;" and Voltaire replies by calling his assailant a "scape-
grace from Geneva, a scoundrel, a mere charlatan, a hypocrite,
an enemy of the human race," &c. Such was the intercourse
between these pretended reformers of society.

Voltaire had formed a complete plan for his warfare with
the Church. He gathered around him many persons like-
minded to himself, who assumed the title of philosophers or
friends of wisdom. They were men of talent, and succeeded
in gaining the public attention to such a degree, that whoever opposed them was sure to be overwhelmed with scorn.
D'Alembert, Diderot, Helvetius, Montesquieu, and others, set
themselves to sap the foundations of religion and of social
order, that, as they said, they might regenerate the world.
Their weapons were falsehood and calumny; their labours
prepared the woes and bloodshed of the last seventy years.
Until their time, the privilege of unbelief was restrained to a
few great or rich people, who sought in scepticism a shelter
for their licentiousness; the people had not learned to despise
the faith of their forefathers, and make a mock of revelation.
But under the auspices of these men, philosophism penetrated
the lower ranks of society. France was inundated with bad
books, adapted to every age, rank, and sex. They were
given away in colleges and country-schools; and every means
was employed to diffuse the fatal poison of unbelief. Thus in
a few years a false philosophy changed the spirit and character
of a great nation, broke every bond of society, and left its disciples no other principle of action but selfishness. Every thing
was prepared for a great commotion, which soon passed from
theory into practice; from the region of ideas into that of facts.
The philosophers foresaw the result of their teaching clearly
enough, and were anxious only to strew flowers over the abyss
they were digging for their country and for the world.

It was not that the court favoured their enterprise. The
queen, Maria Leczinski, the daughter of Stanislaus, king of
Poland, was a fervent Christian, and preserved the royal
family from the contagion of infidelity. Louis XV. himself,
however irregular in his conduct, retained too firm a faith in
the truth of religion to favour the enemies of Christianity, and
rejected with indignation the flatteries with which the philo-

sophers strove to gain his favour. The king was permitted, indeed, to present to the world the scandal of a voluptuous and debauched life; but at length he died in sentiments of true repentance. His daughter, Louise de France, became a member of the Carmelites of St. Denis, where she led a life of penance and mortification; it is to her that her father's return to a better mind is mainly to be attributed.

Thus repulsed by the court, the philosophers found serious impediments of another kind. Each fresh attack on religion called forth a prompt and solid reply; and although their opponents were men of obscure names, and of small influence in the literary world, they considerably impeded the career of infidelity. Among others was the Abbé Bergier, author of *Deism its own Refutation*, and the witty Abbé Guénée, whose *Letters of certain Jews to M. de Voltaire* had a prodigious success, and wounded the pride of the infidel leader to the quick. Still these were only temporary obstructions. The writings of the infidels were welcomed with enthusiasm in other countries; Russia, Prussia, Spain, and Portugal brought them a large number of disciples: and thus was prepared the series of revolutions which have laid Europe waste. The principle of pride on which the philosophism of the eighteenth century rested, was as fatal to the temporal as to the spiritual order. The philosophers tried to hide this inevitable application of their theories; and, postponing the final assault, they contented themselves with plotting the destruction of the Society of Jesus, their most dreaded opponent. These religious, so modest and humble in their lives, so obedient to their superiors and to the Church, stood forward as the intrepid defenders of religion and of society. They were ever ready in the breach, ever on the alert to refute and expose each new sophism of their opponents. They had thus the honour of being the special objects of the hatred and calumnies of philosophers, heretics, and tepid Christians. In Portugal, a man stained with every vice gave the signal for a decisive blow; the Jesuits were involved in a pretended conspiracy against the life of the king, and defamatory libels were circulated to their prejudice throughout Europe. The Pope was required to suppress the order. He refused; and their enemies proceeded to open violence. The houses of the Jesuits were surrounded by soldiers; the fathers were arrested and thrown into prison; some were executed as guilty of treason, and the rest thrown upon the coast of the Roman states without any provision for their maintenance. This was the great stroke of the Marquis of Pombal, at Lisbon, in 1759. It excited great indignation in Europe; but soon a minister of kindred spirit induced the Spanish government to proscribe the order throughout its dominions; and France was induced by the Duke de Choiseul, a partisan of the new philosophy, to follow the example. Without even the form of legal process, unheard, without time to take measures for their vindication, their rules were declared to be impious, sacrilegious, and derogatory to the Divine majesty, by men who did not believe in God, and whose whole efforts were directed to the overthrow of religion; their colleges were closed, their novitiates destroyed, their goods seized, and their vows annulled. This was in 1762. Their judges were parliamentary Jansenists, who rejoiced to humble and crush those who had so long combated their errors and unmasked their disguises. Common sense and law were both set aside in this monstrous proscription; but its victims accepted it as but another occasion of conformity to His image whose Name they bore; and, although accused of a relaxed morality, they refused to take an oath which their conscience could not accept.

But this unjust persecution did not satisfy the vengeance of the philosophers and Jansenists; they resolved to extort from the Pope a decree which should formally and for ever suppress the order. The possessions of the Roman Church in various kingdoms were confiscated; and the Pope was told that they would not be restored until the Jesuits had ceased to exist; and that the suppression of the order was the only means of restoring peace and concord between the Holy See and foreign courts. Clement XIV. exhausted every expedient of delay, but at length, on the 21st July 1773, signed the decree which suppressed the Company of Jesus. The philosophers shouted for joy, and hailed the dawn of the day of their bloody rule; the Christian world was deprived of its most active and learned defenders; and this defeat was the first in a long and melancholy succession of disasters.

The cities of Europe were at the same time perverted by the members of a numerous and powerful society, who called themselves Freemasons, and who held their meetings secretly and in retired places. England, which had first sown the seed of infidel opinions, was the soil on which these dangerous men first appeared. No one has succeeded, as yet, in fathoming the ends and agencies of this secret society; but enough has been recorded to show that its aim was and is to weaken and paralyse religion, and subvert social order. Many of the members know nothing of the real ends and actions of the fraternity; they are allured by the prospect of relief in sickness, and thus become in fact participators in the crimes and guilt of the whole body; only the initiated possess the real secret of the society, and give it its impulse and its movement. On its first appearance freemasonry was denounced as subversive of government, and occasioned great alarm. The members of which its lodges were composed were of evil omen: Voltaire, Condorcet, Lalande, Volney, Mirabeau, and numberless others of similar character and sentiments. The Popes Clement XII. and Benedict XIV., after long inquiry, commanded all Catholics to leave the society on pain of excommunication; but the evil went on increasing, and Europe was enveloped in a net of conspirators, who awaited only the signal of revolt. That signal was given by France. Louis XVI. was then on the throne, and philosophism deemed the time had come to inaugurate its golden age of liberty. We shall see how it succeeded.

§ 3. The French Revolution, 1789.

It does not fall within the design of a history such as this, to describe the grave political convulsions which shook Europe at the close of the eighteenth century, and are shaking it still. These are interesting to us only in so far as they affect the kingdom of God, and we shall notice them only in this relation.

Frightful disturbances were preparing in all directions. We have mentioned two causes which combined to unsettle men's minds,—the infidel philosophism which destroyed all sense of duty and of honour, and the machinations of the secret societies directed against all forms of civil government. To these must be added a third,—the abuses which pervaded every branch of the administration of government. Those who ruled were so corrupted by the impiety which they had welcomed and fostered, that they neglected all the duties of their position, and sought only to enjoy its emoluments; they had rebelled against God; their subjects rebelled against them. An active principle once planted in the heart of society has an irrepressible growth: they who sow irreligion, reap revolution and bloodshed. Abuses were rife every where; the institutions of society had become antiquated and had ceased to suffice for its actual wants. A wise reform might have remedied this evil, and such a reform might have been attempted in an age free from the anarchical theories which were dragging France towards the precipice. A few years showed the advocates of liberty and fraternity wielding a tyranny more atrocious than any recorded in history. The clergy, who were doomed to be the first victims of triumphant philosophism, had foreseen the storm, and, in one of their latest synods, had declared: "A few years more of silence, and there will come a convulsion which will cover France with ruins." The philosophers received this prognostication with a laugh of derision, reiterating, as it were, the impious cry of the Jews, when about to slay the Lord of life: "We will not have this man to reign over us."

Louis XVI., a pious prince, but devoid of the energy needful at such a crisis, was led to imagine that an assembly of the States General would remedy the evils which were distracting society; and the clergy, the nobles, and the third estate met at Versailles. After a conflict, the details of which do not lie within our province, the assembly proceeded to the work of confiscation: it asserted that all the possessions of the Church belonged to the state; that monastic vows were provisionally suspended; and shortly after it sold the greater part of the Church property, and suppressed all religious orders. There existed in France more than 12,000 abbeys, convents, priories, and other religious houses. They had been founded by kings of France, or by private persons, and had a clear right to the protection of the laws. They afforded a shelter to learning and virtue throughout France; and if abuses had crept in here and there, they called for reformation, not for destruction. These houses contained precious monuments of literature and art; all were buried in promiscuous ruin. Philosophism destroyed in one day the work of ages, in spite of the efforts and remonstrances of the bishops and clergy.

When the religious orders were destroyed, the Church itself became the object of attack. Lawyers, imbued with antichristian ideas, drew up a plan of reform. They reduced the number of sees from 135 to 80, one for each of the newly formed departments; they destroyed old sees and created new ones, and suppressed chapters, priories, and benefices. Future bishops were to demand institution from the metropolitan, and not from the Pope; the only act of submission to the Holy See which was permitted, was the forwarding a letter to announce their appointment and to declare their communion with Rome. The choice of bishops and *curés* was confided to electoral colleges, and the *vicaires* were to be selected without any reference to the bishops. This reform was called the "civil constitution of the clergy." It was no sooner published, than it was rejected as schismatical; of all the bishops, four only submitted to it. The king was weak enough to ratify the act, but he soon repented of his weakness and revoked his assent. The assembly then decreed that all ecclesiastics who refused to swear to the new constitution within a week, should be deprived of their cures. The great majority of the clergy preferred persecution, banishment, and poverty, to a betrayal of the Church's rights. They were then deprived, and others were forcibly obtruded on the country. The intrusive Bishop of Poitiers fell dead just as he was about to sign the decree which banished the faithful clergy. A bull of Pope Pius VI., which absolutely condemned the constitution, brought many of the complying clergy to their senses, and restored them to the true and suffering Church. But the assembly found it impossible to retreat. They resolved, in the words of the notorious Mirabeau, to *uncatholicise* France; they wanted to make experiment of their atheistical Utopia. They seized Avignon, which then belonged to the Pope, and put to death 600 of the inhabitants whose only crime was fidelity to the Church. They pursued a similar course throughout France; priests were mutilated for concealing the sacred vessels; at Angers 300 priests were shut up in a prison, and treated with· frightful cruelty; the cathedral of Puy was burnt, that of Avranches was pulled down, and all ecclesiastical costumes were prohibited. The movement went on, aided and encouraged by the unhappy Philip, duke of Orleans. More than 40,000 churches, chapels, and oratories, were torn down by the revolutionists; many more were turned into stables, shops, dwelling-houses, theatres, or club-houses. Bells, crucifixes, chalices, all kinds of church ornaments were destroyed, or appropriated by these pretended friends of the rights of man.

Amidst these horrors, priests, monks and nuns, and simple peasants, received the crown of martyrdom with a fortitude and a serenity which touched their very murderers. Many made their escape into other lands, and prepared the way of the Lord in countries overrun by heresy. The first successes of the refugees against the revolution furnished a pretext for the persecution of the remaining clergy. A great number of priests were arrested and thrown into the prisons of Paris, and into convents or seminaries converted into prisons for the time. During the night of Sept. 1, 1792, placards were posted throughout Paris, announcing the success of the emi-grants; the gates of the city were closed, the tocsin was sounded, and the people were implored to march to the relief of Champagne, which was threatened with invasion. Voices were heard in the crowd: "Run to the prisons; kill the prisoners; they are our real enemies." Assassins were intro-duced into the courtyard of the Carmelite convent (*les Carmes*); the priests were roused at daybreak, and sent into the garden. There they were assailed by the furious emissaries of the revo-lution, and many were at once barbarously slain. Others turned into the church, which was soon strewed with corpses. An *impromptu* tribunal was then constituted, before which the survivors were brought two by two. As they came forward in order, they were interrogated whether they would take the oath of fidelity to the constitution, and on their refusal they were instantly despatched with pikes and poniards. At each fresh murder the crowd renewed its shouts. Meanwhile the prisoners were praying before the altar, awaiting their turn to descend into the fatal court. When their names were called they walked calmly out, engaged in silent prayer, their coun-tenances radiant with joy, and died with the name of Jesus on their lips. Similar scenes of horror were enacted at St. Firmin, at the Conciergerie, and the other prisons of Paris, as also at Meaux, Rheims, Lyons, and Versailles.

We must pass over the judicial murder of Louis XVI. and of the ill-fated queen; nor does it become us to dwell on the succeeding scenes of terror, further than to point out the character of the great reform preached by the philosophers, the regeneration of the world announced by the secret so-cieties, the promised golden age of reason. For ten hideous years the history of religion in France is written in characters of blood; the brilliant episode of the war of the Vendéans alone relieving the horrible monotony of sacrilege and blood-shed.

The Convention then abolished the Christian religion by a solemn decree, and proclaimed the worship of Reason. The first festival of the new divinity was held at Notre Dame on the 10th of November 1793. A woman of infamous character was seated on the altar, and received, together with the adoration of the multitude, the title of Queen of the Gods! The greater part of France followed the example of the capital; the impure abominations of paganism were every where renewed; the churches were pillaged and profaned; the images of the saints mutilated, and crucifixes dragged through the streets with yells of scorn and derision. Madame Elizabeth, sister of Louis XVI., was condemned to death on the 10th of May 1794. The youthful son of Louis XVI. died in the Temple, June 8th, 1795. The death of Robespierre, in 1794, restored some degree of order and peace, but the end was not yet; the work of irreligion was not accomplished so long as the see of Peter, the rallying point of the oppressed and persecuted Christians, stood unharmed.

§ 4. Pontificate of Pius VI., 1775-1799.

The reign of Pius VI. was one long struggle against the spirit of philosophism throughout the whole of Europe. Joseph II., who had succeeded Maria Theresa on the imperial throne in 1765, had learned, from the writings of the so-called philosophers and Jansenists, to distrust religion and its ministers, and he resolved to effect such a radical revolution in the Church as should make it a mere engine of the state. The Christian schools were replaced by secular schools; convents were forbidden to receive additional novices, and all those orders which were not devoted to education were entirely suppressed; seminaries were set up in opposition to the bishops, and the professors were men tainted with the dominant irreligion. He assailed the authority of the Holy See by prohibiting the reception of Papal bulls, briefs, and rescripts, and by appropriating to himself the right of nominating to all sees and abbeys in his dominions. He then required the bishops to assert their independence of the Pope, and their competence to dispense with the common laws of the Church. Pius VI. addressed several briefs both to the bishops and to the emperor, imploring them not to violate the Church's unity, but his remonstrances were vain. He then repaired in person to Germany; he was received with outward respect, but his requests were all refused, and his only consolation was the affectionate homage of the population. On his return to Rome, Joseph II. proceeded further in his career of schism; but the misguided emperor saw his error before his death, and revoked all his decrees on ecclesiastical matters; the revolution had doubtless opened his eyes.

In Tuscany, the Archduke Leopold, brother of Joseph II., had also undertaken to refashion the Church. He followed implicitly the teaching of Scipio Ricci, bishop of Pistoia, a bold and crafty adherent of Jansenist opinions. The archduke prepared catechisms which he required the bishops to teach in the schools; he prescribed the books they were to recommend for the instruction of the faithful; like his imperial brother, he abolished confraternities, forbade processions, and regulated the ceremonies of divine worship, even to the number of candles to be lighted at each function. Ricci set up a printing-press, and published translations of French Jansenistical works; he abolished the Stations of the Cross, and the Festival of the Sacred Heart, and introduced the vernacular tongue into the divine offices. Pius VI. wrote to him, and Ricci replied by summoning a synod, in order to clothe his innovations with a semblance of canonical order. But his career reached its end; he was compelled to resign his see; and, at length repenting, was reconciled to the Church by Pius VII. in 1805.

Some few consolations varied the bitter trials of the Pope. William III., king of Sweden, allowed Catholics to build churches and celebrate their worship in his states; he even came to Rome to inform the Pope of this new decree, and was received with paternal tenderness. At this time too St. Liguori, bishop of St. Agatha of the Goths, in the kingdom of Naples, and founder of the Congregation of the Most Holy Redeemer, was edifying the Church by his extraordinary sanctity. He had vowed never to lose a moment of his time, and he kept his vow with singular fidelity. He had a most ardent devotion to the Blessed Sacrament; he visited It several times during the day and night, and notwithstanding his great age and bodily sufferings, he passed eight hours before It daily. He redoubled his mortifications and penances on Friday, in honour of the cross of Jesus Christ; and he daily made the stations of the cross. He was a most devoted servant of Mary; he recited the rosary daily, and fasted every Saturday in her honour. It is said that he preserved his baptismal innocence unsullied; and yet the details of his penances and mortifications are surprising. He went to his reward on the 1st of August 1787, in the ninety-first year of his age; bequeathing to the Church a valuable legacy of theological and ascetical writings. Thus did the grace of God manifest itself wonderfully in one part of the Church, while it was outraged and rejected in others.

Meanwhile the revolutionary armies had gained many important victories in Italy; and their successes had been followed by the overthrow of the existing governments and the degradation of religion. Rome was the great object of assault. Could they but annihilate the apostolical power in the person of Christ's Vicar, where would be the promises of perpetuity given to the Church? The Gospel would be thus proved to be false. They marched on Rome, after having pillaged the rich sanctuary of Our Lady of Loretto; and the Pope was compelled to consent to great pecuniary sacrifices, and to the surrender of the greater part of his possessions. Only the approach of the Austrians procured him a respite on these humiliating conditions. The death of an obscure French agitator, while endeavouring to excite the people against the Papal government, furnished the pretext for breaking this treaty. Rome was entered on the 12th of February 1798, and Pius VI. was led into captivity. A great number of cardinals and bishops experienced the same fate; and Rome was ruled by a military government. The Pope was placed in a miserable carriage, dragged away during a violent thunderstorm, without being informed of the motives or destination of this compulsory journey. He was taken to Viterbo, then to Sienna, where he remained three months, carefully guarded by day and by night. It was intended to banish him to Sardinia, but the English cruisers prevented the accomplishment of this project. Four months were occupied in wandering from Florence to Valence in France; the Pope was exposed to all kinds of indignities and fatigues, in the hope that his constancy and fortitude might be exhausted. The Holy Father was aged and infirm; the journey was toilsome and painful to him; the most miserable wayside inns were chosen for his resting-places; and his nights were broken by the noise of the soldiers appointed to guard him. He was compelled to cross the Alps in the depth of a severe winter, without any defence against the intensity of the cold. Still, wherever he went, crowds of people came kneeling to receive his benediction, and were loud in their murmurs of indignation against the oppressors of the Vicar of Christ. Pius VI. was surprised to find so much faith in a country where infidelity had led to so many crimes. The Directory wished to degrade religion in his person, by leading him about from town to town in so humiliating a manner; but never did the Pope appear so great and so venerable. Every where his presence seemed to rekindle the almost extinct faith and piety of the people; so that this memorable journey was a series of triumphs for the religion it was intended to discredit. Pius VI. was completely exhausted by the toils and privations of his journey, and by the cares which weighed upon his heart; he died August 19, 1799, blessing his enemies with his latest breath. The revolution could boast one august victim the more; and the Church another holy confessor.

CHAPTER XII.

THE NINETEENTH CENTURY.

§1. Pontificate of Pius VII., 1800-1823.

AT the tidings of the death of Pius VI., the revolutionists and infidels uttered a cry of joy; the Papacy was for ever abolished: they had reached the goal of all their efforts. Religion, deprived of its head, would now disappear from the earth; and the philosophism, of which France had tasted the blessings, would reign in its stead. And, in truth, how could a successor be chosen to the deceased Pontiff? Italy was overrun by the revolutionary armies; all the cardinals were exiled and scattered over the earth. But He who saith to the sea: "Thus far shalt thou go, and no further," put forth His right hand to protect His Church. He spake the word, and the republicans were expelled from Italy; Venice opened its gates to the emperor of Germany, the cardinals were convoked, and entered into conclave on the 1st December 1799. Their choice fell on Cardinal Chiaramonti, who took the name of Pius VII. The Church had mysteriously triumphed in the very moment of its lowest depression, and the powers of hell had prematurely sounded the note of victory. The new Pope repaired to Rome, the gates of which had been opened to him by the victorious Austrians, and was received with enthusiastic joy by the people on July the 3d, 1800.

On the fall of the Directory, General Bonaparte was named First Consul; and under his strong hand some degree of public order was soon restored. Bonaparte saw that a great nation cannot exist without religion; that no government can endure, or be powerful for good, unless it finds a response to its commands in the conscience of its subjects. Philosophism began to allow that it is not possible to rule over a people of atheists. The First Consul immediately took steps to re-establish the exercise of the Catholic religion in France. Negotiations were opened with the Pope; a concordat was signed; and, in spite of every obstacle, the Catholic worship was restored. The happy event was inaugurated in the cathedral of Notre Dame, on Easter-day 1801; the cardinal legate celebrated the Mass; the Consul and all the officers of state were present; and *Te Deum* was sung in thanksgiving. The churches were reopened throughout the provinces; zealous priests returned, and were located in the towns and country villages to instruct the people, and awaken their dormant faith; at the same time some few communities devoted to education were established. An entirely new distribution of dioceses was effected throughout France; the constitutional bishops being every where deposed.

When declared emperor in 1804, Napoleon prevailed on Pius VII. to come to Paris to crown him. It was a journey full of blessing to the countries through which he passed, and of consolation to himself. The pride of the courts which had openly favoured infidelity had been humbled; and on his return to Rome, the Holy Father was busied in providing pastors for the desolated churches of Italy and Germany. Ecclesiastical discipline was restored in those countries, and religion began to flourish again after the disasters which had followed in the train of war. At the very beginning of his pontificate, Pius VII. had virtually annulled the act of Clement XIV., by re-establishing the Society of Jesus in Russia, and reinstating it in all the rights it had possessed before its suppression. Some few years later he entirely restored the

Society; the ruin of which had been the first in a long series of injuries inflicted on the Church. For forty years Rome had not witnessed the touching ceremony of canonisation: Pius VII. proclaimed the *beatification* of five persons, whose virtues and miracles were incontestable; and a princess of the royal family of France, Marie Clotilde, queen of Sardinia, and sister of Louis XVI., was declared *venerable*: she had died five years before, in 1802.

While the Church was thus gradually rising from what seemed to be its ruins, Napoleon was prosecuting his unprecedented career of victories, dismembering empires, creating principalities and kingdoms, and making peace or war at his pleasure. It was not long before there arose a misunderstanding between the Pope and the Emperor. While a victor in Vienna, Napoleon decreed the union of the Roman States to the French Empire. The Pope protested against so iniquitous and unprovoked a spoliation, and, after a long delay, published a bull excommunicating all who were concerned in this measure, without naming any person in particular. On the 4th of July 1809, General Radet entered the apartments of the Pope at night, disarmed his guard, and required him, in the name of the emperor, to renounce the temporal sovereignty of Rome and of the Ecclesiastical States: in the event of his refusal, he had orders to seize the person of the Pope. " If you have thought it your duty to execute these orders because you have sworn fidelity and obedience to the emperor, think," said the Pope, " how we ought to maintain the rights of the Holy See, to which we are bound by so many oaths. We cannot, we ought not, we will not either yield or renounce that which is not ours. The temporal domain belongs to the Church; we are only its administrator. The emperor may cut us in pieces, but he will never obtain this renunciation from us."*   The word of command was given, the Pope was carried off to France, with no other hope than that he should die in exile, like his predecessor. He was first taken to Savona, near Genoa; and all his ministers were imprisoned at the same time. The Roman States were divided into departments, and administered by prefects; and Napoleon conferred

---

* Radet had felt an unusual emotion at the sight of the Pope. He said: " In the street, on the staircases, with the Swiss, all went well enough; but when I saw the Pope I thought of my first Communion, and my heart was moved to its lowest depth."

on his infant son the title of King of Rome. Pius VII. was transferred from Savona to Fontainebleau. On his return from the disastrous campaign of Russia in 1812, Napoleon visited the Pope, in order to wrest from him concessions fatal to the independence of the Church. The Pope yielded at first, but subsequently refused to treat of business except in his own capital. He was then permitted to return to Rome; but scarcely had he left France when the allied armies entered the country. Napoleon's abdication was signed at Fontainebleau in 1814.

Louis XVIII., who then resided in England, was restored to the throne of France; and Napoleon, after his return from Elba and a brief resumption of the imperial power, was defeated in the famous battle of Waterloo (1815), and retained in honourable imprisonment at St. Helena; where he died in 1821, after receiving the last succours of the religion he had so grievously persecuted. Louis XVIII. immediately restored the Papal States, and entered into negotiations with the Pope for the support and extension of religion in France. The number of bishoprics was increased; many religious communities sprang into existence; missions were given throughout the country, and churches were repaired and parishes reconstructed.

The emigrant priests had laboured assiduously in the places of their sojourn, and had done much to lessen the force of prejudice against the Catholic Church. Many conversions had crowned their labours; amongst the converts were men of rank and learning; and never perhaps were so many souls rescued from heresy and schism as at this time. Thus the revolutionary storm had scattered the good seed far and wide, to bring forth fruit in its season. On their return to France, the clergy set themselves earnestly to work to undo the evils of the preceding twenty years. Foreign missions were also wonderfully extended. China had been laid waste by continued persecution; but still a precious harvest of souls was gathered in. A blind Christian was the first instrument of these conversions. Being gifted with an extraordinary memory and with great fluency of speech, he began to teach with singular success. Fresh missionaries stepped forward to occupy the place of those who had fallen, and carried the tidings of salvation throughout that immense empire. Nor was the progress of religion less remarkable in America.

New sees were established in the United States, and the
bishops met in synod without impediment. The divisions
and conflicts of sects had greatly aided the cause of indiffer-
ence and unbelief; but the Catholics increased, and still continue to increase, in numbers and in influence year by year.
The words of life were welcomed also in Corea, a peninsula
almost as large as Italy, on the borders of the Chinese empire,
opposite to Japan. Towards the close of the eighteenth century, a young man, whose name was Ly, the son of the ambassador of Corea, came to Pekin and studied mathematics
under the missionaries. He was induced to read some religious books; and, by the grace of God, he was converted,
and received in baptism the name of Peter. Thenceforward
his great ambition was to be the apostle of his countrymen.
Many were converted by his preaching and were baptised;
so that in five years there were 4000 Christians in Corea.
The government then took alarm, and began to persecute
the Church. Amongst those who were arrested were two
brothers, named Paul and James, who, when interrogated by
the governor, confessed Jesus Christ with a noble simplicity.
Paul began to prove the truth of the Christian religion, to the
surprise of the pagans and the confusion of his judge. The
matter was referred to the king, who ordered that a careful
search should be made for all Christians, who were to be
thrown into prison until they renounced their religion. He
summoned the two brothers, and again interrogated them.
They replied at once: "We profess the Christian religion,
because we have found it to be true; and Christians, if it
please God, we shall live and die." They were then put to
the torture; but their agony could not subdue their faith.
They were then flattered and caressed; but without success.
Whereupon sentence of death was pronounced; and the confessors were led to the place of punishment, followed by a
crowd composed as well of Christians as of pagans. James
was so enfeebled by the torments he had undergone, that he
could only invoke the names of Jesus and Mary; but Paul
preached Jesus Christ aloud all the way they went, to the
amazement of the heathen. When they had reached the
place of execution, they were asked once more whether they
would deny Jesus Christ: they refused. The officer then
ordered Paul to read his own sentence of death. He read
it with a loud and clear voice, laid his head on the block,

breathed a prayer to Jesus, and gave the signal to the executioner. His brother imitated his heroism; and they bore
to the throne of God the first-fruits of the Church of Corea.
The bodies of the martyrs were left nine days unburied. On
the ninth day their relatives obtained permission to bury
them, and they were found untouched by corruption, retaining the hue and flexibility of life; while the blocks on which
they had suffered were covered with blood as fresh and as
liquid as though it had been just shed. Many of the pagans
regarded this as a proof of the innocence of the brothers, and
were converted to the faith. Although the persecution was
again and again renewed, this little Church has continued
to subsist and to bring forth abundant fruit.

Pius VII. devoted himself with ardour to the reconstruc-
tion of the Church throughout Europe. He died on the 20th
August 1823, at the age of eighty-three years; twenty-three
of which he had passed on the throne of Peter. So gentle
was his character, that Napoleon compared him to a lamb;
his piety was solid and deep, and his pontificate will ever
be remembered as one of the most stormy and most brilliant
epochs of the Church's history.

§ 2. From the Death of Pius VII. to the Pontificate of Pius IX.

The revolutionary tendencies of Europe were checked, but
not destroyed. The philosophers and heretics still carried on
their machinations in the dark, and scattered throughout
society the elements of dissolution. The press seemed to
have a special mission to call evil good, and good evil; to dis-
tort the facts of history; to associate religion and civil order
with despotism, retrogression, and ignorance. In France the
restoration was but temporary. During the reign of Charles X.
the revolutionists deemed themselves strong enough for a
decisive assault on the monarchy and on the Church. They
demanded the expulsion of the Jesuits, who were specially
obnoxious to them for their zeal and uncompromising spirit;
and, for the sake of peace, the king consented to sacrifice them.
In 1830 the throne of the Bourbons was overthrown, and
Louis Philippe, the son of the notorious Philippe Egalité,
was proclaimed King of the French. During the fury of this
revolution the crucifixes were thrown down, priests were insulted and threatened, the palace of the archbishop of Paris

sacked and destroyed, and his life placed in extreme peril. The reign of Louis Philippe lasted seventeen years, and threatened to be more fatal to the best interests of the Church and society than the Revolution. Education was not only severed from religion, but conducted by those who were openly and avowedly infidels. The press poured forth its calumnies, history was more and more distorted and perverted, and the chief end of man was made to consist in material prosperity alone. At length the policy of this reign produced its natural fruit, and the king was ignominiously expelled from the throne in February 1848.

Notwithstanding the zealous efforts of infidelity, the Church made progress. The Association for the Propagation of the Faith was begun at Lyons in 1823, and attested the faith of the working-classes, by whose alms it has been mainly raised to its present flourishing condition. Pope Leo XII., who was elected in 1823, laboured to counteract the irreligious tendencies of the age. He gave a great stimulus to education, and restored the Jesuits to the colleges they had occupied in Rome before the suppression of the order. Pius VIII., who succeeded him in 1829, filled the chair of St. Peter two years. He proclaimed a jubilee to draw down the blessing of God on his pontificate; obtained the erection of an Armenian archbishopric at Constantinople; and did much towards the abolition of slavery in Brazil. During his pontificate the Catholics of Great Britain and Ireland, under the guidance of the celebrated Daniel O'Connell, extorted from the Parliament a recognition of their civil and religious rights, and the repeal of those oppressive and persecuting laws which had been so long the disgrace of our legislation. This act of justice had been refused by George III. and by his successor, who feared that the established religion would be endangered if the Catholic faith met it on equal terms. It was at length reluctantly conceded by the Duke of Wellington and Sir Robert Peel on the 13th of April 1829, and the Catholic Church of England entered upon a new and brilliant epoch of its history. The conquest of Algiers by the French, in 1830, not only destroyed the pirates who infested the Mediterranean, and under whose tyranny myriads of Christian captives had groaned for ages, but opened a new range of missionary enterprise to the Church.

Pius VIII. was succeeded, in 1831, by Gregory XVI., a

monk of the order of St. Benedict. He was a pontiff of
distinguished piety and gentleness, who lived the life of a
religious on the throne of St. Peter. He applied himself
to defeat the machinations of the secret societies, to protect
and extend the missions of the Church by the erection of new
sees, and to counteract the strange opinions which appeared
continually on the surface of the turbulent and fermenting infidelity of the day. He had the consolation of bequeathing
to the Church forty new sees in various parts of the world,
and of canonising several saints. His long and arduous pontificate was marked by two great trials. On the death of
Ferdinand VII. of Spain, in 1833, the Princess Isabella, or
rather her mother, Maria Christina, took possession of the
throne, and was strong enough to defeat the legitimate king,
Charles V. This usurpation was followed by fearful viola-
tions of law and equity. When the keystone is withdrawn,
the arch falls in ruins; the violation of the fundamental law
of society paralyses all other laws. The spirit of the revolution made itself master of the Peninsula; the blood of priests
and religious cried to heaven for vengeance; the convents
were pillaged, and the property of the Church seized and
confiscated. Since this disastrous year Spain has known no
rest, and still suffers from the influence of the spirit of evil
it then evoked. In the north, Nicholas I., emperor of Russia,
decimated the Catholic population of Poland by a violent
persecution. Priests and nuns were imprisoned, sent to
Siberia, beaten with the knout, in order to compel them to
submit to the Russian schism. Gregory XVI. exerted himself to the utmost to alleviate the lot of his suffering flock in
Poland, but without much effect. The tyrant and oppressor
of the Church failed in his immediate object, and but lately
sank into a dishonoured grave.

Gregory XVI. had given a great impulse to foreign missions. The light of the Gospel spread further over the earth,
but the blood of martyrs flowed in abundance. This was
especially the case in China. The Annals of the Propagation
of the Faith record the sufferings and fortitude of multitudes
of missionaries, native priests, and laity. One specimen may
suffice of the Church's warfare in this our own time. It was
in November 1835, when Cochin China was groaning beneath
the tyranny of the cruel Minh-Mênh, that a French priest,
M. Marchand, of the diocese of Besançon, was brought before

the persecutor. After a long examination, in which his enemies tried to elicit a confession that he had come to induce the natives to revolt, he was ordered to be tortured. His legs were torn with red-hot pincers, and he was then put into a cage, two feet and a half high, three feet in length, and two in breadth; so that he could neither stand upright, nor sit but with his head thrust down upon his breast. The holy priest remained six weeks in this horrible prison. When the day appointed for his execution arrived, he was led, with several others, to a spot not far from the palace. The king came forth, looked at them, compelled them to prostrate themselves on the earth five times before his majesty, and then gave the signal for their execution. They were stripped naked, and their hands were tied behind their backs. The instruments of torture were heated anew; five executioners at once plunged the glowing iron into the thighs and legs of the martyrs. When the irons grew cool, they were again heated, and again applied to the bodies of the agonised sufferers. M. Marchand was then suspended by the middle of his body on a rude cross, and two executioners took their stand by his side, each armed with a cutlass. The rolling of drums was followed by a profound silence; amidst which the executioners began to slice away the flesh of the martyr in large pieces, avoiding the mortal parts. His arms were laid bare to the bone, his breasts were lying on the ground, they were hewing at his legs, two large slices fell at his feet, when he bowed his head, and his soul ascended to the Lord of life and glory. His remains were treated with the grossest indignity, and at length thrown into the sea.

Thirty-eight orders or congregations are employed in missionary labours, and are filling the earth with the Gospel of Jesus Christ; more than 126 bishoprics are centres of light and of grace to those who but recently knew not the name of Jesus. The missions are divided into five great sections:—1. Those of the Levant, which embrace the Archipelago, Constantinople, Syria, Armenia, Crimea, Ethiopia, Persia, and Egypt. 2. Those of India, extending to Manilla and the Philippine Islands. 3. Those of China, Siam, Cochin China, and Tonquin. 4. America, from Hudson's Bay to the tribes of Paraguay. 5. Oceanica, comprising Australia. These are all governed by the congregation of the Propaganda; and their zealous labourers are furnished by the Jesuits, the Lazarists, the Redemptorists, the Dominicans and Franciscans, the missionaries of the society of Picpus, the Marist Fathers, and other devoted orders of the Church. "Mention," says a Catholic writer, "one point of the surface of the earth, one island of the pathless sea, which has not been trodden by apostolic feet. On what terrible shores have they shrunk from standing to publish the glory of God, or from pouring out their life-blood in His cause? From the icebergs of North America to the burning plains watered by the Ganges, from Corea to the remotest islands of the Pacific, from Thibet to the Cape of Good Hope, the tree of life, whose roots are on Mount Calvary, spreads its sheltering branches and sheds its immortal fruit."

England itself has reaped the fruit of its generous hospitality to the French priests who sought refuge on its shores from the revolutionary tempest. A season of grace seems to have returned; day by day the mercy of God is bringing home to the One Fold some wandering sheep. Many ministers of the Establishment, distinguished for learning and piety, have submitted to the true Church; and multitudes of the laity have followed their example. Churches* and priests have increased with wonderful rapidity since the repeal of the penal laws; and it was reserved for Pius IX., who, in 1846, succeeded Gregory XVI., to restore its hierarchy to England, once the island of saints, but for three dreary centuries the prey of error, delusion, and schism. The old sees, associated with the ancient glories of England, have ceased to exist; and it is now governed by fourteen bishops, presided over by the Cardinal Archbishop of Westminster. Even in Scotland, the stronghold of Presbyterianism, the faith is making steady progress; while Ireland maintains its unwavering fidelity to the see of St. Peter. Religious communities are springing up in all directions. The Jesuits, the Fathers of the Oratory, the Dominicans, Capuchins, the Marist Fathers, the members of the Order of Charity, and others, are zealously labouring for the diffusion of the light of faith; and the education of the young, among both rich and poor, is being undertaken in a spirit which gives the fairest promise for the future of the Catholic Church of England.

* See Appendix.

In France religious works are multiplying fast. Austria has concluded a concordat with the Holy See, which promises to undo the evil work of Joseph II.; Belgium presents to our view a flourishing Church; and although there are signs that the powers of the world will never cease to war against the Spouse of Christ, her progress and her prospects are alike fair and encouraging.

Among the events of the present pontificate, we can notice only the promulgation of the decree which, in 1854, raised the doctrine of the Immaculate Conception of the Mother of God to the dignity of an article of faith. May the time be far distant when the history of his troublous but brilliant pontificate shall be written! We cannot predict its course; but we know that, stayed upon the everlasting promises of Jesus Christ, he will advance from victory to victory. Every thing indicates the approach of great events. We know not what lot awaits the Church, save only that she will ever be found faithful to her Divine mission to console, to bless, to teach, to protect, and to save mankind; ever intent on this her work, whether outwardly triumphant, or in the midst of trials and persecutions. This is her true life, the glory which cannot be taken from her.

Such has been the various and chequered course of the Catholic Church :—prefigured in the old covenant, instituted by Jesus Christ in the fullness of the times, fertilised by the blood of countless martyrs; at first hidden in the catacombs, then glorious and triumphant on the imperial throne; the tamer and teacher of the barbarian hordes of the north, the arbiter of Europe, the protectress of arts, science, and liberty; ever striving against error, and never for a moment wavering in her faith; at times betrayed by her own sons, yet ever consoled by the acquisition of new children; persecuted, but never cast down; assailed by every power of earth, yet ever mysteriously triumphing; unvarying and invariable in her doctrine, her constitution, her discipline; incomparable in the majesty of her institutions, the splendour of her achievements, and the devotedness of her ministers; inaccessible to the fluctuations of the world, while she comprehends and meets all its wants as they arise; towering high above all political revolutions, and continually rising with renewed vigour when her foes were preparing to sing the song of their imagined victory;—ever and in all things she has justified fully and universally the magnificent promises of her Divine Founder, that He would be with her all days, even to the consummation of the world.

The creed which is popularly known as that of Nicæa, tells us what are the distinctive signs by which we may distinguish the true Church of Christ from every usurper or counterfeit. It is One, Holy, Catholic, and Apostolic. And now, when so many sects are pretending to the place and honour of the true Church, there is but one question to be answered, Which of these bodies possesses these four signs or notes?

Take the note of *Holiness*. Where shall we find saints like those of the Catholic Church? Recall to mind the series of her hermits, her religious of both sexes, her missionaries, her doctors, her confessors, her martyrs. She has peopled heaven with intercessors; and she alone now inspires perfect self-sacrificing devotion, covers land and sea with her apostles, and grapples with the evils which are desolating society.

Her *Unity* is incontestable and uncontested. Truth is necessarily one, as God is One from whom it flows. Of what other body can unity be predicated? Is Protestantism one? Is the National Establishment one? Whereas all over the wide earth Catholics profess one and the same doctrine; receive the same sacraments; recognise one and the same visible head.

Every other religion dates from some human founder. Lutherans, Calvinists, Wesleyans, like Arians, Macedonians, Eutychians, began with Luther, Calvin, Wesley, Arius, Macedonius, Eutyches. The schismatic Greek Church dates from Photius. The Establishment from Henry VIII., Edward, and Elizabeth. Whereas the Catholic Church ascends, in an unbroken succession of pastors and of doctrine, to the Apostles. No other date can be assigned to her existence. She alone is *Apostolic*.

Jesus Christ promised that His kingdom should extend throughout the earth; and this is what we mean by *Catholicity*, or Universality. Where do we find this note? The Greek schism is pent up in a corner of the earth, and is smitten with

incurable barrenness.   Anglicanism is limited to the English
dominions.   One sect of Protestant preachers is here, and
another there; but they are not the same body.   Only the
Catholic Church pervades the earth.   The very name is resigned to her by all other sects.

When Jesus Christ constituted St. Peter the visible head
of His Church, He promised that all the efforts of hell should
not prevail against it; that it should last unto the end of all
things.   And what is history but the continuous verification
of this promise?   Every heresy has been broken upon this
rock.   Where are the Arians, who once filled Christendom
with their blasphemy?   Where are the Donatists, the Jansenists?   And where is the Protestantism of Luther, of Calvin,
of Knox, of Cranmer?   Would they recognise their children
in the bodies they founded?   Protestantism has crumbled to
pieces in many places; it is passing away from the field of
argument, and vainly struggling in its agony.   Its strength,
where it is seemingly strong, is the strength of the civil arm.
Only the Church of Christ stands as it has ever stood,—one,
the same, unchanged, unchangeable.   "The rains fall, and
the floods come, and the winds blow, and they beat upon that
house, and it falls not—for it is founded on a Rock."

Sicut audivimus, sic vidimus in civitate Dei nostri:
Deus fundavit eam in æternum.
Circumdate Sion, et complectimini eam ;
Narrate in turribus ejus
Quoniam hic est Deus, Deus noster in æternum, et in sæculum sæculi.
Ipse reget nos in sæcula.

APPENDIX.

—

Page 96.

In Ireland, Christian communities had been founded at a very early date; but the first bishop of the Irish was St. Palladius, who was consecrated at Rome, by Pope St. Celestine, in 431. His success was great; but being compelled by the king of Leinster to leave the island, he returned the same year to North Britain; and the conversion of Ireland was reserved for St. Patrick. This apostolic man is commonly believed to have been born in Scotland, towards the end of the fourth century. At the age of sixteen, he was seized by an Irish chieftain, who had made a descent on the coast, and by him was carried captive to Ireland, where he was set to tend the flocks and herds of his master. After six years of most severe hardships, which he endured in a spirit of penance, he found means to escape, and went to Tours, where, in the school of St. Martin, he applied himself, during four years, to the acquisition of Christian knowledge and perfection. From Tours he returned to his father's house; and there, in a vision, he received his first call to his mission in Ireland. Some years, however, were still to be devoted to study and self-improvement; and it was not until the year 431 that he received from Pope St. Celestine full powers to preach the Gospel in that country. He was consecrated bishop at Evreux.

He traversed the whole island, penetrating into its remotest corners, fearless of danger, and regardless of the opposition and violence which his efforts every where excited. The first fruit of his preaching amongst the barbarous and idolatrous people, was the conversion of a famous poet named Dubtach; soon the most powerful princes of the land listened to his words, and Corrall, a brother of the chief king, was among his earliest disciples. Many of the sons of the chieftains became his followers, and shared in his apostolical labours: many virgins whom he had converted embraced an ascetic state of life; and, in spite of the persecution they encountered at the hands of their parents, persevered in their holy vocation. But the most important conversion was at Connaught, where St. Patrick arrived while the king, with his seven sons and a large body of the people, was holding an assembly; he baptised all the young princes, together with 120,000 of their subjects. He habitually refused the presents which the people, in their gratitude, would have lavished upon him, and in his whole life was a model of disinterestedness and mortification. His labours were attended by numerous miracles : restoring sight to the blind, health to the sick, and raising nine dead persons to life. In the year 439, he was aided by the co-operation of three other bishops ; and, about the year 455, he erected a church, around which arose the city of Armagh, henceforth the ecclesiastical metropolis of Ireland. Soon afterwards he held a synod, in which was framed a series of canons for the regulation of the infant Church. In the last years of his life, St. Patrick wrote his *Confessions;* in which he declares that every where he had ordained priests, and that Christianity reigned amidst the vast body of the people. He died about the year 465, and was buried at Down, in Ulster.

Numerous schools and seminaries were established under the guidance of the bishops ; and, towards the close of the fifth century, St. Bridget founded several convents of nuns, the largest and most celebrated of which was that erected, in 490, at Kildare. During the sixth and seventh centuries, there was not a country in the whole world which could boast of pious foundations or of religious communities equal to those which adorned this far-distant isle. The schools in the Irish cloisters were the most celebrated in all the West ; and, at a time when almost all the civilised world was desolated by war, Ireland alone, at peace and free from invasion, opened to the lovers of learning a welcome asylum. From far and near they came to receive from the Irish people a hospitable entertainment, gratuitous instruction, and even the books that were necessary for the prosecution of their studies ; while, on the other hand, many holy and learned Irishmen left their own country to preach the faith, to establish or to reform monasteries, in other and distant lands, and thus to become the benefactors of almost every nation of Europe.

Scottish historians tell us that the faith was first planted in their country about the year 200, by missionaries sent by Pope Victor ; but it is generally acknowledged that St. Palladius was the first bishop of the North. The southern Picts, however, who dwelt between the Forth and the Grampian hills, were converted to Christianity, about the year 412, by the British bishop St. Ninian ; and the most celebrated apostle of the northern inhabitants was the great St. Columba, who entered upon his labours about 150 years later. St. Columba was born in Ireland in 521, and studied in the famous school of St. Finian. After founding many monasteries in his native land, he passed over, with twelve of his followers (A.D. 563), into North Britain, where he laboured amidst his own countrymen, the Christian Irish or Scots who had emigrated into those parts, as well as in the conversion of the northern Picts, whom he rescued from idolatry by his preaching, virtues, and miracles. He raised to life a youth who died a few days after he and his parents had been baptised, and whose death had given the heathen priests occasion to blaspheme the God of the Christians. St. Columba frequently visited the Hebrides; and in the little island of Iona he built the great monastery which was for several ages the chief seminary of North Britain. St. Columba's manner of living was most austere. He lay on the bare floor, with a stone for his pillow, and kept, as it were, one perpetual fast. Yet his devotion had nothing in it of moroseness; his countenance always evinced a most wonderful cheerfulness, bespeaking the intense serenity of his soul and the ineffable joy with which it overflowed. The Picts, as well as the Scots, held him in the highest veneration; and so great was the influence he possessed, that neither king nor people would do any thing without his approval. After a laborious apostolate of thirty-four years, he sweetly expired, in the year 597, in the seventy-seventh year of his age, praying with his brethren and pronouncing over them his last benediction.

Page 283.

Many chapels were destroyed during the No-Popery riots of 1780. There were about 170 private chapels at this time, and a chapel in each of the following towns: Worcester (built in 1685), Wolverhampton (1743), Preston (1761), Shrewsbury (1764), Cobridge (1780), Garstang (1784), Manchester, Newcastle-on-Tyne, Norwich, Liverpool, and several in London. From 1780 to 1790, some half a dozen chapels were erected in England; but, during the following decades of years, the increase varied from 20 to about 50 or 60, and from 1840 to 1850 it was 144. In 1827, 24 churches and chapels were opened. Besides the churches opened from 1840 to 1850, about 40 new missions were established, in many of which churches or chapels have since been erected; and probably as many, or even more, new missions have been established since the restoration of the Hierarchy; from which time about 100 churches and chapels, many of them worthy of the Catholic name, have been built in England. In the year 1825, the oldest public chapel was that at Wolverhampton, which was built about 1743. But it was rebuilt in 1826; and St. Mary's, Preston, is now the oldest of our post-Reformation structures. Some of our private chapels date as far back as the reign of Elizabeth: and that at East Hendred existed in the thirteenth century. The chapel at Ugbrooke was consecrated for the Protestant service by Bishop Sparrow, of Exeter, in 1761, and was transferred to the Catholics eighteen years afterwards. The chapel at Trelawny, built and consecrated by the Protestant bishop of that name (also of Exeter), was likewise transferred to the Catholic Church, the late Sir H. Trelawny, Bart., a clergyman, having become a Catholic. He was ordained deacon shortly before his death, when he was about eighty years of age. At the time of Bishop Talbot's trial (for saying Mass), in 1770, there were about 30 public chapels in England. Now there are about 700, and the number is increased almost every week. See also *Catholic Statistics*, Richardson, 1853.

CHRONOLOGICAL TABLE.

Chronological Table.

Emperors [with the dates of their accession].		Popes [with the dates of their death].		Principal Events. [The dates mark the beginning of events, and the death of persons.]		Saints [with the dates of their death].	
A.D.		A.D.		A.D.		A.D.	
14	Tiberius.			34	Conversion of St. Paul.	33	St. Stephen.
				38	Gospel of St. Matthew.		
37	Caligula.						
41	Claudius.			51	Council of Jerusalem.	44	St. James the Greater.
54	Nero.			64	First Persecution.	62	St. James the Less.
69	Galba, Otho, Vitellius.	66	St. Peter.				
70	Vespasian.			70	Destruction of Jerusalem.		
79	Titus.						
81	Domitian.	87	St. Linus.				
		91	St. Anacletus.	95	Second Persecution.		
96	Nerva.			97	Gospel of St. John.		
98	Trajan.	100	St. Clement.	106	Third Persecution.	107	St. Ignatius.
		109	St. Evaristus.			107	St. Simeon.
117	Hadrian.	119	St. Alexander I.				
		127	St. Sixtus I.				
138	Antoninus.	139	St. Telesphorus.				
		142	St. Hyginus.	150	Apology of St. Justin.		
		157	St. Pius I.				
161	Marcus Aurelius.	168	St. Anicetus.	166	Fourth Persecution.	166	St. Polycarp.
		177	St. Soter.	171	Montanists.	167	St. Justin.
				174	Thundering Legion.	177	St. Pothinus.
						179	St. Symphorian.
180	Commodus.			189	Mission to India.		
191	Pertinax.	192	St. Eleutherius.				
193	Didius Julianus.						

Emperors		Popes		Events		Saints	
193	Septimus Severus.	202	St. Victor I.	202	*Fifth Persecution.*	205	St. Irenæus.
211	Caracalla and Geta.					206	St. Perpetua.
213	Macrinus.						
218	Heliogabalus.	219	St. Zephyrinus.	220	Clement of Alexandria.	229	St. Hilarion.
222	Alexander Severus.	222	St. Calixtus I.			231	St. Gregory Thaumaturgus.
		230	St. Urban I.				
235	Maximin.	235	St. Pontian.	235	*Sixth Persecution.*		
238	Gordian.	236	St. Antherus.	245	Mission to Gaul.		
244	Philip.			246	Tertullian.		
249	Decius.	250	St. Fabian.	249	*Seventh Persecution.*		
		252	St. Cornelius.	251	*Schism of Novatus.*		
253	Gallus.	253	St. Lucius.	253	Origen.		
253	Valerian.	257	St. Stephen I.	257	*Eighth Persecution.*	258	St. Cyprian.
		259	St. Sixtus II.				
260	Gallienus.	269	St. Dionysius.	275	*Ninth Persecution.*		
268	Claudius II.	271	St. Felix.	277	Manicheans.		
270	Aurelian.						
275	Tacitus.						
276	Probus.						
282	{ Carus, Carinus, and Numerian.	283	St. Eutychian.	303	*Tenth Persecution.*	291	St. Sebastian.
284	Diocletian and Maximian.	296	St. Caius.	304	Theban Legion.	304	St. Vincent.
		304	St. Marcellinus.			305	St. Alban.
306	{ Constantius Chlorus and Galerius.	310	St. Marcellus.	313	Conversion of Constantine.		
312	Constantine.	310	St. Eusebius.	314	Donatists.		
		314	St. Melchiades.	319	Arians.		
		325	St. Sylvester.	325	*First General Council at Nicea.*		
				326	Invention of the Cross.		
				330	Conversion of Æthiopians.		
337	Constantius & his brothers.	336	St. Mark.	337	Arian persecution.		

CHRONOLOGICAL TABLE [A.D. 337 to 709]—continued.

Emperors [with the dates of their accession].	Popes [with the dates of their death].	Principal Events. [The dates mark the beginning of events, and the death of persons.]	Saints [with the dates of their death].
A.D.	A.D.	A.D.	A.D.
337 Constantius & his brothers.	352 St. Julius I.	340 Sapor.	341 St. Paul the Hermit.
		357 Hosius.	356 St. Antony.
361 Julian the Apostate.	366 Liberius.	360 Macedonians.	
363 Jovian.			
364 Valentinian and Valens.			375 St. Athanasius.
375 Gratian and Valentinian II			379 St. Basil.
379 Theodosius.		381 *Second General Council at Constantinople.*	
	384 St. Damasus.	383 Vulgate translation.	389 St. Gregory of Nazianzum.
	399 St. Syricius.	395 Theodosius.	396 St. Ambrose.
395 Arcadius and Honorius.	401 St. Anastasius I.	399 Mission to the Scythians.	400 St. Martin.
	417 St. Innocent.	412 Pelagians.	407 St. Chrysostom.
	418 St. Zosimus.	420 Nestorians.	420 St. Jerome.
	422 St. Boniface.		
425 Valentinian III. *in the West.*	432 St. Celestine.	431 {*Third General Council at Ephesus.*	430 St. Augustine.
	440 St. Sixtus III.	448 Eutychians.	
	461 St. Leo.	451 {*Fourth General Council at Chalcedon.*	444 St. Cyril of Alexandria.
	468 St. Hilary.	457 Vandal persecution in Africa.	461 St. Simeon Stylites.
475 Romulus Augustulus.	483 St. Simplicius.		
Fall of the Western Empire.			
Emperors of the East.			
Zeno.	492 St. Felix III.	496 Conversion of Clovis.	
491 Anastasius I.	496 St. Gelasius.		500 St. Asaph.
	498 St. Anastasius II.		

Emperors	Popes	Events	Saints
565 Justin II.	514 Symmachus.	511 Rogation Instituted.	511 St. Généviève.
578 Tiberius II.	523 Hormisdas.	525 Foundation of Monte Casino.	530 St. Benedict.
582 Phocas.	528 St. John I.	529 Council of Orange.	530 St. Remigius, or Remy.
610 Heraclius.	530 Felix IV.	553 *Fifth General Council.*	545 St. Clotilda.
641 Constans II.	533 Boniface II.	558 Conversion of Visigoths.	565 Gildas.
668 Constantine Pogonatus.	535 John II.	596 Conversion of England.	595 Gregory of Tours.
685 Justinian II.	536 Agapetus.	622 Hegira of Mahomet.	607 { St. Augustine of Canterbury.
	538 Sylvericus.	628 Exaltation of the Cross.	615 St. Columban.
	555 Vigilius.	630 Monothelites.	650 St. Gertrude.
	560 Pelagius.	648 Mission to the Low Countries.	662 St. Maximus.
	574 John III.	651 Aidan, bishop of Lindisfarne.	643 St. Eligius, or Eloi.
	578 Benedict.	680 *Sixth General Council.*	690 St. Benedict Biscop.
	590 Pelagius II.	690 Mission to Friesland.	703 Adamnan of Iona.
	604 St. Gregory I.		709 { Aldhelm, abbot of Malmesbury.
	607 Sabinian.		
	608 Boniface III.		
	614 Boniface IV.		
	618 Deusdedit.		
	625 Boniface V.		
	640 Severinus.		
	642 John IV.		
	649 Theodore I.		
	655 St. Martin I.		
	657 St. Eugenius I.		
	672 Vitalian.		
	676 { Deusdedit II. (or Adeodatus).		
	679 Domnus I.		
	682 Agatho.		
	684 St. Leo II.		
	685 St. Benedict II.		
	686 John V.		
	687 Conon.		
	701 St. Sergius I.		
	705 John VI.		
	708 John VII.		
	708 Sisinnius.		

CHRONOLOGICAL TABLE [A.D. 711 to 1003]—continued.

EMPERORS [with the dates of their accession].		POPES [with the dates of their death].		PRINCIPAL EVENTS. [The dates mark the beginning of events, and the death of persons.]		SAINTS [with the dates of their death].	
A.D.		A.D.		A.D.		A.D.	
711	Leo III., the Isaurian.	715	Constantine.	711	Moors in Spain.	712	St. John of Beverley.
		731	Gregory II.	723	Conversion of Germans.	735	Venerable Bede.
741	{ Constantine IV., Copronymus.	741	Gregory III.	737	Iconoclasts.	738	{ St. Wilbrord of Ripon, bishop of Utrecht.
		752	St. Zachary.	755	Patrimony of St. Peter.	755	St. Boniface.
		752	Stephen II. [died before his consecration.]				
		757	Stephen III.				
		768	Paul I.	766	Persecution of Iconoclasts.	760	Egbert of York.
775	Leo IV.	772	Stephen IV.	778	Conversion of Saxons.		
780	Irene.	795	Adrian I.	787	*Seventh General Council.*		
802	Nicephorus.	816	St. Leo III.	800	Charlemagne crowned.	804	{ Alcuin of York, tutor to Charlemagne.
811	Stauracius.	817	Stephen V.				
820	Michael II.	824	St. Pascal I.	826	Conversion of Danes.		
		827	Eugenius II.				
		828	Valentinus.				
829	Theophilus.	844	Gregory IV.	830	Conversion of Sweden.	835	St. Ansear.
842	Michael III.	847	Sergius II.	844	Conversion of Russia.		
		853	Leo IV.	850	Moorish persecution in Spain.		
		858	Benedict III.	855	Conversion of Bulgaria.		
				856	Rabanus Maurus.		
867	Basil.	867	Nicolas I.	877	John Scotus Erigena.	877	{ St. Ignatius, patriarch of Constantinople.
		872	Adrian II.	880	Conversion of Bohemia.	877	{ St. Neot, abbot of Glastonbury.
		882	John VIII.	882	Hincmar of Rheims.		
		884	Marin II.				

886	Leo VI.	885	Adrian III.	891	Photius.	910	St. Remo.
		891	Stephen VI.				
		896	Formosus.				
		896	Boniface VI.				
		897	Stephen VII.				
		897	Romanus.				
		898	Theodore II.				
		900	John IX.	910	Asser, bishop of Sherborne.		
		903	Benedict IV.	910	Order of Cluny founded.		
		911	Sergius III.	910	Conversion of Normans.		
912	{ Constantine VII., Porphyrogenitus.	913	Anastasius III.			942	St. Odo of Cluny.
		914	Lando.				
		923	John X.				
		929	Leo VI.				
		931	Stephen VIII.				
		936	John XI.				
		930	Leo VII.				
		943	Stephen IX.	950	Persecution by Moors in Spain.		
		946	Martin III.				
		955	Agapetus II.				
959	Romanus.	964	John XII.	964	Conversion of Poland.	961	St. Bruno.
963	Nicephorus Phocas.	965	Leo VIII.	966	Hodoard.	961	St. Odo of Canterbury.
		965	Benedict V.				
969	John Zimisces.	972	John XIII.				
		974	Benedict VI.				
		974	Boniface VII.				
		974	Domnus II.				
975	Basil II. and Constantine.	983	Benedict VII.			988	{ St. Dunstan, archbishop of Canterbury.
		984	John XIV.			992	Oswald, archbishop of York.
		985	John XV.				
		996	John XVI.				
		999	Gregory V.				
		1003	Sylvester II.	1001	Conversion of Hungary.		
		1003	John XVII.				

CHRONOLOGICAL TABLE [A.D. 975 to 1276]—continued.

EMPERORS [with the dates of their accession].	POPES [with the dates of their death].	PRINCIPAL EVENTS. [The dates mark the beginning of events, and the death of persons.]	SAINTS [with the dates of their death].
A.D. 975 Basil II. and Constantine.	A.D. 1005 John XVIII.	A.D. 1005 Invention of the gamut, by Guido d'Arezzo.	A.D.
	1009 John XIX.	1006 Ælfric, the grammarian, archbishop of Canterbury.	
	1012 Sergius II.		
	1024 Benedict VIII.		
1025 Constantine.	1033 John XX.	1041 Truce of God established.	1038 St. Stephen of Hungary.
1028 Romanus III.			
1034 Constantine Monomachus.			
1042 Theodora.	1044 Benedict IX. abd.	1050 Heresy of Berengarius.	
	1046 Gregory VI.	1054 Election of Popes reserved to Cardinals.	
	1047 Clement II.	1055 Schism of the Greeks.	
	1048 Benedict IX. rest.		
	1048 Damasus II.		
	1054 St. Leo IX.		
1056 Michael VI.	1057 Victor II.		
1057 Isaac Comnenus.	1058 Stephen X.		1063 St. Peter Damian.
1059 Constantine XI.	1062 Nicolas II.		
1067 Michael VII.	1073 Alexander II.		
1078 Nicephorus.		1079 Abelard. 1142	
1081 Alexis Comnenus.	1085 St. Gregory VII.	1084 Carthusian order.	1089 Lanfranc, archbishop of Canterbury.
	1087 Victor III.	1095 Council of Clermont for the first Crusade.	1095 Wulstan, bp. of Worcester.
	1099 Urban II.	1098 Cistercian order.	1099 Osmund, bishop of Sarum.
		1100 Godfrey of Boulogne.	1101 St. Bruno.
		1103 Order of Fontevrault.	1109 Ingulphus, abbot of Croyland.
		1105 Peter the Hermit.	
		1118 Order of the Templars.	
1118 John Comnenus.	1118 Pascal II.	1123 Ninth General Council, first of the Lateran.	
	1119 Gelasius II.		1154 St. Norbert.
	1124 Callixtus II.		

Year	Emperors	Year	Popes	Year	Councils & Events	Year	Saints & Notable Persons
1143	Manuel Comnenus.	1130	Honorius II.	1139	*Tenth General Council.*	1153	St. Bernard.
		1143	Innocent II.	1143	William of Malmesbury.	1164	Peter Lombard.
		1144	Celestine II.			1170	St. Thomas of Canterbury.
		1145	Lucius II.				
		1153	Eugenius III.				
		1159	Adrian IV.				
1180	Alexis Comnenus.	1181	Alexander III.	1160	Vaudois.	1197	Longchamp, bishop of Ely.
		1185	Lucius III.	1179	*Eleventh General Council.*		
		1187	Urban III.	1190	Teutonic order.		
		1191	Gregory VIII.	1190	Third Crusade.		
		1198	Clement III.	1200	Universities.		
			Celestine III.	1202	Fourth Crusade.		
1203	Alexis IV.						
1204	Alexis V.						
	Latin Emperors at Constantinople.						
1204	Baldwin I.	1216	Innocent III.	1205	{ *Twelfth General Council.* (Fourth Lateran.)	1221	St. Dominic.
1206	Peter Courtenay.			1209	Carmelites.		
1216	Robert Courtenay.			1210	Friars minor.		
				1212	Clares.		
				1216	Dominicans.		
				1217	Fifth Crusade.		
1228	Baldwin II.	1229	Honorius III.	1224	Mission in Prussia.	1226	St. Francis of Assisi.
		1241	Gregory IX.	1245	*Thirteenth General Council.*	1228	{ Langton, archbishop of Canterbury.
		1243	Celestine IV.	1248	Seventh Crusade.	1230	St. Clare.
		1254	Innocent IV.	1256	Augustinians.	1231	St. Anthony of Padua.
				1256	Sorbonne.	1245	Alexander of Hales.
						1253	{ Robert Grosseteste, bishop of Lincoln.
	Greek Empire.						
1261	Michael Palæologus.	1261	Alexander IV.	1264	Corpus Christi.	1270	St. Louis.
		1264	Urban IV.	1270	Eighth Crusade.	1274	St Thomas Aquinas.
		1268	Clement IV.	1274	*Fourteenth General Council.*	1274	St. Bonaventura.
		1276	Gregory X.	1274	Reunion of the Greeks.		

CHRONOLOGICAL TABLE [A.D. 1261 *to* 1595]—*continued.*

EMPERORS [with the dates of their accession].		POPES [with the dates of their death].		PRINCIPAL EVENTS. [The dates mark the beginning of events, and the death of persons.]		SAINTS [with the dates of their death].
A.D.		A.D.		A.D.		A.D.
1261	Michael Palæologus.	1276	Innocent V.			
		1276	Adrian V.			
		1277	John XXI.			
		1280	Nicolas III.	1283	The Greeks relapse into schism.	
1282	Andronicus II.	1285	Martin IV.	1299	Institution of the Jubilee.	1286	{ Hugh de Balsham, bishop of Ely.
		1287	Honorius IV.	1309	Popes at Avignon.	
		1292	Nicolas IV.	1311	*Fifteenth General Council.*	
		1294	St. Celestine V.	1312	Suppression of the Templars.	1308	John Duns Scotus.
		1303	Boniface VIII.	1320	Trinity Sunday.	
		1305	St. Benedict XI.	1327	The Angelus.	
		1314	Clement V.	1340	Saturday abstinence.	
1328	Andronicus III.	1334	John XXII.			
1341	John V. and John VI.	1342	Benedict XII.			
		1352	Clement VI.	1370	Missions of Tartary.	1373	St. Bridget.
		1362	Innocent VI.	1376	Return of the Pope to Rome.	
		1370	Urban V.	1378	Great schism of the West.	1380	St. Catherine of Sienna.
		1378	Gregory XI.	1388	Feast of the Visitation.	
		1389	Urban VI.			
1391	Manuel II. Palæologus.	1404	Boniface IX.			
		1406	Innocent VII.			
		1409	Gregory XII. *abd.*	1414	{ *Sixteenth General Council* at Constance.	
		1410	Alexander V.			
		1413	John XXIII. *abd.*	1439	{ *Seventeenth General Council* at Florence.	1426	William of Wykeham.
1425	John VIII. Palæologus. Constantine VII.	1431	Martin V.	1439	Reunion of Greeks.	
Emperors of Germany.				1440	Return to their schism.	
1440	Frederick IV.	1447	Eugenius IV.	1449	End of the Western schism.	
				1453	{ Constantinople taken by the Turks.	

				Events			Saints
1493	Maximilian I.	1455	Nicolas V.	Order of the Minims.	1454	1471	Kempis.
		1458	Calixtus III.	Feast of the Conception.	1476	1486	William of Waynflete.
		1464	Pius II.	{ End of Moorish dominion in Spain.	1492		
		1471	Paul II.	America discovered.	1492	1507	St. Francis de Paula.
		1484	Sixtus IV.	Mission to Congo.	1504		
		1492	Innocent VIII.				
		1503	Alexander VI.				
		1503	Pius III.				
		1513	Julius II.				
1519	Charles V.	1521	Leo X.	Lutherans.	1517		
		1523	Adrian VI.	Mission to Mexico.	1524		
				Capuchins.	1525		
				Confession of Augsburg.	1530		
				The Recollets.	1532		
				Calvinists.	1533		
		1534	Clement VIII.	Schism of England.	1534	1535	Sir Thomas More.
				Company of Jesus.	1540	1535	Fisher, bishop of Rochester.
				Mission to India.	1541		
				Council of Trent.	1545		
		1549	Paul III.	Socinians.	1549	1552	St. Francis Xavier.
				Missions of Japan.	1549		
		1555	Julius III.	Missions of Ethiopia.	1554	1556	St. Ignatius.
1556	Ferdinand I.	1555	Marcellus II.	Missions of Brazil.	1554	1558	St. Philip Neri.
		1559	Paul IV.	Carmelites.	1563		
				Council of Trent closed.	1563		
				Seminaries instituted.	1568		
1564	Maximilian II.	1565	Pius IV.	Barefooted Carmelites.	1568		
1576	Rodolph II.	1572	St. Pius V.	Massacre of St. Bartholomew.	1572		
				Missions of China.	1580	1582	St. Teresa.
				{ Reform of the Calendar by Gregory XIII.	1582	1584	St. Charles Borromeo.
		1585	Gregory XIII.				
		1590	Sixtus V.				
		1590	Urban VII.	Order of Ursulines.	1591	1591	St. John of the Cross.
		1501	Gregory XIV.	Abjuration of Henry IV.	1591	1591	St. Louis of Gonzaga.
		1591	Innocent IX.	Persecution of Japan.	1595		

CHRONOLOGICAL TABLE [A.D. 1576 to 1854]—continued.

EMPERORS [with the dates of their accession].	POPES [with the dates of their death].	PRINCIPAL EVENTS. [The dates mark the beginning of events, and the death of persons.]	SAINTS [with the dates of their death].
A.D.	A.D.	A.D.	A.D.
1576 Rodolph II.	1605 Clement VIII.	1602 Mission to Paraguay.	
	1605 Leo XI.	1610 Order of the Visitation.	
1611 Matthias.		1611 Missions of Canada.	
		1613 French Oratorians.	
1619 Ferdinand II.	1621 Paul V.	1621 Bellarmine.	1622 St. Francis of Sales.
	1623 Gregory XV.	1625 Lazarists.	
1637 Ferdinand III.	1644 Urban VIII.	1646 Sulpicians.	1640 St. Francis Regis.
			1641 St. Jane Chantal.
1657 Leopold I.	1676 Clement X.	1679 Christian Brothers.	1660 St. Vincent de Paul.
	1689 Innocent XI.	1684 { Revocation of the Edict of Nantes.	
	1691 Alexander VIII.		
	1700 Innocent XII.	1704 Bossuet.	
1705 Joseph I.	1721 Clement XI.	1713 { Bull Unigenitus against Jansenists.	1719 B. De la Salle.
1711 Charles VI.	1724 Innocent XIII.	1714 Bourdaloue.	
	1730 Benedict XIII.	1715 Fénelon.	
	1740 Clement XII.		
1740 Charles VII.	1758 Benedict XIV.	1742 Massillon.	
1743 Maria Theresa.	1769 Clement XIII.		
1765 Francis I.	1774 Clement XIV.	1774 Suppression of Jesuits.	1783 B. Benedict Labre.
Joseph II.			1787 St. Liguori.
1790 Leopold II.	1799 Pius VI.	1801 Concordat with Napoleon.	1802 B. Maria Clotilde.
1792 Francis II.			

Emperors of Austria.		Popes		Events	
1806	Francis I.		Pius VII.	1809	Captivity of Pius VII.
				1814	His deliverance.
		1823	Leo XII.	1814	Jesuits restored.
1835	Ferdinand.	1829	Pius VIII.	1829	Catholic Emancipation Act.
		1831	Gregory XVI.		
1848	Francis Joseph I.	1846	Pius IX.	1848	Pius IX. at Gaeta.
				1848	Death of the Archbp. of Paris.
				1850	{ Re-establishment of the Hierarchy in England.
				1854	{ The Immaculate Conception decreed, December 8.

INDEX.

QUESTIONS.

CHAP. I. pp. 1-47.

What do you mean by the Church?
In what sense has it a history?
What is heresy?
What is schism?
What is a martyr?
What is a confessor?
What date is usually assigned to the Nativity of our Blessed Lord?
Of what nation, and where, was He born?
How did He found the Church?
Who was the first martyr?
When, and by whom, was the Gospel first preached to the Gentiles?
What is a council?
When and where was the first council held?
How was it conducted?
Which of the Apostles died first?
Which of them lived the longest?
For what is he remarkable?
When, and by whom, was Jerusalem laid waste?
What nation ruled the earth when the Church was set up?
Was its rule favourable to the Church?
Where did St. Paul labour?
Who was he?
Where, and how, did he die?
Give some account of St. Peter's labours.
What books did the Apostles leave behind them?
How do you know them to be the Word of God?
What became of our Lady after the ascension of our Lord?
Why was the Church persecuted?
How many persecutions did she undergo?
What principal martyrs suffered in the first persecution?
What are the successors of St. Peter called?
Name his more immediate successors.
Give some account of St. Ignatius, St. Cyprian, St. Polycarp.
Give some account of the Decian persecution.

When was the Church set up in Britain?
Who is the first British martyr?
Give some account of him.
Is there any memorial of his martyrdom now?
Who were the apologists of Christianity?
Name them.

CHAP. II. pp. 47-93.

How long did the period of persecution last?
What ended it?
Give some account of Constantine.
What was the Labarum?
Did our Lord foresee the persecutions of His Church?
Did they injure the Church?
Who was St. Helena?
For what is she remarkable?
What festival is kept on 3d May?
What did Constantine do for the Church?
Who were the Manichæans?
Give some account of their heresy.
What great heresy assailed the Church after the conversion of Constantine?
Why was it so called?
By whom was it opposed?
Give some account of Alexandria.
How did the Church deal with this heresy?
What is the meaning of the word œcumenical?
What word did the council fix on to distinguish truth from error?
What became of the Arians afterwards?
Where did Constantine die?
What have you to remark on the conduct of St. Athanasius?
What is the meaning of the word creed?
How many are there?
For what is A.D. 350 remarkable?
Give some account of Liberius, St. Hilary, St. Martin.
How did the monastic life begin? and where?
Give some account of the life of Julian.

How did he treat the Church?

What did he try to do in the Holy Land?

Where did he die? and how?

What was the conduct of Valens?

Give some account of St. Basil, St. Gregory of Nazianzum, St. Jerome, St. Chrysostom, St. Ambrose.

What heresy succeeds to Arianism?

How did the emperor act?

Did he *make* the test he mentions?

What council condemned this heresy?

What did the council add to the creed of Nicæa? Was this *new*?

What have you to note in the history of Theodosius?

What great *schism* arose about this time?

How?

What were its effects?

Who was St. Augustine?

What is a Manichæan?

Where, and how, was he converted?

How did he treat this schism?

Were these principles *new*?

Who was Pelagius?

What did he teach?

Why was he wrong?

Who refuted his error?

Who condemned it?

Who were the Semi-Pelagians?

Where were they condemned?

What was the next doctrine assailed by heresy?

What do you mean by the *Incarnation*?

How many *natures* are there in our Divine Lord?

How many *persons*?

How many *wills*?

Who was Nestorius?

What did he teach?

What council condemned him?

Give some account of the council of Ephesus.

What word became the test of heresy?

Was this word any thing new?

Who was Eutyches?

What did he teach?

Who was St. Leo?

When was the council of Chalcedon held? Why?

What have you to remark on the assaults of heresy?

Did they weaken the faith?

Why not?

Give some account of the state of the Roman Empire in the fifth century.

Who was Attila?

When did the Western Empire end?

How long had it lasted?

How long has the Church lasted?

Will it ever come to an end?

Why is the Church always in conflict?

CHAP. III. pp. 93-106.

Who was King Lucius?

What mention is made of the British Church in the first five centuries?

What did Germanus and Lupus come to England for?

How did the Saxons treat the Church?

Give some account of St. Gregory the Great and St. Augustine of Canterbury.

How many Saxon kingdoms were there?

Which was first converted? and how?

Who gave mission to St. Augustine?

Give some account of St. Patrick and St. Ninian.

Who was Clovis?

How did he treat the Church?

Give some account of St. Clotilda, St. Geneviève, St. Benedict.

What is the order of Benedictines noted for?

Give an account of the controversy of *the Three Chapters*.

What have you to remark on this matter?

When did the Persians attack the Eastern Empire?

For what was this war noted?

Give an account of the recovery of the True Cross.

What *festival* commemorates this event?

Who was St. Antony?

St. Hilarion?

St. Denys?

What is the origin of the Montmartre, near Paris?

What effect on the Church had the invasions of the Northmen ?

CHAP. IV. pp. 106-121.

What was the state of the Eastern Church at the beginning of the seventh century ?
How did God chastise them ?
Who was Mahomet ?
How did he spread his doctrines ?
What do you mean by the Hegira ? The Koran ?
What have you to remark on the spread of this false religion ?
What is its state now ?
How do the Easterns differ from the Westerns ?
What were the Monothelites ?
Wherein were they wrong ?
What was the *Ecthesis* ?
By whom was it set forth ?
Who was Honorius ?
What council condemned this heresy ?
What was the Emperor Leo III. remarkable for ?
Who were the Iconoclasts ?
Wherein were they wrong ?
How did they treat the Church ?
When, and where, were they condemned ?
What is the Catholic doctrine on this point ?
Who was the Apostle of Germany ?
Give some account of the spread of the Church into Bavaria, Hungary, Poland.
Who was Pepin ?
How did he treat the Church ?
What conclusion have heretics drawn from his conduct ?
What is the truth on this matter ?
Give an account of Charlemagne.
When was the University of Paris founded ?
How was Charlemagne crowned ?
What is coronation ?
What effects have heresies had on the Church's teaching ?
Who is the author of heresy ?
What great distinctions do you note between heresy and the faith ?
Has heresy ever been universal ?
What does St. Augustine remark on this ?

CHAP. V. pp. 121-146.

Who was St. Anschar ?
For what was the tenth century remarkable ?
How were the Normans converted ?
What title has the King of Hungary ?
Who was Photius ?
How did he attain that elevation ?
How did he conduct himself towards the Pope ?
What were the real grounds of this quarrel ?
What is meant by the Greek schism ?
What effects has schism on a Church ?
Has the Greek Church ever admitted the supremacy of the Pope ?
Give an account of Michael Cerularius ?
What effect had his conduct on the Eastern Church ?
Did the invasion of the barbarians overwhelm the Church ?
Who were St. Bede, Alcuin, Alfred the Great, St. Dunstan, St. Bruno ?
What was the state of England in the tenth century ?
What was the character of the Saxon kings ?
For what are their families remarkable ?
What was the state of Germany at this time ? Of France ?
Give some account of Cluny.
For what was Pope Leo IX. remarkable ?
When did he reign ?
Who was St. Peter Damian ?
When did Berengarius live ?
What heresy did he teach ?
On what principle did he teach it?
What effects had his teaching ?
Who refuted him ?
Who was St. Lanfranc ?
How did the Church treat this heresy ? And its teacher ?
What was the state of the Church in the 10th and 11th centuries ?
What effect had the feudal system on the Church ?
What is investiture ?
Explain the conflict between the Church and the civil power on this point.

Give an account of St. Gregory VII. and Henry IV. of Germany. Of St. Anselm and William Rufus in England. Of St. Thomas of Canterbury and Henry II.

What effects had the excommunication of a king in those times?

How was the question of investiture settled?

What is meant by *the dark ages*?

CHAP. VI. pp. 146-176.

What were the Crusades?

Give an account of the origin, conduct, and effects of the first crusade.

Who was the first King of Jerusalem?

What were the military orders?

Who has possession of Malta now?

How did they obtain it?

Who were the Knights Templars? The order of St. Mary of the Teutons?

How did it end?

Give an account of the life and labours of St. Norbert, St. John de Matha, and St. Bernard.

Who wore the Cistercians?

What effect had the Norman Conquest on the Church in England?

How did Henry I. treat the Church?

Give an account of the second crusade.

By whom was the third crusade undertaken?

Give an account of St. Louis of France.

Did the Crusades succeed?

What effect had they on religion? On civilisation?

What great orders were founded in the thirteenth century?

Who was St. Francis of Assisi?

What was his order called?

Give an account of St. Dominic.

What order did he found?

Against what heretics did he contend?

What have heretics laid to the charge of St. Dominic?

CHAP. VII. pp. 177-189.

Who were the schoolmen?

Give some account of St. Thomas Aquinas and St. Bonaventura.

What steps were taken in the thirteenth century to heal the Greek schism?

What effect had the council of Lyons?

When was it held?

What corrections did the Greeks make?

What is a jubilee?

By whom was a jubilee first granted? and why?

By whom was the jubilee ordered to be held every fifty years?

What did Pope Urban VI. decree concerning the jubilee?

What was the great schism of the West?

How did it arise?

How long did it last?

What effect had it on the Church? On Europe?

What was the judgment of St. Antoninus on this schism?

Did it affect the papal supremacy?

What council was held to heal the schism?

Who was Wickliff?

Who was John Huss?

Where was he condemned?

Did the council violate the safe-conduct granted him?

When, and for what purpose, was the council of Florence held?

What effect had it?

Was that effect lasting?

Why not?

What befel the schismatic Greeks?

By whom was Constantinople taken?

How long had the Greek empire lasted?

To what do you attribute its fall?

CHAP. VIII. pp. 189-214.

Give an account of St. Francis of Paula.

What is meant by reformation?

By whom may it be undertaken?

Who was Luther?

What was his character, conduct, success?

What is the origin of the word *Protestant*?

Who was Calvin?

Wherein did he differ from Luther?

What doctrine did Luther assail first?

Did he confine his attacks to that doctrine?

What do you learn from this?

What effects had Luther's teaching on political and social order?

Who was Servetus?

Has Protestantism any fixed doctrine?

Why not?

Can it teach with authority?

What did St. Vincent of Lerins say in the fifth century?

What effect had this schism on England?

When did Henry VIII. begin to reign?

Why was he called *Defender of the Faith?*

What effects had the Church produced on England?

What was the occasion of Henry's schism?

What was meant by the royal supremacy?

How was it exercised?

How did Henry treat the monasteries?

What changes did he make in doctrine?

Whence was mission to be derived?

On what day was England cut off from the Church's unity?

Give some account of Cranmer and Thomas Cromwell.

What conspicuous persons were put to death by Henry?

Give some account of Sir Thomas More's defence.

How did the schism proceed under Edward VI.?

Did the people accept the schism?

When did Edward die?

What did Mary attempt?

Who was Cardinal Pole?

What effects had her reign on the Church?

Who succeeded Mary?

Why did she support Protestantism?

How was she crowned?

What effect had her reign on the schism?

What was the character of the teachers of the established religion?

How did she treat the Church?

What effect had this persecution?

Was the new religion at one with itself?

Who were the Puritans

How did Elizabeth deal with them?

With what success?

How did the schism affect Ireland? Scotland?

How did the persecution affect Catholics in their property, their liberty, their persons?

Who were the Quakers, Independents, Baptists, Methodists?

What reformers did God raise up at this time?

Give some account of St. Ignatius, St. Francis Xavier, and the Jesuits.

What great council was held by the Church to meet the schism?

When did it begin?

When did it end?

What ceremonies were used at its opening?

Of what matters did the council treat?

What distinguishes it from preceding councils?

What is the creed of Pope Pius IV.? and why is it so called?

CHAP. IX. pp. 214-242.

Who was St. Charles Borromeo? St. Teresa? St. Vincent de Paul? St. Francis of Sales?

Did the schism extend to France?

What is meant by the Massacre of St. Bartholomew?

In what way is the Church concerned with it?

Give some account of the Theatines, the Barnabites, the Brothers of Charity, the Recollets, the Oratory.

Who was Baronius?

What kingdoms of Europe cast off the Catholic faith?

Give some account of Henry IV. of France.

Who founded the French Oratory?

Who were the priests of St. Sulpice?

Give some account of the Blessed John Baptist de la Salle.

For what was the age of Louis XIV. celebrated in France?

What effects had his reign on the Church?

What is the Inquisition?

What is its office?

Is the Church responsible for all the doings of the Spanish Inquisition?

Why not?

What effects had the schism in England *politically? religiously?*

How was the Church treated by James I., Charles I., Cromwell, Charles II.?

How did Charles II. die?

By whom was he succeeded?

What was the conduct of James II.?

What effects did it produce?

What was the origin of the Thirty Years' War in Germany?

What was its result?

How did the schism affect Switzerland? Denmark and Sweden?

CHAP. X. pp. 242-258.

Give some account of the Catholic missions in China, Japan, Paraguay, and Canada.

Who was F. Peter Claver?

CHAP. XI. pp. 259-274.

Who were the Jansenists?

Give some account of Baius.

What was the general character of Jansenist teaching?

By whom were they opposed?

What was the general character of the eighteenth century?

Give some account of the Regent Duke of Orleans, Voltaire, Rousseau, and the French Revolution, so far as they affected the Church.

What was the state of religion in Portugal, Spain, Austria, Tuscany?

By whom was the order of Jesuits suppressed? and when?

What was the conduct of the French clergy during the Revolution?

What decree on religion was passed by the Convention?

Give an account of the Pontificate of Pius VI.

Who was Scipio Ricci? St. Alphonsus Liguori?

How did Napoleon treat Pope Pius VI.?

CHAP. XII. pp. 274-279.

Give an account of the election of Pope Pius VII.

What led to the restoration of religion in France?

Who re-established the Society of Jesus?

How did Napoleon treat Pius VII.?

What effect had the restoration of Louis XVIII. on the Church?

What is to be noted of the exiled French priests?

Give some account of the reign of Louis Philippe in France.

When was the Association for the Propagation of the Faith begun?

What great event befel Catholics in England in 1829?

To whom is that event mainly attributable?

What effect has it on the position of Catholics?

What is the present state of Spain?

Give some account of the recent missions to China.

How many orders or congregations are employed in missions?

Into what sections are Catholic missions divided?

What is to be noted in regard of the Catholic Church in England?

What great change took place in its constitution in 1850?

What is a Vicar-apostolic?

Wherein does he differ from an ordinary Bishop?

What is the state of the Church in France, Belgium, Holland?

For what is the year 1854 memorable?

LEVEY, ROBSON, AND FRANKLYN, GREAT NEW STREET AND FETTER LANE, E.C.